# LESSONS *in* CORRUPTION

## A FALLEN MEN NOVEL

## BOOK ONE



giana darling

Edited by Amber Hodge.
Cover Design by Najla Qambar
Cover Model Preston Trites
Cover Photographer Tlaloc Villarreal
Formatting by Stacey at Champagne Book Design

ISBN: 978-0-9950650-8-6

*"For so I created them free, and free they must remain."*
*John Milton,* Paradise Lost.

To 'Armie' Michelle Armstrong.
For making me laugh when I wanted to cry, for listening to my tales of woe and exclamations of love, but most of all, for making me feel safe.

# One.

I saw him in a parking lot when I was picking up groceries. Not the most romantic place to fall in love at first sight, but I guess you can't choose these things.

He had grease on his face. My eyes zoomed in on the smear of motor oil, the aggressive slash of his cheekbones protruding almost brutally under his tanned skin so that they created a hollow in his cheeks. His features were so striking they were almost gaunt, nearly too severe as to be unattractive, mean even. Instead, the softness of his full, surprisingly pink mouth and the honeyed-coloured hair that fell in a touchable mess of curls and waves to his broad shoulders and the way his head was currently tipped back, corded throat exposed and deliciously brown, to laugh at the sky as if he was actually born to laugh and only laugh…none of that was mean.

I stood in the parking lot looking at him through the heat waves in the unusual late summer heat. My plastic grocery bags were probably melted to the asphalt, the ice cream long gone to soup.

I'd been there a while already, watching him.

He was across the lot beside a row of intimidating and gorgeous motorcycles, talking to another biker. His narrow hips leaned sideways across the seat of one, one booted foot propped up. He wore old jeans, also with grease on them, and a white T-shirt, somehow clean, that fit his wide shoulders and small waist indecently well. He looked young, maybe even a few years younger than me, but I only guessed that because while his structure was large, his muscles hung on him slightly as though he hadn't quite grown into his bones.

Idly, I wondered if he was *too* young.

Not so idly, I decided that I didn't care.

His attention was drawn to the group of college-aged kids who pulled up in a shiny convertible, their brightly coloured polo shirts and wrinkled khakis dead giveaways even if their gelled hair and studied swagger hadn't given them away already. They were chuckling as they reached the two motorcycle men I'd been watching and it struck me that compared to the newcomers, there was no way the sexy blond I'd been lusting after was young. He carried himself well, regally even, like a king. A king at home in a grocery store parking lot, his throne the worn seat of an enormous Harley.

I watched without blinking as he greeted the crew, his expression neutral and his body relaxed and casual in a way that tried to veil the strength of his build and failed.

There was something about his pose that was predatory, a hunter inviting his prey closer. A couple of the college kids fidgeted, suddenly uneasy, but their leader strode forward after a brief hesitation and extended his hand.

The blond king stared at the hand but didn't take it. Instead, he said something that made the fidgeting increase.

I wished I were close enough to hear what he said. Not just the words but also the tone of his voice. I wondered if it was deep and smooth, an outpouring of honey, or the gravel of a man who spoke from his diaphragm, from the bottomless well of confidence and testosterone at the base of him.

The kids were more than nervous now. The leader, one step ahead of the others, visibly shrank as his explanation, accompanied by increasingly more agitated hand gestures, seemed to fall on deaf ears.

After a long minute of his babbling, he stopped and was met with silence.

The quiet weighed so heavily, I felt it from across the lot where I lurked by my car.

The blond king's sidekick—or rather "henchman" seemed like a more fitting word for the frankly colossal, dark-haired friend beside him—stepped forward.

Just one step.

Not even a large one. But I could see how that one movement hit the college crew like a nuclear blast wave. They reeled back as a unit; even their leader took a huge step backward, his mouth fluid with rushed words of apology.

They had obviously fucked up.

I didn't know how.

And for the first time in my life, watching a potentially dangerous situation unfold, I wanted to know.

I wanted to be a part of it.

To stand beside the blond king and be his rough and tumble queen.

I shivered as I watched the men before him cower, his loyal friend at his back. Slowly, because he was clearly a man who knew the impact of his physique and how to wield the sharp edge of power like a literal dagger, the blond king rolled out of his slouched position on his bike and into his full height.

The sight of him unraveling like that made my mouth go dry and other private places go wet.

It had a different effect on the college kids. They listened to what he had to say like men being read their last rites, clinging to any hope he could give them, desperate for salvation.

He gave it to them. Not much, but a shred of something to hold on to because as one they practically genuflected before sprint-walking back to their fancy silver car parked on the street.

Blond king and henchman remained frozen in position until the car was out of sight before they clicked back into movement. Simultaneously they turned, staring at each other for a few long seconds before the laughter started.

He laughed and the sound carried perfectly to my ears. It was a clear, bright noise. Not a chuckle, a guffaw or a mumbled *hahah*. Each vibration erupted from his throat like a pure note, round and loud and defined by unblemished joy.

It was the best thing I had ever heard.

I gasped lightly as his joy burned through me and, as if he heard it, his head turned my way. We were too far away to truly lock eyes but it felt like we did. His friend said something to him but the blond object of my instant obsession ignored him. For the first time since I noticed him, his face fell into somberness and his jaw tightened.

I may have loved him from the moment I saw him but he clearly did not feel the same.

In fact, if the way he abruptly cut away from me was any indication, throwing one long leg over the seat of a huge chrome bike and revving the engine before I could even think to tear my eyes away, he may have even hated me at first sight.

Paralyzed, I watched him peel out of the lot with his buddy. It hurt. Which was insane because I didn't even know the man and more importantly, I refused to be taken in by a pretty face.

The last time that had happened, someone had died.

I pulled myself together, collecting the grocery detritus

that spilled out of some of the melted bags and moved to my car. It was hot as hell in the compact sedan. The leather seats nearly burned the skin off my bottom when I sat down. I got back out of the car and manually cranked open all of the windows before I started the drive home.

Home was a sweet white-shingled house in the quiet residential area of Dunbar in Vancouver where real estate prices were crazy and desperate housewives were a real thing. My husband had grown up in the ritzy grove about eighteen years before I'd been born and grown up in the house next to his. Everyone oohed and ahhed over our little love story, the older neighbor falling for the quiet girl next door.

Once, I'd done the same.

Now, as I rolled up the asphalt drive and saw William's car parked in the garage, I felt only dread.

"I'm home," I called when I opened the door.

I didn't want to say the words, but William liked the ritual. He liked it more when he came home to me already in the house, dinner on the stove and a smile on my face, but I'd gone back to work this year after three years of staying at home waiting for kids who'd never come. I loved working at Entrance Bay Academy, one of the most prestigious schools in the province, but William thought it was unnecessary. We had enough money, he said, and things around the house grew neglected in my absence, especially when you added on my hour-long commute there and back to the small town north of Vancouver that harboured the school. We had no children and no pets, a housekeeper with a more than mild form of OCD who came to the house once a week. I didn't notice much of a difference but I didn't say anything. This was because William wasn't a fighter in the traditional sense. He didn't yell or accuse, bruise with his actions or words. Instead, he disappeared.

His office became a black hole, a great devourer of not only my husband but our potential conflict and our possible resolution. Every fight we could have had lingered in the spaces between his leather-bound law books, under the edges of the Persian carpet. Sometimes, when he was late returning home, I would sit in his big wingback leather chair deep in the heart of his office and I would close my eyes. Only then could I find relief in my imaginations, yell at him the way I wanted to so many days and so many nights across so many years.

We'd married when I was eighteen and he was thirty-six. I was head over heels in love with the curl in his mostly black, slightly graying hair, his incredible *manliness* next to the boys that hung around me in school. I was infatuated with him, with how I looked beside him in pictures, so young and pretty under his distinguished arm. I'd known him my whole life so he was safe but also older and worldlier and, I hoped, dirtier than me. There were so many things an older man could teach a naive girl. I used to touch myself at night imagining the things he would do to me, the ways he could make me pleasure him.

Sadly, I still did.

"Beautiful," William said, smiling at me warmly from where he read in a deep armchair in the sitting area off the kitchen.

He presented me with a cheek to kiss, which I did diligently.

Every time I did, I wished he would grab me, haul me over his lap and lay into my ass with the flat off his palm.

I had these aggressive sexual fantasies often. Wishing that his sweet gesture smoothing back my hair was his fingers digging deep into the strands to puppeteer my head back and forth over his erection. Switching out our separate showers before bed with a shared one, where I bent double with my hands around my ankles as he pounded into me and the water pounded against us both.

I'd tried at first, a long time ago, to make these fantasies realities, but William wasn't interested.

I knew this, I did, but I was more than a little hot from the blond guy in the parking lot, the way he had commanded those men without even lifting a finger. It was only too easy to imagine the way he might command me if given the chance.

It was him that I had to blame for my actions.

I dumped my messenger bag beside William's chair and dropped to my knees between his legs.

"Cressida..." he warned softly.

He couldn't even scold me properly.

I ignored him.

My hands slid up his stiffly held legs until they found his belt and made quick work of undoing it. His cock was soft in its nest of hair but I pulled it into the light as if it was a revelation. It was silky in my mouth and easy to swallow.

William's hand hit the top of my head but didn't grab me, didn't even push me away.

"Cressida, really..." he protested again.

He didn't like oral sex. He liked vaginal sex: missionary, me on top or sometimes, if I forced him, doggy style.

I sucked him hard until basic biology took over and he grew in my mouth. I slammed my head down his shaft, taking him into my throat and loving the way it made me want to gag.

"Damn it," William said, not because it felt good, though it did, or because he liked it, but because he didn't *want* to like it.

I didn't care. I squeezed my eyes shut tightly as I jacked the base of him and imagined the way the blond king may have held my head down until I groaned and gagged around him. How he might have praised me for taking him so deep and pleasuring him so well.

Instead, I got, "I'm going to come and I don't want to do it in your mouth."

"Please?" I panted against his dick, my tongue trailing out to lick over his crown.

It was his turn to squeeze his eyes shut. His legs shook as he orgasmed, his semen landing in my open mouth and over my cheeks. It took him harshly, wrung him dry and useless afterward like a used napkin in his chair.

I leaned back on my haunches and wiped my mouth clean with my tongue and then the back of my hand. My pussy throbbed but I knew he wouldn't touch it so I didn't try to make him. Sex was for the dark hours and I was already in violation of his unspoken code of sexual conduct.

I knew what his reaction would be but, since I was a glutton for punishment, I waited patiently on my knees for him to recuperate. To open his eyes and pierce me with their disappointed, confused condemnation. He reached forward to touch my cheek softly as he asked me, "Why do you degrade yourself like that, Cressie? I don't need *that*."

I closed my eyes against the hot prickle of tears that threatened to elucidate my shame and leaned into his hand so that he would think I was sorry. In a way, I was, because I knew he didn't need *that* to love me. William loved me in a beautiful way, the way one might love a perfectly formed rose, a sentimental trinket. But he didn't love me in the way I needed, the way I'd wanted secretly since I was old enough to feel a heartbeat in my groin, the way one animal loved another.

"I'll make dinner," I said quietly, unfolding from my knees and going into the kitchen.

"That sounds nice," William agreed, easily forgiving me for my exploitation.

He efficiently did up his pants and went back to the book

he was reading while I uncovered the shepherd's pie I'd already prepped that morning.

Our night continued from there in a normal way—happy, trivial conversation about our days over mashed potato-topped meat and veg, an hour or so of reading side by side in front of the fire because we didn't own a TV and then our nightly, separate showers before going to bed. We didn't have sex. We rarely did anymore because the doctors had said that the odds of William having children were slim and my husband was of the mind that sex was for a purpose, not recreation.

So, I lay next to him in our beautiful house long into the night until it was the darkest of the evening hours. Only then did I quietly turn onto my back, lift my nightgown and sink my fingers into my burning hot pussy. I came in under two minutes with my clit pinched between my fingers and another two shoved deep inside, thinking of the sexy young blond king and how he would rule me if I were his queen. It was the hardest I had come in years, maybe ever, and right on its heels came the tears. I cried silently and long into my pillow until it was steeped in salty wet and I was steeped deeply in shame. It was in all two hundred and six of my bones, so entangled with my molecules it was an essential strand of my DNA. I'd been living with it since I was pubescent teenage girl and I was so tired of it.

I was tired of boredom. The monotony of my loving husband and our life together, the hamster wheel of our social life with shallow suburban moneyed folk and the irrefutable fact that I was not attracted to my husband.

I lay in the dark for what seemed like an eternity, dissecting my thoughts like an academic at a conference. Slowly, with no discernable evolution, I was furious.

I was a twenty-six-year-old woman acting like a depressed

middle-aged housewife. I had decades ahead of me still to live, to live a life where excitement, spontaneity and change could be a constant. Why was I lying in the dark like a victim? Because I was ashamed that my perfect life and husband didn't make me happy?

Pathetic.

Then, I wondered if I really was. William loved me because I was beautiful and obedient, because he had trained me to be this way since I was an impressionable girl. He did not love the side of me that was scratching and wailing to break free of the social constraints he'd bound me in so beautifully for years. It was the part of me that wanted to lie, steal and cheat; to sin a little every day and gorge myself on a steady diet of thrills. That side would bring the Irons name shame and the most important thing to William was his wealth and reputation.

It was his wealth that gave me pause. I had no real money of my own unless I counted the few thousand dollars my grandfather put into a small trust for me. I didn't know if it would be enough to start a new life. I didn't even know if I was savvy enough or strong enough to strike out on my own, not after an entire life of obedience to my father, and then my husband.

I didn't know, but as I lay there cradled in the dark night, I decided that I didn't care about the certainty. That, in fact, it was part of the thrill.

I rolled over to look at William lying beside me, his face slack and peaceful in slumber. Reverently, I traced his thick eyebrows, the slightly jagged edge of his hairline down to the winged ear that I liked to kiss. I peeled the covers away from his body carefully so that I could run my eyes over the entirety of my husband for the last time.

The finality settled in me like a bright thing, something light that made the heaviness in my bones fizzle and pop into nothingness.

"William," I whispered, pressing a thumb to the corner of his lips. "Wake up. I have to tell you something."

# Two.

*Three months later.*

Everyone was talking about it.

They'd let one of *them* in.

And not just one of them but the spawn of the devil himself.

Zeus Garro, infamous President of The Fallen MC, the most notorious motorcycle gang in the country, had somehow enrolled his son in the best private school in the province, not to mention halfway through the school year.

Entrance Bay Academy's halls were humming with the news but the teacher's lounge at lunch break that day was practically echoing with it.

"Can you believe it?" Willow Ashby stage-whispered to her best friend and colleague in the music department, Tammy Piper. "They're letting the son of a freaking gang member into the school. How can any of us expect to be safe now?"

I rolled my eyes but pretended to keep reading my heavily annotated copy of *Paradise Lost*. Ostensibly, I was reviewing it in preparation for my lecture in my sixth period advanced English twelve class, but I'd read the epic poem at least twenty-two times, knew the heaviest hitting lines by heart and had prepared my lesson plan to the most minute detail three months ago when my life blew apart and I had nothing to do but read.

Still, pretending to be diligent was better than being drawn into teacher gossip about the new kid. Even after a full semester of teaching, I was surprised by how much teacher culture mirrored teenage culture in the hallowed halls of EBA. When I'd been happily married, my life had revolved around William, so I hadn't noticed as much but now that I was single, the dramatic pull was nearly inexorable.

"What if he brings a gun to school?" Tammy asked.

"It'll be drugs," Willow said. "Just you wait. Before we know it, the academy will just be a front for drug running."

"Don't be an idiot, *Pillow*," Rainbow Lee, a fellow teacher, said as she came into the lounge and walked past the two gossips. "If everyone judged books by their covers, there is no way you would be allowed to teach people. You look like a slutty Malibu Barbie."

I hid my snort behind my hand as Rainbow continued over to where I usually sat and curled up on the banquette by the bookcases. She winked as she sat down on the couch across from me, ignoring the sputtering noises Willow made as she tried to think of a comeback.

"You really shouldn't call her Pillow," I chided her with a friendly smile, even though Rainbow had made overtures at friendship with me before and I had gently rebuffed her.

William didn't like to socialize unless it was necessary to do so at one of his firm's functions, so I'd stopped making friends a long time ago.

I was a new woman though, I had time for friends, especially ones as sassy as Rainbow Lee.

She shrugged her bony shoulders. "Those fake boobs are enormous. She clearly wants attention drawn to them so I don't see the problem."

A rough throat clearing over my shoulder caught my attention, pulling my gaze from Rainbow to a fairly attractive brunet man with a beautifully groomed beard and thick-rimmed black glasses. He wore a brightly coloured plaid shirt beneath his tweed blazer with a matching kerchief tucked in his front pocket. I recognized him from the halls but I'd never spoken to him before. He reminded me of a younger William, obsessed with his looks and his own charms.

My lips pursed before I could help it.

"Hello," he said with a gracious smile, as if his attention was something I should be grateful for.

My hackles rose but a lifetime of manners and etiquette prompted me to say, "Hello," instead of ignoring him as I wanted to.

He waited a beat for me to elaborate and when I didn't, his grin widened. "You're the new IB English and history teacher, Cressida Irons."

"I am, but I've been here for six months now. You're a bit tardy with your introduction," I pointed out helpfully.

He laughed and I got the feeling that he thought we were flirting.

"Mitch Warren," he introduced himself anyway, sitting down on the edge of the little coffee table in front of me. "IB biology and freshman science. It's nice to have some fresh blood infused into this place."

I didn't really know what to say, so I didn't say anything.

I shouldn't have worried because he was undeterred. "You should come out with us tonight. The staff always gets a drink at McClellan's on Wednesdays to make hump day a little easier. I could give you a ride if you need one?"

He was being sweet and considerate. It wasn't his fault that

I was more than shy, a little scared and definitely hopeless. So, I smiled back at him, a small smile because I'd forgotten how to give a genuine one.

"I have a car but a drink sounds lovely. What time should I be there?"

He blinked at me for a moment before rolling back his shoulders and beaming at me. I had to admit, he had a very pretty smile.

"Six o'clock too early? We try not to stay out too late with school and all."

"Makes sense. I'll see you then." I smiled before pointedly turning back to my book.

He waited a moment, his eyes hot against my face, before he moved away. I sighed a quiet breath of relief.

"I know, he's hot but a serious pain in the ass," Rainbow warned me even though her eyes were dancing with amusement.

I closed my book again to smile at her. "I'm just trying to be more social. Trust me, I'm not looking for a new romance."

"Hey, sprite," Rainbow called to someone over my shoulder.

I looked up to see a diminutive woman with short, spiky black hair and delicate features flop down in the chair next to me as if she weighed a ton, when she couldn't have been more than a hundred pounds soaking wet.

Tayline Brooks frowned. "Don't call me that, it makes me feel silly."

"Maybe next time don't flounce into the room, then," Rainbow shot back.

Tayline stuck her tongue out and I laughed at them.

She rolled her huge, brown eyes as her head lolled against the backrest and she continued talking as if we were mid-conversation. "Rainbow's always been a bit of a name caller. She grew up with a home-stay family that *clearly* didn't teach her any manners."

"I have manners. I just prefer truth to bullshit," she retorted.

"That's the better option," I agreed.

They both looked at me with mild surprise and then, startlingly, evaluation.

"Heard you got divorced," Rainbow said. "Does that mean you finally found a spine?"

"Rainbow!" Tayline protested.

"What? She just said she prefers honesty."

"That was more cruel than honest."

"I don't mind, really," I interrupted, and I meant it. I was done with being mild-mannered and subservient, with observing everything but never giving my input. I stared hard into Rainbow's dark eyes and said, "I found a spine."

"Cool. I noticed the sad eyes." She gestured to my outfit, a sleek black turtleneck dress. "This new you is better."

"Agreed."

Tayline had gnawed on her full bottom lip as she watched our exchange, but now she leaned forward with an earnestness that warmed my heart. "Seriously though, you're okay?"

I swallowed the lump in my throat unsuccessfully. "I'm getting there."

"You moved here, right? From Vancouver."

I nodded. "I bought the old cabin on Back Bay Road."

Tayline screwed her nose up adorably but Rainbow snorted.

"Yeah, it needs a little work," I admitted.

"You'll need a thousand hands and scads of money to make the place habitable."

I peered at Rainbow shyly. "I don't have many hands or scads of money."

"Your husband wasn't rich?"

"He is."

They stared at me, drawing their own conclusions.

"Asshole," Rainbow swore, shaking her head.

I shrugged because she was right, but I wasn't at the point where I felt comfortable talking badly about William.

"We could help, if you needed more hands," Tayline offered, her doll-like eyes wide with sincerity.

"I'd like that," I said.

"Cool," she said with a massive grin. "I'm so excited we can be friends now!"

"Every other woman at Entrance High is engaged or married," Rainbow explained, as if marriage was to be avoided at all costs.

Given my experiences, I was inclined to agree with her.

"Not Willow," Tayline amended.

"No, but she's a bitch so we don't hang out with her."

"And not Kathy."

"No, but she's a certified hermit and, God love her, she's ugly as sin so we don't hang out with her either," Rainbow explained.

I blanched at her candor, which made both of them laugh.

"Now that you live here, you should know now that nearly everyone in Entrance is freaking gorgeous," Tayline said, leaning forward in her chair to stare at me with large, earnest eyes. "Like seriously, there just may be something in the water here."

"I think it's that like draws like," Rainbow commented.

"For whatever reason, there are a shit-ton of pretty people in this town and us, the smart *and* pretty ones, we've gotta stick together."

I had no experience with women like this, with girlfriends or even any friends at all. The only relationships that I had ever known were with my conservative parents, my husband or the shallow acquaintances I had with other housewives back in Vancouver. Even in high school, I hadn't socialized much. I was too busy being groomed by my parents and William to be his future wife.

Moving to Entrance was about more than finding my independence from them, it was about learning how to *live.* Having friends even, and maybe especially friends like Tayline and Rainbow, seemed only fitting.

So, I smiled genuinely at them and said, "Seems like a good idea to me."

They both beamed back at me as the bell for sixth period rang out.

"So, we'll see you tonight at McClellan's?"

"Totally."

# Three.

McClellan's was cool. It was all wood, different colours and textures but totally beautiful, the big square bar most of all. It was packed with people, even on a Wednesday night, so it was filled with the sound of good humor and camaraderie. A happy place for happy people.

It made me feel odd, taking a part in the scene when normally, I only read about them. It was difficult not to sit back, acting as silent narrator as my companions, Rainbow, Tayline and Warren, who went by his last name, among them, laughed and reminisced about past school years and made predictions about the future. They were including me, everyone seemed determined to do so, but it only made it harder for me to let loose.

"I've got fifty smackaroos that the new MC kid sleeps with the entire grad class within the first six weeks," Willow said over the rim of her fancy blue-sugared cosmo.

"Willow! You shouldn't bet on the students' love lives," Harry Reynard, our soft-spoken librarian, protested.

She snorted. "Oh come on, Harry, you have eyes. That boy is *fine.* Another few years, and I'd take him for a ride, if you know what I mean?"

"I think everyone knows what you mean," Tayline said.

"But I have to agree, he is seriously gorgeous. I forgot how to conjugate the verb *faire* in class today, I was so stunned by his pretty face."

Everyone laughed so I took the moment to quietly tell Rainbow, "He was a no-show in my class today."

"No way. Did you tell the headmaster?"

I shook my head, biting my lip. "I wondered if maybe he got confused with his schedule. I want to give him the benefit of the doubt, especially with all this talk about him and his father. He probably feels unwelcome enough."

"You're a softie, eh?"

"Twenty bucks says that Tay hooks up with her biker again," Warren said as he sneered down at pretty, little Tayline.

She glowered at him but the blush riding high on her cheeks ruined it. "Fuck off."

"Hasn't asked you to go steady yet, then, eh?"

Even I frowned because Warren was being nasty, searching for a soft spot to poke at. I didn't know this "biker" but it was obviously a sensitive subject.

"Back off, Warren," Rainbow hissed.

"Seriously," said Georgie, our receptionist and an adorable middle-aged woman with bouncy blond curls.

Tayline didn't care for their protection. She bared her little teeth, leaning forward so that she was almost falling off her stool. "Careful now. I may just call up *that biker* and get him to remind you why we treat The Fallen with respect and more than a little bit of fear in Entrance."

"Oooh, I'm so scared." Warren laughed and a couple of his buddies, the biology and gym teachers, laughed with him.

Tayline leaned back on her stool, her face cast in the shadows of the low-lit bar, and spoke softly, "You should be."

A shiver worked its way down my spine. I was easily

spooked these days but even though I realized that, it did nothing to waylay my terror.

I knew of The Fallen MC, obviously. Everyone in British Columbia, on the west coast of both Canada and the USA, in all of the United Kingdom, knew of The Fallen. They were the modern-day warlords of those lands, the men who created their own rules and held ironclad rule over the rest of us. The police had tried for years to close them down but had given in to a tentative understanding when nothing, not since their inception in 1960, had brought them low. They were known and feared but they were not brutal the way some of the motorcycle clubs in Texas and the east were. The public shootings, pile-ups of dead bodies and poorly hidden marauding were a thing of the past. Their power was so absolute in BC that they ruled without contention.

I knew all of this because I did my research before moving to Entrance and because my brother was into a lot of bad stuff but he had never, not once, been stupid enough to get involved with The Fallen.

I found it hard to believe that pretty little Tayline was involved with an outlaw but I thought of the blond king from the parking lot so many months ago, his aura of menace and totalitarian-like control. He was the most attractive man I had ever laid eyes on, in no small part because of his unlawfulness.

As if sensing my thoughts, Tay pushed her stool closer to mine as the conversation resumed around us.

"You look interested, princess," she said with a sly kind of smile. "Have you ever had a biker before? I have to say, you don't look like the type but I don't know you well enough to see what's beneath the prettiness you've got going."

I stayed silent because what she said annoyed me but I didn't have enough experience to offer a scathing retort.

Tayline softened visibly, shedding the animosity that she'd shrouded herself in when Warren was attacking her. "I'm sorry. Cy is a touchy subject for me. My best friend is a cop. My kind of, sorta boyfriend is a one-percenter. You can see how it's a source of contention."

"I can." I hesitated. "Why do it, then?"

She stared off into the distance for a long moment. "A man without respect for the law is not a man without respect for anything. All that intensity, that devotion, is channeled toward other things, mostly their people; the brotherhood, family, their women. You can't experience anything like it until you've had it."

I swallowed thickly, surprised by the shiver of want in my bones. "A difficult thing to give up, then."

"Yes," she agreed softly.

We were quiet for a moment before she broke free of her contemplation to slam back the rest of her beer. She smacked her lips, wiped her wet mouth with the back of one hand and announced that the next round was on her.

I watched her go to the bar, which was when I noticed the blond king leaning against the far end, one booted foot crossed over the other. He was watching me in a way that said he had been watching me for a while. His handsomeness hooked painfully in my gut, pulling me toward him inexorably. I coveted that beauty; it filled me with greed and possessiveness. My hands itched to walk the clifflike drop of his steep cheekbones, to shove themselves into the thick, kinky mess of his golden hair.

I watched his intense stare transform into a brilliant smile. My breath left me all at once but I didn't care to get it back. I'd never breathe again if it meant seeing that man with that smile made especially for me.

*Come*, he mouthed.

I could almost hear his voice whispering the command in my ear, his hot breath against my neck. I shivered as I slid off the stool, making my way toward him without any conscious thought.

"Cress?" Tay called after me.

"Bathroom," I mumbled.

The blond king watched me cross to him for a moment before he turned around and sauntered out the back door.

I followed him.

The night air was cool and fragrant with sea salt and cedar, so fresh it made my lungs tingle. I took a moment to breathe deeply because I couldn't help it.

In that second, hands came at me. They pressed me by the shoulders to the wooden exterior of the bar but I didn't cry out because I knew it was the blond king who held me. The yellow light of a distant street lamp fell across the side of his face, cutting it into black-and-white relief that made him both staggeringly beautiful and utterly terrifying.

He stared down at me, studying me without words or care for as long as he wanted to. I let him because apparently, I was having an out-of-body experience.

We were breathing in tandem. It was a strange thing to notice, but I loved watching the way our combined breaths mingled together in white clouds in the cool fall night.

I'd wondered what colour his eyes would be but no amount of guessing could have prepared me for the absolute wonder of his gaze. His pupils were a bright, beautifully pale blue shot through with deeper demarcations and spots of brighter hue like imperfections in an ice cube.

Finally—his lips, too pink for a man, really—opened and I felt anticipation pull my body tight against the wall.

"Hey," he said softly.

I blinked up at him, shocked at the simplicity of his greeting.

"Hey," I said back.

Humor tugged at his mouth. He had more restraint than me. I smiled fully. His eyes tracked every nuance of the expression across my face before they darkened with unmistakable lust.

"You were in the parking lot of Mac's Grocer," he continued as if it were only moments after our bizarre almost encounter three months ago. "Pretty little thing standing dumbstruck beside a piece-of-shit Honda Civic."

Instantly, I bristled. "It's rude to insult someone's car."

It was his turn to blink, which he did before he tipped back his head and erupted in that clean, bright laughter again.

I tried not to fall to my knees at the beautiful sound.

"That's the truth, babe," he agreed after he'd settled down. "That's the damn truth. But I have to say it anyway, that car does not suit a smoke show like you."

"Smoke show?"

This had to be the strangest conversation I'd ever had.

His eyes sparkled, gleaming such pale a blue they looked almost colourless. "Yeah, babe. You're too hot for such a shit car."

Before I could get annoyed again, he chuckled and dipped down to speak just beside my ear. "Look good on the back of my bike though."

A little thrill shot through me. He must have felt the shiver through the hands still cupping my shoulders because they flexed against me in response, pulling me closer so that there was only a sliver of vibrating space between us.

"I don't even know you."

"Pressed up against me on the back of my bike, you'd get to know me pretty quick," he retorted.

His fingers were playing with a lock of my hair, which was incredibly distracting.

"You know, it's polite to introduce yourself to a lady before you hold her captive in a back alley," I explained lightly and even though what I said was true, it didn't mean that I didn't like it.

His grin flashed against his face. He knew I liked it. "Name's King."

I jolted, my eyebrows raised and my mouth open in shock. "Are you making fun of me?"

He tipped his head to the side. "No."

"Your given name is King?"

What were the odds that my little nickname for him would turn out to be so literal? Then again, what were the odds that I would run into the same man who had radically changed my life three months ago just by being alive, vibrant and beautiful in a way I'd never seen before?

"King Kyle Garro, babe."

"Why in the world would your parents name you that? Talk about unrealistic expectations," I muttered.

He laughed again but this time it was low, husky. "Not so unrealistic in my case."

*Oh.*

His eyes were laughing at me as he leaned even closer. The scent of him, the sweet tang of male sweat, the clean wholesome fragrance of detergent, legitimately made me weak in the knees. I was strangely grateful for the hands pining me to the wall.

"I was born to be King," he said, his voice so full of laughter that I wondered how he could speak past his humor.

I snorted before I could catch myself and, because he had my arms pinned so I couldn't cover my mouth in shocked horror at my uncharacteristic display of rudeness, I widened my eyes at him. "Sorry, that was rude."

"That was honest, babe. Don't worry, I dig it. Besides, you don't know me yet but soon as you do, you'll get it, my name and how it fits like a fuckin' glove." He grinned at me as he spoke, as he pressed himself even closer so that we were plastered together from thigh to chest.

"Um, King, you're a little close given that I literally just met you," I muttered.

I tried to shift away but the movement just made my breasts brush back and forth over his hard chest. His eyes darkened at my wiggling and one hand slid from my shoulder, past the outer edge of my breasts to curl around my hip.

"Like the feel of you against me."

I'd never met such a brazen man in my life. People weren't allowed to touch strangers like that, to say whatever crossed their mind. There were *rules* in modern society. But it seemed King Kyle Garro was cool with breaking them.

"Do you have no shame?" I asked.

He took in my tilted head, the earnest set of my features and didn't bother to keep himself from laughing at me. "Nah, never seemed like a great thing to have."

Well, I couldn't argue with that.

"That's fair," I said.

His gorgeous, crystal-clear eyes sparkled like they were faceted. "Yeah."

We stared at each other for a long time. He pressed so close to me that I could feel his heart beating. His pulse was a slow, hard drumbeat, whereas mine pattered wildly in my chest. He held me tightly, stared at me intimately as if he had a right to me, and more, as if he had been holding me and staring at me all our lives.

It was disconcerting only a bit more than it was enthralling and both emotions overwhelmed me.

"Are we going to do this all night? I've got colleagues inside waiting for me," I finally said, going for sassy but failing because my voice was breathy.

He grinned at me and up close to it like I was, it almost knocked me out with its perfection. I'd never seen such a beautiful smile, not even in a movie or a magazine.

"Could do this all night, for sure, but I'd rather have your fine ass on the back of my bike. Let me take you for a ride."

"A ride?"

He chuckled, but I caught the flash of erotic excitement in his eyes. "Yeah, a ride on my bike. It's a good night for it. You ever been up the Sea to Sky?"

He was referring to the Sea to Sky highway that started at the border to the United States, ran through Vancouver, Entrance, Whistler and all the way up to Lillooet. It was one of the most beautiful drives in the world, threading as it did all the way up the coast of British Columbia before it disappeared into the mountains. I'd followed it up to Entrance where it settled just north of Vancouver, but I'd yet to drive any farther.

So, I said, "No."

"You ever been on the back of a bike?"

"No."

This time a grin so wicked that my heart lost a beat to its beauty. "Lookin' forward to breakin' your cherry, babe."

He laughed at my scowl as he unpeeled himself from me and then me from the wall. I was opening my mouth to scold him when he reached out to smooth a hank of golden brown hair back from my face.

"Got a lot of hair, babe," he said.

"Ugh, yeah," I answered.

"Looks good."

"Um, thanks," I murmured, caught up in the warmth of his small grin.

"Right, you go in there, tell your girls that you're heading out and I'll meet you out front in five."

"Ah…" I hummed, uncomfortable with the entire situation now that his delicious body wasn't pressed up against mine and his yummy hormones weren't messing with my brain.

"No 'ah' about it. Get in there, get set and let's fuckin' go. Meet you out front in five, babe, yeah?" he ordered, leaning forward to grab the back of my neck and bring me close so that we were nearly nose to nose again.

I made the mistake of inhaling, taking in a deep lungful of that heady fresh laundry and male musk scent of his.

"Yeah," I agreed.

He squeezed my neck, grinned into my face and stepped away so quickly that I nearly fell forward. He was laughing softly, hands in his pockets, as he walked away around the corner. I blinked after him for a minute, chewing my bottom lip and worrying.

I'd moved to Entrance to get away from my boring, strictly regimented life. I'd never been hit on in a bar, never kissed a stranger, never rode on the back of a motorcycle or done anything I shouldn't have done. I was so dull, it was a wonder that I didn't put myself to sleep.

So, with renewed energy and a kick of pure enthusiasm, I skipped into the bar to tell my new friends that I was leaving. When I approached our group of tall tables, everyone was still there but they'd collected a few more people. One of them was crowding Tay—which was easy to do considering her size and then, considering his own—and he wore a black leather vest embroidered with the image of a skull that dissolved into brilliantly detailed angel wings. It was a striking and disturbing image, almost too beautiful to represent a motorcycle club. The Fallen MC was patched above the winged-skull and, if there had been any doubt, when the tall man turned toward me as I approached, it was obvious that he belonged to the outlaw band of brothers that silently ruled the province. This was obvious because he was a tall, broad-shouldered man with aggressive muscles that bulged under his black tee, a thick albeit beautifully groomed beard that partially hid the massive scar that sliced from the top of his left eye, ran behind a black eye patch and reemerged across his cheek to disappear in the hair covering his jaw. I'd never seen a man with such a disfiguring scar, let alone a man without an eye and I was struck dumb not with horror but curiosity. I'd learned a long time ago that my curiosity could get me in some serious trouble, so I quickly composed myself and walked up to the duo as if they were my best friends.

The one-eyed man stared me down with his single, dark brown eye as if daring me to be disturbed. I had the feeling he enjoyed frightening people.

I smiled at him. "Hi, you must be Cy. I'm Cressida Irons. It's nice to meet a friend of Tayline's."

Cy stared at me for what felt like forever before his glare lessened—though didn't leave completely—and he tipped his chin at me. I realized that it was the only acknowledgment I was going to get and I was okay with that.

When I turned to look at Tay, she was trying to rein in a smile.

"I'm leaving," I said, glad that Tay had her beau to distract her from my departure and that Rainbow was nowhere to be seen.

I'd only known them a day, but I had a feeling those two had already inducted me into their sacred sisterhood and I also had a feeling they didn't mess around with their girl's-night-out commandments, so letting a fellow girl friend leave on the back of some stranger's motorcycle would probably *not* be okay with them.

There was a small voice of reason in the back of my head that reminded me of the last time I'd left a bar with a random stranger. If no one had known where I'd gone, that night would have ended a lot differently for me. A lot worse.

So, I quickly leaned in to tell Tay, "I'm going on a ride with one of the bikers. Say bye to Rainbow for me. I'll text you when I get home safe, okay?"

"You have my number," she said but she looked uneasy. "Which biker?"

Before I could answer, Cy moved closer to her, knocking her knees apart with his wide hips so he could settle between them. When she struggled slightly, his hands clamped down on her hips to still her.

His woman secured, Cy looked at me and grunted, "Leavin' too. Later."

I smiled again at him, this time genuinely because I thought he was funny. "Later," I echoed with a chin lift before I grabbed my purse from Tay's chair and headed out the front doors.

# four.

In the moment when I was pushing the door open, I worried that King had decided not to give me a ride, that he realized he was wasting his time on a no-fun, dull-as-death woman who wouldn't know how to live even if she was given a second lease on life. The panic that followed that highly depressing thought swept through me, spiking my adrenaline so that I ended up pushing the door too hard and spilling out into the street with what looked like—and was—desperation.

Happily, and unhappily because I had just made a fool of myself, King was there. He sat on his huge Harley in the exact same pose he had that day in the parking lot. He was even wearing the same outfit, worn jeans that fit him like a woman's dream, clunky motorcycle boots that were surprisingly sexy, and a new tee, this one a dark grey that made his pale eyes glow like mercury.

He was smiling arrogantly when my gaze finally landed on his.

"Got your fill?" he asked.

Heat flooded my cheeks.

First, I literally trip on my way to see him and then I get caught *ogling* him.

God, I was such a dork.

I pushed my hair back behind my ears and shrugged helplessly as I explained, "I'm a massive dork."

I watched him throw his head back, and when I say throw, I mean he thrust it back with such force that I worried he would topple backward over the bike, then he proceeded to laugh uproariously at me for a good thirty seconds.

Seriously, I counted.

When he was done, he wiped his eyes with the back of his hand and then grinned at me. "You're easily the funniest woman I've ever met."

"You obviously don't know a lot of women," I countered.

His lids lowered and his eyes lost their sparkle as they heated. "Babe, I think we both know that I've known a fuckuva lot of women."

Yeah, I didn't doubt that. The man looked like a Greek god. There was no way someone that good-looking remained without a bedmate for long.

Still…

"You may have made your point but now I don't really want to get on the back of your bike."

His lips twitched but he bit his lip to hide the grin. Even though it was a poor attempt to veil his obvious amusement with me, I was glad because I'd adopted my Serious Teacher Pose, hands on hips, weight on one leg with the other extended so I could tap my high-heeled toe, and chin tilted down so that I could glower through my lashes. If he didn't take *that* seriously then I knew I would never stand a chance of making him listen to me.

"Babe," he said, as if that negated all of my doubts.

It didn't. At least, not really. I did like it when he called me babe, even if it was because he didn't know my name.

"You don't even know my name!" I accused, shocked that

I'd only just noticed.

"Yeah."

"You've been calling me babe because *you don't even know my name* and here I was, *liking* that you called me babe," I explained with my hands now fisted on my hips.

He cocked his head as he stared at me, still smiling. "Don't see the problem if you like it."

"But you probably call every girl babe," I pointed out. "And you probably don't know their real names either."

His lip twitch was my only answer.

I made a noise of frustration, something between a low shriek and a growl, and turned on my heel to go back inside.

"Babe," he called, proving that he had serious nerve. "You like being called babe by any guy?"

I hesitated, not understanding where he was coming from. "Not particularly."

It was kind of misogynistic, I guessed, but, truthfully, no one had ever called me that before.

"Right. But you like it when *I* call you babe."

It went without saying—because I had already said it to him—that I did.

"Babe," he repeated, humor vibrant in his words as he held out a spare helmet for me. "Get over here and get on the back of my bike."

I could feel the war raging inside my chest. It wasn't the sane or safe choice to get on the back of a bike with a complete stranger who, while out of this world beautiful, could easily overpower me if that was his intention. My heart rallied against that logic, pointing enthusiastically at his aforementioned beautiful face and his pure, bright smile. A man like that would never take advantage of a woman, right?

Besides, my heart had longed for such romance for a very

long time and here was an opportunity to literally ride off into the night with a handsome stranger. I mean, come on. How much better could it get?

In the end though, it was my gut that decided things for me. It was the same feeling I'd had when we were breathing the same air. My skin prickled, waiting for the touch of his strong hands, my nipples pebbled in anticipation of being pressed up against the cool leather of his back. The animal side of me, one that I had seen in so many other humans but never felt myself, called out to him.

I heeded that call even though I knew listening to instinct over reason would probably get me in trouble.

I knew it, and I wanted it.

So, without a word, I turned and made my way over to the bike. With an easiness that hid my unfamiliarity with motorcycles, I swung my leg over the silver and black beast and settled myself on the perch just behind him. The skirt of my dress rode high on my thighs so that only my underwear separated my core from King's broad back.

I shivered as he tugged my arms around his slim torso and I fell flush against him.

"Don't be afraid to scratch or bite me if you get scared," he said over his shoulder.

I didn't have to look at his face to know he was smiling.

"I won't get scared," I lied.

"Don't be afraid to scratch or bite me all the same," he retorted.

Before I could say anything, although I had absolutely *no* idea how to respond to that, the bike came to life with a low roar and King was pushing off the ground and into motion. We turned off Main Street immediately and found ourselves on a long backwoods road that led us directly onto the highway.

As soon as we hit the open road, King let out a loud, carefree shout and gunned us forward. My arms convulsed around him in fear.

The Sea to Sky highway was a windingribbon of pavement that followed the edge of the coastline. It was beautiful, especially as the sun winked out behind the mountains and spilled vibrant pinks and oranges across the sky. It was also freaking terrifying. King took us around the corners so fast that we were close enough to the pavement on one side that I could have touched it *easily*.

"King," I tried to shout, but my voice was breathless with fear.

His laughter rumbled through him and against my chest. It warmed me against the cool lash of wind streaking past me, through my hair and over my skin. It made me realize how good the air smelled, so sharp and fresh. I could feel my heart acutely in my chest, the way my breath churned through my lungs and escaped in excited puffs through my open lips. I felt alive, utterly recklessly, *beautifully* alive.

"This is great!" I shouted into the wind.

King laughed harder.

We rode for a long time, until my butt ached and my thighs burned.

"Feel the burn?" King shouted over his shoulder at me.

I did, in more ways than one with my body pressed so close to his. I could feel the muscles shifting in his back, rolling like waves against the shore of my pelvis.

"Yes," I answered, laughing.

"Wouldn't want to ride you too hard," he yelled back.

I buried my face in his back so that he could feel my laughter against his body.

We finally pulled off to a bar on the side of the highway,

tucked away in an artificial clearing between a thick copse of evergreens. It was a long, low rectangle of poorly painted turquoise wood panels with a small sign above the door that read Eugene's in neon pink lights. I squinted at the old-school movie theatre sign that had the words "When life gives you lemons, grab the tequila" slotted into it.

"You play pool?" King asked as he easily swung off the bike and spun to face me.

He moved with such vitality it was like watching an athlete play his sport, with a grace and energy that took my breath away. I was relatively sure I could watch him play ping-pong and find it utterly captivating.

I gasped when he stepped forward to pluck me off the bike and set me on my high heels.

My legs wobbled as if I'd been at sea when I took my first few steps. King chuckled as he slid in to wrap an arm around my waist.

"Steady on," he teased.

"I'm perfectly capable of walking by myself," I sniffed.

His free hand firmly gripped the back of my neck so that I was forced to look up at him. It was a possessive, overtly familiar gesture, but I had the feeling that King was a man who took what he wanted.

And for some insane reason, at the moment, that seemed to be me.

"Maybe I just wanted an excuse to take you in my arms," he whispered huskily, dipping down so that his lips were so, so close to mine.

"You don't seem like the type of guy who needs an excuse," I breathed, my sass lost to the desire that flared at his proximity.

His eyes flashed and he tugged me close with a jerk that had our bodies flushed together thigh to thigh, groin to groin, chest to chest. I shuddered against him as his hand slid from my hip over across the small of my back to the opposite side of my ass and gave it a squeeze.

"Thank you for reminding me," he said before he kissed me.

He swallowed my gasp with his lips and filled my open mouth with his skilled, silken tongue. His taste erupted in my mouth, a combination of hot, sweet cinnamon candies and a flavor uniquely his own. I groaned and he swallowed that too. When my knees grew softer than warm butter, he banded a strong arm around my waist to keep me propped up.

When he finally broke away, I kept my eyes closed, lips open and damp, savoring every last minute of the kiss even as it dissipated like a melting candy on my tongue.

"Good?" he asked with a grin when I finally opened my eyes.

"Awesome," I breathed. "I freaking loved that."

"The kiss or the ride?"

"Um, both?" I'd seen kisses in movies that looked pretty impressive but they should've hired King to show them how it was really done. My knees were still shot, or at least I told myself they were so that I had an excuse to keep my hands fisted in his tee.

"Yeah?" His grin expanded, impossible bright. "Cool."

"Yeah, cool," I said, unable to do anything but grin back at him like a fool.

"So, pool. You play?"

"Never," I admitted.

I was seriously pathetic.

But King only continued to beam down at me. His excitement was so contagious that it obliterated my momentary self-hatred.

"Glad to be the one to teach ya, babe."

"Me too."

He chuckled as he pulled me tight into his left side under the long reach of his arm slung across my shoulders. I fit perfectly there, small in the crook of his long, strong body, cradled there as if I already meant something to him. He smelled like heaven, like fresh air and laundry. I dragged a deep breath into my lungs and giggled when he stared down at me with a raised eyebrow.

I shrugged a shoulder, trying to play it off. "You smell amazing."

"So do you, babe, but I've known you 'bout an hour so I was gonna wait to sniff you that obviously until at least the second date."

I choked because I was embarrassed but I laughed because he'd just improved on perfection by being funny on top of everything else. He tugged me even closer as we walked across the lot, either because he wanted me closer or because he was aware that walking on gravel in high heels was as seriously precarious exercise. Either way, it made me want to swoon.

"Now that we've passed that beginner shit, I'm warning you, I'm going to have my nose at your throat a lot taking hits of that sugar-and-spice smell you got going."

I laughed as he pushed open the door to the dark bar. Music rushed out to meet us, wrapping me in one of my favorite Elvis songs, "Jailhouse Rock", that made me want to dance.

"Fan of the King?" my mysterious biker asked me as he ushered me over to the bar.

"My dream vacation is to go to Graceland," I said in answer.

He laughed. "Glad to hear you got good taste in music, babe."

I nodded absently but my mind was busy processing the scenery.

The interior of the bar was warm but not unbearable and tinged blue, green and pink from the wickedly cool neon light art that hung around the one huge room. Smack-dab in the middle of the space was an enormous wooden bar, brightly coloured and beautifully artistic graffiti scrawled across the base of it while the large podium in the middle was shelved with row after row of liquors and shining glassware. To the left was a kind of gaming area with two burgundy red felt pool tables, three dart boards, a Pac-Man arcade game that I immediately *had to play* and two of those mini basketball hoop arcade games that I'd only ever seen at the fair. On the other side was a small raised stage that was currently empty and most of the seating, and a little dance floor between the tables and the stage. The walls were black with those cool neon lights twisted into an assortment of images like guitars, flamingos and also cool sayings like Wild At Heart and, the biggest one across the main wall behind the bar that said Shut Up and Drink.

It was, without a doubt, the coolest place I'd ever been to.

"Wow," I mumbled as King led us directly to the bar.

He grinned as he once again lifted me by the hips to place me on a stool. "Cool, right?"

"Very," I agreed.

"What can I get you?" he asked, leaning in so that I was caged between the bar and his long, lean body by the arm he braced on the counter.

I tried not to sniff him again but it was hard.

"Gin and tonic?"

"Is that a question or your drink order?" he asked me, eyebrow raised.

"Um," I hedged. William had always ordered my drinks

for me. If it was a casual before-dinner drink, it was always a gin and tonic; if we were at dinner, it was always wine or champagne. "I don't really know what I like. I don't drink very often."

His right eyebrow joined the left high on his forehead. "You're how old? By the time I was fifteen, I knew I was a beer and whiskey man through and fuckin' through."

"That's early," I pointed out, to take the spotlight off of me. "You know you are six times more likely to develop alcoholism if you drink before the age of fifteen."

He smirked. "Only addiction I got is to bikes, books and babes."

"Books?"

He laughed that gorgeous laugh right into my face. "You judgin' a book by its cover?"

I blushed. "Sorry, a lifetime of shallowness has left me a little judgmental. I'm trying to change that."

"Now you surprise me," he peered at me, fingering a lock of my pin-straight hair and rubbing it between his fingers. "Pretty like a fuckin' princess but smart like a queen."

An enormous man, taller and broader than anyone I had ever seen in my life, appeared in front of us so quietly it was as if he had materialized there. He wore his long, glossy black hair tied back in a thick, messy man bun at the base of his brown neck, his plaid black-and-red shirtsleeves rolled up haphazardly over quilted forearms the size of one of my calves. The features he held in stern repose were roughly cut, a bump from a once or twice broken nose, cliffy cheekbones and a jaw so squared it created right angles under his ears. Even his mouth was hard, flat lined over a dimpled, scruffy chin and his eyes, though thickly lashed, were a flat brown. He was a brute, the poster child for the Canadian outback.

"Eugene," King greeted warmly. "Sup?"

The man, inexplicably and horribly named Eugene, grunted in response.

King didn't seem perturbed by the bartender's lack of social grace. He angled toward the bar but slid a hand under my hair at the tender skin on the back of my neck and squeezed possessively.

"Listen, man, this lady doesn't know her drink preference yet, if you can fuckin' believe it. Do me a favor and bring us a selection of cocktails and beers you think she might like."

"Sweet, sour, bitter or clean?" Eugene asked, leaning his trunklike arms against the bar so he could look me in the eye. I tried not to flinch when I saw the sheer size of his hands. They were enormous, more animal than human. I had no doubt he could crush me with those hands if he wanted to.

"Um, not too sweet, sour and smoky, maybe?" I answered, still staring at those paws.

They flexed and then clenched into a fist the size of a baby's head. My gaze snapped up to his to find him grinning, but even that expression was vaguely terrifying because it looked unused and awkward on his all-man face.

"Skittish one you got there, King," he rumbled in a deep rough-edged voice.

King chuckled. "She's new."

"Yeah, to Entrance?"

"To livin'."

Eugene pursed his lips and finally locked eyes with me. I was surprised by the intensity of his gaze, the scrutiny that made me feel he was giving me a full up-and-down even though he only looked directly into my eyes. He was turning me inside out to make sure I was good enough for his buddy. I let him, even though it made me squirm, because I liked that King had someone looking out for him.

"Good woman," Eugene finally noted, somberly and academically as if he was reciting his doctorate thesis to the board. "Deserves a good *man*."

I frowned at his odd emphasis on the word "man" and so did King. He growled low in his throat, a sound that made me embarrassingly hot.

"If you're gonna cock-block me, get someone else to make our fuckin' drinks."

"No one'll make 'em better than me."

"She wouldn't know the difference."

My head swiveled back and forth between them like I was watching a tennis match but a deep unease flickered at the back of my thoughts, a candle flame trying to illuminate the things that lurked in the dark.

King finished the stare-off by turning to me, blocking Eugene from my sight. Without thinking, I reached up to tug on a lone, perfectly formed curl in his riot of kinky and straight hair.

I felt his irritation fall away as he watched me watch the slide of his silky locks between my fingers.

"You wanna play with me, babe?" he asked.

I knew he was referring to pool, but it sounded like he could have been referring to something else, something more. A little thrill of fear and anticipation zipped up my spine.

"Can we do some shots first?" I asked.

He raised his brows at me. "You done 'em before?"

"Once," I said.

I'd done shots the one night I'd tried to deviate from my life path, at my bachelorette party thrown by my brother for just the two of us. The night I'd learned not to let my inner deviant out to play.

"Eugene, give us two shots of tequila too," King called out

without taking his eyes off me, then said, "I'll let you get tipsy, babe, but just enough to loosen you up. You know how to do a tequila shooter?"

"Lime and salt, right?"

He grinned at me as the shots were put in front of us with a salt shaker and a bowl of limes.

"First you lick," he said, picking up my left hand and locking eyes with me as he licked a sinuous path along the back of my palm between my thumb and forefinger. "Then you salt. Get your shot in the other hand just like that. Good. Then, lick the salt, slam the shot and finish with the lime. Ready?"

I hesitated because Eugene was watching me and chuckling and a few other patrons toward the end of the bar were openly staring at the grown woman who had never done a tequila shot.

"You got this, babe. Trust me, this is good tequila and the burn is even better. Why don't you let me show you how it's done first, yeah?"

I nodded, relieved because I didn't want to make a fool of myself in front of the regulars.

King's smirk turned mischievous as he sank his hand through my hair to the back of my neck and tugged me toward him. Once I was near enough, he threaded his fingers through the locks at the nape of my neck and tugged to the side so that the left side of my neck was exposed. I stopped breathing when he ducked down to run his nose over the skin there.

"Told you I'd have my nose at your throat," he reminded me. His voice was rough like wheels over gravel but his tongue was silken as it darted out to run the same path his nose had just done down my neck.

I shivered violently, which made him laugh against my cool wet skin.

"Watch me," he ordered as he leaned back to grab his shot.

He didn't have to. I was certain I could spend the rest of my life watching him and never get tired. My weird compulsion lent me new understanding toward reality TV. Watching beautiful people live was definitely something I could get behind.

King gently tilted my head and sprinkled salt on my wet skin, then swayed forward to languidly lick it off. I sighed into his bright mass of hair, unable to stop myself from running my hands through the side available to me. How a man could have hair that soft was beyond me.

I waited until he slammed back the shot and sank his teeth somewhat erotically into the fruit, before I asked my question.

"Do you deep condition or what?"

"Excuse me?"

"Deep condition your hair," I explained patiently. "It's so soft."

"Ugh, babe, I'm a man."

"Yes," I said, because I was *very* aware of that. "A man with seriously soft hair. I need to know what conditioner you use so I can get some for myself."

"Babe," he said slowly, deliberately. "I'm a *man*. You seriously think I use conditioner?"

"Yes, but specifically deep conditioner," I explained. "Otherwise, you wouldn't have hair softer than Vicuna cashmere."

"What the fuck is Vicuna cashmere?" King asked, laughing, leaning back to prop his elbows on the bar so that he could rest comfortably between my legs but not touch me, close but not crowding.

"It's *the* finest cashmere in the world. So, don't tell me you don't use deep conditioner, King. We just met and lying doesn't make a good first impression."

He stared at me for a long minute and I stared back, my eyebrows raised and lids narrowed in a modified version of my No-Nonsense Teacher expression. Finally, he blinked and burst out laughing.

I tried to be annoyed but couldn't. His laugh was seriously the best thing I'd ever heard.

"King," I protested, but he was already leaning forward to wrap his arms around me, cocooning me in his laughter.

It was *awesome*.

When he quieted, he pulled back just enough to look down at me with sparkling eyes. "You're hilarious, babe, you know that?"

"I was serious."

He chuckled again, shaking his head as if I was too much. "Take your shot and let's play pool. Winner gets a kiss, yeah?"

"That means loser gets a kiss, too," I pointed out.

King winked at me. "Perfect."

# five.

It was after another tequila shot, three cocktails (a gin and tonic, something called a Moscow Mule that was fabulous and a cosmo martini that I thought tasted like liquid sugar, so *yuck*) and a Blue Buck beer for me and just the one shot and a beer for King.

It was after I'd lost at pool four times but kicked ass at Mrs. Pac-Man and after I'd met some of the regulars, all of them old men except for a nerdy ginger-haired guy working on his computer named, inexplicably, Curtains.

It was, in all, after the best date and probably best night of my life, and King and I were heading back to Entrance because it was well past midnight and I had school the next morning.

The happiness I felt drove me to distraction, which was why it took me a moment to distinguish the new sound from the rushing wind, the gun of the motorcycle and the increasingly loud vibration of machines against pavement as they gained ground. Before I could make sense of it, they surrounded us.

I gasped and pressed myself even closer to King, who swore viciously under his breath.

Bikers on all sides of us, two closing in front of our bike so we were forced to slow down.

My eyes swept over the litany of chrome, black and leather,

the flurry of bearded faces and tattooed skin. The skeletal face of The Fallen MC's infamous patch stared at me from all angles. It was like something from a horror film.

Immediately, I knew I deserved whatever horrors came next. This was what I got for taking a risk.

"Don't be afraid, babe. I'm gonna pull off at the next shoulder," King called through the roar of wind and gunning engines.

I didn't bother trying to answer both because it would be impossible to match the volume of the wind and because we had already begun to pull off the road.

We were barely stopped before King was gently peeling me off the bike, mindful of my aching, inexperienced body.

"I want you to stay here and don't say a word, yeah?" he murmured to me as he settled me carefully against his bike.

"Okay," I whispered, my eyes darting to the small group of leather-clad men pulling up beside us.

"Hey," he said, pinching my chin between his fingers so that I was forced to look at him. "Nothing is gonna happen here. These guys, they're my family. They saw me with a chick and they probably just want to razz me about it. No worries. Just let me deal with it alone. They aren't the kind of men someone like you would understand."

Something flashed across his face, something that looked an awful lot like regret followed swiftly by shame, but he was moving away from me before I could decipher it.

I watched his loose, rolling gait with a little bit of lust despite my discomfort. He called something to a short, stocky older man wearing all black with a shock of white hair he had spiked all over his head. They gave each other one of those manly, slam-a-fist-on-the-back kind of hugs before grasping each other by the back of the neck to bring their foreheads together as they spoke quietly about something.

The other guys hung back, laughing and shooting the shit, looking at me curiously but keeping their distance. One guy started to walk over but King's hand flexed and released—a subtle sign, but one that the advancing man heeded instantly.

I noticed the enormous white, dark green and black patches on the backs of their jackets and vests and tried to swallow my apprehension. I'd been right all those weeks ago to think that King was involved with something dangerous in that back parking lot of Mac's Grocer. He was part of The Fallen MC, the criminal gang that had cornered the market on the marijuana trade not only in Vancouver, but throughout the entire province and most of western North America.

I would be a fool to get involved with someone like that. A criminal. Because if King was a biker in The Fallen, that was exactly what he was. I'd wanted some excitement in my life, a change from William and our modern-day suburbia, but that didn't mean I was ready for outright anarchy.

I couldn't deal with another person I loved going to prison and coming out so irreversibly fucked up that they were a different person. I couldn't do the visitations, their evolution from forced cheer to inadequate silence to nothing because in the end, after things had gotten really bad, my brother, Lysander, had refused to let me see him anymore.

My eyes settled on King again, seeing him throw back his head and laugh that laugh I had fallen in love with in the parking lot, that laugh that had been the final catalyst in my marriage. I barely knew the man, who he worked for, what he believed in, what he desired, and yet he had already irrevocably changed my life.

I dropped my gaze when he turned around to gesture at me with a smile and a wink as he'd obviously said something about me to the older biker. I didn't want them to talk about me. I didn't want these outlaws to know my name. I'd trained my whole life to be a good girl, a good wife and woman, and I told myself that I wasn't going to throw that away for a pretty face.

I peeked through my hair to see King laugh again and groaned.

A *damn* pretty face.

"Sorry 'bout that, babe," King said as his clunky boots filled my vision.

It disturbed me how sexy I found the sight of those manly shoes, so different from my husband's loafers and Sperry boat shoes.

"Babe?" His fingers found my chin and raised it so I was looking into his amazing ice-blue eyes. "You good?"

"I need you to take me home. This was a mistake."

He reeled back slightly, his mouth slack, big body loose then suddenly tight with tension. I watched as he closed his eyes for a moment, as he dragged in a fortifying breath. When he opened them again I was surprised by the guardedness of his expression.

"What changed in the last three minutes?"

I fidgeted because I didn't want to seem like the stick in the mud, snobby asshole that apparently I was to my core. "Nothing, I just had a minute to see the error of my ways. I don't even know you, and this"—I gestured vaguely—"isn't me."

His eyes narrowed on me. "I thought we agreed the best way to get to know each other was with you on the back of my bike? I don't take that shit lightly. In fact, I haven't asked a chick to ride with me like that in my whole fuckin' life. So, I'm going to ask you again, what the fuck changed in the last three minutes?"

My eyes flittered nervously over the bikers congregated over his shoulder. They were still chilling, some of them smoking cigarettes and what smelled like pot, two of them were arguing almost violently but then they burst out laughing.

When I brought my eyes back to King, his were sparking with fury.

"It's the MC."

It wasn't a question, but I nodded hesitantly. "I'm trying not to judge you, King, honestly. It's just, I'm not that kind of woman. Trust me, I wish I were. I've always wanted to be the kind of woman that lets her hair down, dances on tables in bars and goes skinny-dipping on the beach. I'm just *not*. I'm the kind of woman who curls up with a book in front of the fire, who doesn't drive at night in the rain because it isn't safe, who has never even left the country."

Shame burned through me like brush fire, a sudden evisceration of my confidence and will. I felt hollow and worthless as I looked up into his eyes again, unafraid of the condemnation I found there because no one felt that more deeply than I did.

"It's not that I don't want to do this with you," I said through the sting of tears in my throat. "I just know that I can't."

"You don't know anything about me. You don't even know if I'm part of that life you're so fuckin' afraid of."

"Are you?" I asked softly.

His jaw flexed. "Yes, but not in the way that you think."

I waited but he only stared at me, the muscles in his corded throat starkly defined in his anger.

"You're not gonna give me a chance, no matter what the fuck I say, eh?"

I swallowed noisily but didn't say anything. Truthfully, I wanted him to push me. I wanted him to be the first person in my life to throw me into the deep end, to drag me from the light into the darkness and the shadows to show me what lurked there, to teach me how to play with the monsters instead of fear them.

Instead, my stupid lower lip trembled and I rolled it into my mouth to stop the shakes.

King stared at me hard for a moment before he cursed violently and ran his fingers roughly through his unruly hair. "Fuck me for fuckin' digging some chick without the balls to see it through."

I flinched but he was right.

"I'll take you home."

He was quiet on the ride back into town. The spark between us was still there, and I had a feeling it would always be there like an electrical hum at the supermarket, but it was blanketed. His frustration rolled off him, made his body tense in my hold.

I pressed my forehead to the back of his leather jacket, noticing for the first time that it didn't have The Fallen MC patch on it. As the wind rushed past us, leaving this biker and me in a strange bubble of isolation amid the dark Canadian wilderness, it was easy to analyze my fears.

When the only time you've ever let go and really lived resulted in your brother going to prison for five years, you learn to keep a tight leash on your impulses. The only time I'd let my inner wild child out in the intervening years was in random, unsuccessful attempts to seduce William to the darker side of my lust. Now, here was King, trying to blow open the lid on my conservative values and lifelong propriety. Recklessness had never got anyone or me anywhere. Being a teacher, my favorite historical examples included Napoleon's rash march on Prussia and Picasso's depressive suicide over his lack of artistic skill mere days before his first critical acclaim. Literary cautionary tales also abounded, Romeo and Juliet being the most infamous, but more, Abelard and Heloise, and my ultimate favorite, Satan's crusade against the all-powerful God. My life and my studies had taught me that nothing good came from the unpredictable and I truly believed that even though I'd left William for a more exciting existence, dating someone like King would only destroy me.

Even as I solidified that opinion, there was a small part of me—that darker, crazier Cressida that lurked inside me like a schizophrenic bitch—that reminded me of one of my favorite *Paradise Lost* quotes, "The mind is its own place, and in itself can make a heaven of hell or a hell of heaven."

It was that small, sunken part of me that wondered if maybe it wasn't William or my parents who still had me in their cage, or if I was just too cowardly to walk through the very doors I'd pried open for myself.

I was so deep in thought that I jumped when we pulled into McClellan's parking lot and came to a stop beside my ugly Honda Civic. This time when King swung off, he didn't help me. Instead, he leaned against my car with his arms and booted feet crossed, guarded and angry.

"For what it's worth, I had fun tonight," I said quietly because my conviction was shallow and I was barely able to form the words.

King stared at me hard, it pushed at my chest and made it even harder to breathe. I tried to look away from the condemnation in his stare and failed.

"Fuck that," he bit out.

"Wha—"

He was on me so fast I had no time to bring up my hands or to close my lips before his open mouth landed hot on mine, his tongue stroked against mine in a way that easily erased the words poised there. His lean hips pinned me against the bike, his hand found my neck and I was a goner. There was no hope for any girl when a man like King had them in his arms. Scratch that, no man but King had this kind of power and now, he wielded it over me mercilessly.

"King," I gasped when he almost viciously bit my lip, dragged it through his teeth then sucked it like a candy.

"Yeah, baby. Tell me again how you can't do this," his voice rasped against me.

"Do you want me to give in like this? Because you're kissing me and not because I think it's a good idea?"

He closed his eyes, tipped his forehead against mine and sighed over my lips. "No, Cressida. What I want you to do is go home to your cold, lonely bed and think about doing all the dirty stuff you know I wanna do to you. Then I want you to wake up, make breakfast and think about how if I was there, I'd make it for you. After that, before school, I want you to bring your piece of shit car into Hephaestus Auto so I can take a look at it."

I was nearly dazed by his sweetness, about to ask how he knew I was a teacher when I was pretty sure that I hadn't told him about my job, and how he knew my name, because I wasn't sure I'd told him that either, until he started talking about my car.

"Betty Sue is fine. Besides, what do you know about cars?" I demanded.

His lips twitched and he tugged playfully on a lock of my hair. "If you could stop ogling my fine ass for two seconds, you mighta asked me where I worked and I woulda told you Hephaestus Auto and Mechanics."

My blush made him laugh, but he sobered pretty quickly

when I tried to push him away.

"Promise me you'll bring that car in. Not comfortable with you driving something that may be unsafe, yeah?"

"I don't know whatever it is you want with me, King, and honestly, I, uh, don't have the money to get my car fixed."

He scowled. "Knew it had problems. Now if you don't bring it in tomorrow, I'm going to have to send a fuckin' guy out to tow it and I won't be happy about it. Bring it in, Cress. Just because you don't wanna pursue what we got doesn't mean I want you drivin' a death trap."

"Okay, King," I said softly, both because my tequila buzz was veering straight into pure exhaustion and because he was being sweet in that badass biker way I found myself liking.

He nodded then smirked cockily as if he knew it was already a forgone conclusion that he'd get what he wanted from me. Before I could snap at him for it, his mouth was hard on mine and then he was maneuvering me to my car, tapping me on the ass and heading back to his bike.

"Didn't mention it before but I won't mind if you think of me in the shower tomorrow too, yeah?" he added just before the roar of his bike starting up drowned any possible hopes I had at retorting.

It was just as well. I was *definitely* going to think about him in the shower.

# Six.

I told myself I was spending extra time on my appearance that morning because I was evolving into a new post-William me, a woman who wore what she wanted even if it meant lipstick in the morning on a Thursday and a dress with a form-fitting bodice and short, flirty skirt that almost showed too much leg. It was mostly true, so the little lie was easier to swallow.

I smoothed the silky fabric over my thighs as I pulled into Hephaestus Auto and Mechanics and turned off the engine. The garage was surprisingly large and thrumming with activity even at seven-thirty in the morning. I spotted over a dozen men milling about the lot, working on cars or chatting over parts. The garage had a reputation all across Canada for being the best at automobile upgrades and motorcycle additions but I could never have imagined what a colossal venture it would be.

Suddenly, I was intensely aware of my rundown, fourth-hand Honda Civic. I pulled into an empty spot between some kind of Ferrari and a sleek black sports car with an insignia I'd never even seen before. I sat in my car, stroking the wheel absently to soothe us both as I took stock of the operation.

Hephaestus Auto sprawled across an enormous industrial lot that bordered the "good" side of downtown Entrance from the seedier neighborhoods. The parking area was large and bracketed an undesignated pathway that led up to a small brick building that must have housed the office areas and reception. To the left were the garage bays, five huge caverns all currently open and filled with at least one or two cars. To the right was a little park area, incongruent from the asphalt jungle, verdant with a small garden and huge earthenware pots and troughs that held long grass and, in the spring, would probably bloom with beautiful flowers. Beyond that lay another long, low brick building with a huge black door studded with metal and very few windows. There was a super cool graffiti sign to one side of the door that showed a terrifying skull bracketed by huge charred and tattered wings with "The Fallen" written in black letters across the top. I figured that it was some kind of clubhouse or meeting hall where they conducted all their criminal business.

My lips thinned as I thought about King's part in all of that.

I'd done my research last night after an hour of lying in bed wired and unable to sleep. The Fallen MC was the premier source of BC marijuana in the province and all of North America. They ran into problems with gang warfare only in the southern states of America and California where they crossed territory with the Mexican drug cartels but otherwise, they'd cornered the market. They didn't deal in other drugs, which I found kind of strange, and the rest of their alleged criminal enterprises consisted of munitions dealing and money laundering.

I had been born and raised by older, conservative parents who didn't believe in divorce. Then, I'd been married to a deeply reserved, repressed lawyer who felt about nothing so passionately as he did his own social standing.

I'd wanted to shed my old skin, those old connections, but did I really want to do a 180? If I took up with a biker, there was no chance William or my parents would take me back. I tried to tell myself that I didn't care about that but I did. Even though they didn't make me happy, they had been my entire life and I wasn't ready to irrevocably emancipate myself from them yet.

I sighed deeply, steeling myself against King's inevitable temptation. Just because he was the hottest thing I had ever seen—living or dead and that included Elvis Presley who was *the* original hottie—didn't mean I would lose control around him and say, fall to my knees and beg him to bed me like I'd fantasized about in the longs hours without sleep the night before. No, I was a strong, independent woman.

Still, I flipped down the mirror to check and then reapply my deep berry lip stain before I got out of the car.

Before I could approach the reception area, an enormous man covered in tattoos from chin to finger tips, approached me with a crooked smile.

"Lost, lady?"

I swallowed back my unease because the guy was both scary and ridiculously attractive. His tattoos were all done in blacks as deep as his unkempt hair and long-lashed eyes, and they contrasted deeply with his porcelain skin tone.

"I'm looking for King. He told me to bring my car in for servicing."

The stranger's inky black eyes trailed the length of my car. His lips twitched but at least he didn't laugh. "You sure he didn't mean to send you to the dump?"

Shame rippled down my spine. "I'm sure. Betty Sue is all I can afford and she just needs…a facelift."

"Thinking if you can't afford a new car, you sure as hell can't afford the facelift this piece of crap needs to stay running," he told me.

I blew a huff through my lips and planted my hands on my hips. “Listen, that’s exactly what I told King but he wouldn’t listen to me. I’ll just get in my car and go, then. I’m sorry we both wasted our time.”

“Whoa, hold up, Sassy. If King told you to bring it in, he musta meant to fix it within your price range, all right? Stay here. I’ll get ’im.”

I realized that I was pouting and pulled my curled lower lip between my teeth before I nodded. The stranger smiled, wiped his dirty hands on his dirty navy blue mechanic overalls and extended it to me.

“Bat Stevens.”

I stared at his outstretched fingers and corded forearm, covered in an inked flurry of bats.

“You must love bats,” I deadpanned as I shook his hand.

His lips quirked, softening the hard lines of his face and his overall badassery. “Hate ’em, but I make myself live with them.”

I frowned after him as he turned away to find King. He wore the standard black jumpsuit of a mechanic but I knew without having to ask that Bat Stevens was a one-percenter and I didn’t know if it said good things about me that I was astonished by his parting words of wisdom. Could a biker really be a philosopher or was he just tripping on something and I was so desperate for insight that I was looking for it in unlikely places?

“Babe,” the already familiar boyish huskiness of King’s voice called to me from across the asphalt.

I looked up with a nervous smile that immediately fell off my face as I took in all that was King as he approached me. He was wearing another tee, this one a dark navy that set his eyes to the colour of Arctic-blue, and his signature low-riding, totally worn out jeans over ridiculously sexy motorcycle boots. I watched as he wiped his grease-covered hands on an even greasier rag before slipping it into a back pocket. His hair was messy, a chaos of golden kinks around his wide-smiling face. He looked like a freaking angel.

My heart stopped for a long pause. Restarted with a clunking thunk that made me think I was dying.

He slowed as he reached me, his smile twisting into something less pure, corrupted with the arrogance he felt when he saw how much he affected me. I tried to be annoyed but it was hard when his beauty literally made it difficult for me to breathe.

How a man who looked like him could exist in real life was really beyond my comprehension.

"Babe," he repeated, this time quietly but his voice was filled with laughter.

"King," I said, my voice cracking. Heat sluiced from the top of my head to my toes and I knew I was blushing but I cleared my throat and powered on. "You told me to bring my car in so here I am."

"Here you are," he agreed as his eyes dragged like a physical touch over my body. "Lookin' fucking gorgeous. I can't believe the guys have left you alone."

"I haven't been here long," I admitted.

"Yeah, that must be it."

We stood staring at each other and I worried it was awkward but I couldn't bring myself to stop staring at him. He seemed to be experiencing the same problem.

"Still determined to stay away from me?" he asked with that signature cocky grin I was already helpless against.

"It's for the best."

"I gotta disagree with you there, babe."

I watched him lean against my car, one booted foot crossed over the other, his arms folded so that the fabric of his shirt pulled tight over all those lean muscles in his chest. He was so beautiful but so cliché, I had to laugh.

"You are such a rebel without a cause," I teased.

His eyes lit as they raked me up and down. "I got a cause, babe. Gettin' you on the back of my bike and gettin' you to stay there."

My laughter died in my throat, clogging it like road kill. I swallowed thickly. "You're tenacious, I'll give you that."

"You should give me a lot more but I'm willing to earn it. Just need the chance."

I threw my hands up. "You don't even know me, King. Why in the world are you trying so hard?"

His eyes narrowed and the cocky, boyish charm he usually exuded fell away like a wolf its sheep-shorn disguise. I took a step back, which was a mistake because he was on me, so close but not touching, rangy arms bracketing my body against the car and bent slightly so that he could bring his face close to mine.

All I could see were those silver-blue eyes, wolf bright.

"Attraction ain't something you can fake, babe, and soon as I saw your sweet self across the parking lot that day, my breath left my body like a punch to the gut. Never seen someone or anything so beautiful as you."

"Beauty isn't everything," I protested weakly.

His eyes remained somber but there was twitch in his lips that told me he fought a smile. "Nah, it's not. Lucky for you, I also happen to like dorky, sweet librarian types with a hidden wealth of sass."

"Gosh, that was sweet," I whispered before I could stop myself.

His grin nearly blinded me but it was the hand that worked its way under my hair to cup the back of my neck that made my knees shake.

"I got a lotta sweet to give if you promise to look at me like that every time I give it."

"Look at you like what?"

"Like I'm worth somethin' special. Don't get that much and babe, I gotta tell you, it makes me feel like I'm King of my own fuckin' castle."

I closed my eyes and dropped my head against the car with a groan. "I never stood a chance against you, did I?"

"Not really," he laughed.

I peeked at him through one squinted eye. "My life is a mess and I'm not jumping up and down at the thought of dating a criminal."

"Like I tried to tell you yesterday, I'm not a criminal. My family is involved with the club but I'm not." He sighed and dragged a hand through his curls. "I'm not yet, at least. Gotta be honest here babe, if you're gonna give me a chance, it's a very real possibility that I might be a brother one day. Some might even say it's a forgone conclusion."

"But it isn't?" I asked, clinging to the slight possibility.

"Nah, but turning my back on family isn't really in me. Even if I didn't patch in, this place, the brothers and the lifestyle… I couldn't ever turn my back on 'em."

I chewed on my bottom lip for a long moment. Too long apparently, because King gently pulled it with his fingers and smoothed his thumb across it.

"Never told anyone I wasn't sure if I was gonna patch in," he muttered.

A little thrill went through me at the intimacy of him sharing such a big secret. "I won't tell."

"Know that, babe," he said as if we'd known each other forever and he'd been sharing his secrets all our lives.

We stared at each other and I felt suddenly like crying.

"You're too much for me," I whispered through my tightening throat. "I swear, you'll be bored in a week. I'm no fun."

His thumb brushed back and forth over the corner of his jaw, his eyes soft as over-washed denim. "The bones are already there, Cress. You're the same girl who climbed on the back of a stranger's bike and beat my ass at pool using some pretty dirty tricks. I just gotta corrupt you a little and, just sayin', I'm lookin' forward to that part."

I blushed which made the hand on the back of my neck tighten, so I knew before he did it that he was going to kiss me. It was a long, languid kiss that started out with closed lips then open mouths and finally tongues, molasses-smooth and sweet swipes and tangles that made my belly quiver.

"Nice piece," someone shouted.

"When you're done with her, I wouldn't mind a round with the bitch," another man yelled from across the lot.

Shame burned through me, William's voice suddenly in my head telling me not to be a slut. I tried to push King away but he was immovable. He frowned but I knew the expression wasn't for me when he looked over his shoulder and spotted the second guy who had called out.

"Shut the fuck up, Skell. My woman wouldn't give you a second fuckin' look if you were the last man in Entrance."

*His woman*?

"Your woman, eh?" The man named Skell barked out a laugh. He was a terrifying-looking guy, with tattoos all up his neck, a few on his face and silver bits stuck in his brows and ears. "Bit young for a ball and chain, King."

"You see her?" King called back.

There was a pause. "Yeah, man. Saw her clear across the lot, wanted her. I get closer, might have to find a way to convince her to give another brother a chance."

"Then you know, you find something this sweet, you get it on lockdown. So, if you're done being an asshole, leave me to doing that, yeah?"

Skell jerked up his chin in the universal sign for male respect and walked back into one of the garage bays.

When King turned back to me, I was the one frowning.

"What?" he asked.

"I can't resist you if you keep going all sweet in a cool, badass biker kind of way that's also sexy," I informed him.

His lips twitched, then he did my favorite thing by throwing his head back to laugh. I stared at his beautiful throat, unaware until him that a throat *could* be beautiful, and absorbed the awesome sound of his humor.

"Babe," he said, squeezing me tighter, "you don't want to resist me. The sooner you realize it, the happier we'll both be."

He was so right. It didn't say much about me, except that I had a very narrow mind, but I was constantly surprised by King's sweetness and smarts. They seemed totally incongruent from the image of a biker I had in my head.

"Okay," I said softly, looking up into his face so I could watch the warmth flood his icy eyes.

"Good, babe," he whispered back in the same gentle way.

God, a tall, rough-edged biker man who could also be thoughtful, smart and kind?

He was too good to be true.

I just wished I'd known how literal that was at the time.

"Pick you up tonight at eight."

"Okay, where are we going?" I asked.

There were only four restaurants in Entrance proper: the

two formal, Donovan's Steakhouse for family dinners and celebrations, and La Gustosa, *the* place to impress anyone and everyone with their phenomenal authentic Italian food; the informal, Stella's Diner and an Earl's, the one and only chain restaurant to infiltrate the town. I had only been to Earl's and even then only once because when I was married, I'd needed to be out of the classroom and on the road home by four-thirty at the latest in order to have dinner on the table for William by the time he got home from work.

"Somewhere outside of town."

"Oh." I pouted slightly. "I'd love to go somewhere here. Maybe Stella's?"

He raised a brow at me. "Woulda taken you more for a La Gustosa kinda woman."

I shrugged. "I've heard Arturo and Anna Lucia make the best pasta outside of Italy but I've been to lots of fancy restaurants and I have to admit, I haven't had a really good burger in years."

King reeled back as if I'd hit him, his eyes wide and mouth slack with horror. I giggled, as I'm sure he meant for me to.

"Well, we can't have that. Burgers it is, but not Stella's. Best place for a burger and fries is Pourhouse in Vancouver. You up for another ride on the back of my bike?"

"I like riding on the back of your bike," I said, because it was true but also because I wanted to see his eyes turn to fire.

They did not disappoint.

He groaned, pressing my body fully into the car with his weight flush against me and his forehead tipped to mine. "Sexy as fuck, you like my bike."

"Glad you think so," I said, as if I wasn't down to my toes thrilled that someone as freaking unbelievably attractive as King thought I was sexy.

"Now, I'm gonna kiss you 'til your toes curl then I'm going to get one of the brothers to give you a ride to where you got to be."

I was stuck on the kissing thing, my lips tingling and my gut tightening, so I didn't object to making some stranger go out of their way to give me a ride to school.

"Okay."

He grinned, then moved closer to press that smile to the corner of my mouth. "Like that word from you, baby."

I opened my mouth, hopefully to say something feminist and independent but probably to say "okay" again and again until he kissed me senseless but he was already on me, kissing me just like that.

He tasted good, fresh and clean like a drink of cool water. His hand found its place under my heavy hair, wrapped around my neck as if he knew I needed the support to hold me up in case my knees gave out.

"Be at yours at eight. You own a pair of jeans?" he asked after one last lingering kiss.

My eyes were still closed and I was considering the possibility that just a kiss could bring me to orgasm. With King, I honestly thought it might be achievable.

"Babe," he called.

"Here, just recovering."

His chuckle wafted over my lips. I licked them, tasting him on me, thinking his laugh had a taste and it was *freaking awesome*.

"You own jeans or just these sexy skirts?"

"I own jeans." I opened my eyes under furrowed brows and huffed. "Of course, I own jeans. I'm Canadian. It's a toss-up between jeans and Lulu Lemons, which is our national uniform."

He grinned. "Coulda just said yes, Cress."

I rolled my eyes. "Yes, King, I own jeans."

The hand holding my neck squeezed then slid a long, languid path down my back and over my bottom. I shivered and King watched me do it, his eyes tracking the goose bumps that rippled up along my neck. He ducked his head to run his teeth and the very tip of his tongue down the side of my throat until he reached the juncture of my shoulder and gently bit there.

"Oh," I gasped.

He pressed a chaste kiss to the top of my shoulder. "Gotta get goin'. Wish I didn't."

"Me too."

"Tonight, Cress." He pulled away, both hands at my neck, bracketing it firmly so that he could look me in the eyes.

"Tonight, King. Got it."

"I'm gonna show you how to live, if you let me in to do it."

I knew it. I knew it better than I knew *Paradise Lost* and I'd written my honors English thesis on it. I knew it better than I knew William's schedule and I'd lived by it for eight years. King was a man who could change my life, throw me into the deep end when I'd only ever kept my feet in the warm waters of the shallows. I didn't know if I was ready for such a massive change. I was still technically married, I had no experience to keep a man as wild as him anything close to satisfied let alone tame, and I had less than two thousand dollars in my bank account. Not exactly living the dream I'd dreamt of my whole life. But on the back of a bike with King, riding to nowhere with the smell of hot asphalt and his clean laundry scent in my nose, I thought that could easily be a new dream to dream and maybe, unlike the others, attain.

"I'm counting on it."

# Seven.

"It's that time of year, people," I said, turning toward the board so that I could write the name of our next unit in blue marker on the white wall. "*Paradise Lost*."

My intimate group of IB grade twelve English students actually gave a little cheer, a small burst of applause. I'd only been teaching at the school for a semester but I was already well liked and especially well known for my love of John Milton and his epic poem. The kids had been excited all year to discuss it. I was too. The only damper on my mood was that this was the fourth class in a row that the new student had missed and I wasn't looking forward to catching him up on an entirely new unit when he did deign to show up.

"Tell us again why Satan is your ultimate book boyfriend," one of my students, a scrawny but beautiful boy named Benito Bonanno, called out.

The other students snickered.

I braced my hands on my hips and fought against my smile as I faced them. "Benny, you clearly haven't read the book yet if you have to ask me that."

"You're such a dork," one of the jocks, Carson Gentry, mocked me as everyone laughed again.

It was good-natured though; like I'd said, the kids loved

me, mostly because I loved every single one of them.

"I am," I agreed with a proud wink at Benny, who blushed.

"Never seen a dork look that good in a skirt before."

I frowned, ready to scold the unfamiliar voice, possibly a visiting parent, for demeaning me in front of the kids but when I turned to face the man who spoke, I choked on my reprimand.

As in, I literally choked. Tears welled in my eyes as I started coughing harshly into my hand but I could still make out the blurry outline of a tall, lean as a whip, blond man in front of me.

I prayed with more piety than I had ever before possessed that the man in front of me was not the blond king.

Carefully swiping under my eyes so I didn't disturb my eyeliner and mascara, I blinked slowly and focused harder.

God, it was him.

King stood in the door frame, his long body leaning against the jam with his hands in the pockets of his black trousers, a charcoal-grey sleeveless hoodie pulled just tightly enough across his obviously muscled chest. His hair was a riot of sexy rumpled waves, little curls pushed behind his ears that I wanted to wrap around each finger of my hand. It was his eyes, though, which held me arrested. They were a bright and pale blue, so light they seemed to glow like burnished steel. The lazy confidence in his stance did not reflect in those hazardous eyes. Instead, they were sharp with intelligence, creased at the corners in a sexy squint that was born of wicked intent.

I stood there and stared and stared and stared.

Truly, I could not fathom doing anything else, even with a class full of students baring witness, even with my scolding words cooling and forgotten on my tongue.

It could have been the impossibility of seeing him in my

classroom but I knew the truth of my stupefaction.

He was just too beautiful to bear.

Fortunately, it seemed the rest of the class thought so too.

"Are you an angel?" one of my favorite students, a curly-haired and pimply-faced Margaret asked earnestly.

It spoke to the class's serious interest in the newcomer that no one laughed at Margaret's ludicrous question.

King's lush mouth curled on the left side of his face, cutting something like a dimple but manlier into his cheek.

There was a collective sigh from every female in the room. Shamefully, that included myself.

"I'm no angel, doll," he said to Margaret and even though his words should have been contrived, his combination of bad boy aura and the genuine kindness that shone in his eyes as he stared at the mortified girl, made it possible for him to pull it off.

"I beg to differ," Talia, one of the popular girls, muttered.

Her posse giggled.

"Okay," I said, finally snapping out of it. "Angel or not, may I help you with something?"

I was teasing him. We'd gone to dinner at Pourhouse in Vancouver the night before and it had been *awesome*. I loved riding on the back of his bike even though it totally wrecked my hair and I just straight up loved spending the time with him. He was playful and arrogant in a boyish way that was like catnip to me, but manly in all the other ways that counted, fairly bossy, certainly thoughtful and definitely deviant. We hadn't done anything more than make out hot and heavy on his bike in my driveway when he took me home but it had been hot in a way I'd never experienced before. As soon as we were parked, he'd turned just enough to lift me and swing me, smooth as if I weighed less than nothing, until I was perched slightly on top and in front of him. Then without hesitation, his hand found its place on the back of my neck, fingers in my hair tight enough to puppet my head to the right angle as he'd kissed me.

I'd wanted to invite him in, which was so unlike me that I'd actually laughed a little hysterically when I'd asked him. To my infinite surprise, he'd gently rejected me, kissed me again so thoroughly it had taken the sting out of it and then told me he wanted to take things slow.

I didn't know bikers had a slow function but I was curious enough about him and nervous enough about satisfying him, to agree.

Now, he stood before me, clearly trying to surprise me at work like some kind of superstar boyfriend. So, of course, I was teasing him.

"I'm Kyle Garro," he said, which seemed bizarre because I very obviously already knew him.

Something about his abbreviated name sparked in the back of my mind but I was too distracted by the slightly defeated angle of his smile to figure it out.

I watched as he reached into an open backpack at his feet and retrieved papers. My pulse fluttered manically in my throat as he crossed to me, stopping close enough to touch. The scent of laundry and clean, male sweat made me woozy so it took a moment for me to realize he was holding out the papers to me.

"King?" I asked dumbly as I took the papers and realized what they were. "Are you kidding me?"

His smile tightened. He shoved his hands into the wrinkled pockets of his uniform trousers and shrugged somewhat sheepishly. "Nah. I'm King Kyle Garro, your new student."

"No," I bit out.

"Yeup," he said, rocking back on his heels.

Oh my God. Oh my God. Oh my God.

I'd sucked face with a student.

I'd let a *child* make love to my mouth the way most women never let any man take them, ever.

Oh my God. Oh my God.

"Oh my God," I whispered.

The class laughed and Benito, my class aide, rushed forward to give King his new textbooks and show him to his seat. I watched dumbly as he chose between one of two empty seats but I knew before he was offered which one he would choose, front row, dead centre in front of my desk.

A whimper rose in the back of my throat but I swallowed it.

"Are you okay, Mrs. Irons?" Aimee asked sweetly.

I was still reeling from the shock of having King *as a student* in my class but I'd had years of practicing my façade and I was more than capable of containing my freak-out until later.

"Yes, thank you, Aimee. Well, I'm sorry about that disruption, class. What were we talking about?" I prompted them.

"How hot Satan is!" a few of the girls shouted.

I laughed with my students but I could feel the blush stain the exposed skin at my throat and collarbones. Though I didn't look at him, I could feel King's gaze like a hot brand on my face.

How could he have forgotten to tell me he was only *eighteen* bloody years old? Had he known he was my student? Was this all some horrible joke that he and his teenage friends had decided to play on the older teacher?

Mortification poured over me like hot lead, burning my eyes, choking me as it spilled down my throat.

"Satan is the villain of *Paradise Lost*," Benito explained helpfully to our new student.

His voice was higher than normal, which led me to believe that Benny liked King just as much as I did. He wasn't out of the closet yet but he'd given me the privilege of being "in" on his secret and nothing, not even William's marriage proposal, had ever made me feel more honored.

"Is he, though?" I asked, shaking off my thoughts to indulge in a teaching moment. "Or is he the antihero? Can anyone tell me what I mean by that?"

"A character that assumes the guise and most of the characteristics typical of villainy but throughout the narrative, the reader develops empathy for him or her," King drawled.

I forced myself to look at him. He sat sprawled in his chair exactly like a typical indolent teenager, but the sharp edge in his diamond bright eyes undercut his youth, gave it a weight and somberness that made me feel less skeevy about previously believing he was an actual adult.

"Correct," I said, after clearing my throat. "Characters like that have been attractive to readers for generations. Nothing is so black and white, just as Hester in *The Scarlet Letter*, Mr. Darcy in *Pride & Prejudice* and Jay Gatsby in *The Great Gatsby*. These are deeply flawed characters that we still found ourselves aspiring to be. Why is that?"

"We're complicated," King said again without raising his hand. "People judge everyone based on shallow crap: how hot they are, how rich and academically accomplished. It's bullshit, because at the end of the day, the one thing everyone can relate to is the grind to get to that place. We all suffer, we all fucking grieve and sin every damn day. It's that dark stuff that makes those characters real to us."

"Wow," Benny said, his huge brown eyes locked in wonder on the new student.

"Ohmigawd, he is so hot," Maya Person whispered loudly to her best friend, Talia.

I hated that I agreed with her.

"Watch your language in this class, Mr. Garro. And we raise our hands here, if you wish to be called on," I reprimanded him.

"Satan didn't believe in obeying The Man and you think he's a babe. Didn't think you'd mind," he had the audacity to say.

I stared at him in muted anger. My tummy filled with static electricity that I feared would show in my eyes.

"You will respect me in my classroom," I finally declared with a chin tilt that I felt underlined my point very well.

His eyes freaking *twinkled* in response. I watched him lift his hand in a two-finger salute before he said, "Wouldn't dream of disrespecting you in that way, Miss Irons."

I couldn't tell if I was imagining it or not but I could have sworn he put the emphasis on *that way*, as if he could think of other, much more pleasurable ways to disrespect me in my classroom.

A flush sluiced down my front from my cheeks to my chest where my nipples furled into hard points behind my flimsy bra.

"It's Mrs. Irons," Aimee corrected.

King frowned, his countenance changing so quickly from carefree, cockier than Satan before the fall, to something darker, broody and infinitely more Byronic. "Married?"

There was no reason for me to feel guilty. If anything, he should feel guilty! He was the one who had seduced a grown woman while he was underage.

"I don't discuss my private life in class," I said, turning back to the whiteboard to write some preliminary notes.

"She does," Talia murmured. "She's separated from her husband and she just bought this little cabin over on Back Bay Road. She commuted from Vancouver last year but now she offers extra help every day after school. Trust me, you'll need it. She's cool but she's a total hard ass."

"Talia," I scolded, but there wasn't much bite to it.

I did talk to my students about my personal life to a certain extent because I wanted them to know that they could talk to me about anything going on in *their* lives. It was the same reason that I offered extra help every Monday through Thursday after school, because I wanted them to have a safe place to go.

Entrance was a rich community but the underbelly was poor and unfortunately riddled with drug use and violence. Some of my kids hung out in my office after hours just to forestall going home.

"Mmm," King hummed, and I didn't have to look at him to know that he was pleased with Talia's intel.

I'd never wanted to run out of my classroom before but the look in King's eyes, the predatory hunger there, and the fact that apparently, I had hooked up with one of my freaking students, had me ready to hightail it out of there.

"Okay, I'd like you all to read Canto IV, when Satan meets Adam and Eve. Take notes. There may or may not be a pop quiz about it tomorrow morning."

Everyone groaned but I knew they didn't mind too much. I'd successfully infected them with my enthusiasm for *Paradise Lost* and most of them, even the boys, were already quietly reading by the time I closed the door on them.

I kept my head down as I quickly made my way to the staff restroom at the end of the hall, somehow managing to keep my breakdown at bay until I shut the door and turned on the lights.

A student.

I'd broken the cardinal rule of teaching and hooked up with a student.

It wouldn't matter to anyone that I hadn't known at the

time that he was my pupil. People didn't look too hard at the details when they were presented with a scandal, and this was a *scandal*. The married (no matter that I was legally separated) teacher with The Fallen MC's prodigal son?

Yeah, no. I was fucked.

I was groaning into my hands when the door opened into my back and sent me reeling forward.

"What the—"

King ignored my indignation, stepped into the room and locked the door with an audible *snick* that sounded to my ears like a bomb going off.

"Get out," I ordered.

"No, you're gonna listen to me."

"I am *not*. Get out," I said as I righted myself and spun to face him with my hands planted on my hips.

King had the audacity to cross his arms and lean, freaking lean like he had no worries, against the door. "No. You're gonna calm down for two fuckin' minutes and listen to me."

"I am not. And, newsflash, you are my student! I am the one who lays down the rules here, buddy. So, get out of my way or I'll send you to the headmaster's office."

His lips slid to the left in a lazy smile that reached through my rage and confusion to spark the lust that lay like kindling at the pit of my stomach whenever he was near.

"You won't do that."

"Are you trying to blackmail me?" I asked.

I didn't think King would do something like that but he was from a criminal family and he'd been lying to me since the moment I'd met him, so what did I know?

"Shut your mouth before you say something you can't take back and really piss me off."

I emitted a strangled cry of rage. "Are you freaking kidding me right now? You lied to me, you led me on and you've humiliated me. I could lose my job for this, King. I have no money to my name. I *need* this job."

Hysterical sobs bubbled up and rose into my lungs so that I had to pant to breathe through the pain. Spots danced in front of my eyes and I could feel my body sway but could do nothing to stop it. Rough, warm hands caught me, one at its spot on the back of my neck and the other over my hip.

"Take a deep breath, babe."

On auto-pilot, lost to the psychedelic chaos of my panic attack, I obeyed.

"Another."

I took another.

"Good girl," he murmured into my hair as he pulled me into his body.

I breathed deep, dragging his intoxicating scent in over and over again. It calmed me, being held against his hard chest, cocooned in his strong arms, but it also made me want to cry. I'd been frightened before just knowing that he was the kind of man—boy—who could change my life, who had already changed my life just by *being*. I'd only just come to terms with the gamble, accepted the odds even though, historically, they had never played out in my favor.

I'd accepted that fact that he was essentially a criminal.

I couldn't accept the fact that he was my student because that would make *me* a criminal.

"This happen often?" he asked me.

His hand on the back of my neck pressed me firmly into his pecs, his thumb a pendulum swinging back and forth over my hairline. It was both bossy and tender, a contradiction that I'd already figured out was King's modus operandi. I hated how much I loved it.

"Sometimes," I answered.

I'd been having panic attacks on and off since the day my brother had left home for good. It was, without a doubt, the worst day of my life but also, depressingly, the day I'd felt most alive.

It was also ironic, given that I'd essentially helped to kill a man and now here I was, obsessing over the possibility that King was a criminal.

I pulled back from him so abruptly that he actually let go.

"You do not get to touch me or comfort me, especially when you are the one who caused the problem. Please, please, tell me you didn't know I was your teacher?"

He finally had the decency to look mildly abashed. It was boyish and charming the way he tucked his hands in his pockets and rocked back on his heels. I reminded myself that I wasn't in a position to be charmed by a boy.

"Saw you the first day of school, remembered you from that fuckin' parking lot. Hottest day in September and there you stood, plastic bags melting all around you, just fuckin' staring at me. At first, I thought, what kind of bitch just stares at a guy like that? But that was before I actually saw you. Told you once, I'll tell you again. Took my goddamn breath away, babe. Never coulda known I'd feel that way about someone just lookin' at 'em but I did."

He paused, and the only sound in the room was the shaky rattle of my breath through my lungs. It felt like my entire nervous system was shutting down.

"Didn't seem fair the next time I saw you, you were my goddamn teacher. I knew if I just had a chance to get to you, you'd be mine. Knew it then and know it now even more. You're mine, Cress."

"I am *not*," I snapped but I sounded like a child denying

something the adults knew she wanted.

How was it that this eighteen-year-old boy could reduce me to the youngest parts of myself? He made me yearn like a teenager that had never rebelled, the child who wanted what she could not have.

"You are and you know it. You want this," he said, stepping closer again. His voice was forceful but there was anxiety in his normally smiling eyes, tension in the hands that flexed at his side. I knew he wanted to go to me, to put his hand on its place at my neck.

I took another step away from him and spoke before I could succumb any further to his outrageous appeal.

"I'm only going to say this once, so listen up. You lied to me, you took advantage of me." He opened his mouth to protest but I held up my hand. "Whatever your reasons were, even if you did like me or whatever the hell you kids call a crush these days, what you did was manipulative and disgusting. Even if you refuse to show up to class, I *am* your teacher. From here on out, I expect you to be in that class, to participate by raising your hands and respecting my authority in that classroom and to hand in your work on time. That is all I expect from you. What I will not accept from you is any reminders about our more intimate time together, no overtures at reconciliation and no inappropriate comments. From here on out, King, I am so far from 'yours' that I would rather be *anyone* else's. Is that understood?"

He stared at me for too long. I could feel the cool calm of those pale eyes douse my anger again and again until I felt waterlogged and fizzled out but I held out hope that he would get me, that this nightmare of a situation would just end before it turned into real drama. Job-ending drama, being forced to return to the husband who refused to divorce me kind of drama.

Finally, he sucked in a deep breath and nodded curtly. "Sure, Cress, I gotcha."

"Mrs. Irons," I corrected him.

His shoulders rounded and he scuffed his shoe on the linoleum floor like the child he was so that at first, I thought I had him in his place all safe and sound. It wasn't until I'd moved passed him to the door and was already moving through it that I realized I'd underestimated him again.

"For now, *Miss* Irons."

# Eight.

Another apple.

It sat on the left corner of my desk like a cliché. Shiny, red and bright. It wasn't the same kind of apple every day. It had been nine school days since King had made his big reveal as my student so I'd had nine different apples: Ambrosia, Granny Smith, Golden and Red Delicious, Gala, Honeycrisp and McIntosh. My impulse the first day he had arrived in class, walked to my desk and left the apple tied with a little note card to the stem, was to throw it out. Actually, I'd wanted to hurl it at his pretty face so that it smashed all over him, bruised and messed him.

I hadn't done either, so points to me for impulse control.

Instead, each day I put the note in my desk drawer without reading it and left the apple on the edge of my desk until I could reward it to a student for a question well answered. I thought this approach showed that King's antics were fruitless but he persevered, which made me wonder if he knew that I pulled out the notes to read them every day after a class. They were both a torment and a treat, lines of poetry scrawled in block letters. I'd memorized them all but the one from the day before, Monday's was on repeat in my head.

*Dreams shine like pearls in her eyes. I become an artist,*

*a collector, stringing saltwater gems on necklaces that she may wear.*

I sighed heavily but the kids didn't notice. I was a sigh guy by nature so they were used to it. Besides, they were busy working in small groups on reading questions from *Paradise Lost* and EBA was a good school, the best, so the kids were good ones who were mostly happy to get down to work.

Only King watched me and I knew he did, not because I looked at him (I made it a point to only glance his way when it was absolutely necessary), but because I could feel his eyes like sunbeams against my face. They warmed me always, made me feel watched in a way that was pure admiration, like he was a painter and I his muse. In a way, through his little apple poems and one-line compliments, I was.

After years of pinning for my dream man, I'd found him. A tall, golden blond Adonis, cool in the way only true rebels can be, kind in the way I'd never known a man could be, totally into me, and completely off-limits.

I'd never entertained anarchist or blasphemous thoughts in my life but the unfairness of the situation made me want to punch God (if there was one) right in the throat.

A loud giggle drew my attention to the group working in the front left of the classroom, their single-person desks arranged in a tight clump. I sucked air in through my teeth when I saw it was Talia laughing, her beautiful, professionally highlighted blond hair pulled over one shoulder so that she could play with it coquettishly while she leaned into King. For his part, he was sprawled across his small seat, a position I'd come to learn was customary for him. He had his pencil to his paper but I could tell that whatever he was writing wasn't for the assignment because he had a wicked smirk on his face. Talia was leaning over her desk to read what he wrote, uniform unbuttoned to reveal a deep parenthesis of cleavage.

"Talia?" I asked, before I could help myself. "Care to share with the class what is so amusing about John Milton's greatest work?"

Normally, I didn't mind if the kids goofed off a little while they worked. I wanted them to like my class, like me, so that the work they did would be less like homework and more like curiosity-propelled research. Talia knew this so she frowned at me the way one friend would frown at another who was interrupting her flirtation.

Too freaking bad.

"The fall of humanity from Eden was instigated by a fuckin' apple. You tell me how *Paradise Lost* isn't a kind of comedy," King taunted, leaning forward on his forearms so that his defined biceps flexed beautifully under his dress shirt.

*Focus.*

"Either elaborate or admit you were slacking off in class, Mr. Garro," I retorted.

The class raised their collective eyebrows and a few students made *oooh* noises as if we were two boxers entering a ring.

"There is a thin line between tragedy and comedy, yeah? Well, the comic tragedy of Milton's poem is the contrast between mankind's practices and preaching of virtues and morality in the face of reality, which holds temptation after temptation. Basically, they don't stand a chance of staying on the path to heaven. Satan is so easily able to corrupt Eve because he only has to open her eyes to the endless possibilities of life instead of the narrow scope that God and his religion allowed her previously. One bite of the apple, one taste of temptation, and it's fuckin' hard to go back to."

"That's depressing," Aimee murmured.

"Yeah, don't know what kind of comedy you watch, man, but that shit is not funny," Carson drawled.

"It's not funny like that. It's *ironic. Paradise Lost* is supposed to be about the fall of man from Eden, the fall of Satan and his angels from heaven, about their follies as they compare to the grace and power of God. It's God that's supposed to be the hero, the perfect character, but it's Eve and Satan that we empathize with the most."

This was, unfortunately, true. It was the very reason that I so loved *Paradise Lost*, why I was desperate to go back to school for my Master's degree and eventually my PhD. The idea of delving further into the contradictions that made up Milton's masterful poem had formed the first time I read it at seventeen. It had appealed to the tension within myself, the need to sin and the learned inability to do so without systemic grief.

That King got the conflict nearly undid my resolve.

"Totally," Benny agreed, his voice dreamy as he stared across the room at the biker boy. "It's like Milton kept trying and failing to make God and Michael and Jesus his heroes but even he couldn't get behind them."

"Even God thinks it's fuckin' funny," King continued, gazing lazily around the class at his captive audience. "During the battle between the angels, he literally sits 'above and laughs the while.'"

"Because?" I prompted as I stood up to round my desk and rest my bottom against the front of it.

Typically, I didn't like to be behind my desk when I was discussing with the class but lately, I'd been using it like a shield against King. I remembered why when his eyes raked up and down my body. My outfit was conservative, a thick, chunky knit sweater with great woven ropes up the arms and across the front in a cool stone colour over a tight black knit skirt that came to the tops of my knees. There was no reason for his eyes to darken, for them to linger over my tidy braid like he wanted to dig his fingers in it, use it to hold me still while he plundered my mouth. No reason at all because I was careful with how I dressed now that he was my student.

Yet, I knew he wanted me. Badly. And the thought sent power and lust spiraling through me.

"Because even God knows he has created creatures who will only ever be imperfect and he has given them impossibly lofty fuckin' goals," King said.

"Some would say that they aren't 'goals,' that he doesn't expect them to live up to all the ideals he sets for them but that he gives them those aspirations to guide them toward a good path," I countered.

He snorted. "Look where those got 'em, kicked out of beautiful places and unable to appreciate the beauty of their new reality. Only Satan, the 'bad guy,' makes something of his new circumstances."

"Yeah, but only because he's angry," Margaret countered.

King shrugged one shoulder. "Doesn't matter why. If you want to evolve you gotta accept your circumstances, your reality. That's one of the problems with the pious in *Paradise Lost*."

I had never heard King speak so eloquently, with so few curse words. The effect was staggering. He was wonderfully intelligent, which wasn't surprising given that he passed the rigorous exams to get into EBA. It was surprising because I had bought into the cliché, a biker as a dense, potentially violent man without social mores.

King was nothing like that.

I on the other hand, was exactly the suburban housewife stereotype; small minded, bigoted and afraid of the unknown.

My eyes caught on his bright gaze as I surveyed the

students, still caught in debate. He watched me as if he knew me, knew the horrible bits of me but accepted them. Even more, he looked at me like he could see the dark heart of me and liked it.

Later that night, after a long day of back-to-back classes because I'd taken on teaching both grades eleven and twelve advanced English and History in an attempt to make some much-needed money, I finally closed my online grade book and got ready to head home. It was late, after six-thirty, so most of the students and teachers had long ago headed home unless they were part of the basketball team currently practicing on the other side of campus in the gymnasium.

It was knowing this that I finally allowed myself to open the left-hand drawer in my desk and pull out the little pile of apple poems that I'd tied the other day with the pink ribbon I'd worn in my hair. There were nine of them, tiny scraps of paper, some written on the backs of receipts, some on standard-issue notebook paper and one on real, old school parchment. It was that one that I smoothed out with shaking fingers now.

Fit to me
Made for me
Bone of my bone
Broken
Lost or freed
You are a state of mine
Eternal
Bone
Of my bone

How could a boy so young write something so exquisite? I felt each word throb through me, in tandem with my heartbeat so that I found myself rereading the poem in that intimate cadence.

He couldn't love me, of course. He didn't know me. I was a game to him, an older woman he wanted to conquer so that he could crow to his friends about his prowess in the bedroom.

At least, that's what I told myself. Even though I didn't know him very well, it felt fundamentally wrong to think he was capable of such calculated cruelty. His sense of right and wrong was his own but I didn't think he was a deliberate heart-breaker. I saw him flirt shamelessly with girls in my class and the halls of EBA but he never took it too far and despite speculation, I hadn't heard concrete evidence that he'd slept with any of them.

It was more than that though. I kept telling myself that I didn't know him, but secretly, I felt like I did. I knew that he was smart as a whip, both intellectually curious and thoughtful in my classes and in others. He'd been given a scholarship to EBA, though rumor was his father was richer than Crocus off his illegal drug trade, and even though everyone kept waiting for him to screw it up, he was a model student. Everyone loved him; even the acerbic teachers mentioned how well he was doing in their classes despite coming in at midterm in the second semester.

I knew that he was a shark at pool, that he liked local IPA beers and tequila shooters, preferred burgers above all other food, and bizarrely, loved Elvis nearly as much as I did. I felt I could guess at the other stuff too, the abstract that made up the spirit of him. He was tender but possessive, soulful but cruel when crossed. I'd witnessed these things but more, he'd given me a window into his elemental self by writing me those poems.

He wanted me to know him. How could any woman resist

a man who opened his beautiful heart to her without knowing what she would do with it?

I could have turned him in for inappropriate behavior the second I found out he had been lying to me about being my student, or the first time he gave me an apple poem. I didn't and it astounded me that he knew I wouldn't.

I sighed heavily as I rewrapped the poems and placed them back in my desk before I gathered my things to walk home because my car was still at Hephaestus Auto.

Entrance was also not exactly the picturesque west coast town that I had been imagining when I moved here. The downtown core was sizeable and beautifully maintained, with a huge main plaza dominated by an elegant fountain, wrought iron chairs and a tended garden. The buildings were old, Victorian inspired or redbrick and all meticulously restored. The only blight on the town was a sprawling industrial lot on the east side of town beside the river where a garage, a tattoo parlor and a little strip mall stood. This was the side of town that the down and out citizens of Entrance lived. There weren't many of them and they weren't truly impoverished even if the single-level bungalows had seen better days. No, it was the chain-link fences locking in frightening beasts that had maybe, at one time, been dogs, and the pungent scent of marijuana that seemed integral to that specific burg. As a girl who had spent her entire life in the affluent and posh neighborhood of Dunbar in Vancouver, the seedy side of Entrance terrified me.

The little cabin I had bought sight unseen online was ramshackle. The heat was on the fritz, which had been fine when I first moved in during September but during December, January and even now in February, it required me to wear at least three layers of thick knits and invest in multiple blankets. The hot water held out for about three minutes and I was the kind of woman who took half-hour showers. Most of the kitchen cabinets were broken, the fridge groaned like a bear emerging from hibernation, and the sloping garden that led to the ocean—my entire reason for buying the house—was an overgrown thicket of thorns and tangled bushes. I was still reeling from my disappointment even though I'd already been there for six months.

Still, a thrill shot through me at the sight of the little cabin on the side of a steep cliff beside the ocean. There was a thick coating of moss on the steepled roof, the screen door was hanging crookedly on its hinges, the garden was so overgrown that it crawled up the sides of the peeling, shingled walls and onto the sparsely graveled driveway. It was an absolute mess. But it was mine; I owned it outright. The real estate agent had balked at the plastic bag of cash I handed to him to complete the transaction but he took it all the same and now, for the first time in my life, I owned something just for myself.

I named the house Shamble Wood Cottage and I planned on painting a little sign to put on a post at the start of the long driveway. It was well down my priority list but I couldn't wait to claim the land the way I wanted to, making it exactly my own.

The interior wasn't much better. The best thing about it was the open plan layout, unusual in an older cabin. The kitchen led to a slightly sunken living room and dining nook that was delineated with an old, hand-carved oak bar that was decorated with raised designs of ivy and delicate tree branches on the front so that it was visible from the living room. The entire front wall at the back of the house was constructed of large windows and sliding glass doors so that every room had a perfect view of the sloping yard and the gorgeous sprawl of the blue ocean unfolding from the rocky beach.

I didn't have much furniture, but the deep leather couch

and huge matching chocolate brown armchair I had perpendicular to each other in the seating area in front of the enormous stone fireplace were cabin chic and super comfy. I'd finagled a makeshift coffee table out of wooden crates until I had the time and money to buy a real one but I was desperate for a few bookcases that could house the boxes of books I had set to one side of the couch.

After putting away the groceries, I made myself a bowl of oatmeal with fresh berries and maple syrup. Breakfast for dinner or lunch and breakfast for breakfast was pretty much my go-to. I was a morning person and I loved everything about the first meal of the day, including coffee. After eating, I grabbed my mug of decaf and moved to the huge armchair in front of the crackling fire. It had taken me a couple of tries to get it lit but I was glad I had bothered because the sea salt in the logs turned the flames a gorgeous blue and green.

It was quiet and beautiful and I wanted to love my life now that I was free, but even liberty couldn't close the yawning abyss of loneliness in my soul. It overtook me in the darkness between falling asleep and slumber and in the fragmented moments of quiet between periods at school. When lovebirds brushed together beside me, intrinsically bound to each other like magnets, like two things elementally meant to be. I knew it came mostly from being isolated my entire life, cloistered away by my ultra-conservative parents because of the mistakes they had made with my brother. I'd had no friends, only family, and even that was fractured irrevocably by the time I was eleven.

It also came because I was a romantic and yet, I had no romance. Not ever. Lusting after King and the brief time we had spent together was the greatest connection I'd ever forged.

Before I had left, I might have had a home and a husband, but I'd never been loved, neither had it or lived with its pulse inside of me. I'd lain awake while William snored softly beside me, imagining the kind of life I might have lived if I had been strong enough to run away, to fight against the destiny that had been plotted for me by my parents. I dreamt of a man who would utterly possess me, rip me from comfort and safety and plunge me into passion and chaos. A man who would look at me, instead of through me as my husband had. A man who was a real man, maybe one who chopped his own wood and fixed his own leaky pipes. Not a thirty-six-year-old lawyer from a small, deeply religious town in the prairies who had befriended my parents and took me as an eighteen-year-old bride because I was pretty, practically virginal and had no greater aspirations for myself than those set by my parents. I'd dreamed the dream for eight years before finally doing something about it.

Now, I had my beautiful, ramshackle little cabin in a lovely town with a teaching position at one of the best schools on the west coast. I should have been content; I should have been the happiest person in the world. Yet, as I sat by the fire and delved into one of my countless paperback romances, I found myself crying silently as loneliness sat beside me, my only companion. At one point, I imagined the throaty thrum of a motorcycle moving past the mouth of my long driveway and thought about a future I could never have with King, and the tears fell a little harder.

# Nine.

"Go out with me."

It was a chilly but bright late winter day in Entrance. The sun filtered through the thin layer of clouds like silver, falling across the blossoms that burst forth early on the west coast as soon as the last of the snow melted. The air was cold and clean, so fragrant I kept dragging in deep breaths that made my lungs tingle with cold. I was still bundled up in an old white suede coat with a fur collar that I'd bought at a vintage store in Vancouver for a steal, pale pink gloves on my hands and a toque on my head. I was also holding a coffee from Honey Bear Café. It was a dirty chai latte, my favorite. How King had known that, I couldn't be sure, but it was sitting on my desk after third period, which I knew he had free (because I'd used my teacher's authority unethically and printed off a copy of his schedule).

I knew it was from him because instead of my name written on the side of the cardboard, it said "babe."

I hadn't had any interactions with him outside of class and those crazy beautiful apple poems in two weeks and he was still trying to get to me. I was terrified that it was working.

"Cressida?"

I jerked out of my thoughts and finally tuned to Warren,

who had been sitting beside me at the picnic table while we ate our lunches. Ostensibly, we were meant to keep an eye on the kids as they loitered about the soccer field, the tiny copse of trees to the left and the ultra-cool outdoor gym to the right. Many of the students lay on the grass drinking sodas and enjoying the sunshine even though it was still uncomfortably cold out.

At some point, Rainbow and Tay had been with us but evidently, they'd left sometime during my daydreams about King.

"Sorry," I murmured. "What did you say?"

Warren smiled winningly at me, his Ken doll face fixing into a perfectly symmetrical grin. "Go out with me."

"Oh." I wasn't surprised by the invitation; Warren hadn't exactly been subtle in his admiration of me since he'd formally introduced himself two weeks ago. Still, I'd been dreading this moment, tried to delay it by being friendly but coolly disinterested in him. Maybe the Cressida I'd been at eighteen, desperate for love and completely naïve, would have enjoyed Warren's attention. As it was now, I found him kind of annoying. He wore Axe body spray, for one. What grown man wore Axe body spray?

"Oh, yes, or oh, no?" Warren joked.

I opened my mouth to respond when I felt eyes on me. It didn't make any sense but I knew the texture of the gaze, the way they fell hot on my skin then slid possessively through my hair over my cheeks and neck like a physical caress. There were words in that gaze, ones that spoke of deviant plans for my body, promises that they would one day come true.

King's eyes on my skin spoke to me more eloquently than any man ever had before, excepting him. It made me wonder what his hands would say on my skin if given the chance.

Now, I could feel their jealousy heavy and hot as I leaned

into Warren.

"Oh, no," I said softly to my colleague. "I'm sorry, but I'm not even technically divorced yet. It's too soon."

Warren was already nodding, leaning toward me with an accepting smile. "Of course, I knew you'd say that. I can wait."

"Really, I wouldn't. I was married for eight years. It will take a while to get over that."

His eyebrows shot up. "You're not old enough to have been married that long."

Irritation prickled through me. "Well, I was."

"You must have been a child bride," he joked. "No wonder it didn't work out.

I winced because his words hit a little too close to home. Eighteen *was* too early to get married and my parents should have known that instead of cultivating it. They'd practically handed me over to William the minute the ink was dry on my high school diploma.

My phone pinged loudly in my pocket. I checked the screen, thankful for the reprieve until I saw the message there.

**Lysander:** In the parking lot.

Nothing good could come from my ex-con brother loitering at my place of employment, especially at a prep school like EBA where everyone was judged on their wealth and propriety.

"Excuse me, Warren," I muttered without looking up as I slipped my phone in my pocket and speed-walked around the corner to the parking lot.

The U-shaped lot was mostly empty, students and faculty off-grounds for lunchtime, and I didn't know if Sander had a car or not. I stood near the science building, squinting into the sun trying to find him when a large hand clamped down on my shoulder and dragged me behind the bushes.

I let out a loud squeak before I could control the reaction

and then glared up at Sander once he had me settled between himself and the wall.

"What in the world are you doing here?" I hissed.

My big brother crossed his arms across his barrel chest and glowered down at me. I hadn't seen him in three months but he wasn't much changed. Prison had done that to him two years ago. He'd never been an upstanding citizen but after six years behind bars, he'd emerged tatted and roughed up in a way he'd never been before. There were scars on his hands, hands that I knew could make beautiful music, and harsh lines between his brows from a now permanent scowl. He was still beautiful to me and until I'd met King, I'd believed him to be the most handsome man in the world. What little girl doesn't think her older brother is hero worthy? Especially when they very literally save your life?

His stern face broke into a small smile. "Good to see you too, princess."

My heart broke open, crashing through my stupid anxiety at anyone seeing me with my thuggish-looking brother. I threw my arms around his thick neck and peppered his face in kisses. His rumbling laugh worked through me as he wrapped me up in his bear hug.

"Missed you," I whispered brokenly.

"Missed you too."

We held each other for a long minute before he carefully placed me on the ground. I kept his hand in mine, rubbing the ridged calluses with my thumb.

"You look good," he said. "Divorce never looked so good."

"Thanks." I beamed. "But not divorced yet. William still won't sign the papers."

Immediately Lysander's face turned stony. "No fuckin' way."

"Sander, please." I put my hand on his arm to calm him because there was no one more volatile than my brother. "Don't worry about it. I'm doing really well."

He stared hard at me for a second before nodding curtly. "Seems so. Got yourself a fancy teaching job at a fancy school. Thought you wanted to go back to school?"

"I need money for that. But I'm happy here for now, really. The other teachers have been really welcoming and the kids are good, really bright."

"How you doin' for money?" he asked, cutting right to the point of his visit.

I bit my lip. It was never easy to say, when Lysander brought up money, if he was going to ask for or offer it.

"Tell me," he ordered.

"I'm fine, honey. I bought a tiny house by the water. It needs some fixing but it's all right."

"Got furniture?"

"A bit," I assured him with a little shrug and a smile. "I pilfered some stuff from our storage unit before I moved up here."

"Your mum and dad help?" It was always "your" parents with him even though they were his as much as mine by blood. He hadn't talked to them in years. The last time they did was seared on my brain, my father's face as he shouted at Lysander for leading me down the wrong path right along with him and my mother's wailing sobs. Now, they didn't even mention Sander. He was worse than dead to them. It was as if he had never existed.

So, I got why he called them mine and not his.

I shrugged carefully because I didn't want him to fly into a rage as I knew he would if he felt someone had wronged me, even if it was my own parents. "They aren't very pleased with me right now. You know how much they love William."

They still spent every Sunday night having dinner with him. Dad went fishing with him the first Saturday of every month just as they had done since before I hit puberty, and mum made him casseroles to keep in the fridge now that his (and I'm quoting her on this) "wife had abandoned him."

I spoke only to my mother, and even then, only when she called me in an attempt to guilt-trip or shame me into going back to William.

I didn't say any of that because Lysander was unpredictable, loyal beyond belief to those he loved (only me, that I was aware of), and a little bit crazy.

"They should love you more," Sander said.

I shrugged again. It hurt even though I wanted it not to. I was coming around to the fact that they weren't great people, that very nearly *gifting* their daughter to their best friend who was nearly twenty years her senior was *not* okay, and that cutting her off without emotional or financial support when she finally left him was ridiculously cruel. But I wasn't there yet.

"You love me enough for anyone," I said, squeezing his hand. "And anyway, I'm making it work. It's good for me to be on my own and struggle. I've never done that before."

"Good," he said, meaning it with all his heart even though he only gave me a brisk nod.

There was a little pause where I waited for him to tell me his real reason for ambushing me at my school and he pretended his only motivation was making sure I was all right.

"Need you to do something for me," he finally grunted.

Damn.

"Okay, what do you need?" I asked as if it was no big deal.

And it wasn't. Lysander never had much of a future. He hated our parents, began binge drinking and partying at the age of twelve and never turned back from a life of poor decisions.

Our parents threw him out of the house when I was ten and he was fifteen but he'd still found ways to see me, to buy me little gifts and take me out to the movies. He was and always had been my little secret, my minor rebellion. I'd been giving him money since I was eleven, first from my allowance and then from my joint account with William. It wasn't unusual for him to ask. He'd had only odd jobs before and now that he was an ex-con, it was even harder for him to find work.

Only now, I didn't have my parents or William's money and I barely had any of my own.

So, I was hoping whatever he needed didn't involve a whole bunch of zeroes.

"I heard you been spending some time with a brother from The Fallen MC," he said instead.

*What?*

I gaped at him as shock, horror and disbelief raged through me. How could Sander have possibly known that? I knew he liked to "keep an eye on me" but how far did that extend, because he would have literally had to be stalking me to find out about the minimal time I spent with King.

And if he knew, who else did?

I shuddered.

"How did you hear that?" I demanded, only it was too breathless to really be an order.

He crossed his arms again and stared at me, not willing to answer.

"For Pete's sake, Sander, I spent like two days with the guy. How do you know about that?" I cried, heedless of keeping a low profile now that I was panicking.

People finding out I had an ex-convict as a brother was way lower on the totem pole than them finding out I'd made out with a student.

"Doesn't matter. I need you to get me a job at Zeus Garro's garage."

"What?"

He repeated his statement then said, "I wouldn't ask you if it wasn't important, princess."

I blew out a frustrated breath. "I don't know where you heard I was hanging out with a biker but the fact is, I'm not. I ended it before it even started. I mean, come on, Sander, me with a man like that? I don't think so."

I laughed nervously because there was a large part of me that wanted to be the kind of girl who would attract and keep a man like that.

Sander raised a brow at me. "Don't need to know the details. Don't even need you to date the guy. Do need that job, Cressida. Like I said, wouldn't ask if it wasn't super important."

It was easy to understand what he meant. He wouldn't ask unless it meant the difference between staying out of jail or going back in, or maybe even the difference between life and death.

I wanted to be appalled, but even though Lysander had never asked me to personally extend a favor like this to him, I'd seen him do it to others before. This was the way of his outlaw life, favor exchanges, manipulations of people and laws, demands and acts that would make a normal human crumble. He thrived on them now, excelled at his criminal life.

I didn't judge him for it. I'd helped buy it for him so I never judged him for it.

But he'd never asked me to take part in it.

"You can't ask him yourself?" I ventured.

"Nope. Zeus Garro's a smart guy, wouldn't let someone on to that compound unless he was trusted."

"*I'm* not trusted. I've never even met Zeus Garro."

“This guy that you aren’t seein’ anymore. He go quietly when you cut him loose?” he asked, somewhat bizarrely.

“Ugh, not really,” I admitted.

He nodded. “Then I’m thinkin’ you’ll meet Zeus Garro sooner than you think. Gotta get goin’. Text me when you’ve sealed the deal for me.”

“I really can’t promise anything,” I tried again, desperately. “I can’t see that guy again, Sander. And even if I did, I don’t think he’s the kinda guy to just blindly do what I ask.”

My brother hesitated then lifted his big, scarred hand to palm my cheek. I pressed myself into it, as always starved for affection.

“I need you to do it, you’ll do it. Best thing in my life, princess. I know you won’t let me down.”

I stared at him as he patted my cheek then turned and disappeared around the corner.

“Well, crap,” I huffed as I closed my eyes and hit my head against the wall.

When I opened them again, King was there.

# Ten.

He was on the other side of the bushes, in the narrow pathway between the science building and the forest that bracketed the left side of the property. At first, I thought he was just leaning against the wall smoking, looking like a modern-day James Dean with his worn black leather jacket shrugged on over his school uniform, the curl of smoke escaping from his lips like a white scarf lifted in the cold wind. His hair was down and chaotic even though I'd noticed over the past few weeks that he liked to harness it with a little bit of leather cord he kept tied to his right wrist. He looked like a poster child for the original bad boy.

I was startled out of staring at him by the arrival of the same hulking man from the parking lot at Mac's Grocer who'd acted as his sidekick. He approached King with a chin lift, and then they did that ultra-masculine hand-clasp back-slap thing that I'd only seen people do in movies.

"Don't like this," King muttered as he threw his cigarette to the ground and crushed it with his boot.

"Bro," was the only thing his friend said, yet it seemed to convey more.

King's shoulders were hitched to his ears, his hands in his pockets as he kicked at the grass. "I know it's gotta be done.

Don't like this shit at EBA, just sayin'. I worked fuckin' hard to get in here, Mute."

Mute. Appropriate name. He grunted in response.

"I mean, fuck, I get it. No one messes with The Fallen. But doin' this at school is sketchy," King griped, his hands in his hair making it even messier.

"Might not come to anything," Mute suggested but King slanted him a "get real" look and even he didn't look too convinced.

"King, my man!"

All of our eyes shot to Carson Gentry. He was by far and away the richest boy at Entrance Bay Academy, and also one of the prettiest. As in, his eyelashes got caught in his eyebrows and his irises were a golden brown so deep a girl could fall into them like molasses. He had good hair, good teeth and a body honed by endless soccer practices. The EBA girls loved him more than they loved anyone. Or they had, until King Kyle Garro showed up in his leather jacket with all that golden hair and a corruptible grin.

As one, King and Mute jerked their chins at him.

It wasn't a practiced move but it screamed cool in a way that had Carson Gentry's rich-guy arrogance wilting.

"So, ugh, you got the good stuff?" he asked them.

Adrenaline coursed through me until the hair on the back of my neck stood on end.

*Oh my God.*

Was I witnessing what I thought I was witnessing?

I frantically looked for a way out of the situation. If I could sneak away before I truly heard anything, I didn't have to report it, right?

But there was no way to slide by undetected in the narrow pathway or slip unseen between the bushes by the wall. I was skinny but I wasn't that tiny.

"Maybe. Depends on what information you got for me," King rumbled.

His voice was octaves lower than his normal charming tones, almost always filled with laughter even when he wasn't being funny or amused. Now, it was dark and forceful. A shudder ripped up my spine, leaving behind a tangible ache.

"What are you talking about, my man?" Carson said with an uneasy smile.

"Not your man, Carson. Heard you've been getting your shit from some other dealer. What's up with that?" King questioned.

"Don't know where you heard that, man, but it's not true," Carson repeated, but he shifted his weight from foot to foot uncomfortably.

I hated that one of my students was asking for drugs but I hated particularly that it was Carson. He was a bright kid with sad eyes, probably because of the bruises that he often claimed were from football practice but that the coach and his teachers knew better were from his wildly unpopular in town father.

King and his friend shared a brief look that was merely a flicker of eye contact before Mute took one large menacing step forward. With his enormous bulk, a six-foot miniature Hulk with severely buzzed black hair and a huge neck tattoo of some kind of red reptile, it didn't surprise me that Carson's shaky grin disappeared to be replaced with an "oh my goodness, I'm going to crap my pants" expression.

He held up his hands beseechingly. "Dude, *one* time I get product from someone else and you're flipping out?"

King stood up from his lean against the wall and uncrossed his arms as he turned fully away from me to face Carson. "Flippin' out? If you think this is me *flippin' out* then you better brace yourself because if you don't tell me in two fuckin' seconds who supplied you, I'm gonna show you what it actually looks like when I flip the fuck out on your ass."

"Whoa, whoa, *fuck*, okay!" he practically yelled as Mute slowly moved toward him, hemming him into the wall. "I got some mediocre weed from this guy named Hector."

"Mexican," Mute grunted.

King ignored him, his entire body stiff and radiating fury, but I had a feeling this was a significant insight.

"Where'd you hear about 'im?" King asked.

"Dude," Carson whined.

King stepped closer and calmly hoisted Carson by his dress shirt into the air before he thrust him hard against the wall.

My gasp was drowned out by Carson's warbled whimper. I knew it was well beyond time to do something about what was taking place but I couldn't bring myself to move. It wasn't so much that I was scared, though I was. The problem was, I was only scared just enough to ignite the desire at the base of my belly. The monster that slumbered like Sleeping Beauty's dragon inside my gut was rumbling, stretching and yawning as it had when I'd viewed a similar scene with King in the grocery store parking lot. Just like then, she wanted in on the action, to laugh in the face of the scared punk who dared to fuck with such a beautiful King. She wanted to revel in their power, bathe in Carson's fear and try her own hand at manipulation.

It was totally and completely fucked up.

The Cressida I was didn't live to scare people, she didn't even live to intimidate people. I helped old ladies cross the street, I baked cookies for my neighbors and sat with students when they needed a good cry. I did this because I was a good person.

Only, King made me want to be not such a great person.

He made me want to indulge in all things that had tempted Eve: sex, gluttony and larceny. King was my apple, my Satan, my ultimate fall from grace.

And as I stood there riveted by his cruel power, I hated myself.

"*Fuck*, okay, I didn't hear about him, all right? He found me at Evergreen Gas Station. Said if I wanted to find him again, that's where he would be. But I didn't, okay? His shit is nowhere near as good as yours," Carson was babbling.

But I was done, on fire with shame and scrambling to put out the flames.

So, I made a rash decision.

I stormed out of the bushes.

Or, at least, I tried to storm.

But I was wearing impractical but utterly beautiful high-heeled leather boots that made my legs in their olive-green riding pants look *awesome*, so I tripped. Badly. I fell through the bushes and onto my hands and knees just behind the trio who all turned their heads to witness my disgrace.

"Mrs. Irons?" Carson croaked, half mortified and half thrilled because he recognized that I was his savior even if I was doing a really terrible job of it.

Embarrassment lit my skin like a second-degree burn but I righted myself with minimal awkwardness and fisted my hands on my hips. "Yes, Carson, Mrs. Irons. The same Mrs. Irons who has just witnessed a drug deal and an attack against another student on school grounds."

Carson's hope drained from his face as he realized that he too was in trouble. King and Mute didn't move.

"Drop your arm from Mr. Gentry's throat, Mr. Garro, and you both come with me. As for you," I turned to Mute, "get out of here before I have to find out who you are and what you're doing here and then call your parents."

I watched through my indignant fury as Mute's mean face relaxed enough to twitch just barely into a smile. "Sure thing, *Miss* Irons."

My mouth fell open as he turned on his heel, jerked his chin at King and ambled out of sight around the building. Rage built even brighter inside me as I realized that King had told his friend about me.

"Gentlemen," I practically screeched. "Follow me to the headmaster's office."

Entrance Bay Academy was one of the top ten prep schools in the country and as such, it was ludicrously expensive to attend and boasted a gorgeous campus. Headmaster Adams's office was probably the nicest office I had ever seen in my life, and William was a lawyer so I'd seen a lot of them. The lower half of the walls were paneled in deep mahogany wood with navy blue paint on the rest, the other school colours reflected in the yellow accent pillows on the leather couch and the emerald green curtains and lush grey-green rugs. Adams himself sat in an enormous wing-backed, tufted leather chair with, I kid you not, a pipe growing cold in its placeholder on his ornate desk.

He suited the room. It was more than just his grey-and-green tweed blazer with the elbow patches and his beautifully maintained moustache. He oozed authority and social elegance. He was large, having once been young and fit whereas now he was old and soft over a layer of lingering muscle. His great big cloud of white hair was parted to reveal his florid scalp and he was taken with crossing his hands over his chest like some kind of academic Santa Claus.

I quite liked him. He was easy for me to read and even easier for me to please because he was the type of man my father and William had been.

I did not like him at the moment, as he scowled at me from under his fuzzy eyebrows.

"You've put me in quite the position, Mrs. Irons," he said finally, after studying me for several moments.

I didn't understand how it had come to this. I'd arrived, irate, with a terrified Carson and an unflappable King in tow, explained how things had unfolded to the headmaster, then I had been promptly ordered to wait in the reception while he spoke first with both of them, and then individually to each.

Now, he had beckoned me back into his office and I felt very much like a naughty child once more called into my father's study.

"You see," Adams continued, "Carson Gentry's mother is the sister of Mayor Lafayette's wife and his father owns half of this town. It would be unfortunate if I had to telephone them about this little mishap as they contribute annually and *generously* to this school."

"Headmaster—" I started.

He lifted a single finger and wagged it. "Now, I agree there must be something done about Mr. Garro. Normally, I would suspend him at the very least but his father has made it quite clear that he expects Kyle to be treated with above-normal reverence."

"Not above normal anything," the deepest voice I'd ever heard sounded from over my shoulder. "My boy fucked up, fine. Strike one. You want 'im out of your prissy little school because you think my boy is beneath you when the truth is, he's fuckin' better than us all."

I swiveled in my seat, eager beyond belief to match the voice to the name.

Zeus Garro filled the doorway the way I knew he would and still he took my breath away. Not like King did, with his sheer beauty, but because Zeus was the biggest, scariest man I'd ever laid eyes on.

He was at least six-foot-five and quilted with muscles so dense that I'd break my finger if I poked him, I was certain of it. Like his son, he had a riot of curly, wavy hair but it was longer and darker, brown at the roots lightening to sun-soaked golden at the ends. It was touchable hair that gave him a "just fucked" quality that didn't help dampen his incredible sexual charisma. He had a lush mouth surrounded by a short, well-groomed beard, and thick-lashed eyes just a shade more silver than King's. He should have been beautiful, a kind of gorgeous that you could have cried over. Instead, the hard set of his jaw, the bumps in his strong nose that denoted it at least twice or thrice broken, and the hard glint in those icy eyes turned me to stone with fear.

Zeus Garro was not someone you fucked with.

And it was clear as he moved his enormous, tattooed bulk through the elegant room to stand before the desk with crossed arms that he felt Headmaster Adams was trying to fuck with him.

Adrenaline kicked into gear through my blood and brought me to that dark place of joy as I waited for him to rip into Adams.

I wasn't disappointed.

"Mr. Garro, you have to understand that Kyle was trying to sell drugs to a student," Adams began righteously.

"The fuck he was," Zeus growled. He tipped his head my

way without looking at me. "She tell you that?"

"Well, of course!"

Zeus swiveled his head my way in a move so smooth and menacing that it made goose bumps break out over my skin. "You tell him that?"

I swallowed. "Technically, I told him that Carson was trying to buy drugs but King didn't seem to be selling any."

This appeared to be the right thing to say. I was grateful for this for two reasons. One was that as soon as I'd been told to wait in the reception, I regretted turning King in. He was clearly doing something he shouldn't have been but I really didn't believe he deserved to be expelled for it. Not just because I'd grown accustomed to wearing his gaze like a crown or because I lived for his apple poems or because no one else had ever made me feel so alive. Truly, King deserved to be at EBA because he was incredibly smart and gifted, capable of going to one of the best universities and away from his criminal family. He deserved that opportunity and I couldn't stand the thought of being the one to take it away from him.

The other reason I was grateful for my quick-thinking response, was that, as I'd said, Zeus terrified me and I very much did not want him to kill me (something that I was certain he was capable of meting out with his bare hands).

Zeus squinted at me before his face relaxed slightly and I noticed that the crow's feet beside his eyes radiated in pale lines, saved from his deep tan because he spent all his considerable time outdoors squinting into the sun. It was a surprisingly attractive detail, and one that made him more human to me. I wasn't sure if I liked him or not. Could one like the President of a known criminal enterprise? But I loved that he was going to bat for his son and I loved that he was flustering the normally imperturbable Headmaster Adams.

"Right. As I understand it, Adams, my boy was merely trying to stop the spread of drug use at this school. That Gentry bastard approached him lookin' to score just because King rides a bike and King was tryin' to turn the kid to the right path."

I tried, with all my might, not to burst out laughing at the load of crock he was spewing. Somehow, even though my belly ached with the effort, I succeeded.

"He was bein' a social justice warrior," Zeus added for effect.

I covered my snort with a cough.

Zeus clapped me helpfully on the back.

Headmaster Adams, it seemed, didn't know what to do with this information. He sat with his mouth open and his brow furrowed, staring at the MC President as if he had two heads.

So, I jumped into the fray, leaning forward to smile softly at him. "Be that as it may, there *was* the matter of King being rough with Carson, which is inexcusable at EBA. Therefore, I suggest that King be given detention for the rest of the semester to pay penance and learn from his mistakes."

"Fuck that," Zeus barked, but it was just that, all bark and no bite.

He shot me a look out of the corner of his eyes that I knew meant he was pleased with me, that we had somehow ended up on the same team protecting King.

"Excellent idea, Mrs. Irons," Adams declared, recovering enough to slam his fist on the desk with authority. "Kyle needs to understand that he is at EBA now, a school of higher education and decorum. Rough housing and violence will not be tolerated. So, detention with Mrs. Irons every day after school for the next four weeks of the semester."

“What?” I squeaked even as Zeus slammed his own palm down on Adams’s desk, jolting both the headmaster and myself in our seats as he said, “Done.”

“But Headmaster Adams, I don’t oversee detention,” I pointed out.

“You don’t,” he agreed. “But I know you could use the extra money and you are already here until five every day at least, helping the other students. Kyle may complete his homework silently while you conduct your study sessions.”

No, no, no.

How did this happen?

Zeus stared at me out of the corner of his gaze, assessing me with that eye more thoroughly than anyone ever had out of two. I held still, barely breathing under his scrutiny and at the thought of having even more time with King, especially if it was one on one.

“From what I hear, *Miss* Irons, you’ll set my boy straight about his behavior and have him actin’ like a gentleman in no time.”

I swallowed thickly as Zeus nodded curtly at the headmaster and swaggered (that really was the only word for it) out the doors.

# Eleven.

It couldn't be explained, the way I wanted him. It felt unnatural, beyond a craving, more like a possession, some alien force taking control of my body, urging me to do things that I *knew* were morally corrupt, socially unsound. It was already overwhelming to be in the same room with him day after day, as he was in two of my grade twelve classes. I was not looking forward to that afternoon after school when we would have our first detention together.

Sweat beaded like a crown of shame on my forehead as I sat in my sixth period English class, consumed with my internal struggle.

Don't look at him too often.

Don't walk past his desk.

Again.

Okay, this would be the last time.

The struggle was very real and my only relief came from knowing that he was experiencing the same thing. I was the focus of this class, his contemplation based on the angled slope of my breasts beneath my silk blouse, the exact shade of each strand in my long cascade of golden brown hair. I knew this because his eyes had become an accessory I wore with pride, a necklace I wore pressed tight to my throat, hot and heavy on the exposed skin above my décolletage.

Also, I knew because he told me so.

With his apple poems, but also in the margins of his tests, across entire pages of his notebook where he drew beautiful little sketches of me, fragments of my person so that only someone well acquainted with me would recognize their likeness. I knew even as I sat at my desk while the students wrote poems as a creative writing exercise, that his lean, strong fingers were tracing the tip of his pencil around the lines of my face.

"All right." I stood up to address the class. "Who is ready to share?"

I smiled when Benny's hand shot into the air. He had been particularly motivated since King joined our classes.

I was strangely shocked to see King's hand up, lazily propped on the edge of his small desk. He participated frequently in class discussions, especially during our *Paradise Lost* unit, but I hadn't expected him to be willing to share his poetic side to a greater audience than me. For some reason, it made my heart pang.

So, even though I knew it was a bad idea, I found myself calling on him to read. Our eyes clashed as I did so, the impact so tangible that I was sure the class heard the crackling clang of electric chemistry between us. King smiled that long, slow curl of the lips that unwound something inside me before he stood up.

"Why don't you read the poem for us, then we will question you as a class about your intentions?" I suggested, somewhat breathily.

He nodded and didn't take his burning gaze off of me as he began to recite his poem.

"A secret in her smile
Tucked in a rosy furl
I want to pull it out with my teeth
Soothe the paper cut with my tongue
Dip in the well of her blood and write
My own secret on her lips
So that every time she talks
Every lick of those lips
And drag of breath through her mouth
She feels me
Her tongue scrapes the scar of my secret on the inside of her pout
And she can't deny the truth of it
Of me
Of us
I've branded her with it
She's mine."

The silence in the class was impenetrable. It cloaked me in faux privacy, enabled me to indulge in a moment of pure, unadulterated awe and lust. There was no doubt in my mind that King was speaking about me. The glittering ice-blue of his eyes shone on me spotlight bright. I fidgeted nervously under his possessive regard, fiddling with my left ring finger where my wedding and engagement bands used to rest.

The girls in my class had collectively lost their breath to him, their pheromones heating in the small room so that the cloying scent of their adolescent sweet perfume grew stronger.

Seventeen-year-old girls, and I was no better.

In fact, I was significantly worse.

I'd been a married woman, lived enough years to control my baser instincts, especially after William had successfully cauterized them for so long.

Yet, there I stood in front of my classroom, thighs rubbing together, nipples beaded under my shirt and pulse throbbing like strobe lights, calling King to claim me, to take me like I knew he wanted to.

As if reading my salacious thoughts, King sank back into his chair and winked at me. "So, whaddya think, teach?"

I was grateful for the reminder that I was, indeed, his teacher.

"Interesting, King, I'll give you that. But why don't we see what your classmates have to say?"

Immediately, nearly everyone's hands flooded the air.

King chuckled and slouched farther back in his seat, a lazy smirk on his face. "Well, look at that, at least someone liked it."

Talia laughed and flounced over to King from her seat on the other side of the room. With an ease that belayed their familiarity, she flopped into his lap and wrapped her arms around his neck.

"You are so silly. Of course, I liked it," she crooned to him as she pressed a kiss to his cheek.

I wasn't sure who looked more devastated, Benny or myself. My breath froze in my lungs, the iced air expanding until my lungs ached.

King smiled fondly at Talia but gently urged her off of his lap. "Wasn't about you, sweets. You're not the only beautiful girl around here, you know."

*Sweets*. He had a nickname for all the girls. Sweets was more unique than babe, it was probably unique to her and he called every random girl who rode on the back of his bike, *babe*.

She giggled. "Whatever, handsome."

I pursed my lips and forced my posture straighter. This was fine, good, even. King was a *teenager*. He should be with another teenager. It made sense. Plus, he and Talia were both lovely blondes. They would look good together.

Yes, I was happy. It was nice to see two students link up and find joy in each other.

*Bullshit*, crazy Cressida raged inside the cage of my ribs, shaking them so violently that my breath began to rattle in and out of my mouth. *He's yours!*

He wasn't, had never been and wouldn't ever be.

Still, rage burned through my veins turning blood to hot lead.

Talia caught the expression on my face and laughed lightly as she settled back in her seat. "Sorry, Mrs. Irons. I'm sure you get me though. He's so hawt."

I did get her.

"No worries, Talia," I said drily as I turned away to sit behind my desk again, needing the space. "Next time try to control yourself though, okay?"

I could feel King's eyes on me, the necklace now a choker of barbed wire around my throat but I refused to look at him for the rest of the class.

Unfortunately, our class was sixth period so King stayed in his seat while everyone else left the classroom. Talia lingered for a few minutes, leaning against his desk so that her breasts were in his face but I was able to ignore them fairly well as Maya stayed behind to ask me a question about her *Paradise Lost* final paper. I continued to ignore him when both girls left, the door closing with a sinister *snick* behind them.

I had papers to grade from my grade eleven history class and a lesson plan to make for my substitute teacher next Friday for when I had to go back into Vancouver for a mandated mediation session with William. It all needed to be done efficiently, because I was frequently interrupted by students seeking extra help or kids who just needed a good listening ear. I fully expected Benny to show up to voice his woes about Talia and King, for example.

So, I bent my head with a curtain of hair between King and myself, and set to work.

This lasted for a surprisingly long time. So long, in fact, that I became jumpy and easily distracted by every single noise. Benny did come, his eyes wide and frenzied but upon seeing the object of his tizzy, they widened even more in agony and he quickly backtracked from the room.

My favorite student, an eleventh grader named Louise Lafayette who was built like a blonde bombshell already but dressed like she was sixty and who had, just last week, been diagnosed with cancer, came in for her customary cup of tea. We shared one every Thursday afternoon, the only free time she had between classes, volunteering and dance lessons. Now, the dance lessons would have to stop because she was beginning chemotherapy in two weeks. We had our cup of tea, talking quietly huddled together on my side of the desk so I could reach out to push back her hair, touch her hand. Her father was the mayor of Entrance, a busy man with no time for his daughter, and her mother was the unofficial queen of society, so she too made no efforts with Louise or the younger daughter, Beatrice. Therefore, our tea dates were the only times Louise got any sort of affection or attention and I made sure to give it to her in spades.

Detention was nearly over by the time she left, smiling slightly despite her situation. I was grateful for my hour with her even though I didn't get any work done, because I truly adored her. She was as close to perfect as I believed a person could get; outstandingly beautiful, funny with a quick wit, and kind enough to spend hours every week volunteering at the local autism centre. I was happier than I could say that she trusted me to be there for her, just as I felt overwhelmingly privileged every time one of my students confided in me. Even though I didn't want to teach forever, it was by far my favorite part of the job.

I was also grateful because for one hour, I'd been wholly distracted from the blond king sitting five metres away diligently working on his assignments.

Only when Louise had left and I'd turned back to my grading, did he quietly speak.

"You were so good with her."

I stiffened. Of course, he could have overheard our quiet conversation and Louise knew we had an audience so she wouldn't have said anything she didn't want shared, but I still thought it was rude of him to eavesdrop.

So, I told him so.

His soft chuckle gave me goose bumps. "Not gonna lie, babe, I'll take any opportunity I can get to learn more of you so I can get closer."

"King," I protested quietly, still gazing, unseeing, at my papers.

"Had to give Kelsey Hopkins twenty bucks to spill how you take your fuckin' coffee. Worth it to see the way you savored every fuckin' sip. Made me think of how you'd savor me, I ever get in there with you."

God*damn*, why did he have to be so sweet and sexy all at the same time?

I finally looked up at him, seeing him leaning forward in his chair, forearms on knees, hand resting between his thighs, head tilted down but eyes tipped up so he could look at me from under his golden brows, his eyes blue and pure as a tundra sky. My breath left me in a soft gasp at the sight of all that beauty in one man.

"There they are. Missed those whiskey eyes of yours," he said, quietly.

We were both aware of the possibility of being walked in on. It was late, just after five o'clock, but there were still students going home from music and sports practices, teachers loitering over unfinished marking. It lent my classroom an intimacy that I'd never experienced before, our secret attraction making even the rows of metal and wood desks, the textbooks lining the shelves along the back wall and my standard-issue yellow wood desk romantic and cozy.

"You can't say things like that to me, King," I said, completely without conviction because I was a bad woman in a good girl casing.

"Not gonna stop, Cressida," he retorted.

I sucked in a breath and held it as he unfolded that long body and ambled over to the classroom door. He caught my eyes as he slowly turned the lock, pulled the thin paper curtain over the little window in the door so no one would see in, and turned off the artificial lights so only the pastel hues of the setting sun lit the room.

My quick breath and the loud tick of the clock over the whiteboard behind me were the only soundtrack to my seduction as he strolled over to my desk and leaned down over it. My eyes skirted over the corded tendons in his forearms, the way the blue of his rolled-up sleeves made his arm hair look like pure gold, his skin another shade of the same colour.

"You look at me like I'm a king. Can't even hide it," he said and his voice was filled with awe, as if me thinking he was anything beautiful and good was inconceivable to him.

I frowned. "Your arrogance is clouding your judgment. I look at you like the capable and intelligent student you are."

He made a face, his lips twisting as if to bottle up a secret insecurity that wanted to spring forth.

"Do you doubt you're smart?" I asked without thinking first, shocked at the possibility.

King shrugged and leaned back to perch his butt (cute, high and tight, I knew, even though I'd tried not to notice) on the edge of my desk. "Gotta be smart to get into this place. Worked my ass off to get the marks, take the exams. Even had to get special dispensation to join the IB program late."

"So, smart," I confirmed.

"Sure."

I narrowed my eyes at him. "False modesty doesn't look good on you."

Finally, he grinned. "Not false, babe. Been smart my whole life, read a book a day since I could read at six years old. Got a head for numbers too and I've always been good with tech."

I'd heard enough through his teachers to know the truth of what he was understating. "You're a bit of a biker genius, eh?"

He blinked at me then laughed his musical laugh. I lived for the way his throat moved while he did it.

"Whatever. Truth is, I know I'm smart, yeah, but if everyone I've ever met doesn't think so just 'cause of who my dad is and what I look like, does that still make me smart? Without the opportunity to use that intelligence?"

It was a really good question. One I didn't have an answer to.

"That's why you worked so hard to get into EBA," I deduced, amazed by his tenacity.

"Wanted options," was his answer.

I bit my lip, desperately wanting to know the answer but aware that it would give away my hand, a hand full of hearts. "You aren't sure if you want to join the club? Or are you already a member? I'm not really sure how it works."

He cocked his head at me. "You really wanna know?"

I nodded.

"You patch in to the club after spending time as a 'hangaround' then more seriously, as a prospect to prove your worth. Could be a month, could be three years, depends on how long it takes to show the rest of the brothers your spirit and your loyalty. Once you're in, you don't get out, yeah? So prospecting is important. Don't want a brother who doesn't want to be there or can't fit in. The Fallen is a family at the end of the day. It just so happens that it's literally my family."

"I met your father when he came into the headmaster's office the other day." I hesitated. "He was interesting."

King laughed again. "He's a scary motherfucker but he's a good dad, good Prez."

"He wants you to, um, patch in?"

"Yeah. It's a legacy thing. My great-great-grandfather founded the MC back in the '60s to take advantage of the hippie movement."

Also known as taking advantage of the booming drug trade.

"And you don't know if you want to be a part of all that?" I asked tentatively.

King plucked the apple that still sat on my desk, a Granny Smith, which was my favorite and he seemed to have guessed that because it was the only one I got repeats of, and tossed it idly in one hand.

"Love the life. Gettin' on the back of my bike with my brothers and ridin' 'til we gotta stop or starve. It's a good life, babe, not gonna lie, I could live it. I just wonder, if I got this head, shouldn't I use it? I applied to some of the best universities in the country. Can't prospect if I'm in school."

"No," I agreed because I didn't know much about life in an MC but I did know something about student life. "I went to university and even though I didn't take advantage of all the extracurricular activities and parties, it kept me really busy."

He nodded. "So, like I said, wanna keep my options open."

"That makes sense. Can I ask you something though?"

"As my teacher?"

I bit my lip. It would be entirely inappropriate to ask him as anything else, obviously, but I had the feeling he would clam up if I said so. Instead, I shook my head but left it at that.

He rewarded my vagueness with a gorgeous smile that crinkled the skin beside his glacial water blue eyes. God, he was so gorgeous it made my stomach ache.

"Shoot."

"If you could do anything in the world, regardless of your actual skills or education, what would you do?" I asked.

It was a question no one had ever asked me. My parents and William had encouraged me to go to university because, to them, it was uncivilized not to have a higher education. I'd become a teacher after that because it was the only career they felt would give me the time I needed to take care of my husband and, eventually, a family. It was only after I left William that I realized it was a question I should have and could now ask myself.

King's lips pursed as he thought about it. I loved that he did that, contemplated everything carefully before he answered. It was part of what made him such a good student but also why he was so irresistible. At the end of the day, I was a woman starved for authentic attention just like Louise, and here was a man capable of giving it to me in spades.

"I'd run my own businesses. More than one because diversification is important but also because I get bored easily."

"Sounds like university would be a good idea, then," I suggested.

He laughed but it was hollow. "Thinkin' about it, babe. Don't push a man when he's on the fence about somethin'. He'll keep clinging to it 'til his dying breath if he feels he might land on the wrong side with the right push."

I knew from my experiences with William and my father that he was right, so I nodded even though I dared to ask, "Are you saying I could give you the right push?"

This time, his laughter was that beautiful bright peel I found myself living for.

"Says she isn't interested then likes the idea of havin' sway over me," he muttered as he shook his head at me.

I glared at him. "Arrogant boy says he's interested in me then flirts with another girl right in front of me."

Triumph lit his eyes, turned them into silver medallions. He was on me like a flash, caging me in my chair with his strong forearms, his face a hair away from mine and angled so he could speak right up against my mouth.

"You want me, babe. I see it every time I'm near you. Won't look at me but I look at you and I see the raised hair on your arms, the quick breaths that make your sweet tits strain against your prim shirts and the way you rub those thighs under those sexy-as-fuck skirts. You want me so badly that if I tucked my fingers beneath your panties, you'd soak my whole hand."

A groan escaped me before I could stifle it. King's eyes darted down to my lips a second before he swooped down to claim them for himself. His hot tongue owned my mouth, sweeping across my teeth, over my tongue in a wet roll that had my thighs trembling. When I groaned again, he matched it with one of his own. One of his hands fisted in my hair and tugged my head back for greater access to my mouth. I couldn't move but it made the kiss hotter, knowing that he was in control, taking what he wanted from me. I'd never been kissed so thoroughly, so possessively. It set my skin on fire. My fingers itched to rip off my suddenly uncomfortable clothes and let his wet tongue attempt to put out the flames.

His mouth angled away from mine, his lips wet against my cheek as they brushed down to my neck. I panted loudly when he used his teeth to scrape a slightly painful path down the line of my throat.

"Want to take you right here, right now. Spread these thighs and bury my face in your pussy, see if you taste as sweet as you look. I wanna eat you until I've had my fill, and Cress babe, I'm a growing fuckin' boy so I'm *starvin'*."

"Ohmigawd," I whispered because I'd lost all capacity for rational thinking.

The minute his mouth hit my skin I'd been a goner.

I'd thought I had imagined how good his hands and mouth felt on me during our two kind-of-dates but I was wrong, my memory was a weak thing and the reality of it all over me was kicking its butt.

My head lolled backward against my chair as his lips travelled lower, following the path his clever fingers opened for him over my breasts. He didn't open my blouse the whole way, just enough to lick, suck and bite at the swell of both breasts above the white lace bra I wore.

My hands fisted in his hair as he almost viciously sucked one of my nipples through the abrasive fabric.

"King," I called breathlessly.

He used his teeth on my nipple, just hard enough to have my hips surging off the chair. His large hands came to my legs, shoved my tight woven skirt up my thighs around my waist, and then they wrapped over my hips and back between my thighs so he could wrench them open and hold them down.

I looked down at him as he stared like a pious man at the altar of my panty-covered mound.

"Been dreaming of this pussy, Cress, need it now. Gonna take it hard and I need you to stay quiet for me, babe, yeah?" he ordered, his voice so gruff with desire that I could barely discern it.

I nodded frantically as I watched him touch his finger to the panel of lace between my legs and slowly come away with a string of my wetness still attached to him. I'd soaked through my panties.

He dipped his head, lapped his flat tongue over the lace then sucked briefly on the fabric over my clit. I made a garbled sound of ecstasy, unable to help myself.

"Stay quiet," he reminded me as he hooked two fingers in my panties, shoved them aside to make way for his tongue.

I shook my head back and forth, trying to get a grasp on the slippery slope of euphoria I was quickly ascending as his tongue dipped, hot and greedy, inside the well of my arousal.

"Fuck yeah, you taste like fuckin' sugar," he groaned into the side of my inner thigh then sank his teeth there. "Look at me as I eat this cunt, Cressida. Watch how much I fuckin' *love* it."

I saw stars behind my eyes as he attached his mouth to my sex, but it absolutely blew my mind to look down to see him feasting on me, his mouth open wide over my pussy so he could fuck me with his talented tongue. His golden head rocked slightly as he thrust in and out. I tightened my fingers in his silky locks and ground against him, my inhibitions incinerated by each flaming lash of his tongue.

Little sounds started to filter from my mouth but I couldn't stop them as my orgasm worked like a tsunami inside me, sucking away all my willpower, rearing back with everything I had, everything I was, to crash into me full force.

"King," I called weakly.

One hand snapped up to muffle my voice. As soon as it was secure, I broke open, that huge tidal wave shattering against me, drowning me almost alarmingly in brutal pleasure. I sank beneath the sensation and rode it out until I gently washed back onto the shore of my consciousness.

When I did, I opened my heavy lids to see King's head resting on one of my inner thighs, a hand soothingly stroking the tender skin on the inside of my opposite leg. He looked up at me like a cat that ate the canary.

I stiffened immediately, reality flooding back in the wake of my release. I scrambled away from him, tugging down my skirt, righting my panties and trying to do up my shirt buttons all at the same time. King calmly sat up on his knees again, took my frantic hands in one of his and used the other to redo the clasps on my blouse and smooth my hair down.

"Perfect," he stated when he was done.

I fell into his cool blue eyes, drowning in a different way at the hands of the same man in less than five minutes.

"King," I croaked, my throat sore from my muffled groans. "This wasn't right. I, I'm sorry, but this won't happen again. I told you before and I'll tell you again, I am a good woman, I'm not comfortable crossing these boundaries with you. I'm the adult here, the authority figure and I should have said no, most of that responsibility is on me." I sucked in a deep breath to settle myself. "But you can't do this anymore. I just proved how pathetically weak I am and I need you to stop putting yourself out there for me."

His face remained stoic throughout my speech but when I was finished, he stood up to look down on me. I swallowed thickly at the expression on his face because it wasn't disgust or fury that lurked there, but fierce determination.

"Never met a woman like you. Know I won't again. You find somethin' worth keepin', you find a way to fuckin' keep it. Not gonna stop, and just so you know, I got it that this could get you fired, that this could cause you embarrassment but what I got to say to that is this: whatever pain and ugliness I bring you by bein' with you, I promise I'll bring you double that in sweetness and beauty. You hear me on that, because I may be a man without a normal moral compass, but I'm a man who makes a woman a promise, and I'll die before I break it."

# Twelve.

I didn't sleep well and I woke up in a foul mood. To make myself feel better, I put on beautifully sexy lingerie in a deep rose colour that looked great on my pale gold skin with all my honeyed hair. The dress I wore was new, from a really cool vintage shop in town called Entrance Only, and it made me feel like a ballerina because it wrapped using a big bow at my little waist that was pale pink. I curled my long hair into loose waves, slicked a subtle dusky lipstick over my naturally pouty lips and nodded curtly at my reflection in the mirror. I looked like the ultimate lady, the wife of a lawyer, the daughter of a professor. I looked like myself.

I hated it.

It didn't really feel like me, not the new Cressida who rode on the back of motorcycles, got drunk on weeknights with strangers and let teenage boys feast on her pussy in the middle of her classroom.

Which was exactly why I donned my good girl armor. I couldn't let those things happen again. Not only because it was morally suspect but because I simply couldn't afford to lose my job. Shamble Wood Cottage needed a ton of repairs, I had to fund my voracious book-buying habit and I was racking up law fees because William refused to sign our gosh-darn divorce papers. Without a divorce settlement or alimony from him, I'd need to work at EBA for the next five years before I could even make it financially possible to go back to school.

So, armor and good behavior.

Warren picked me up for school at quarter to eight, his smile bright as I entered the car.

"You look amazing," he complimented as I buckled up.

I smiled slightly at him. "Thanks. I had a rough night and wanted to feel pretty."

He laughed as we pulled out of my driveway. "Fair enough, but you look pretty nice every day."

"That's sweet, Warren, but I'm still not going to sleep with you," I reminded him drily.

He laughed again and shook his head. "I didn't offer to drive you to school so you would sleep with me. I mean, that would be chill, but honestly, I live close by and I'm not crazy about the idea of you walking across Entrance by yourself."

"I've been fine," I pointed out. I'd been making the walk for the past two weeks while my car was at Hephaestus Auto. When I called them the other day, a gruff man had told me that my car was better off in the dump but that they were working on it. So, I'd been walking until yesterday when Warren had noticed and offered me a ride.

We rode in silence listening to an oldie's station Warren let me choose and Elvis Presley's "Heartbreak Hotel" came on. My gut clenched as something sour blossomed inside me. I both hated and loved that both King and I loved Elvis especially because I listened to his music all the time. It meant that even when I didn't want to think about my too-sexy-for-his-own-good student (which was always), I did. The song reminded me that I'd have to find a way to stay unmoved by our transgressions of the day before and reaffirm my position as *just* his teacher.

Warren and I had just pulled into the parking lot when my phone rang. Focused on facing King in our fifth period, I didn't look at the screen before I answered.

"Hello?"

"Cressida Irons," my mother's voice trilled over the line. "I've been calling you every day for the last week. Where in heaven's name have you been?"

I dropped my forehead against the glove compartment with a painful thud. The one thing I didn't need this morning was a lecture from Phoebe Irons.

"It's my mum," I told Warren with a wince as I covered the speaker on my phone. "Unfortunately, I have to take it. Do you mind?"

Warren smiled and handed me the keys. "I have a mother too. Take your time and just get the keys back to me sometime later today."

*Thank you*, I mouthed as I raised the phone to my mouth again.

I waited until he'd exited the car to say, "Hi, Mum, just been busy with school. It's the last two and a half weeks of the winter semester."

She made a disappointed noise in her throat. "Not an excuse to leave your mother's phone calls unreturned."

"No," I said when she paused for my response.

"Really, Cressida, I know you are going through some kind of horrible midlife crisis—"

"Quarter-life crisis," I corrected her automatically because I'd never been so aware of my age before. "I'm only twenty-six years old, Mum."

"Twenty-six years old *and* married. You're hardly a spring chicken anymore."

*Ouch.*

"I want you to come to Sunday dinner this weekend. You haven't been home since Christmas," she ordered.

I hadn't been home since Christmas because it had been an absolute unmitigated disaster. I'd given in to my loneliness and my mother's insistence and attended the family celebration because I was a weakling. Christmas Eve hadn't been too horrible. It had started off with awkwardness between my parents and me, which was unusual because we used to be so close. My father was a professor of Greek and Roman studies at the University of British Columbia so it was safe to say that I'd inherited my dorkiness from him. We read the paper first thing every morning, first together at the kitchen table when I still lived at home and then over the phone for a morning debriefing when I lived with William. He loved to quiz me on current events, debate with me over moral quandaries in the media. He was my husband's best friend, which meant that I saw my dad just as much as a married woman as I did when I was growing up.

My mother and I were part of the same book club, we went for power walks every morning before I went to work at EBA, and we talked on the phone at least once a day. Since leaving William in September, all of that had stopped. My parents hadn't allowed me to move back in with them. They couldn't fathom why I was leaving such a good man and they were actually angrier than William had been when I'd told him I wanted a divorce.

So, I'd taken what meager money I'd had in my own bank account to get a little apartment too close to East Hastings Street for comfort and, when that money started to run out, I'd turned to Lysander. With the money he'd lent me, I'd bought my little house in Entrance six weeks after leaving William and I'd never turned back.

That Christmas Eve was the first time we'd seen each other in two months and I'd foolishly thought they'd embrace me. Mum would make me her famous hot chocolate that was more chocolate than milk and dad would whip out his latest research for me to read over and give him notes on.

Instead, the awkwardness had been followed by a house-shaking fight.

I'd never fought with my parents like that before. We all shouted, called each other names and, regrettably, I'd told them that they were awful parents for giving me to William.

The night had ended in tears on all sides.

The next morning, despite assurances that they wouldn't ambush me, William had been next to our Christmas tree when I descended from my room. When I'd immediately turned to go back upstairs, my mum had demanded that I speak with him or she would never see me again.

I'd spoken to William. He'd graciously forgiven me for my "tantrum" and asked me to come home. In response, I retrieved the divorce papers I'd tried to send him in the mail four times from my briefcase by the door and handed them to him. In an uncharacteristic bout of anger, he'd tossed them in the flaming hearth then told me I wouldn't survive without him to guide me or without his fortune. He'd stormed out, my parents began to shout again and I'd hastily retrieved my bags and left.

So, you can imagine that I wasn't looking forward to a repeat performance.

"I can't make it this Sunday, Mum. As I said, it's end of term and I'm swamped with work," I said, studying the texture of Warren's dashboard like it held the secrets to the universe.

A loud, nails-on-a-chalkboard silence followed.

"William was here yesterday. One of his colleagues asked him out, you know. You probably remember her from his work functions because she is uncommonly pretty. Natalie Watson, her name is."

Great, we'd moved onto target practice. My mum liked to shoot arrows at random tender spots until they stuck. If she wasn't my mum and I wasn't her bullseye, I would have respected her for her ruthlessness and tenacity.

"Great, Mum, you should encourage him to say yes," I said.

Another silence, shorter this time while she collected herself for another attack. "He would be better off with someone like her who could properly appreciate how much William works."

I rolled my eyes. For some reason, my parents and William were convinced that I'd left him because he worked too hard.

If only it had been that easy.

"Probably," I agreed lightly. "Listen, Mum, I'm at school and I have to go in now. I'll answer next time you call, okay? Maybe we can talk about what you've been reading lately. I just finished a great book, *The Ghostwriter* by Alessandra Torre."

She sniffed. "I read that ages ago when it first came out."

Anger pricked over my scalp. "It only came out a few months ago, and I don't have much time to read for pleasure now that I'm trying to make ends meet."

"You wouldn't have to make ends meet if you'd stayed at your proper place by your husband," she fired back immediately.

I leaned back in my seat, ran a hand over my closed and throbbing eye sockets. "Okay, have a good day. Talk to you later."

"If you don't talk to William, Cressida, don't be surprised if he takes matters into his own hands," she warned ominously before hanging up.

*Great.*

A knock rattled against my window. I screamed, dropped

my phone into my lap and whipped around to see Tayline's face pressed grotesquely against the glass, Rainbow holding her stomach and belly laughing behind her.

"You freaks," I yelled through the door. "You gave me a freaking heart attack."

Tay peeled her mouth off the window so she could join Rainbow in her cackling. I shook my head but their antics immediately made me feel better after the toxic phone call with my mother. I grabbed my messenger bag from the ground at my feet and swung out of the car.

"That was almost murder by surprise," I lectured them both with my hands on my hips, using my best Teacher in Charge voice. "You're lucky I have a strong heart."

Rainbow wiped the tears from under her eyes. "Dude, that was priceless. We should start every morning like that."

"Agreed," Tay said, bumping my thigh with her hip because she was so short. "Thanks for the laugh."

I rolled my eyes at them but couldn't control my smile. "You guys are children."

"Yeup, takes one to know one. It's what makes me such a good teacher." Tay nodded sagely as we made our way into the school together.

I'd taken to spending all of my breaks with the duo and I found myself in the surprising position of having my own friends. It was incredibly pathetic that I was in my mid-twenties and I'd never had girlfriends outside of my mother's book club.

Needless to say, I was enjoying Rainbow's calculating wit and Tayline's goofiness. They didn't take life too seriously, which I loved because it meant I couldn't take myself too seriously.

"So, I heard Warren finally asked you out and now you're

sitting in his car in the parking lot. What gives, Cressie? Don't you remember that conversation we had at the beginning of term? We're best friends now, we've claimed you, which means we should be the *absolute first* people who know about your love life," Tay lectured me as we pushed through the doors to the main hall and entered the calamity of students and teachers rushing around before classes started.

"Honestly, I kind of forgot about it," I admitted with a sheepish look that made them both burst into laughter.

Rainbow even slapped her knee. "That is *wicked.* If Warren knew that, his manhood would be in serious question. You know Pillow has been trying to catch his eye all year?"

Speaking of the woman, Willow floated down the hall past us on a cloud of very expensive and very strong Chanel perfume. Tayline coughed loudly but raised her eyebrows in innocent query when Willow shot her an irritated look.

I shook my head. "Children."

Tay stuck her tongue out at me.

"So, you've been separated for months and you aren't getting a little antsy for some action?" Rainbow asked.

They both followed me to my classroom, waited for me to unlock the door and turn on the lights before stepping inside with me. Rainbow sat in King's seat in the first row right in front of my desk, which made the blush I'd been trying to keep at bay, flame to life.

"*Oh*, she is!" Tayline crowed.

"Hush."

"Do you have a crush?" Rainbow asked, her eyes narrowed on me.

Insanely, I wondered if sitting in King's desk was giving her some kind of intuition about us.

"Get up, get out of my classroom, children!" I ordered,

clapping my hands to hurry them along. "Some of us have work to do before class."

"Yeah because you were too busy crushing on someone to do your work after school," Tayline called over her shoulder as I literally pushed her out the door.

"Don't think you're getting off this easily," Rainbow warned even as I closed the door in their faces. "You've got until lunch, sister."

They both stared at me through the window in the door but I turned my back on them before they could see the depth of my flush.

I collapsed at my desk with my head in my hands and asked myself when my life had gotten so complicated.

The answer came to me easily: the day I'd seen King's gosh-darn beautiful face across the parking lot of Mac's Grocer.

I should have known it was coming. Mum had practically announced his arrival in her phone call that morning. Still, I wasn't prepared for the announcement that came over the PA system at the end of my fourth-period history class.

"Mrs. Irons, please report to the front office. Your husband is here."

Immediately, my students shifted in their seats. I was close to my students so they knew that, in my mind, I didn't have a husband anymore. My hand remained poised over the white board midway through writing out the conditions of the Paris 1918 Peace Treaty. I could not believe that William was at EBA.

"Miss Irons?" Benny called tentatively. "You want me to go with you to the office?"

Immediately, my chest tightened with love and dread.

Benny; my sweet, sweet boy.

"Or I could go for you and tell him to fuck off?" Carson suggested as I turned around, catching sight of his massive football player arms flexing in teenage bravado.

Every since I'd turned him into the headmaster, Carson had been surprisingly active in my classes. He'd always been a fairly bright student but I got the sense he was ashamed of his behavior with King that day and wanted to prove to me that he was a good kid.

No one laughed at his suggestion, but a few other students nodded their heads as if that was an acceptable option.

I wrangled up a smile and affixed it awkwardly between my cheeks. "Don't be silly, guys. He may not be my husband anymore but he isn't a monster. Remember, there are two sides to every story."

"Every time you talked about him, your face went blank," Ally Vandercamp told me with a wise nod. "We never liked him. You're way too pretty to settle for some old, boring banker guy."

"Lawyer," I automatically corrected. "And Ally, you shouldn't jump to conclusions like that."

She was right; William was old and boring, but that didn't mean she should think that.

"I heard Mr. Warren thinks you're hot," Ally continued, unperturbed. "You guys would make a super cute couple."

"Totally," Aimee chirped.

I was beyond grateful that King was not in this class.

"Okay, enough about my personal life," I told them sternly. "I'm going to the office to deal with this and you all are going to open your textbooks to page 318 and read more about the Paris Peace Conference."

"Yes, Miss Irons," they all parroted back at me.

I shot them a droll look that had some of them laughing as I collected my purse and headed to the front office.

My steps were slow and heavy taking me there but still, I arrived before I was fully ready.

William stood before the reception desk with his hands in the pockets of his neatly pressed flannel trousers, his thick salt-and-pepper hair brushed back beautifully from his high forehead. His elegant, masculine beauty was impossible to deny even though I was no longer drawn to it. He presented himself impeccably from the Phillip Patek watch at his wrist to the glossy sheen of his expensive Italian loafers. His suit was custom-made, one I'd ordered for him last Christmas from Ermenegildo Zenga Bespoke for twenty-five thousand dollars, and I knew that if I drew closer to him, he would be wearing the cologne I'd first begun to buy him when I was a fifteen-year-old girl with a crush. I'd saved up my allowance for six months to afford the Clive Christian C cologne but the expression on his face when I'd given it to him in the back hall that Christmas had made it totally worth it.

My estranged husband stopped talking with Georgie the moment I stepped through the doors, but he took a moment to collect himself before he turned to face me. When he did, his face was a handsome mask. I knew the sight of me had to have affected him but there were no tells, no tick in the jaw or flexing of the hands. Just nothingness.

"Cressida," he said in his smooth, dulcet tones.

A friend of his had once told me that William was like a Canadian James Bond without the smarm. I hated that I agreed with him though it was for different reasons. Like the fictitious spy, my husband was incredibly two-dimensional.

"William," I returned. "What are you doing here?"

"I'm here to see my wife."

I stood, slightly stunned by his audacity, as he strode forward, took me by the shoulders and pressed a kiss to my cheek.

"What are you doing?" I hissed into his ear as he pulled away.

He smiled but it didn't suit his face the way it suited King's. It was impossible not to compare the two now that I'd sort of had both. They were the only two men to ever touch me sexually and now William was *here* at school, in King's domain. Goose bumps broke out like a premonition written in Braille over my skin.

"You won't return my phone calls or my emails so I decided to see you in person," he said as if he was the most reasonable person on the planet and I was a shrew. "I have a very important client dinner to attend at the end of the month just outside of town here and I thought you could accompany me. I even bought you a new dress."

I seethed. Visions of punching William in his clean-shaven throat, slamming his head into Georgie's half-moon-shaped desk until his perfect head was bloodied, swam through my mind like shark-infested waters.

The audience, Georgie and now Shawn Walters, one of the math teachers, were now both avidly watching and kept me from acting upon my baser instincts.

Thus, I cleared my throat of fire and said, "I've mailed you the divorce papers four times now, William. I see you every other week at court-mandated couples counseling for exactly this reason, so that we can talk about our problems in an *appropriate* venue. What in the world would make you think that the middle of the day at my place of work would be a good time to discuss the dissolution of our marriage?"

It was William's turn to frown. "Cressida, there is no need

to speak so harshly."

Oh my God. I was *this* close to tearing out my hair and I freaking *loved* my big head of hair.

I took a deep breath as I vaguely registered two more people slipping into the room.

"I'm sorry if it seems like I'm angry though, to be honest, it is almost undoubtedly because I *am* angry. I do not appreciate being ambushed at my place of work," I told him in what I felt was, irrefutably, a calm tone.

"You tell him, girl!" Tayline chorused from where she suddenly stood with Georgia, Shawn and Rainbow behind the desk.

I shot her a look but she only raised her hands in the air in the universal sign for "preach." Giving up on her before smoke came out of my ears, I turned back to William and made my voice sweet because I knew honey worked better than vinegar with men like my ex.

"Why don't we go outside? We can speak more privately there."

He hesitated, which was smart because I was being tame with our audience but would absolutely not be if I were alone with him. I decided to take the decision from him and immediately pushed through the door that led to the teacher's parking lot. A moment later, William followed. I knew if I cared to look that the little grouping left inside would have their noses pressed to the windows but I focused on William instead.

"Seriously, what were you thinking coming here and making a scene like this at my school?" I asked, my anger still starch through my muscles but the hurt was creeping in, wrinkling my resolve.

Did he really care for me so little?

"I wasn't the one making a scene. I merely wanted to speak

with you, Cressida. You didn't give me the chance at Christmas and those sessions are a joke. I wanted to give you a chance to tell me what you think went wrong in our marriage so that I can attempt to fix it with you," he said.

It was a good response. Or it would have been if I hadn't had the exact same conversation with him a good twenty to thirty times before.

I ran a hand through my hair and tried to find my inner Zen. "I honestly don't know what to say to you anymore, though. I don't love you, William."

He stared at me for a long moment before he nodded curtly. "I understand that I work a lot—"

"It wasn't about the work," I practically growled. "You can't give me what I need anymore."

He snorted. "There are very few things that I can't afford to give you."

"For Pete's sake, I don't mean financially. I mean emotionally, sexually."

"You're just going through something right now. In another six months, you'll be begging me to let you back into the house," William said for the umpteenth time; he just kept extending the timeframe it would take for me to return to him.

"I won't," I said gently, stepping forward to touch his arm lightly.

His huge dark brown eyes stared down at me, confused and belligerent. "You're being ridiculous. You have to know that I can't give you any money when you're acting like this. It wouldn't be fiscally responsible of me to support your midlife crisis."

"Quarter-life," I corrected automatically, just like I had that morning with my mother.

"You know I have this big merger coming up and your

mother is almost literally sick with worry every day that you keep up this charade," he pushed, driving the bamboo slivers farther and farther under my nails.

"Stop it, William. Now, you're just trying to be mean."

"She's going to the doctor next week. Your father is very worried," he continued with the same infuriating calm.

"I said stop it," I hissed, stepping closer and up on my toes so I could try to get in his face.

"No, not until you come home. You think I don't care, Cressida? I'll show you just how much I care if I have to tie you up and lock you in our bleeding closet," William said, again, calm as can be.

A shiver worked itself up my spine like a creepy, crawly thing.

"You good, teach?" a new, hoarse voice said from behind me.

Normally, I tried not to curse but I felt that the arrival of Zeus freaking Garro warranted it.

"Fuck."

"Cressida?" William asked, instantly straightening and moving into me so he could place his hand in a possession of ownership on my waist. "Do you know that…man?"

"Better question is, does she know you?" Zeus demanded, stepping into my line of sight.

He was wearing his leather cut over a skintight white T-shirt that defined his abs in a way that was somehow more indecent than being totally bare-chested. The purity of the shirt contrasted beautifully with the plethora of black outlined feathers that wrapped around his biceps and upper forearms like the tips of angel wings and the other tattoos that crept up his neck under his beard. He looked like a menacing, badass biker; the villain in this bizarre scene.

Instead, I knew he was the demon on a black hog come to save me from my knight in shining armor. Unconsciously, I took a step away from William and closer to Zeus. Sensing this, the biker snagged me by the wrist and tugged me forward so that I fell in beside him.

"Yes, William," I said, although Zeus's actions had rendered it unnecessary. "I know him. This is Zeus, um, Garro." I turned my head up to look at the man looming over me and winced slightly. "I'm so sorry, I don't know your real name."

Zeus stared down at me for a long beat as if he wasn't certain if I was human or alien. Then he said, "Zeus is my name on the streets and in the books now, teach. Don't sweat it. Now, tell me what's goin' on, yeah?"

I sighed heavily, waved my hand in a very shocked William's direction and explained, "This is my soon-to-be ex-husband. He would already be my ex-husband if he agreed to sign our very fair divorce papers but instead, he's holding our joint account hostage until I go back to him."

I watched Zeus's face go from diamond-hard to graphene, the hardest material in the world. I thought for a moment that he might just be the hardest man in the world and I wondered what I'd done bringing a man like him into this conflict with my husband.

My fears gave way to shock when he slung a weighty arm around my shoulders and kissed, *kissed*, my temple.

"Ah, the one you told me about last night before bed," he said.

I blinked.

William blinked.

Zeus continued to speak. "Knew he was a fuckin' piece of shit caught in your tire treads, darlin', but didn't think he'd be low enough to show up at the school to fuck with you."

"Me either," I squawked when he squeezed me to prompt a response.

He jerked his chin up at William. "You listen to this and you listen like your life fuckin' depends on it because, Willie boy, it fuckin' *does*. This lady is now with a Garro man and in case you're so stupid you don't know what that means, I'll let you know. She belongs to The Fallen MC and no one fucks with The Fallen. Not even soon-to-be ex-husbands with wallets bigger than their tiny pricks who think they can blackmail a woman into bein' with 'em."

"Oh my God," I said with the last of the breath left in my lungs.

I tried to inhale but choked on my inability to understand what was happening and started to cough. Zeus (not so helpfully) thumped me on the back with a mighty fist.

"Are you actually saying that you're dating my wife?" William confirmed, his jaw unhinged with the weight of his doubt. "That my wife of eight years, the same woman who won't watch sex scenes in romantic comedies and who hasn't spoken with her brother in the nearly nine years since he went to jail because he's a convict, is involved with a notorious motorcycle gang?"

"Club," I croaked out at the same time that Zeus corrected him too.

We shared a weird little smile.

"That's exactly what I'm saying. So, if you're 'bout done here, you can let Cressida go back to work and you can go back to whatever cage you came from and keep livin' your narrow fuckin' life," Zeus ordered.

William stared at him.

I stared at him.

Zeus moved.

He used the arm around my shoulders to swing me into his front and then he tilted his head toward me so all William (and the nosey folks in the office) could see was his riot of crumpled, shoulder-length brown waves. It probably looked exactly like he was giving me a big kiss. Instead, he pressed his lips close to my ear and said, "Just claimed ya, teach. Hope to fuck my son knows what he's doin'."

"I—I don't know what, I mean…" I tried to say but Zeus lifted a hand and pressed it gently over my mouth.

"Don't lie to me, teach. Wouldn't'a helped you if I didn't think you were a good woman. Now, I want you to step back when I let you go, look at me with stars in those beautiful brown eyes and then hightail it back into your classroom. Yeah?"

His eyes were so close to me I could see the loops of different blues and grays that made up his irises. Unlike King's whose were perforated and so pale a blue they glowed just like Arctic ice, Zeus's were ringed like the trunk of an old tree. They were wise eyes despite their brutality and before I could overthink it, I nodded my acquiescence to his demands.

We broke apart, I looked up at him dazedly (not really an act as I was seriously bemused) and then with one last sidelong look at a ruffled William, I hightailed it to my classroom. Only when I was at the doors to the humanities building did I look back to see Zeus leaning against his massive Harley with his arms crossed over his chest, watching as William's car peeled out of the lot.

# Thirteen.

"What's wrong?"

I jolted out of my thoughts at the rumbling, annoyed sound of King's voice. He stood in front of my table in the library office. It was surrounded on two sides by glass walls so I could see the students working quietly at their tables. Now King was the only one left in the lull between class time and after-school study sessions. It wasn't lost on me that our lovely librarian, Harry Reynard, had left me the office in peace when he'd realized I needed a little alone time.

It had been a long twenty-four hours, the longest of my life, so I didn't hate myself too much for assigning a last-minute in-class essay on *Paradise Lost* in my last period English class just so I could have fifty minutes to figure out what had happened in the parking lot between my estranged husband, the President of The Fallen MC and little ole' me.

Even after the class ended, I hadn't figured it out.

The silver lining of this was that I didn't feel awkward around King even though I should have been blushing and fidgeting like a shy schoolgirl after what I'd let him do to me this time yesterday afternoon.

Still, a thrill of anxiety and the delicious echo of pleasure pulsed through me and tightened my nipples at being in the same room alone with him. King's eyes ducked down to the sight but, surprisingly, his frown remained.

"What are you talking about? I dismissed class. You can take a walk or something before detention starts in ten minutes," I said, because I didn't know what else to say.

*Well, King, William showed up at school to make a scene but don't worry, your crazy hot, insanely scary dad stepped in and, I think, claimed me like a piece of property so that my ex wouldn't fuck with me anymore. That's what's wrong.*

King's eyebrows locked together, casting deep shadows over his glacial eyes. "Don't give me that bullshit. Something's been up your ass all day and I wanna know what it is."

"How is that any of your business?"

A sneer twisted his beautiful mouth as he leaned forward on my desk, cornering me like a predator would his prey. "'Cause if you tell me, I'll take care of it for you."

Gosh freaking darn it, I did not have the strength to deal with his strangely endearing brand of biker sweetness today. "King, not only is it not your job as a student to take care of anything for me except your homework, I am also incredibly uncomfortable with the idea of you 'taking care of' anyone."

Hurt flickered across his features, brief but stunning and wrong like a midnight eclipse.

"Just 'cause I'm the son of The Fallen doesn't mean I take care of every problem with my fists."

Shame rose in my throat, a bitter and nauseating cocktail. He had never given me any indication that he would deal with his problems like that and especially after our heart-to-heart yesterday about people judging him as a brainless, violent thug, I felt sick for jumping to that conclusion.

"I'm sorry," I said with my aching heart between my lips.

When he didn't move, I placed a hand on one of his fists and ran my fingers lightly over the golden hair across his knuckles.

"That was wrong of me," I continued softly. "I spoke hastily but honestly, it had nothing to do with my real impression of you."

"Yeah, and what's that impression?" he asked, leaning down closer so that the tendons and muscles in his arms popped out in stark relief.

I licked my lips because I couldn't lick him.

King's eyes tingled like bee venom over my mouth.

My eyes skittered to the door and back to him.

Taking that as the sign it was, he reached out to slide his palm around the back of my neck under the thick fall of my hair. It felt oddly vulnerable, his big palm wrapped around my slender neck against my hummingbird pulse, his fingers slotted between the vertebrae of my spine effectively locking me in stasis so I was forced to look into his eyes and nowhere else.

"Tell me," he urged.

"Okay," I agreed. "I think King Kyle Garro is a man who plays at being a boy to dupe the dumb, a predator to scare the weak and a pretty boy to manipulate the trite."

His eyes flashed and a low rumble worked through his throat. "And how do I act with Cressida Irons? Who am I to her?"

"You're a King who makes her want to be his rough-and-tumble Queen," I said before I could stop myself, our whispered conversation lending a confessional tone to our words.

I couldn't lie. I didn't want to.

Damn the consequences.

"Screw detention. Come with me right fuckin' now," King ordered roughly but it was the edge of desperation in his voice that had me dutifully following him.

It was only when he moved toward the labyrinthine rows of books in the back of the library and not the door that I came down from my King-induced high.

"No way am I doing anything with you in the freaking library." I tried to tug my hand out of his hold with both of mine to no avail. "King!"

He ignored me until we were in the sweet, paper-scented depths of the library, sequestered away in Row WXYZ.

"Oh my God," I gasped as King turned on me.

He slammed me up against the shelves, anchoring me to the rows of books with his lean hips. His growl vibrated against my lips as he took my wrists in one of his big hands and pinned them above my head.

Before I could regain my breath, I tasted his. His mouth claimed me, searing the secret his apple poem had promised me into the delicate skin on the inside of my lower lip. He bit me there, scraped his teeth over it again and again until I writhed against him.

He broke away with a snarl to say, "You think just 'cause you're the teacher, I gotta follow your rules? Well, you're wrong, babe. Between you and me, I'm the fuckin' authority figure. If I gotta fuck you in the library to show you what's what, I'm only too happy to fucking oblige."

I licked my dry lips, fighting to remind myself why I should say no to this, to this inappropriate man in this highly inappropriate place but my sex was throbbing a heavy, steady beat that scrambled my good intentions. I rubbed my sticky inner thighs together to try to alleviate the ache but King stopped me by kicking my legs farther apart with one booted foot. Before I could protest, his hand was between my legs, slapping the bare skin of my wet inner thigh so hard it stung then cupping my entire mound in his huge palm.

"This cunt is wet because of me. It's exactly my depravity, my *wrongness* that gets these sweet juices flowing. You like me bossing your sweet ass around, don't you?"

"No," I said, but it came out breathy.

There was a haze around everything but King, his hand on my cunt, his breath on my face and his eyes, those huge pale blue moon eyes, boring into my face, daring me to lie to him.

They flashed at my blatant untruth. I gasped as two of his thick, callused fingers plunged beneath the placket of my underwear and curled inside me, pressing hard against my front wall. My knees collapsed at the intensity so that the only thing holding me upright was the strong hand pinning my wrists and the two fingers impaling me.

"You want to be dirty with me, *Miss* Irons," he taunted me, drawing his tongue down the edge of my jaw until he reached my chin. I gasped when he nipped it between his teeth. "Can feel your pussy tighten around my fingers when I talk like this to you? Looks like I'm fulfilling two fantasies by fuckin' my hot-as-fuck teach in the stacks."

I bit my lip to keep from groaning as he twisted his fingers inside of me, drawing out a pleasure so deep it made my legs shake.

"Turn around, hands on the shelf and don't fuckin' let go," he ordered.

Instantly, I whirled around. I stood straight up and down but curled my fingers onto the shelf just below my shoulders.

King's laugh caressed my neck but he didn't touch me. "Show me you want it, Cressida. Present that sweet ass for me."

I tried to swallow my small cry of desire but my throat was parched, all the moisture in my body pooling between my thighs and leaking down to the tops of my stockings.

Desperately, I jutted my bottom back, deepened my lean until I was at forty-five degrees.

"Better," King praised me.

My gasp punctuated the deep library quiet when he grabbed both my hips and pulled me back farther, right into the rigid length tenting his trousers. I panted against my arm as he pushed my back down then flipped up my skirt. He took a step back so cool air wafted over me and I shuddered, so turned on that a stiff breeze could have sent me over the edge.

"Look at that," King murmured hoarsely. Two knuckles reached out to run down my crease from my asshole to my pussy. "So wet for her student."

I bit my arm and groaned, shoving my hips back into him.

Heeding my unspoken plea, those fingers turned vicious and tore off my lace underwear. The pain it evoked made me break out into shivers and I was still recovering from the overwhelming hotness of the gesture when a hot tongue replaced the fingers.

I reared back into the sensation even though it embarrassed me to think of King on his knees behind me, his face buried in my ass.

A shockwave of pleasure throbbed through me as his nose brushed my opening and his tongue curled around my still sensitive clit. I threw my head back as he bit the sensitive skin on the inside of my thigh and pinched my clit hard between his fingers. The book titles in front of my face grew fuzzy and my legs began to shake. Vaguely, I heard the sound of a zipper being lowered then King's long, tortured groan.

"Could come just from your taste," he said, licking at the wetness that had trickled down my right thigh.

Simultaneously, he drove three fingers into my wet heat and sucked my swollen clit deep into his mouth. So easily, he tipped me humpty dumpty over the edge of pleasure and crashing into pieces on the other side.

"Fuck, my girl is so easy to please," he said against the side of my thigh as the orgasm fragmented my thoughts.

Even through the delirium, I knew the words were praise and it spurred me on.

I thrashed helplessly against the books, sending some tumbling to the floor as his words combined with the fingers inside me and his mouth fused over my clit made me come for longer than I thought possible.

King straightened from the floor, flipped my molten body over and upright then pressed my back against the books once more. He pushed his forehead hard to mine as he gently played with my wet pussy, careful with my sensitive clit now that I'd come.

"Really wanna fuck you, Cress."

I twined my hands around his neck and dropped my head to rest against his shoulder. He smelled warm and male in a way that had my gut clenching. I wasn't ready to condone out loud what we had done, what we were actively doing at that very moment, but after two mind-melting climaxes, I somehow wanted him inside me even more than before. So, I pressed my lips to his thundering pulse in silent consent.

He rolled his head against mine. "Nah, not gonna happen like that. Meant what I said, babe, tired of you thinkin' you can shut me out and keep me down. I get in, and I mean I *get in* with you, I need the words. I need you to give me that soft and sweet you got inside you. I want to hear my Queen beg for her King, you hear me?"

I squeezed my eyes shut but rubbed my nose against his because it was right in front of me and I found I couldn't stop myself. God, but I heard him. There was almost nothing I wanted more than to wrap myself around him in that moment and into the next, to ride him now and later on his bike. To stand beside him the way I'd first imagined that day at Mac's Grocer.

But reality had come crashing into my daydreams in a very real way just hours earlier and I just could not deal with declarations and possibilities that hung just outside my reach like Eve's glistening apple.

"I had a really bad day today, King," I admitted softly right up against his lips, which was somehow so much more intimate than just kissing him. "I can't tell you what you want to hear. I can't *be* who you want me to be to you. But this afternoon, after a really *really* bad day, all I wanted was to be here with you."

There was a brief silence where our breaths tangled hot and intertwined between our open lips. I wanted to know what he was thinking, wanted to ask him if he was crazy and if I was crazier for embracing in the freaking library when we both needed to stay at EBA in a very real way, if we were delusional the way Eve and Satan were, for thinking that we could alter our reality to suit our desires.

Instead, I twined my fingers in his golden curls and gently pulled him to me, groaning into his mouth when his fingers flexed hard on my hips.

"Cressida?" Harry Reynard's lilting British voice echoed through the rows of books. "You still in here? I bloody hope so because your purse is still in my office. If you're back there reading, come out and grab it. I need to lock the door and go home."

I froze but King only buried his face in my hair and chuckled softly.

"Holding a wooden plank in my hands instead of the woman I brought back here," he teased.

"Shut up and get off me," I whispered harshly, shoving at his shoulder.

He continued to laugh but let me go.

As I straightened my clothes, I told him how things would go. "Okay, I'll head out first and distract Harry while you sneak out…" I trailed off when I looked up to see King no longer in front of me.

"Gosh freaking darn it," I mumbled, smoothing my hair frantically before making my way silently through the stacks.

When I got closer to the sitting area and the office, I heard male voices laughing.

"Yeah, Mr. R, what can I say, you know how I get when I'm readin'," King was saying.

I peeked around the corner to see him leaning against the door to the office, blocking my view of Harry.

"I don't believe I've ever met anyone who could read through an apocalypse, King, but if anyone could do it, it would be you," Harry replied.

King shrugged. "You grow up readin' in a loud, smelly, hot garage and you learn to shut shit out."

"I imagine so." Harry laughed.

It was clear to me that the two were well acquainted, which was interesting because Harry was the full-time librarian and didn't teach any classes. If they were close, it meant that King spent an inordinate amount of time in Entrance Bay Academy's two-story haven of books. For some reason that insight made my heart palpitate painfully.

"I heard you say Miss Irons left her stuff behind. Do you want me to drop it by her classroom on my way to the parking lot?" King offered innocently.

"Would you mind? My wife gets a tad frustrated with me when I'm late for dinner, since I'm the one who insists on eating so early."

"No problem," King said, heading into the office.

I took the opportunity as it was meant and snuck out of the office. I didn't go back to my classroom, which was already locked up for the day because I was a coward and I couldn't face seeing King again. I had a spare set of keys to the cabin in a little hollow alligator sculpture I kept by the front door and my car was still in the shop so, as I'd been doing for the past two weeks, I began the forty-five-minute walk home.

I was passing along Main Street, enjoying the way the blossoms had begun to coat the streets like spring snow banks, when the roar of a motorcycle disturbed my thoughts. It wasn't exactly a surprise when I turned around to watch it pull up beside me but it was when a man other than King emerged from the helmet.

He could have been a model. In fact, if he wasn't, it was a criminal offense to women all over the world that he kept a face that pretty off of magazine covers and advertisements. Despite the full-sleeve tattoos and the unmistakable Fallen MC cut, the guy was all prettiness with eyelashes like mink fur and gorgeous wavy brown hair he kept cropped short at the sides and overlong at the top.

Even before he opened his mouth, I knew he'd have a good voice, unfairly melodic for a man. "Cressida Irons, sup, girl?"

"Um." I shifted on my high heels, wishing not for the first time that I'd gone back to my classroom to get the Converse trainers I usually wore to walk home. "Nothing, stranger. Just walking home from work."

He nodded, swung off his bike and swaggered forward with a multi-ringed hand extended to me. "Name's Nova."

"It seems you already know my name," I replied even though I shook his hand.

The grin he flashed me was practiced, a study in beauty and arrogance. "King sent me to give you a ride home. He wanted you to know he woulda done it himself but was needed at the compound. He also wanted me to ask how the fuck you been getting home when your piece of crap car is still at the shop?"

I bristled. "I've been walking. You tell King if he didn't want me doing that then he should have been working on my car so I could get it back."

Nova crossed his arms and stared down at me. "That kid has been working on that good-for-nothing car every spare moment he's got."

"Oh." I sighed, frustrated with myself. Why did I turn into a raging judgmental bitch the first second I was reminded of King's biker status or faced one of his biker kin?

"Listen, I'm sorry. It's been a really long, tiring day but that isn't an excuse to be rude," I apologized.

Nova's face broke into an even more beautiful smile. "No worries, doll. Both King and Zeus told me you got spirit, not at all surprised to find they spoke the truth. Wouldn't like you much if you didn't."

"They both told you?" I echoed dumbly.

"Sure. Zeus was spittin' mad when he came back from pickin' up Harleigh Rose from school and there you were bein' fuckin' accosted by your slime ball ex. That's why King's not here to take you home. He and Zeus are fixin' to do something about that motherfucker."

My eyes widened until they hurt. "What?"

He laughed. "Don't worry your pretty face about it. We got your back, girl."

"I don't need you to 'fix' the problem with William. It's my problem and I'm going through the appropriate channels to fix it myself," I told him firmly.

I trusted King not to do anything extreme but his father was another story.

Nova peered at me. "How's that workin' out for ya?"

I was silent because we both knew the answer to that question.

"Right, so, are we gonna stand here all day or am I gonna take you home?"

"Take me home," I muttered mulishly as I followed him over to his bike.

He laughed then laughed even harder when he saw my expression of wonder as I took in his huge, sleek motorcycle. It was even bigger than King's and had The Fallen insignia painted in dark green and white on the side.

"A girl who looks like you and can appreciate a good ride?" Nova said as he swung a long leg over his bike and waited for me to settle. "Easy to understand what's got the Garro men all riled up. Doesn't hurt that you look like a fuckin' delicate little princess too."

"Queen," I corrected before I could think about it. "Like a queen."

He looked over his shoulder at me with new questions in his heavily fringed eyes. "Sure, like a queen."

I bit my lip and resolved not to say anymore but happily, I didn't have to because Nova started his bike with a loud roar and took off toward my cabin. I pressed my cheek into his back and huddled against him as the cold air whipped over me.

It said something about King that he would send one of his brothers after me even though he had to have been angry with me for running away. It probably pissed him off to realize that I'd been walking to and from school every morning too. I wondered if he would be at my door the next morning to drive me on the back of his bike and the thought made me sick and excited all at the same time.

"Queenie," Nova said after he'd pulled down my driveway and come to a stop in my sloping front yard. "Please tell me this ain't your place?"

I dismounted, pleased that I was getting the hang of it, and fisted my hands on my hips. "It is and before you say something mean about it, I'll have you know, I'm very proud of Shamble Wood Cottage. I'm fixing her up myself."

"Seems you could use a fuckin' hand," he grumbled, his pretty face creased as he took in the disastrous yard and the peeling paint. "Looks like a fuckin' Halloween haunted house."

I bit my lip but didn't say anything because I had gotten a lot of trick-or-treaters that fall.

"Thanks for the ride, Nova," I said, then it dawned on me and I laughed. "Casanova, right?"

He winked at me. "It's that obvious I'm magic with the ladies, eh?"

"It's that obvious your arrogance knows no bounds," I quipped pertly, which made him laugh. "It seems to be a trait you Fallen men share."

"It's not written in the handbook but yeah, it's pretty common," he said when he finished laughing.

"You have a handbook?" I asked eagerly, thinking I'd like to read it.

He laughed again. "Nah, bikers aren't really handbook kinda people, Queenie."

I blushed at the nickname, loving it.

"Gotta go, so get into the house and lock the door," he ordered kindly.

I did as he asked but just as I was about to disappear inside, he called out, "And, Queenie, don't think I won't be tellin'

King that your car and your husband aren't the only pieces of shit he has to make right."

I frowned as he roared out of the drive and pet the doorframe of my cabin, murmuring, "You're not a piece of shit. Ignore him."

# Fourteen.

I woke up to thunder.

It took me a moment to understand that it was man-made. The deep growl of motorcycles as they travelled as a group through the streets of Entrance had become familiar and I recognized the sound now as it descended on the front of my property.

I jumped out of bed, mindless of my pretty little rose-patterned nightgown, and flew to the window to draw back the curtain just in time to see at least ten bikes roll down my steep driveway. I spotted the golden blond head of the man responsible for my rude wakeup call immediately.

Without thinking, I pushed open the old window and leaned out to yell, "King Kyle Garro, what in the hell do you think you are doing bringing this riffraff to my home at the crack of dawn on a Saturday?"

He continued swinging off his bike and ignored me as a huge white truck came down the drive. I watched as he directed it to the only space left to park at the front of the house, on an old flowerbed that was now just dry dirt.

"King!" I called again.

"Hold on a sec, babe," he called without turning around.

"I'm not your babe, I'm your teacher," I yelled at him.

A few of the men chuckled but otherwise, everyone ignored me.

As soon as the truck was parked, the men converged on it, pulling tools, buckets and heavy equipment out of the loaded cab. Most of The Fallen men wore their cuts but tons of them were shirtless beneath them, some had even shrugged off their jackets to reveal worn, dirty tees over old jeans and athletic shorts.

"What the fuck are you doing?" I called again, so furious and confused that I didn't even blush at the curse.

"Why don't you come down and find out?" King shouted, finally turning around to face me hanging out of the window. "But before you do, put on some clothes, would you? My brothers don't need to see how fuckin' cute you look in that nightie."

"Might motivate us to work harder," Nova suggested.

King hit his friend on the back of the head but I ducked out of the window, suddenly intensely aware of how much skin I'd exposed to all the guys out there. I rushed to my closet, donned an old pair of jeans that I'd long ago cut into shorts and one of my book T-shirts, this one with *The Great Gatsby* cover on the front. I dashed into the bathroom, stared at my sleep-swollen eyes and rumpled golden brown waves but decided I didn't have time to do anything but secure my hair back with a lavender bandana wrapped around the crown of my head.

"King," I called even before I had the front door fully open.

"Yeah, babe?"

I stopped abruptly as I watched him carry a huge bag of soil out of the truck and dump it on a growing pile beside my front yard. Four bikers followed suit while the rest had disappeared.

"The others are round back. Told 'em to finish the weedin' so we can move on to the serious stuff," King said as he dropped the bag and ambled over to me.

I stood stupefied as he leaned in to press a kiss to my cheek.

He smelled like laundry and sweaty, hardworking man. My knees wobbled but through sheer strength of will, I remained standing instead of diving into his arms.

"What are you doing here?" I said instead.

He cocked his head to the side. "Whaddya mean?"

"What. Are. You. Doing. *Here*?"

"Babe," he said with a frown. "You needed help with your yard, yeah? I brought my brothers. We're gonna spend the morning working on it and you're gonna reward us by making some of that pulled pork Rainbow Lee is always talkin' about."

"King," I started, incredulity and awe at odds in my voice. "I'm not even going to ask you how you know about my pulled pork. But you're my student, not my boyfriend. You can't just be at my house and you certainly can't bring gang members here!"

His frown screwed tighter. "Right. Let me get this straight. My brothers show up to help you with your yard work because they wanna help you out and you call them fuckin' *gang* members? What the hell, Cress?"

Shame doused my anger like a bucket of cold water. "Ugh, I'm sorry. I didn't mean it that way, I just—"

"Shut up, I wasn't finished," King growled, stepping close to me so that he could lean down into my face. The only thing that kept his posture from being totally threatening was the hand that found its way to the back of my neck, under my hair. I realized that he did it when he wanted to connect with me, when he needed to reassure both of us that I was his. It scared me how much I liked it. How much I needed it too.

*He is your fucking student, Cressida,* the adult, respectable, and moral side of me reminded myself.

*He is also hot as fuck when he's like this*, the other side, the darker, deviant one that had always lived deep inside me but was steadily clawing closer and closer to the surface of my being.

"Second, you're right. I'm not your fuckin' boyfriend. Children have girlfriends and boyfriends. Idiots let their women walk around unclaimed, secured by a fuckin' hope and a prayer because they don't make their women feel owned, cherished like the ultimate prize. No, I am your man, babe. The fuckin' man that sees you strugglin' to make ends meet because of your prick of a soon-to-be ex-husband, so he calls in his brothers to help her out even though he knows they'll give him shit for being pussy whipped. I'm your fuckin' man because I love being that for you. Now, do you hear me?"

My breath panted out in the sliver of air between us. His words had me wound up like a toy, ready to spring further without any thought to the consequences. I tried to think of all the reasons I couldn't let this man be my man and the first one that sprang to mind was, stupidly, what I went with.

"You can't be my man because you're still a boy. You're eighteen, King."

Even though his eyes were pale, like sunshine on ice, they were perpetually affable. He was a happy, social guy with innate charisma and a wealth of charm, a guy who loved life and was generally stoked to be living it. So, it was with actual terror that I watched those eyes drain of all warmth.

His hand on the back of my neck squeezed almost painfully.

"I got work to do, so I'm going to ignore your repeated attempts to piss me off until after the guys leave and I can show you just how much of a fuckin' man I am."

I swallowed painfully at the look of disgusted reproach in his eyes as he pulled away from me, already shouting orders at the men.

"It's real hard to piss that boy off, but sure looks like you succeeded," the deep rumble of a familiar voice came from behind me and I knew before I even turned around that Zeus Garro was standing there.

He looked as enormous and dangerous as ever, too hot for anyone's good, hotter even than his son if you liked a man who looked like he could literally and easily kill someone with his bare hands.

Unlike the other guys, he was still leaning against his bike, wearing his leather jacket, smoking a cigarette in a way that said he knew how to make love to a woman and, conversely, that he didn't give a fuck about your opinion of his cancer stick.

Still, I said, "Those will kill you."

Because I was looking for it, I saw the flash of humor light his eyes, nearly the same colour as his son's but more silver than pale blue.

"Maybe it's not such a surprise you piss him off," he amended.

I shrugged helplessly and went over to his bike to lean on the huge metal beast with him. There was something about King's father, someone whose very posture dared anyone to fuck with him, that put me oddly at ease. I knew he wasn't interested in me, that he didn't condemn me for lusting after his son or having an ugly yard or a messed-up marriage. Zeus Garro didn't give a fuck about anyone until he did, and then he didn't care who you were or what you'd once done.

I had a feeling that I was edging into the latter category and it made me warm inside the way pleasing my parents to keep their affection, or obeying William because it was my duty as his wife, had never done.

Zeus offered me the damp tip of his cigarette. When I raised my eyebrows at him dubiously, he hitched a shoulder and said, "Can't hate it if you've never tried it."

I peered at him, thought about how I'd never done drugs, not even smoked a joint, never had sex in public, stolen a lighter from the gas station or kissed a stranger. I thought about how I'd left William so that I could finally live, let the darker me finally breathe, and I'd barely done that.

I took the cigarette and put it to my lips, drawing in a tiny puff. Zeus watched me, his lips already curled before I started coughing like my lungs were on fire. He chuckled deeply as he thumped me on the back with a meaty paw.

"Not for everyone," he admitted.

"You," I said between fits of hacking, "knew I would hate it."

"Woman, there isn't much I don't know and most I learned, I learned from tryin'. Purest way to live life."

"Why don't you stick to the biker marauding and I'll do the teaching," I advised drily, tossing the cigarette to the ground to stomp on it with my bright pink flip-flop.

When I was done, I stared up at Zeus with a sassily tipped chin.

He burst out laughing; throwing his head back the way King did, exposing his thick, beautifully corded throat. I was shocked into silence by the magnificence of the man and of the privilege I knew it was to see him laugh.

"Hey, old man," King shouted from the side of the house. "Just 'cause I'm mad at her doesn't mean you can hit on my woman. Find someone uglier who's willin' to put up with your horrible mug!"

"For Pete's sake, I am *not* your woman," I yelled back, hands immediately fisting on my hips.

Zeus stared at me, humor forgotten. "Boy's got it bad for you, teach. He's made no fuckin' bones about it. He wants you.

In his mind, it's a done deal. Raised 'em spoiled but you can't blame me. My ex-wife is a crazy cunt, so I mighta overcompensated, but he's a good kid, a good son and brother, and one day he'll be a good man for The Fallen. He'd make a damn good partner too, all that love and loyalty wound up in him just waitin' to unspool and attach itself to the right people."

"I see where King gets his poetic talent from," I said quietly, because I wished I didn't have to say it. "But I'm his teacher. No matter how we met, it doesn't negate the fact that being with him would not only be unethical, it would be socially unacceptable."

"Never grew up carin' about what people thought of me so can't speak from experience when I say who the fuck cares?"

"Ugh, the school board, maybe? I need this job," I reminded him. "Not everyone can run a marijuana empire."

Zeus's eyes flashed. "Like your sense of humor, teach, but that ain't something you should joke about, ya hear me?"

"Yeah." I swallowed back my instantaneous fear. "I hear you."

He nodded curtly, uncrossed his arms to rise fully to his impressive height and faced me. "Point is, I don't give a fuck if you wanna be with my son. Far as I'm concerned, you're both consenting adults and you seem like a decent broad, a little skinny for my tastes but hey, if my son likes it..." He shrugged, humor dancing in his eyes as I drew up to snap at him. "Easy, teach, I get you. Life's tough when you care what people think. You got a job, friends who might judge you. Just sayin' you can always get another job, new friends. The bitches at the MC aren't bad women. You'd like 'em. Decide you want to do this, I'll get Maja, Buck's woman, to give you a call. She runs the MC bitches."

"This is the weirdest conversation I've ever had," I

admitted. "And, just to say, calling women bitches in 2017 is totally misogynistic."

He shrugged one huge shoulder. "Like I said, don't really care 'bout those kinds of things. She's a fuckin' peach, changed Buck's shit luck for the better. I think the world of her, so what difference does it make?" He watched me absorb his compelling but bizarre biker philosophy and nodded. "And, just to say, you'll probably have more of 'em, you stick with my son. The kid's a piece of work."

"Thank you, by the way," I said quickly, sensing he was about done with me. "For yesterday. William is being surprisingly tenacious."

His eyes swept over me. "Not so surprising."

"That's nice but really, he didn't care much about me when I lived with him so I don't really get why he cares now."

"Men don't like losin' what's theirs, especially if it's a pretty little teacher with sass but a serious thirst to please. He's pride hurt and a man like Willie-boy can't stand that. I'm workin' on something so he gets the fuckin' picture but for now, he thinks you're with me and, he's a lawyer and a smart man, he'll back off."

"I think more than just William thinks I'm with you," I ventured, thinking about those noses pressed to the glass while we had our parking lot altercation.

It occurred to me that a lot of life-changing events happened to me in parking lots.

Zeus shrugged his mighty shoulders. "What do I care if people think I got myself some hot teacher ass?"

"King's, um, okay with that insinuation?"

"For now."

I swallowed painfully but didn't question his vague and terrifying response.

I stood up and moved away from the bike because even though I was reeling, it was clear he had said his piece and was going to leave. The Prez of the club had more important things to do than help a lady in her garden, but I deeply appreciated, in a strange way, his taking the time to comfort me, to give me his take on the situation. It also disturbed me to know I essentially had his parental consent to fuck his son.

# Fifteen.

It was later, after an entire morning and afternoon spent working in my mess of a garden side by side men who were, convicted or not, criminals. Still, I'd found myself charmed by one after another as we toiled away in the soil. I wondered if it had to do with bonding over something as elemental as the earth and a hard day's work, if it was because I felt beholden to them for their charity and they were curious enough about my relationship to King to be attentive or if it was because King had rallied the most charismatic of his troops in an effort to woo me to the dark side, to convince me that at least one of the obstacles in the way of our relationship—his criminal family—was inconsequential.

It was after I'd made them all my famous pulled pork, which I'd fortunately already had marinating in the fridge and popped into the slow cooker before helping the guys in the yard. They'd inhaled the pork, slaw and brioche bun sandwiches I'd made them, decimating the food that I'd planned to use in my meal plan for the next few weeks in under half an hour. I'd never seen a group of grown men eat and it was both a terrifying and a heady thing to be the one to feed them. They'd all grown silent as they devoured the food and chips I'd laid out, most even ate a bit of the simple green salad I'd made, and then complimented me with grunts, belly pats and sincere smiles. It was more satisfying than any gourmet meal I'd made William during our marriage.

So, when Nova continued to hit on me despite King's growls, Buck belched so loudly it literally shook the table, a crazy biker named Lab Rat got drunk as a skunk on some mysterious liquid he kept in a jeweled skull encrusted flash at his hip and started speaking in really bizarre riddles, I only laughed. I laughed because it felt like living, and I loved it.

King watched me the entire dinner, his anger banked or forgotten, his eyes star bright as he showed me a slice of his family. They seemed to beckon me closer, enticing me to adopt his family as my own. He would, I knew, give everything in his life to me, unashamed, totally generous. Just as I knew that he wouldn't expect blind obedience in return, dinners on the table at six p.m. sharp, laundry done and folded back in its drawers as if it had never been dirtied. King wanted me to live and he just wanted the opportunity to help me do it.

The men hadn't lingered after dinner, only to respectfully leave their dishes by the side of the sink (they weren't heathens but they were bikers so they weren't going to do the dishes for me). I closed my eyes where I sat at the dinner table, listening to King murmur quietly to Mute while the roar of bikes started up outside. I was tired after the long day and the socializing, physically exhausted but also mentally, it was hard work struggling through a lifetime of preconceived notions to see the men who dedicated their Saturday to helping me on the other side.

So, I knew I was prepared to face King, to have the conversation I needed to have with him about boundaries, about me being the teacher and him the student. I didn't have it in me to lie to him.

The truth was, I'd fallen in love with him in the parking

lot of Mac's Grocer five months ago and since then, I'd only sunk further. He was it for me, and it could have been the book geek in me, the eternal romantic suffering from a lifelong lack of romance, but I really believed that. King was everything I'd dreamed a man should be; a real man built of loyalty, tenacity and verve, who laughed like the world was made just to entertain him and loved like crazy. I could never have known that the other things, his youth and its resulting vigor, his lack of morality and the liberation it gave him and, by extension me, would be my kryptonite.

I was a good woman who had fallen in love with the ultimate bad boy.

Now, I just had to figure out what to do about it.

"I could hear you thinkin' all the way in the kitchen," King said, and I knew he was standing beside my chair, hands in his pockets, faux-casual, while his eyes burned hot on my face.

I peeked at him from under one eye. "I've got a lot to think about, King."

"Care to share with the class?" he taunted me, referencing our professional relationship because he could be an asshole, especially when he didn't think he was going to get what he wanted.

"I'm too tired to do this right now."

"Fuck that."

I sighed. "If I told you that your cursing bothered me, would you stop?"

"If you were my woman, I'd think about it. Hard habit to break after eighteen years, but I'd give it a shot," he responded instantly.

Rage suddenly burned in my gut, rushing through my throat and onto my tongue like acid reflux. The unfairness of the situation, of loving a boy and of him pursuing me with this doggedness, of my husband refusing to divorce me and holding his money ransom, of my brother relying on me to somehow secure him a job through my nonexistent relationship with King… I opened my mouth and wrath spilled off my lips.

"Jesus, King, how can you expect this from me? I'm a grown woman, I've been married for Christ's sake, and you're still just a boy."

King's pale eyes narrowed on me, glinting in the moonlight streaming through the huge windows like the light off a blade.

"Do I look like a boy to you?" he asked, his eyes locked on me while he drew his hand, a hand I knew to be strong and rough with calluses, along the ridges of his abdomen I could see even through his shirt.

I was arrested by the sight of him as he unfastened the first few buttons on his jeans. He paused, his eyes pulsing like a beacon. It was a dare for him to continue. I gritted my teeth against the desire that lived between my thighs, burning hotter than lit coal. It was irritating that King always pushed me, forced me up against the boundaries of my propriety like he wanted to fuck me from behind in front of an audience of my personal demons. It was even more irritating that it made me feel electric with tension and vitality, that the colours of the world grew neon and sharp.

He took my hesitation as the positive encouragement it was and dipped his hand under the denim. "A boy knows how to please a woman like you? How to make her feel like a queen?"

I swallowed drily as he wrapped his fingers around the ridged length trapped against his thigh beneath the unforgiving denim. Slowly, deliberately, he tugged himself upward so that the swollen purple tip of his cock appeared above the waistband, the head wet with precum that I wanted badly to paint across my panting mouth, lick off with my eager tongue. I licked my lips, lost to the fantasy.

My gaze clung to his groin but I knew he watched me, knew his eyes would be bright with power and longing. He played me perfectly, manipulating me with his beauty, teasing me until I was on the precipice of begging to see his dick.

"You want this cock, babe?" he growled.

My God, but I did.

My mouth was too dry to answer so I nodded.

"Grown women don't get on their knees for boys, do they, Cressida? So, you have a choice. You can tell me to get out or you can get on your knees for me now and I'll show you how a real man treats his woman, starting by letting you worship my dick with that beautiful mouth of yours like I know you're aching to."

My mind emptied of everything as the power of his words, his stance and challenge washed over me. Unconsciously, my body swayed toward him, caught in the current of his persuasion. Before I could help myself, my knees were hitting the cold hardwood at his feet and my mouth was open, tipped up and waiting for him to grace it with his dick.

He stared down at me, his face fierce and harsh with longing but touch gentle as he reached out to slide his hand around the back of my head, tangling in my hair as he brought me closer.

"Good girl, you made the right choice. Now take me in your mouth and show me just how much of a man I am."

My tongue flicked out to lick the bead of moisture off his tip, the flavor exploding on my tongue as a low groan exploded from King's throat. I stared up at him as I gripped the edge of his jeans with my teeth and tugged hard. The denim fell to the ground, his belt dropping with a clang, and I was rewarded with the sight of his gorgeous cock, thick and long against his hard belly.

"Fuck, that look in your eye," King groaned, both hands sinking into the hair above my ears. "You look like you want to fucking worship me."

"I do," I said. "I shouldn't want to but I've never wanted anything more."

I'd dreamt of this since puberty but only in the darkest hours before morning, my fingers sticky from my leaking pussy as I imagined all the ways I could be made to please a man who had the power to bend me to my knees. Now, I had the freedom to unleash my dirtiest fantasies on a man who was too sexy to be true.

As if he knew I needed it, his hands pulled back my hair on each side of my temple and fisted there, tightly. He tipped my head up so that I was looking into his stern face.

"Tired of you fighting it. Tonight you're mine."

"Yes," I panted, mouth inches from his pulsing shaft.

"Get to work."

I moaned as I immediately pressed my cheek to his hot skin, nuzzling my face into his groin to drag in a deep lungful of his manly scent. My tongue darted out to lap softly, teasingly at the base of his cock, over the skin of his balls. His hands tightened in my hair as I suck hard at the junction there, tasting his salty, delicious flavor.

He was exceptionally long and as I traced the thick vein on the underside of his shaft, I worried that I wouldn't be able to take all of him. Determined to try, I lapped my tongue over the sensitive underside of his head, looking up at him to see him watching me with eyes like melting ice. I shivered with bone-deep pleasure as I opened my mouth wide and took him deep.

"Motherfucker," he cursed softly, as his hands spasmed in my hair.

I groaned wantonly, aware of the vibration of the sound all around his dick as I nestled it at the back of my throat. King tried to rock his hips forward but I gagged around him.

One of his hands found my throat, pressed lightly there as he instructed me, "Open that throat, babe. Gotta get in there."

I moaned again, desperate to do as I was told but unsure how to do it.

Sensing my conflict, King widened his stance and rotated his hips slightly back and forth, fucking my mouth in shallow thrusts.

"Swallow as I press forward."

His hot shaft pulsed forward again, breaching my throat and I swallowed convulsively.

"Ah, fuck, that's it," he growled, thrusting forward slow and steady until he was rooted deep down my throat.

I swallowed again, drool running from my stretched lips and down my chin as I looked up at him. My thighs were slicked with moisture at the thought of how shameless I looked like that, mouth filled with cock, cheeks flushed from the struggle of taking it so deep.

"You look fuckin' gorgeous with my cock in your sweet mouth," King rasped out, dragging himself slowly out over my tongue. "Stick your tongue out for me."

I did, not feeling silly or ashamed as he slapped his swollen purple head against it once, twice, three times before I caught it between my lips again. My mind emptying of everything, each care and worry I wore like a heavy mantle sloughed off and I focused only on the man that stood before me like my King. It was the sexiest thing I'd ever done, licking and sucking on him freely, sloppier and sloppier as I made him wet with my mouth, loving his taste and the noises we made together.

Finally, I couldn't take it any longer and I reached my hand down to press between my thighs.

"Stop," he barked.

I froze immediately.

Oh my God, what was I doing?

Shame burst inside me like an overripe fruit, spilling through me until everything felt rotten. I tried to scramble away from him but his hands were still woven in my hair and they clenched painfully until I gasped and stopped moving.

"Let me go," I begged.

It sounded like a sob and I realized that I was close to tears.

I couldn't help it. I'd finally let myself want someone, act out that desire in a way that I *knew* some people thought was disgusting but I hadn't thought that King…

His hands yanked my head until it was tilted up to him.

I kept my eyes downcast.

"Fuckin' look at me, Cress. Where did you go?"

I swallowed hard but said nothing.

"Look at me."

I bit my trembling lip, noticed it was swollen from him, and winced.

"Did I hurt you?" he asked, his voice suddenly soft.

When I didn't immediately answer, he sank to his knees so that he could look me in the eye. His hands shifted down my neck, his thumbs at my chin to tip it up gently.

"What the fuck happened there, babe? I'm getting' the hottest damn blowjob I've ever got in my life and then my girl freaks. I need to know what I did so I don't do it again, yeah?"

"You didn't do anything," I murmured, because I couldn't stand him thinking it was him who had done something wrong.

I was the one who had turned into a class-A slut.

"Cressida," he growled. "You don't answer me, you won't like what you get."

My gaze snapped up to him, his threat sparking something inside me. "I didn't *want* anything from you. You're the one who made me do this so don't be angry with me for acting like, like that."

"What the fuck are you talking about?"

"Don't blame me for acting like a whore!"

His face solidified then collapsed as if I'd taken a hammer to it. Swiftly, before I could even squeak, he was lifting me off the floor and into his arms. Automatically, I wrapped my limbs around him to hold on as he moved us across to the kitchen. He deposited me on the scarred counter but kept one arm wrapped around my lower back while the other found and gripped my chin.

"Cress babe," he started saying before I could open my mouth. "You gotta know I don't think that of you. Trust me, you are the furthest thing from a fuckin' whore that I have ever seen. You think I'd want you the way I do if I didn't think you were a queen?"

I drank his words down greedily but ducked my head to press my forehead into his neck so he wouldn't see my blush. "I get a little…carried away sometimes."

"Yeah?" he asked, dreamy surprise in the one syllable. "Babe, you think I'm gonna complain about that, you got another think comin'. Never, not ever, seen something so hot as me in your mouth like that. If you'd stop bein' ridiculously insecure about it, I'd have you on your knees again in a minute."

A shocked giggle burst from my lips. "Really?"

"Yeah, babe," he confirmed, using the hand around my back to take a handful of my ass and give it a squeeze. "Really. Only reason I was tellin' you to stop was so I could be the one to make you come." He smiled boyishly. "I'm greedy like that."

"My, ugh, my ex-husband wasn't a fan of it," I explained even though it mortified me to do so.

"Already thought the guy was a fucker, didn't need more of a reason to hate 'em but I'll take whatever you wanna tell me, if it makes you feel better."

That was sweet, sweeter somehow even than his telling me I wasn't a whore.

"You didn't hurt me," I decided to divulge. "I like having my hair pulled."

A low growl rumbled through his chest, vibrating against my lips where they were pressed to his golden throat.

"Babe, you're killin' me."

"I like it when you talk dirty to me and are a little rough with me," I continued.

"Shut up," he ordered, as he whipped my concert tee over my head.

"And when you put your hand on the back of my neck to hold me how you want me while you take my mouth."

"Babe," he warned in a low voice that sent a thrill of fear and desire shooting straight between my legs.

I squirmed as he made quick work of my jean shorts and plain white panties, tugging them off while he lifted me with one hand.

"I think I'd like it even more if you put your mouth on me," I ventured as I leaned in to run my tongue up his neck.

He tasted so good, all clean salty male. I groaned.

"You want my mouth on your pretty cunt?" King said as he tipped his head down to stare between our bodies at the apex of my thighs.

I followed his lead and watched as he slid his index finger from the tiny patch of hair over my clit through my wet slit all the way to my opening. He dipped his finger inside me then drew over my clit lightly with one knuckle. I shuddered violently against him then again when his smoky chuckle wafted over my ear.

"Tell me you want it."

"I want it."

"I expect you to say my name when I make you come, babe. I want you to own that it's me between these pretty thighs," he said as he dropped to the floor.

My breath came fast and hard through my parted lips as I watched him spread me open with his fingers and swipe his knuckle over me again and again.

"So fuckin' pretty," he murmured before he replaced his knuckle with his mouth.

I gasped, my hands flying to his hair to steady myself as he tugged me to the edge of the counter. I was perched precariously but I didn't care, not when his mouth was fused to my wet folds, mapping them with the expertise of a cartographer. He moaned into my flesh then took my throbbing clit into his mouth and sucked hard.

"King," I said as I tipped my head back, my long hair brushing the countertops.

I caught our reflection in the floor-to-ceiling windows beyond the kitchen and living room and bit my lip to keep from whimpering. The yellow lights of the kitchen perfectly illustrated us against the black night outside. King on his knees, his impossibly broad shoulders pushing my legs wide and his golden hair a halo in my dirty hands. Strangely, it was the sight of me, bowed with pleasure but riding him like a seasoned jockey, that ratcheted my arousal into the stratosphere.

"Wanna taste your cum, babe," King growled against my swollen flesh as he eased two fingers inside me and curled them wickedly. "Be a good girl and come for me."

And I did, spectacularly.

I lost sight of myself in the blackness that reared up inside me, swallowing me whole and turning me inside out. Vaguely, I realized that King had stood up, shoved his jeans down and wrapped his beautiful dick in a condom.

"Fuckin' beautiful," he grunted as he took my lax legs in his hands, tipped my hips and plunged into me in one hard thrust.

I screamed, still riding the tail of my orgasm so that the intense sensation of his length inside me sent me spinning into another, smaller climax.

"Fuck, dreamed about it, it was never this good," he bit out then clamped his teeth on the side of my neck and rode me hard.

I knew he was leaving a mark but I loved the way the pain beat around the pulse in my neck like a second heartbeat, one that pumped pure pleasure through my veins. I wanted the pain he could give me, I wanted his tongue and teeth to write his poems on my skin, wicked ones written in bruises and sweat, flourished with tears and cum.

"Yes," I hissed, tipping my head to give him even more surface area to bite.

My legs convulsed around him as he continued to beat into me. His cock played my wet pussy like a drum, pounding over and over in a delicious rhythm that had me vibrating and emitting sounds I'd never heard before.

Just as a third, seemingly impossible, orgasm was about to claim me King nipped my earlobe and said, "Love the feel of your tight, hot pussy all around me. Gonna fuckin' live between these thighs, gonna make you give it up to me all the time. Claim you in your bed before school then make you teach class without any panties, watch my cum leak out of you while you talk about Eve's fall from Eden." My breath hitched as I wavered on the edge of my climax. "Yeah, you like that, babe? Thinkin' of my cum trickling down your thighs, knowing how hard it would make me to look up under one of your skirts as I did the homework you assigned?"

"Fuck," I cried out as pleasure electrocuted me.

My legs shook almost violently around his lean hips and my nails raked down his back to pull him even closer to me. I heard him curse, thrust once, twice more, hard pumps that prolonged my own orgasm, before he held himself deep inside me and came with a manly, sexy-as-hell grunt.

I held him to me as we both came down from it, my hands fluttering tenderly along the defined ridges of muscle in his back. There was a deep dip down his spine, delineating the muscles like a crevice between mountains. For some reason, feeling that made my mouth water.

"How often do you work out?" I asked lazily, my eyes closed and my chin perched on his shoulder.

His body rumbled with a low chuckle. "Shit, she's even funny after I've fucked her senseless."

"I was genuinely curious," I protested tiredly, yawning into his neck.

"Still funny, babe." He shifted his arms tighter around me, slipping them under my bum to lift me in the air.

I murmured a little protest but wrapped my heavy limbs around him as he started walking us through my little house. Already half asleep, I was only slightly aware of King stopping to turn off lights and lock the doors before he carried me up the stairs.

"Heavy," I protested as he climbed.

He snorted into my hair, gave my ear a little nip that almost made me stir again. "You can't be more than a hundred and twenty pounds soaking wet, Cress. Trust me, I got you."

And he did. My body felt like warm wax as he maneuvered me into my bedroom then the adjacent bathroom where he propped me up on the little counter there. He left me to my business then came back in a few minutes later carrying one of my little cotton nightgowns, this one pale pink with gold lace edging. It was then that I realized he was buck-naked and I was still wearing most of my clothes. My eyes conducted a brief but thorough search of his nudity before I could control myself. I hummed my approval, too exhausted to mind that I sounded like a harlot.

"Need help putting this on?" he teased me as he handed over my nightie.

"Did you snoop through my things, King Garro?" I asked with faux indignation.

Truly, I was too tired to care and so attached to him after he'd gifted me with three consecutive, mind-blowing orgasms in a lifetime of mediocre sometimes but not always finishes with William, that he could have broken into my bank records, email and the tiny safe I kept tucked at the back of my closet and I still would have forgiven him.

He chuckled. "You have a spare toothbrush I can use?"

I blinked up at him, my levity forgotten. "A spare toothbrush?"

"Yeah, babe. I like the taste of you but I'd rather kiss you with a clean mouth before we head to bed."

I blinked again. "Oh."

It was a bad idea, him staying the night. I knew there were a lot of reasons for this, but for the life of me, my sex-addled brain couldn't rummage them up.

"Under the sink in the blue plastic Tupperware," I said instead of telling him to leave.

His resulting grin was wide, his lips even pinker than normal from kissing me so much. "Get into bed."

"Okay," I mumbled, scrubbing a hand over my freshly washed and moisturized face as I shuffled out of the bathroom.

It was strangely intimate to hear another person getting ready to join you in bed. I crawled beneath my pretty patchwork quilt and cream-coloured sheets and put my pink facemask on my forehead in preparation for sleep. I felt awkward lying there waiting for him to join me. I'd never had a man other than my husband share a bed with me and I was suddenly conscious of all the ways I could embarrass myself in sleep. Did I snore, toss and turn, expose every dark secret I had (though there were few)?

I was still obsessing over it when King entered the room, flipped of the light and crawled onto the right side of the bed as if he'd been doing it all his life. My breath whooshed out as he snagged a strong arm around my middle and hauled me over to him, settling my body so that I lay mostly on top of him instead of the mattress.

"This can't be comfortable for you," I mumbled.

It was amazingly comfortable to me. I never could have known that a body made from marble could feel so good beneath my slight curves.

"Wouldn't put you here if it wasn't," he responded.

"I need the facemask or else I wake up at the butt crack of dawn," I explained. "And I don't know because I've only ever slept with my ex-husband but I may snore or, I don't know, fart in my sleep or something equally horrific so I apologize in advance and I won't be offended if you want to go home."

King's hand stroked warm and heavy down my back and it was lulling me to sleep despite my anxieties.

"Doubt you do anything gross, Cress. You're a fuckin' lady

if ever I met one."

I tried to shrug but my position sprawled across him wasn't conducive to it. "Just warning you."

"How 'bout I let you know in the morning if you're anything other than fuckin' adorable, yeah?"

"That's fair," I whispered.

King's soft chuckle rustled my hair. He reached over to tilt my facemask down over my eyes for me and then fitted his hand in the groove of my hip as if it had been carved out just for him.

"Get some rest, babe. Gonna wanna have you in the morning too."

"Perfect," I tried to say, but I was already gone.

# Sixteen.

I woke up to the sound of thunder again.

Confusion and déjà vu disorientated me for a moment until I realized that this sound was far gentler than yesterday, far closer than the rumble of bikes had been then. I smiled before I was even consciously aware that the rumble in my ears was the low, gentle snores rolling through King's chest.

Carefully, so I didn't wake him up, I lifted my head to stare down at the gorgeous blond man in my bed. We had fallen asleep with my cheek to his chest, his arm around my waist to hold me tight to his side and I loved that we'd woken up in the same position, as if even in sleep our bodies were drawn together.

His face was breathtakingly beautiful in slumber, soft and boyish in a way that emphasized his youth. It should have made me disgusted to have an eighteen-year-old in my bed but it didn't, not after last night. What boy took care of the woman he cared about like King did me? What boy dedicated his entire Saturday to doing her lawn work? What boy wrote such heartrending poems, discussed literature and history like an academic and looked so freaking manly in a tee and jeans?

No, King Kyle Garro may have been my student, but there was no doubt in my mind that he was a man.

I trailed my fingers lightly over the ladder of square abdominal muscles on his lower stomach and thought about last night. Sex in the kitchen was something I'd never done before but I was thinking now that it should become a staple. There was something so dirty about fucking on the counter, in such a mundane, family place. I knew I'd never be able to cook in it again without thinking of King's hot mouth between my legs, his fingers inside me preparing me for his big dick.

A shivered rippled through me as I looked back up at his face to find his eyes open under heavy lids, watching me.

"Mornin', Queen, enjoying the view?" he asked in a sleep-roughened voice.

I blushed but tried to shrug casually. "If I'm going to hell, I might as well enjoy the view."

His eyes turned sharper than a knife's edge at my words. "Don't do it, Cressida, not this mornin'."

"Do what?"

"Make this thing we got goin' shameful."

I nibbled my bottom lip but kept my hand smoothly stroking his chest to soften my words. "I don't regret last night, honey, but you have to realize that what we're doing, what *I* am doing, is wrong. It's a hard adjustment for me to make after a lifetime of struggling to be good and pure."

King dislodged me as he sat up abruptly, pushed himself back against the headboard and plucked me out of the sheets to set me in a straddle over his lap. I could feel his morning wood between my thighs but his priority was tucking the blankets around my naked hips so that I wouldn't be cold in my poorly insulated room.

So sweet, my biker.

"Purity is a social trap," he started to explain after he had us both settled in how he wanted. "No one is ever pure to everyone and I guarantee you that no one that pure is happy. Happiness is streaking bare-assed naked down the wet sand into the waves, it's drinkin' too much and laughin' too loud with your friends, it's lovin' so hard you want to devour the flesh, soul and mind of another person. None of that is fuckin' pure and all of it is fuckin' sublime."

He leaned in to frame my face with his big hands. "The only thing dirty about this is the people who will try to shame you. You do not need to be pure or ordinary to be good, babe. You just need to live and love without guilt and I swear to you, you'll leave the world a better place than you entered it."

Jesus, he was such a poet.

"Okay, King," I said, because in the moment, I believed he was right.

He stared hard at me to assure himself that I was telling the truth before he said, "Good. You with me, then?"

"Yeah, I'm with you," I whispered softly, returning his gesture by framing his handsome face in my hands. I pressed a gentle, openmouthed kiss to his lips. "But we've got to have rules."

"You can take the teacher outta the classroom but you can't take the teacher outta the girl, eh?" King laughed into the crook of my neck before he pressed a kiss behind my ear.

I shoved at his shoulder but I was smiling. "I'm serious, King! We can't just date."

"Who says I wanna date?"

I froze, my eyes widening until I felt like my eyeballs would fall out. Had I read every single signal wrong? Was I jeopardizing my career and my reputation for a good roll in the hay (correction: a super life-changing roll in very awesome hay)?

King's loud hoot and subsequent laughter jerked me from my horrified thoughts.

"You *asshole*," I cried, thumping him on the chest and shoulders with my fists. "You complete *dick*! I can't believe you'd joke about something like that."

Still laughing, he rolled us until he had me pressed on my back in the bed. My anger immediately fled as he licked then bit at my neck. "Love you riled, babe. Nothing better than seeing my girl's whiskey eyes lit up and alive."

"Meanie," I grumbled but my heart wasn't in it because it was his, tucked away safely and securely in a place only he could find.

"Totally," he agreed, biting down hard over my jugular in a way that had me wet in an instant.

"King," I gasped. "We were going to talk about the rules."

"Yeah, okay, babe. Rule one: no talking when I'm inside you unless it's about how good it feels, yeah?"

"You aren't even inside me… oh!" I said, then shut up because rule number one was a rule I could get behind.

****

Later, after sex so awesome it made my toes curl so hard they cramped, and a shower where, I kid you not, King washed my hair for me after washing other more intimate places *very* thoroughly, I was in the kitchen with my head in the fridge trying to decide what to feed him. He'd disappeared after the shower but I knew he was somewhere around the house because his Harley was still out front and I knew he wouldn't leave without saying anything.

I was deciding between granola and yogurt and bran cereal when hands clamped over my hips and King stuck his face into the fridge beside mine.

"Find treasure or somethin', babe?"

I laughed. "I'm trying to decide what to make you for breakfast."

"I want pie."

I tipped my head to look up over my shoulder at him. "What?"

"Pie," he repeated before kissing me hard and moving away from me. "Apple pie."

I closed the fridge and turned to lean against it with my hands on my hips as I watched him cross to the dock station I had on the counter under my ancient microwave. He began tinkering with my old iPod, his lip between his teeth as he scrolled through my music.

"King, apple pie for breakfast isn't a thing," I informed him.

"Sure it is, you make it for me," was his illogical but somewhat rational reply.

A giggle rose in my throat but I swallowed it down. "What are you, twelve? Adults eat real food for breakfast, not dessert."

King didn't shift his head up to look at me but he shot me a sidelong glance that burned through me. "You need me to show you again how much of a man I am, babe? Remember, I'm eighteen, I can go all day and all fuckin' night, you need me to."

He watched me shiver with arrogant satisfaction before he added, "Do a better job of it if I had pie."

I threw up my hands as I gave into laughter. "Okay, fine, I'll make you pie but we have to go out for apples."

He didn't respond. Instead, he plugged in my iPod and Elvis Presley's "Burnin' Love," one of my all-time favorite songs, came over the speakers. He'd known I loved Elvis but I loved even more that he'd put on that particular song this morning. I opened my mouth to say so but he had already disappeared out the side door into the garden.

I shook my head at him but couldn't stop smiling as I pulled out the butter, lard, salt and flour to make the crust.

Minutes later, I heard the screen door slam and looked over my shoulder to see King amble into the kitchen carrying a small crate filled with different apple varieties. When I frowned up at him, he shrugged.

"Apples," he said inanely.

"Yes," I agreed. "Why do you have a box of apples on hand?"

He cocked his head at me like I was the one being silly. "Babe, I give you an apple a day. I gotta stock up. It's cool and dark in my trunk so I keep 'em in there."

I blinked and blinked, trying to stop the flood of tears threatening to drown me.

"Cress, it's not a big deal, babe. All the best students give their favorite teachers apples, yeah?" he joked.

I shook my head unable to speak because I didn't want to dissolve into tears our first morning together.

"Besides, you smell like 'em. Ever since I got you on the back of my bike that first night at the bar, I've been obsessed with them."

"God, you're perfect," I blurted out.

King laughed, dropped the crate on the counter and caught me around the waist to hug me from behind, burying his face in my apple scented hair. "Only for you, babe."

I sniffed back the tears but allowed myself to sink back into his hold for a moment before I shooed him away so I could finish the crust.

He poured us both coffees before he jumped up on the counter beside me to keep me company while I rolled out the dough. I loved having him close, loved having him reach out randomly to claim a kiss or rub flour off my face. We talked about his brothers in The Fallen, who were crazy but I'd learned last night that it was mostly in a good way. I asked him why he didn't have any tattoos, and he'd laughed when he told me there wasn't anything he liked enough that he wanted it permanently on his skin. I made the filling while the crust rested in the fridge, making salted caramel to add into the apples, an idea that King rewarded with a long, deep kiss.

I had so much fun just hanging out with him that when there was a knock at my front door, I didn't even think about going to answer it. It seemed like a normal, if beyond fantastic, morning between a customary couple.

"Babe, you sure you should answer that?" King called when I was already halfway to the door at the left end of the kitchen.

I halted immediately, turned to survey the student sitting (deliciously) bare-chested on my counter then to look down at my outfit, which consisted of a short, pretty rose-embroidered robe.

"Probably not." I grinned at him. "Whoever it is will just go away when I don't answer."

"Good. C'mere and give me your mouth," King ordered with a crooked grin.

I skipped over to him, which made him laugh, planted my hands on his strong thighs and jumped up slightly to lay a big one on him.

"Not so fast," he said, grabbing me by the hips so that he could hold me suspended in the air over the ground.

I sighed at the manly act before he took advantage of my parted lips and kissed me thoroughly.

Another knock sounded on the door but I didn't think of it because I was busy kissing a god. It was minutes later that I registered someone calling, "Cressida, I know you're in there and I'm not leaving until you let me in."

King's hand immediately spasmed on my hips and I wrenched myself back in his hold so I could stare at him in horror.

William was at the door.

# Seventeen.

"I'm dreaming," I told myself. "This is not real."

"It's real, babe," King growled.

"Ohmigawd, ohmigawd, ohmigawd," I chanted, unable to move and tied to the tracks as the train barreled toward me.

"Cressida, babe," King's voice cut through my panic. "Listen to me. Answer the door and get rid of him. If he doesn't go, I'll sort it out, yeah?"

"You can't," I said, my voice in an octave I'd never heard before. "He can't see you here. He thinks I'm dating your freaking father and you're my freaking student!"

"Deep fuckin' breath right now, babe. If you freak out, I'll rage out and we can't have me killin' your ex-husband, yeah?"

"Yeah," I agreed because I definitely didn't want him to go to prison even if I kinda sorted wanted to see him beat William up.

"We're going to get through this together. It's super fuckin' bad timin' because I had plans to eat my apple pie then eat you but we'll put those on hold. I'm not trippin' about being here. I'm glad because I'm gonna help you get rid of 'im for fuckin' good. Now, go answer the door." He pressed a firm kiss to my mouth like a punctuation mark and hopped off the counter.

I waited for him to disappear somewhere in the house, taking the time to breath deep and get my shit together.

"Cressida," William called again from behind the door.

"You can do this," I told myself. "You are a strong, independent woman and you can *do* this."

I started toward the door then paused and rubbed my hands over my face. "You're also a shameless harlot who just spent the night boning the gorgeous much-younger man who, along with his father, is 'fixin'' to do something about the husband currently demanding entry to your house while said younger man is hiding somewhere inside it."

Another knock at the door and a hissed, "Answer the fuckin' thing, babe," from somewhere else in the house.

"Ohmigawd, I'm so going to hell," I mumbled.

Then I opened the door.

And to my continued horror, it wasn't just William who stood before me, but also my mother.

"Well, it's about time. It's inconceivable that you would leave guests out on the stoop to freeze to death while you dawdled around inside. My goodness, it's nearly eleven o'clock. What are you doing still in your robe?" Phoebe Garrison said as she pushed past me and into my home.

I stood dumbly in the door, my eyes locked on William and my father as they retrieved something from the car and made their way toward me.

*Oh my* fucking *GOD!*

"Cressida, please don't tell me you're making pie for breakfast?" my mother called from inside.

My eyes darted between the approaching men and the mother currently rummaging in my house and I made the quick decision to focus on the worse threat. I dashed inside to find her opening and closing all my cupboards.

“You told me this place was charming,” she accused but didn’t stop her snooping. “It’s an absolute *sty*.”

“It’s a work in progress,” I defended. “As you may remember, I didn’t have any money when I left William.”

“Yes, I remember. So how exactly did you afford even this pile of kindling?” Phoebe asked me, finally turning to pin her eyes on me.

They were my eyes staring at me, which I’d always found comforting but now I found it incredibly perturbing because they looked at me with the same judgmental condemnation that I knew I’d used my entire life on people like King and his brothers. It gave me a stomachache to think about it.

I also couldn’t tell my mother that I had taken money from Lysander because, to my parents’ knowledge, I had excommunicated him from the family church years ago.

So, instead, I went on the offensive.

“What are you doing here, mother? I seem to remember you saying something about never visiting me here because you didn’t want me to get used to the idea.”

Her lips pursed but William and my dad entered the kitchen before she could lecture me about my rudeness.

“Princess,” my dad called out as soon as he saw me. I was in his arms in the next second, his cigar and newsprint scent as familiar to me as my own.

Peter Garrison was not a bad man, but he was a simple one and that was in and of itself a bad thing. He got up every morning at six a.m., read the entire *Globe & Mail* newspaper back to front then went to work at UBC where he taught the same six courses every year in the Classics department, then he was home to Mum and dinner on the table by six-thirty p.m. after which he spent the night working or reading in his study. Simple life. Simple man. And, in his eyes, simple relationship with his daughter.

He loved me very much but he didn't understand me and it was beyond his capabilities to try.

So, I hugged him back and enjoyed my brief moment of peace in my daddy's arms.

"Why aren't you dressed yet? It's nearly eleven o'clock?" William asked me, echoing my mother's words as he waited his turn to press a kiss to my cheek.

I accepted it but took a large step back when he was finished. "Why are you here at eleven o'clock on a Sunday? Why are you here at all?"

He blinked at me. "You wouldn't come home and then when I saw you with that awful biker man, I knew I had to take matters into my own hands."

"So you brought my parents and ambushed me on a Sunday?" I asked acerbically.

"Yes," he stated.

"I could hit you right now," I gritted out between my teeth.

"Cressida Phillipa Irons, do not speak to your husband like that! I know I taught you better," my mother rebuked me even as she unloaded the groceries that the men had brought inside.

"Mum, why are there groceries that I didn't buy in my house?" I asked, in a surprisingly calm voice.

How in the world was I going to get them to leave when they were very clearly settling in? I thought of King somewhere in my house and anxiety spiked my blood like lead poisoning.

"We're having Sunday dinner here because you refuse to come home," she said into the oven as she checked its cleanliness (found it sorely lacking) and preset the temperature.

"No, you are not. I don't go to your house for family dinners anymore because *it is no longer my home*," I cried.

Childish rage and frustration built inside me ready to

stomp its feet and throw its fists in the air. The reversion made sense if only because they made me feel like a child, helpless against their "adult" mandates of superiority, as if my opinion wasn't valid given my age.

When I thought about it like that, it made sense that I'd been drawn to a (much) younger man. I was tired of old people and their stuck-in-the-mud ways.

"You need to leave," I ordered.

No one listened to me.

In fact, my dad was already taking his beer from a cooler that they'd also brought in from the car, the same one he and William used every Saturday when they went fishing. Without heeding my order, he descended the four shallow steps separating the kitchen from the living room and took a seat on my cracked leather couch.

"Not bad," he mumbled, patting the cushions.

My mother continued to set out the ingredients for what looked like a real turkey dinner and William just stood there staring at me as if he was waiting for me to perform.

Oh, I'd perform all right, but I was certain he wouldn't like the show.

I opened my mouth to throw a tantrum, perversely looking forward to it, when the low distant rumble of a motorcycle sounded in the distance.

"I'm waiting for you to tell me what you were doing with that criminal," William prompted me.

"How do you even know he's a criminal?" I shot back. "Just because he has tattoos and rides a bike doesn't mean he's done anything illegal."

"He's the President of The Fallen MC, of course he's a criminal. If you knew even half the things I knew about him, you'd run back to me and *beg* me to keep you," he returned.

"How do you know anything about him, at all?" I asked, curiosity warring with my rage.

William blanched slightly and I wondered if it was because he'd hired a PI to tail me.

My God, I hoped not.

"I'm a lawyer, Cressida, I know these things," he said vaguely. "I'm not here to argue with you, anyway. I'm here to talk you into coming back home with me."

"If you wanted to talk to me about that, you could have waited until our session next Friday," I retorted. "Right now, I really want all of you to leave."

"We were concerned about you, Cressida," my mother chimed in. I shouldn't have been shocked to see her in the red-and-white checked and frilled apron that she wore whenever she cooked at home. Of course, she'd brought it with her. In less than ten minutes, she'd somehow yet effectively made me a guest in my own house.

The growl of the motorcycle was louder now, coming down the seaside road to my driveway. I didn't know what King had done exactly, but I knew he'd called in reinforcements.

Knowing this, I said, "Fine, but you should know that I have company coming over for dinner. They should be here soon."

Immediately, three heads turned to look at me.

"Company?" William and my mother said at the same time.

"Do they like *Jeopardy*?" my dad asked, because priorities.

"Yes, company. No, Dad, I'm absolutely certain that they do not like *Jeopardy*."

We were all silent as the sound of tires pulling down the driveway became distinguishable.

My mum turned to me with an expression of horror, her

hand at her heart. “Please tell me that isn’t the horrible biker William told us you’re dating?”

As if on cue, there was loud rap at the door before it pushed open to reveal Zeus and, to my utter confusion, a fully dressed King. My mouth dropped open at the sight of them but my jaw completely unhinged when an absolutely stunning streaky-blonde teenager followed in behind them and I got my first look at the youngest Garro.

As one, my family blinked at King’s.

I opened my mouth to say something, though I didn’t know if my acting skills were up to playing whatever part they expected me to play, when King stalked forward to stand beside me. As he did, the blonde girl moved to my other side, throwing me a little wink as she jumped up on the counter and snagged an apple from the crate King had left out.

“Hey, babe,” Zeus rumbled in a voice very similar to the sound of his revving motorcycle. “Who the fuck are the old folks?” Before I could answer, he turned to William. “And why the fuck are you in my woman’s house, Willie-boy? Thought I warned you to stay away.”

“We, I’m, you…” my mother stuttered as her brain overloaded with fear.

“Mother.” I beamed at her as Zeus joined our united front. “This is Zeus Garro and his two children, King and Harleigh Rose.”

“Sup?” Harleigh Rose nodded at my mum and spoke through the apple she was noisily masticating.

King just crossed his arms and glared at them. Unconsciously, I moved closer so I could press my shoulder against him.

“Cressida,” William started, his face set as he took a step forward to show the biker family suddenly inhabiting my kitchen that they didn't intimidate him. "Your parents and I came all the way up to this podunk town to spend the day with you. As I told you before, your mother is literally sick with worry. The least you can do is respect us enough to send these…" he struggled for a word "…*people* away so we can spend time healing."

"Healing?" King repeated incredulously. "Your wife left you and you cut her off from your joint accounts and from her fuckin' parents. While you were married, you made her feel like a *whore* and a neglected housewife. Have you seen her, buddy? She's a fuckin' knockout and you ignore her? I think it's you who needs some goddamn healing in the head."

"Preach," Harleigh Rose said, lifting her hands in the air.

I felt like I'd been dropped into an episode of *Family Feud*.

There was a long standoff where I was seriously unsure if a fight was going to break out (this vibe emanated from the Garro family) or if the police were going to be called (my family).

It occurred to me then that I was the pinnacle of the situation and hiding behind the Garro family was cowardly. I wanted to do it anyway. I'd been playing dead for years, following the path of least resistance and always doing what I was told. Because I was a dork, I'd always wished vampires were real but now more than ever, I wished I could die and be reborn as a Garro, someone wicked in ways both smart and cruel, selfish just enough to get ahead and take what you wanted, and beautiful in strange ways that echoed both inside and out.

So, I stepped away from the biker family at my back and into the middle of the silent war so that I could die that metaphorical death. Appropriately or not, I couldn't decide, "Sympathy for the Devil" played over the speakers as I took my stand.

"William, I want you to leave. I'm sorry that you can't

understand why I don't want to be with you but I feel that I've done my best since the beginning to tell you why that was and you seem to be incapable of empathizing with me. I want a divorce. I will say it again and again until my dying breath. Even if you refuse to sign the papers, I will never come back to you or the life we had. My life is here in Entrance now and, honestly, I don't think I'm the kind of person you'd like anymore."

"Clearly," he agreed firmly. "But marriage isn't something that you just end on a whim, Cressida. We've been together for eight years. Everyone says we are the perfect couple and we are, can't you see that? Doesn't that mean something to you?"

"Unfortunately for us both, it doesn't mean much," I admitted softly. I knew he wouldn't agree with me.

I turned to my mum who was wringing her hands in front of her and darting her eyes back and forth between King and Zeus. Honestly, I got it. I'd never seen them side by side and I was grateful that they were behind me because they were a distracting duo. Of course, my mother was probably imagining all the ways they could kill her while a normal woman would be driven to distraction by all the ways they could *do* her, but it was kind of the same thing.

"I would love it if you wanted to stay and get to know my new friends but I understand that this is hard for you. I've been dependent on you my entire life, even when I was with William, so I can give you the time to adjust if you need it. That said, I need you to understand that this 'pile of kindling' and these 'bikers' are my life now. I. Am. Happy. In fact, I'm happier than I've ever been. So, if you need to go then please do, because *they* are staying."

I crossed my arms and, like a boy band following the lead singer, the Garros crossed their arms in unison behind me.

My family hesitated a beat too long because King lunged

forward, snapping his teeth and barked at William, "Beat it before I beat you."

As one, my parents and William collected their belongings and headed out the door without a backward look. I watched from the window over the sink as my mother hesitated by the car, her hand on my father's shoulder, probably wondering if it was safe for me to be alone with criminals. Whatever it was, my father closed it down and they got into the car and took off.

"Fuck," I whispered brokenly as soon as their car disappeared up the steep drive.

Immediately, King pressed against my back and his arms looped around me tighter than rope. "I got you," he murmured.

I turned into him and burst into tears.

Dimly, I was aware of Harleigh Rose and Zeus moving into the living room to give us a modicum of privacy, but I was too busy soaking the front of King's tee to mind.

"They don't deserve your tears, babe, but if you gotta cry, do it now and get it out. Don't want you to do it alone," King murmured.

I cried harder.

What in the world had I done to deserve a man like him?

And what in the world had I done to deserve meeting him as his freaking teacher?

"Okay, time to stop now," King ordered after a good five minutes.

"Okay." I sniffed but didn't take my head from the front of his shirt because I had snot trailing from both nostrils.

With firm but gentle hands, he pried me from his shirt, stared down into my disgusting face and then leaned over to rip off a piece of paper towel. I took it from him and blew my nose slightly turned away from him. When I turned back he was smiling at me and I knew he was going to tease before he said, "It's a good thing I slept with you last night and you showed me how sweet you can be between the sheets, otherwise I'd probably be out the door after the fuckin' Stepford family standoff." He shuddered dramatically. "Don't know how you lived with 'em for so long, babe."

"I *was* one of them, King," I acknowledged. "I still kind of am. I'm so beyond grateful to your family for white knighting me out of that situation but there's still a part of me that they reared that says you guys are criminals and it's scary for me to be a part of that, especially after my brother went to prison when I was eighteen." King's face widened then creased in surprise. "And there's another part of me that William created that doesn't even understand why you'd be into me in the first place. You're eighteen years old with your entire life ahead of you. You are so smart and gorgeous and charming… Why in the world would you choose to hitch your wagon to me?"

"Maybe because you're fuckin' adorable when you say things like 'hitch your wagon' and 'for Pete's sake' like you're from nineteenth-century England," he joked.

When I only smiled weakly, he raked a hand through the hair I'd tousled myself only that morning and hoisted me onto the counter. He spread my legs with his thighs and put his hand in its place on the back of my neck.

"Don't like to explain myself at all, let alone more than once so listen close, Cress babe, because I'll only tell you the one time. I saw a woman across a parking lot in September. It was fuckin' hot as sweaty balls that day, could barely see across the asphalt through the heat waves, but I saw you and you saw me. Don't know what you saw but I saw a fuckin' babe. All that sun-kissed hair and huge eyes—couldn't tell the colour—but could tell they'd suck me in and devour me whole. Little slip of a thing starin' at a biker like you had the right to me, like you'd climb on the back of my bike, on the top of my dick and ride 'til you couldn't take it anymore.

"Saw you in class months later and this woman I'd been obsessin' over was supposed to be my goddamn teacher? No fuckin' way. Not before I'd fucked you." I flinched but he caught my reeling chin between his fingers and laid an openmouthed kiss across my closed mouth, coaxing the seam of my lips open until he could touch his tongue to mine. "Then I kissed you and I'm tellin' you, I could never sell a drug headier than your kiss. I was already hooked but that was the reel."

"King," I breathed.

But he continued, "Got shit for it when I was a kid but I'm a romantic. Read fuckin' *Wuthering Heights* when I was eight and got hooked on the classics. Always knew I'd meet a girl, want her, take her and keep her forever. That would be it for me." He shrugged like he was telling me what he wanted to eat for supper. "Didn't expect it to happen when I was eighteen but you roll with the punches, ya know?"

"I know you're being sweet but you're also freaking me out," I admitted.

King nodded. "You asked, I answered. Don't ask me questions that you don't want an answer to, Cressida, warning you right now. I'll always give it to you straight. It's on you to be careful with that, yeah?"

"Yeah," I agreed, thinking that I wasn't ready, after all of that, to ask him about his current or future dealings in The Fallen MC.

"You were good today, brave with them," he praised, bending his knees slightly so he could look me level in the eye. "Sexy as hell and super badass."

"Yeah?" I asked, brightening because I'd always wanted to be sexy and cool but didn't think I had it in me.

"I'll show you just how sexy I thought it was later," he promised, pushing his hard length firmer against my sex, barely covered by my parted robe and nightgown beneath.

I gasped and grounded myself against him, watched his eyes flash like lightning then did it again just to see the same reaction.

"Dad, H.R.?" he called out to his family. "Gotta talk to Cressida alone for a bit. She's real torn up about all the family drama and shit. You cool to hang?"

Zeus just laughed.

Harleigh Rose popped her head up over the couch to frown at her brother. "Fine but be quick about it, yeah? I haven't even really met the woman yet."

"Might take a while, H.R., she's really riled up," King responded with a wicked grin.

I opened my mouth to scold him for being so freaking obvious but a screech came out instead when he tipped me off the counter and over his shoulder. He walked out of the room with me kicking and giggling until he gave me a brisk swat on the ass. Then, after he dropped me down on my unmade bed, he set about riling me up even more.

# Eighteen.

"Take it."

*God.*

I thought I already was taking it.

But as King rotated his hips against my ass, I realized that he hadn't even begun to fuck me. His fingers curled over my waist, tilting my bottom up from the bed even as the rest of his hard body pressed me into the mattress. His cock hit something in me that lit up my body like a Christmas wonderland.

"Oh my God," I cried into the mattress, aware that King's family was waiting for us downstairs and that technically the stairs that led to my attic room didn't have a door.

"Wanna hear it, babe," he grunted, lifting his lean hips so his length dragged agonizingly slow out of my clutching heat.

"Oh God, please make me take your cock," I panted, looking over my shoulder to see him watching his cock as he pushed it slowly back into my eager pussy, as he ground his hips against me. "God, that's so hot."

"No God in this bedroom, Cress. Call me what I am: your King," he growled, rearing up to catch a fistful of my hair and jerk my head back.

His lips descended over my neck and he sucked hard at the base of it. Distantly, I was aware that he was marking me, hurting me, but I loved it so much, I couldn't bring myself to stop him. I wanted to turn my body into one of his poems, an ode to me written in my skin and bones.

He started slamming into me, fucking me so hard his thighs slapped loudly against my ass, his hands around my hips that were starting to bruise. A black hole of pleasure grew in my mind, sucking up any thoughts or worries, leaving behind ever-expanding bliss.

"Look so fuckin' pretty taking my cock," King grunted into my ear. "Look even better comin' all around it."

His hand went from my thigh down to the tamed curls between my thighs. He pressed the heel of his palm against the skin there while two fingers rubbed hard, tight circles over my slippery clit.

"It's not enough until I hurt you, is it, babe?" he crooned into my ear.

A flush erupted across my skin, turning my already flaming skin to ash. "Yes," I whispered.

In the next second, he reared back onto his knees, lifting my hips high in the air so that I was on all fours. The second after that, his huge hand landed on my ass with a resounding *thwack*. I rocked forward from the impact of the punishing slaps and his brutal thrusts as he beat me with both of them simultaneously.

"Yes," I hissed, fisting my hands in the sheets so I could slam back onto him.

I was so close to climaxing it set my teeth on edge.

All it took was King wrapping my hair around his fist like a leash and jarring me so I sat back down against his cock and he could thrust up into me, his lips on my ear growling, "Mine," to finish me off.

Seconds later, he followed with a hoarse shout that may

have been my favorite sound in the entire world.

We collapsed, his weight heavy and delicious on top of me.

"Better than any fantasy," he muttered after a few minutes of recovery.

"You're awfully sweet for a biker," I teased him.

He rolled off me slightly to land a hard smack to my sore ass. "Did I or did I not just fuck you senseless while spankin' that fine ass?"

I snorted. "Crude."

"True."

I turned my head lazily to find him smiling at me. I smiled back.

"Dad and H.R. are downstairs," he reminded me. "Gotta get showered and ready for the day, babe. Got things to do."

"Oh God, I can't believe your dad and your sister know we just had sex," I groaned into the mattress.

King's hand slid from the top of my head to my tailbone in a languid show of possession. "Don't mind they know I'm fuckin' you."

"You're my freaking *student*," I cried, rolling over so I could toss my hands dramatically into the air.

"Yeah," he agreed easily.

"King," I said, utterly exasperated with both of us. "What the fuck am I doing?"

"You're livin'."

"Does living mean feeling like you're constantly on the edge of making the wrong decision?"

"Yeup."

"Do you ever get used to that?"

King cupped my face, his thumb swiping across my cheekbone. "No, you don't."

I sighed gustily. "I think I need therapy."

His smirk was small but tender, as if he thought I was a dork but an endearing one. "Surprised you don't need it more, comin' from a family like yours."

"Yeah, that's fair," I said.

"Now, you gotta get showered so you and H.R. can start cookin' that huge ass turkey your folks let behind."

"And what are you and Zeus going to be doing while the women cook?" I asked with a raised brow. "This isn't the fifties, you know, and I just spent the last eight years cooking dinner every night for William, with special family dinners every, single Sunday. Besides, I didn't ask you and your family to stay. I appreciate you calling in the troops to help me, I really do, but it would be… I don't know, super weird for us to all have Sunday family dinner together."

King sat up, ignoring the way my mouth dropped open at the sight of his beautifully masculine naked chest. "Weirder than fuckin' while they're waitin' on us downstairs? Weirder than the fact that my dad's pretending to date you to give you protection against your motherfuckin' asshole of an ex? Weirder even than the fact that you just took my cock, a-fuckin'-gain and you fuckin' love it more and more each time?"

"There's no need to be crass," I told him.

"There's also no need to be a bitch for the sake of fuckin' propriety. I'm into you in a big way, Cress, think I've made that pretty fuckin' clear. What you also need to be clear on is this; I may be younger than you, I may be your student in the classroom, but here, with us and in real life, I'm a man who knows what he wants and takes it. No questions asked and definitely no regrets. That's the kind of *man* I am. Now, I get that you don't really know what kinda woman you are because you were tied like a puppet on strings for your ex and your parents. I get it. Doesn't mean I'm going to stick around and put up with this bullshit. I'm not making excuses or apologies and I'm tired of yours. I'm not judgin' you for your past but you keep judgin' me for mine. You want this thing to work, *you* gotta make it work for you, Cress, and fast."

"This thing? King, honey, seriously, we cannot have a thing," I said softly, but even to me I sounded like a broken record.

"Yeah?" He crossed his arms over his chest and glared at me. It would have been funny, the idea of this gorgeous blond man sitting cross-legged and cross-armed naked in my bed trying to convince me to be with him. Any sane or insane woman would jump at the chance.

I know I did.

"Tell me why we can't do this," he dared me, as if he was asking me to debate something difficult, the ethics of capitalism or the merits of torture techniques in modern-day interrogation.

"Um, okay. One, I'm your teacher and therefore in a position of power over you." I ignored his ignoble snort and continued. "So even though you are technically an adult, I can still very much be fired and raked over reputation-ruining coals if anyone finds out about us. Two, the age difference. I may have just gotten out of a mediocre marriage but that doesn't mean I'm over the idea of having a husband and a family someday in the future. You're eighteen and you have your whole life ahead of you. And finally, you're seriously involved with a criminal organization and whether you decided to patch in or not, that will always be a significant part of your life seeing as your father is the President of The Fallen. I'm a soon-to-be divorcée who has only done three bad things in her life and doing them nearly gave me a heart attack!"

"What three things?" he asked, making me feel like he wasn't really listening to me.

I counted them off on my fingers for him. "I took a drag of your dad's cigarette yesterday. When I was eighteen, I accidently led a man on when I was really drunk at a bar. I slept with you."

"Slept with me implies you've only done it once," King pointed out reasonably. "I've been inside you four times in the last twenty-four hours and I had my tongue in you twice before that."

"I think you're missing the point," I reminded him.

He shrugged one shoulder. "You always tell us in class to be specific so, I'm just sayin', be specific."

I rolled my eyes and leaned forward to punch him in one of his delicious pecs. "Do not use my own words against me!"

He snagged my wrist and tugged so that I toppled over onto him and he fell flat on his back. "I'll do whatever I gotta do to get you to hear me. One, we're careful. I'll probably still fuck you at school because, babe, you bein' my teacher is not a turnoff, but we'll be careful. I know you need the job, I got it. Two, I may be a high school student but like I told you, I'm a man. We see where this goes and we like it, I'm into babies and in a way that's more than just likin' the idea of planting them in you." He waggled his eyebrows and cupped my bare sex, still wet from our sex.

I shoved at his hand but only to distract myself from the thought of blonde, pale-eyed babies that looked exactly like King.

"As for the criminal stuff, I don't got much to defend myself other than to say, I'm not asking you to push drugs or lie to the police or carry a gun. I'm asking you to trust that I won't get you involved in any of that. But honestly, right now, I'm just askin' you to give the life a try."

I bit my lip as my thoughts spun fast and clunky like an

overfull washing machine, churning our combined baggage over in my mind.

This was what I'd asked for, what I'd only dared to dream of for the past twenty-some-odd years. A life of adventure with a man strong enough to anchor me through it.

I looked up through my eyelashes at King and asked a question as my answer. "You think I'd look good in leather?"

He blinked then wrapped his arms tight around me and burst into laughter.

"Oh my God, that is totally smokin' on you!" Harleigh Rose shouted at me even though I was only a metre away from her in the small change room of Revved & Ready Clothing.

I also did not think the tight leather mini dress with a V-neck that plunged down to my naval looked "totally smokin'" on me. I thought I looked like a poorly made blood sausage.

I told her so.

She laughed, but I'd already learned that, like her brother, Harleigh Rose loved to laugh and she did so freely, beautifully, with her mouth spread wide over her teeth and her hand pressed to her belly. She was only fifteen but she was already a knockout, with a huge head of streaky blond hair, enormous eyes that were a deep, true blue, and legs so long they seemed to sprout from her ears. Now, if anyone could pull off the dress I was currently trying to wear, it would have been her.

"Yeah, it's a bit much," Maja agreed.

This was Buck's "old lady" (a term I'd just learned meant something a little more intense than "girlfriend" but could also mean "wife"). She was wearing skintight, distressed blue jeans that rode so low on her hips, I could easily see the stamp across her back that declared her "Buck'ed up." A fifty-something woman, she wore the outfit surprisingly well, probably because she looked like a) she didn't give a fuck what you thought and b) if you voiced your unwanted opinion about said outfit in any way, she'd fuck you up.

Seriously, the woman carried a gun in her metal-studded clutch purse.

I knew because she'd showed me in the car on the way to the store.

"I think you should try on the pink one," Tayline commented from her spot on the floor. She held a tub of popcorn on her lap that she'd bought from the old-school movie theatre across the street. Apparently, she never went shopping without sustenance.

"Agreed, we need to sex her up a bit," Cleo chimed in. She was two years younger than me and her dad was also a member of The Fallen who apparently went by the name of Axe-Man.

I didn't know where they came up with these names and when I'd asked the ladies, they'd laughed at me but not in a mean way, more in a "bikers are crazy people, what can we say" kind of way.

"I think King wants to sex her up enough as it is," Harleigh Rose told the others with a wrinkled nose. "He spent like an hour and a half upstairs 'comforting' her after her crazy parents and ex-hubby blew through."

"Jealous," Cleo breathed with stars in her eyes.

"Rock on," Lila crowed. She wasn't anyone's old lady or relation but she seemed to be an intrinsic part of the group that had assembled at the store to help me pick out something appropriate for me to wear to my first biker party.

When I blushed, Hannah, the owner of Revved & Ready

and a woman who showed most of her skin but most of it was tattooed so it was somehow cool instead of indecent, waved away my embarrassment by saying, "Girl, I've been livin' in Cougar Town a long time. Can't say it's a bad place to be. Those boys can keep a woman satisfied all through the night."

"Um, ew." Harleigh Rose made a puking sound. "We're talking about my brother here, Han. Can you maybe rein in your inner pervert?"

"One day you'll meet a man and you'll understand," Hannah told her.

Harleigh Rose made a face but then quickly ducked behind a thick sheet of her hair so she could hide her flush.

Interesting.

But I was really done with the talk of my sex life with my student so I retreated back into the change room while mumbling something about trying on the pink dress.

Seconds later, Tay pushed through the curtain with her popcorn bucket tucked under her arm and took a seat on the stool. When I paused in my undressing, she said, "Oh go on, it's not anything I haven't seen before."

"Yeah, on yourself. Not on me," I pointed out.

"Girls get naked in front of each other, Cressida, it's not a big deal," she said as if I was stupid but then she winced. "I'm sorry, I know you're new to the whole 'normal social behavior' thing."

"Somehow I doubt *this* is normal social behavior," I answered drily but I did wiggle out of the leather dress.

"So, are we going to talk about the last forty-eight hours or what?" she asked just before she unhinged her jaw and shoved a fistful of popcorn into it.

I sighed, but I'd known this was coming since the moment the bell chimed above the door as Harleigh Rose dragged me into the store to meet some of the biker babes and Tayline ended up being one of them.

After King and I finally got out of bed to shower (together in the end, so it took a little longer than normal), we'd joined Zeus and Harleigh Rose in the living room where they'd made themselves totally at home. The pack of beer my dad had left behind was beside Zeus as he reclined in my huge leather chair and he was already on his fourth one while Harleigh Rose had appropriated one of my romance novels and was reading it while sitting upside down on the couch.

I'd worried that it would be awkward because, well, it was awkward. Instead, the Garro family had all acted like we spent every Sunday together like some kind of screwed-up modern-day family.

It was the best Sunday I'd ever had.

Harleigh Rose helped me cook. Not because we were ladies, but because the men were bikers and the only things they could successfully do with their hands were make engines roar and ladies purr (this they told me themselves). When I'd opened my mouth to sass them, King's sister had quietly informed me that they would cook if I wanted them to but that it would be far from edible.

So, we cooked.

And I found out that Harleigh Rose was hilarious, confident in the way of only the most well-loved kids, and utterly genuine. She gabbed away the entire time about boys (of all whom seemed to like her but none of whom she seemed to like), girls (much the same deal), and how awesome The Fallen was. I wondered if Zeus and King had elected her the MC spokesperson because she waxed on about how they organized huge charity fundraisers every year, how well renowned the garage was in the automotive community and how cool it was to grow up with so many "aunts" and "uncles." It struck me hardest when she talked about her mum and how much of a "total bitch" she was but how much it meant to her to have all the biker babes to talk to about things she couldn't go to her mum about.

I wanted that.

It was obvious that Harleigh Rose noticed because when we all sat down to dinner at my rickety dining table that I'd bought from a garage sale for forty bucks, she'd informed the guys that they were going to throw a BBQ to celebrate the start of spring break and to properly introduce me into The Fallen.

I was terrified and I objected until I was blue in the face, but both Garro men seemed to think it was an awesome idea so by the time I served the apple pie I'd made for King that morning, the news had spread through the biker network and plans were set.

Which led me to that moment in the changing room with Tayline, trying on clothes because Harleigh Rose had raced up to my bedroom after dinner to check my closet for "party gear" and found nothing suitable. She'd rounded up some of the biker babes, calling it a "total fashion emergency, like '9-1-fuckin'-1'" and dragged me out of the house to meet them all at Revved & Ready.

My heart had been lodged somewhere in my throat even before I'd seen Tayline. Telling more people our secret didn't seem "careful" of us but when I'd tried to express that to King, he'd laughed and said, "babe," in that way of his that was supposed to be enough of an answer.

I told him he did that and I didn't like it, which made him laugh some more. But then he'd said, "Babe, The Fallen is a fuckin' vault. You think anyone is gonna narc on the fact that the son of the Prez is fuckin' his teacher? Not fuckin' likely."

When he put it like that, it was difficult to argue with him.

Tayline knowing was a whole new kettle of fish.

For one, she was my friend and she now knew that I'd kept a pretty colossal secret from her. Our friendship was new but I loved it, loved her. She was tiny but enormously personable, pretty but unafraid of the ugly truth. Tayline Brooks was the kind of woman who lived the way I wanted to live and I'd be crushed if I'd lost out on having a friend like her because she decided I was a gross perv for sleeping with a student.

Then, of course, there was the unassailable fact that she was my colleague at the school where said student and I conducted our professional (and sometimes overly personal) relationship. Ethically, she was honor bound to tell the headmaster about my inappropriate transgressions. This time tomorrow morning, I could be out of a job and known across Entrance as a whore.

"Told you that night in McClellan's." Her soft voice pulled me away from my miserable inner monologue. "A man without respect for the law isn't a man without respect for anything. That kind of man sees a woman he wants, he's gonna have her even if she doesn't want him at first. Fuckin' wear her down 'til she can't even remember the reasons he wasn't supposed to be her dream man."

I slowly turned around to look at her, my heart jumping from my throat to my mouth. I felt like I was going to throw it up.

Her huge brown eyes were wide and sad on me. "I'm trying to tell you that I understand. First off, the kid is sinfully hot. Like honestly, they shouldn't send a student like that to anywhere but a monastery. Even then"—she shook her head—"he could probably give them some lessons in corruption if you know what I'm saying."

Despite myself, I snorted with laughter.

She sobered quickly. "I'm telling you I get it but I'm also really worried, Cress. I know you look like a Disney princess but this is real life and I think you know enough to understand that happily-ever-afters don't happen real often. Not saying it couldn't happen for you and King but given the circumstances, you can't think the odds are in your favor."

"Trust me," I muttered. "I don't. Honest to goodness, Tay, I don't even know how I got here. One second I'm married and miserable, the next I'm sleeping with a freaking teenage boy."

"And loving it," Tayline guessed accurately.

I nodded and slumped against the wall, only vaguely registering that I was still half naked. "Loving it. He's even hotter than Satan, Tay."

"You're so weird."

"And he's sweet too, in a badass biker kind of way that's even better than normal levels of sweet because it's so manly." I shivered delicately.

She laughed and stuffed another handful of popcorn in her mouth. "Cy is the same way. You've got to watch yourself, The Fallen men take you by surprise. They look broken in ways that can't be fixed but once you get to the heart of them, you find the kind of men most women would pray for, beg, and bribe to be with."

"Yeah," I agreed softly. "And mine just happens to be eighteen."

"In ten years, you'll love the age difference."

"You sound like King. I'm not even legally divorced yet, he's still in school and he's talking like we'll be together for… a while." I shivered, this time in discomfort.

Tay cocked her head and peered at me. "Do you really think you'd jeopardize your career and your reputation for something that *isn't* going to last ten years?"

Her question hit my soul like a hammer to a gong, reverberating through me. The blast set things that had fallen off-kilter in my whirlwind affair with King back into place but at new angles.

I wanted the same things that I always did. Love, laughter and living large right beside fear, anger and tears. I wanted it all, every single thing life had to offer me. It was actually fitting that each one of those things was wrapped up pretty in King Kyle Garro. Like all good covetable things, he wasn't wholly good for me, which made him all the more desirable.

"Glad I could talk some sense into you," Tay joked when she'd had enough of my dazed epiphany.

I laughed. "I love you, Tayline. Really. Thank you for trying to understand."

She stood up, carefully placed her popcorn on the ground so it wouldn't spill, and crossed the two steps it took for her to wrap me in her little arms for a big hug.

"Welcome to crazy town, population badass bikers and their bitches. Us sane ones have to stick together."

Later, after I'd tried on six more outfits and finally settled on one that I knew would blow King's mind, the biker babes and I were at Eugene's just outside of town drinking a Eugene classic cocktail he'd made up called a Maple Sour that was basically just a whiskey sour with maple syrup. It was delicious, and I told Eugene it was officially my drink of choice. I was on my third one.

"The man's got one eye, how the fuck does he stay on target?" Maja asked Tayline who had just recounted a tale of her sexual escapades with Cy (apparently short for Cyclops) on a trampoline in some random backyard one night after they'd been drinking.

"He compensates in other, more important areas," was Tay's sly response.

We all burst into cackling laughter. Harleigh Rose was still there despite being severely underage but she wasn't drinking and apparently, no one would care even if she was because Maja had offered to grab her a beer or cider when we ordered our first round. It was clear that Eugene's was a biker-friendly bar, but I wondered how they got away with things like that with the police.

"Buck may be an old coot now but let me tell you, that man is hung like a horse. Used to be in the early days, I'd walk around bow-legged. That's why the old-timers call me Bow-bow."

I giggled. "And they gave Buck his name because he was your bucking bronco?"

Maja slapped her hand against the table and hollered with laughter before she answered, "Nah, though I fucking love that. He's called Buck because his idiot brother shot him with a rifle when they were teens and he's still got buckshot lodged in his ass."

I covered my mouth with both hands so I wouldn't spit out the sip of cocktail I'd just imbibed.

"They're crazy cool, eh?" Harleigh Rose whispered as she pressed harder into my side.

She had been beside me the entire night, constantly involving me in conversation, touching my hair or grabbing my hand frequently. Despite her cheeriness, I noticed the way she hung on to each ounce of female affection these ladies showed each other and I loved that she'd taken an immediate liking to me. I didn't know if it was weird for a twenty-six-year-old and a fifteen-year-old to be friends, but I had a feeling the deed was already done and I wanted to do nothing but blow the ink dry on the dotted line.

"Crazy cool," I affirmed in a conspiratorial whisper.

She beamed at me.

"You know, I left William the same day I saw King in the parking lot of Mac's Grocer for the first time," I said into the ensuing silence.

The whiskey had made me uncharacteristically communicative.

The girls loved it.

I didn't know if I'd be as big a fan in the morning.

"Fuck off," Hannah said, because she was coarse but also *awesome.*

"No, seriously." I laughed nervously but I'd already committed to telling them. "I was getting groceries and thinking about how my night was going to be the same as every other night I'd had for the last eight years, make William dinner, read then go to bed, only since I'd started working again, we'd probably have an awkward conversation added in about how I shouldn't have started working again. I didn't even realize how boring and sad I was until I saw him and Mute intimidate some preppy college guys."

I shrugged and frowned into the bottom of my empty glass when I went to take another sip. "Saw him and it hit me between the eyes like a lightning strike. Even if I never saw him again after that, he would always be the guy who changed my life."

"Wow." Cleo sighed with her head on her hands. "That's so romantic."

"Be more romantic if my woman actually said shit like that to my face instead of gabbing about it with her girls."

I froze with my empty glass halfway to my mouth (I'd been about to lick the remnants of sweet and sour foam from the inside rim). The women at the table, all loose with liquor and easy with good friendship, grew alert.

"King," I said in a voice that was more breath than sound as I turned to find him standing beside our big booth table.

He was wearing an indecently tight round-neck tee as he usually did when he wasn't in uniform, and his rumpled halo of gold hair was down around his broad shoulders. The way he stood with his hands in his back pockets presented the insane breadth of his chest like a billboard for male beauty and I licked my lips at the sight of it. When I brought my eyes back up to his, they practically glowed in the dark like the neon blues light art behind him.

"Time to go, babe," he ordered darkly.

I gulped loudly and lowered my glass to the table. "I think, um, we were all going to get another drink."

"Darlin'," Lila said as she tried to hide her smile, "your man wants to go, you go."

Instantly, I frowned. "What if *I* want to stay? I'm having fun and I've never had real girlfriends before. I like it."

Collectively, the hard but beautiful faces of the biker babes, Tay (who was somehow only a pseudo biker babe), and Harleigh Rose (who was too young and bright to be hard) softened in empathy.

The sight of it burned down my whiskey-hot throat. I wasn't sure if it was a good feeling or bad.

"We'll be here, you need another girl's night," Cleo said, reaching across the table to give my hand a squeeze.

"And we'll be seeing you Friday at the BBQ in that smokin' hot new outfit," Hannah added with a waggle of her tattooed eyebrows. "You see it, King, and you won't want your woman to leave the house."

"Definitely time to go, Queen," King repeated, his impatience fraying at the edges like rope.

I had the ridiculous urge to ask him to bind my body with his ropelike words, to bend it and secure it into new shapes using just the weight of that tone. Desire must have flashed across my face because he was reaching over Tayline to lift me forcibly out of my seat.

I let him because I loved the way he did it, like I was nothing but a feather. He settled me on my feet, snagged my purse and coat from Tayline's outstretched hands then settled one arm over me. Every time he did that, it felt like a mantle of power across my shoulders.

"Careful," I said even though I loved the gesture, because we were in public even though we were outside of town at *the* biker bar.

His lips twitched. "You don't want to be careful."

I rubbed my legs together to relieve the sudden ache between them.

"Right," he said with a nod.

I watched him drop my stuff into Tayline's lap again and then his arms were around me, one banded across my back and the other in its spot under my hair.

"Been four hours and I already miss this fuckin' mouth," he muttered before he closed his lips over my mouth and ate at it.

Lust rushed through my veins, enlivened by the alcohol I'd consumed. I was drunk on my new favorite cocktail, Canadian maple syrup, Canadian rye whiskey and the seriously delicious taste of all-Canadian guy.

Only when my knees softened like butter and I almost fell against him did King pull away from me. Without releasing his hold, he turned to our table of avid spectators and said, "Thanks for takin' care of my woman. Tryin' to keep her, so it means a lot you took her under your wing."

"Okay, cue the swoon," Cleo said, her eyelashes fluttering like fans.

"Even I have to admit, that was pretty sweet," Harleigh Rose allowed with a little wink sent my way.

"Okay, bye!" I said so loudly it was a shout because suddenly I was the one eager to leave.

The ladies laughed at me as I tugged my badass biker guy out of the bar and into the night. We were both so preoccupied, we didn't notice the unfamiliar bikers hanging out in the corner of the parking lot as we swung onto King's bike, but they sure noticed us.

# Nineteen.

For the eighth morning in a row, I woke up beside King. Or rather, I was sprawled diagonally across him as if he were an island salvation in the midst of a mattress ocean. One of his long arms held me to him, anchored over my shoulders by the other hand that twined in the hair at the base of my neck. Even in sleep, he held me like he would never let me go.

I lay there beside a man-boy I never should have known and loved him secretly, desperately with every atom of my being. I'd loved him since the moment my eyes had landed on him in the grocery store parking lot and since then, he'd not only given me more than enough reasons to continue to love him, but also the means to begin to love my life.

Before King (B.K.), I'd enjoyed my books, going on long quiet walks through Stanley Park and hanging out with my parents.

A freaking pathetic list.

Now, I loved riding on the back of King's black-and-chrome customized Harley Davidson with my breasts to his leather jacket and my hair to the wind. I loved feeling his hands on my skin tuning and revving my engine with his sometimes rough but always-reverent touch. I loved the biker babes and the rest of the Garro clan, the least traditional family I had never interacted with and also, somehow, the most genuine. I loved my students, sweet Benny and misunderstood Carson, beautiful but broken Louise and even Talia and her crew of beautiful but vain girlfriends. They all trusted me to teach them and to love them from afar so even though teaching had never been my original dream, I found myself loving even that.

King had arrived in my life like an angel fallen from heaven and ascended from hell, like my own real-life Satan who whispered rebellion in my ear so winningly I had no choice but to answer his call.

I didn't know if Eve was happy in the end, uprooted in her new life and new world with Adam, but I knew I would be if that future was available to me.

"Shut up," King croaked.

I propped my elbow on his chest, placed my face in my hand and stared down at him. "I'm being quiet."

"'Bout as quiet as a souped-up Mustang drivin' down the Sea to Sky," he muttered without opening his eyes.

"Are you saying I breathe loudly or something?"

"I'm sayin' I never heard someone think as loud as you."

I glared at him, and feeling it, he opened one sleep-heavy eye to see it.

He grinned.

I glared harder.

Then he chuckled, a low sound so deep that moved under me like shifting tectonic plates. I hung on tight and waited for it to pass, liking the way his laughter felt and that I kept discovering new ways to appreciate it.

"Time?" he asked, closing his eyes again but shifting to align me front to front over top of him.

I abandoned my position to press my cheek to his lightly

furred chest, tuck my arms under his back and up over his shoulders. His workingman hands abraded the skin at the base of my spine just over my ass as he stroked me in lazy whorls.

"Early. We've got an hour and a half before school," I told him.

We rode in together sometimes, but not always. I'd objected at first because it seemed blatantly inappropriate to go to school with the same teenage lover that I taught in fifth period English, but King had pointed out that everyone thought I was dating his father so it wouldn't be odd to catch a ride with him in the morning as we were going to the same place. To keep it safe, sometimes other bikers would take me in. Nova volunteered for the job most of the time, which made King especially grumpy, but so did Zeus, Priest, a quiet but beautiful man who didn't ever speak to me unless it was to confirm a question I'd asked, and, surprisingly, Buck. The latter drove an absolutely enormous motorcycle with tall, swooping handlebars called "ape bars" and the engine growled so loudly, I wore earplugs even under my helmet. I loved riding with him though because he told me stories about King and even Zeus, whom I was surprised to learn was only thirty-four. We also always made a point to stop at Honey Bear Café and Bakery so Buck could get his daily donut and I could get a coffee.

"Good, I'm takin' you to school today," King mumbled.

"Okay," I said, smiling against his heartbeat. I may have loved going to school with Buck because he was kind of making it his duty to be my "biker dad" but there was nothing better than riding with King.

"Get up and get ready, babe. I'll be up soon," he ordered sleepily because I needed more time to get ready than he did, given he was a man who rolled out of bed, took a two-minute shower (that is, if I wasn't in it) and left.

I pressed a long kiss to the skin over his heart, infusing the moment with every single ounce of forbidden love I felt for him. Suddenly wanting to cry, I broke away and hustled into the bathroom.

My morning routine consisted of a short shower to wash and shave (a daily necessity now that I had King in my bed every night) and about thirty minutes to blow dry my hair, put on my minimal face of makeup and dress. I stood in my closet trying to pick out a dress or skirt (pants were harder to get off in a hurry if King wanted me during detention, which he often did and I just as often gave in because I was weak and he was *hot*) when I noticed how the small walk-in had changed in the last week.

A surprisingly neat stack of clean T-shirts, all in neutral colours, sat beside a pair of well-loved once-white-now-kinda grey sneakers that King used when he went running every day, usually right after school. Beside those, there was a not-so-neat pile of dirty laundry, men's boxer briefs, again in neutrals, gym socks and his black mechanic's onesie with *Hephaestus Auto* stitched on the pocket.

King had invaded my closet.

It did not bother me.

I was a neat person by training; William and my parents were as close to OCD as you could get without being formally diagnosed. But the sight of King's mess cluttering my closet floor made my heart warm and throb like an open wound. I was a masochist so I poured salt into it by reminding myself that one way or another, this affair would end. Probably in disaster, but definitely, when he either went off to UBC or patched into The Fallen. I was realistic. No freshman university student wanted a girlfriend, let alone a twenty-six-year-old divorcée, and no hardcore biker would want Miss Irons as an "old lady."

I slipped on a light blue cotton button-up dress and a matching headband with a little daisy on it. I caught sight of myself in the full-length mirror as I made to leave and frowned at my reflection. I looked like a freaking grade school teacher—adorable, yeah—but in no way equipped to deal with a biker. Biting my lip, I looked down at the matching cardigan in my hand, dropped it to the floor and grabbed the little black leather jacket I'd bought with Harleigh Rose the other day at Revved & Ready. It was a little incongruous but somehow it looked cute and I decided the bizarre contrast perfectly suited the new me.

I was reading *Zen and the Art of Motorcycle Maintenance* when King joined me in the kitchen a few minutes later. He immediately moved to the coffeepot to pour himself a cup using one of my bookish mugs that illustrated the snitch from *Harry Potter* and said "I'm a catch." It was so fitting, I giggled behind my own coffee cup.

His school dress shirt was still unbuttoned, revealing a tanned column of muscular torso that made my mouth water. He scratched at his abs, caught me staring and smirked.

"No time for a quickie this mornin', babe. 'Less you want to suck me off real quick?"

I blushed but tossed my book at him. "You are such a twerp."

He caught the book easily in the hand not carrying the coffee and shook his head at me. "You need to start cursin', Cress. You teach high school, not elementary school."

I ignored him, plucked my book from his hand when he came over to the table to grab one of the bagels I'd put out for us, and went back to reading.

He laughed. "Like your choice of readin', babe. Like that you're finally tryin' to understand."

I shrugged as if it wasn't a big deal when inside, I was happy dancing that he'd noticed I was making an effort. "It's a classic. It was remiss of me not to have read it already."

A loud pounding at the door made us both freeze. I looked to King but he was already up buttoning up his shirt and moving toward the window over the sink so he could peer around the bushes at whoever stood at the door.

"Huge ass man at your door, Cress," he said. "Do I need to get my gun?"

"You have a gun?" I asked, because that's what seemed important at the moment.

He slanted me a look. "Got more than one. I'll take you to Smoke's Range one day and teach you how to shoot so you can defend yourself when I'm not around. For now, tell me if havin' a huge-ass man at your door is something usual for you."

I thought about it for about two seconds before I was shooting out of my chair and wrenching open the front door.

"Sander?" I asked, my hands flying over my dropped mouth as I took in the sight of my "huge ass" brother.

His handsome face was black and blue. Twin bruises ringed his beautiful dark eyes and another marred his scruffy jaw. His lip was cut and when I reached out to snag his hands, so were his knuckles.

It wasn't, unfortunately, unusual for Lysander to show up at my door bruised and bloodied. Like I'd said, he lived a tough life and didn't seem to be able to get away from it. So, I was prepared for the sight of him.

"Come in, come in," I urged him, gently tugging on his hand when he hesitated.

I settled him at the little table in the breakfast nook and smoothed back his hair so I could press a kiss to his forehead. "Just going to grab the first aid kit, I'll be right back."

He looked up at me with deep, dark eyes that seemed to me like the exact colour of sadness. When he nodded, I hurried down the hall in the opposite direction to grab the kit under the powder room sink.

"Babe, you gonna tell me what the fuck is going on?" King asked as I swept back into the kitchen and straight to my brother.

I halted in opening the metal box and whirled to face him. "Oh God, um, right. I guess, well, King, this is my brother Lysander Garrison. Sander, this is King."

"King Kyle Garro," my brother clarified, speaking tenderly through his swollen mouth.

He shot me an eloquent look, part hurt and part frustration. It had been weeks since he'd asked me to secure him a job at Hephaestus Auto, and I hadn't forgotten, but it wasn't as easily done as it was said. I didn't know why he wanted a job there and now that I actually knew Zeus and his clan of kids and bikers, I wasn't sure if I felt comfortable foisting my sketchy brother off on them.

"Seems you have the advantage," King said, his voice pitched low in that badass biker tone he used when he was pissed. "Only heard about you for the first time a few days ago and I was under the impression you were still locked up."

*Shit.*

Both men shot me looks of glittering betrayal, as if I'd plunged knives into their backs.

"Be grateful. Normally, she doesn't tell anyone about her fuck-up older brother," Sander said finally, but his posture had shifted from pained and tired to straight-backed.

Tension thrummed through my small kitchen for the second time in less than a week.

"Sander, you are not a fuck-up," I began, moving forward

with my initial act of tending to him. As I was pulling out the gauze, the instant ice packs and the hydrogen peroxide gel, I told King. "I don't really talk about Sander because he's private. Seeing as I'm, um, dating you, I realize that maybe I should have told you more about him."

Sander grunted at both my words and his pain as I pressed the ice pack to his jaw. "Don't need anyone knowing my shit."

"Tough fuckin' luck," King snapped.

He was leaning against the kitchen counter across from us in his school uniform minus the striped tie and navy blue blazer. It occurred to me that he should look like a schoolboy waiting for a ride to class. Instead, he looked like a wolf in sheep's clothing, a creature of violence and instincts and sex wrapped up in shiny packaging meant to make him innocent. Instead, it amplified his threat.

"What's your beef?" King asked.

Sander glared at me as he reluctantly answered. "Second-degree murder."

King's eyebrow rose as he coolly appraised the other man. "Bum charge?"

"No." My brother shifted uncomfortably as I gently tended to his cut knuckles. "Did it, did my time for six years and got out for good behavior."

"Why are you showin' up at Cress' door first thing in the morning lookin' like you've been run over by a sixteen-wheeler?"

I was glad King had asked the question because I was dying to know the answer.

"Got caught cheating at cards at Lake Edge Casino," he grumbled with a shrug. "Shit at cards and shit at cheating so it was a dumb idea but I needed the money. It's not easy finding work when you're an ex-con."

I carefully tied the gauze off and tied it at the backs of his hands then placed a kiss on each of his big palms. "So sorry, Sander," I murmured quietly.

He used one of those hands to cup my cheek for just a second before he dropped them back between his spread thighs. It was his way of telling me that he didn't have any regrets.

"How much do you need?" I asked, still soft because I didn't want to ask King to leave but I didn't want him around for this particular conversation either.

Lysander had been my secret, my responsibility and my cross to bear for so long that I almost wasn't ready to share him with anyone else.

"No," King's voice cracked across the floor between us harsher than the flick of a whip. "You are not givin' him any of your hard-earned fuckin' money, babe. You barely have any as it is."

"King," I hissed, because Lysander didn't know that.

"The fuck?" my brother asked, his injured hands coming out to grab my waist when I tried to pull away from him.

"Get your hands off her," King growled.

"Okay, okay, let's lower the testosterone in the room for a second," I suggested brightly, my nerves translating strangely into faux confidence.

"What is he talking about, princess?" Lysander asked me.

It occurred to me that I no longer liked the nickname that, ironically given their differences and estrangement, both my father and brother used on me. Queen and Queenie sounded so much better.

"William took my name off our joint accounts so I was left with nothing when I asked him for a divorce. It was why I had to ask you for the loan," I admitted.

"You told me that situation was temporary," Lysander accused, getting to his feet but swaying when he reached his full height.

"You're sayin' you care? From what I understand, seein' you here right now askin' for money, you're just as bad as her scumbag ex," King snarled.

I pushed him firmly back into the seat and held out a hand to an advancing King. "Stop it, both of you! King, go to the counter and lean on your freaking hands. I do not need you punching my brother when he's clearly already received his beating for the day. Sander, calm down, you're probably concussed and I don't need to be dragging your heavy ass to the emergency room before I go to school. Which, by the way, King and I have to be at in forty-five minutes so we need to wrap this up because he also has a present for me, and no way am I missing out on that because you can't cheat at cards!"

They both blinked at me and when I glared at each of them in turn they finally did as they were told.

"William has turned out to be, unfortunately, more than just a total bore, he's a complete asshole," I told my brother but quickly looked at King to see him smiling at my choice of curse word. "I was really lucky to have my job at Entrance Bay Academy already because, honestly, Dad got it for me through his connections. It's enough to live on but I wanted a place for myself and I wasn't sure if I'd ever get any money from William, so, I asked you for the loan. I'm sorry if it put you out. You told me you were doing well and I believed you."

I had. Lysander had started to be the one to treat me to dinners, to pay for my ticket to the movies and he'd even got me a really cool necklace with the Grim Reaper etched on a silver medallion. I'd never worn it because it didn't really suit me but the thought was lovely.

It was stupid of me though. I should have known by now, looks could be deceiving and just because he'd seemed to have more money, nicer things, it didn't mean he actually *had* the money.

I wondered where it had come from but that wasn't the point of this conversation and was better delved into when King wasn't there to witness it.

"I offered you the money," Sander grumbled. "You couldn't have known. I was working down on Vancouver Island for a bit but I wanted to move back here when you left William." My heart ached with love for him as he shrugged like a grumpy bear. "Harder to find work than I thought it would be."

"That's why you asked for a job at Hephaestus Auto," I concluded.

He nodded. "Heard about it through the grapevine. They aren't afraid to hire ex-cons there and I'm good with my hands."

"Honey," I said moving forward to hug the only man who had ever really loved me. "You could have told me that."

"Yeah," he admitted gruffly. "I cause too many problems for you as it is."

"I caused the worst one," I retorted.

"Shut up, Cress."

"Okay, Sander."

We hugged it out for a long minute, our hearts beating in tandem the way they always did. We were two completely different people who came from a set of parents who were in turn completely different from us, but we loved each other despite of or maybe because of those divergences.

I pulled away to say, "I don't want to see you get beat up anymore, okay? I have some cash on hand." I always did just in case he needed it. "Wait a second okay?"

He nodded but his eyes cut over my shoulder to King. I ignored that and made my way upstairs to my bedroom where I kept Lysander's emergency cash hidden in an old leather boot in my walk-in closet.

I knew without turning around when King entered the doorframe.

"I'm giving him the money, King."

"Not happy 'bout it, Cress babe, but I understand why you feel you gotta do it."

I fell out of my crouch so my knees hit the carpet and I could turn my torso to look at him. "You do?"

His long, rangy form entirely filled the entry as he lifted both arms to hook his hands over the doorframe. The pose made his body into a piece of art, defined by ropes and lengths of hard, flat muscles from his pectorals to his groin, which peeked out from his shirttails like a sexual promise.

"I do. He's your brother and you feel you owe him loyalty. The Fallen operates on that kind of faith, so trust me, I get it. What I don't get and what I am one hundred percent not okay with, babe, is not knowing shit about his circumstances or how he affects your life. He comes to you for fuckin' money? He gave you the cash to buy this house? Don't like that, Cress. That guy fuckin' screams bad news."

I didn't say anything as I rooted around in the boot heel for the wad of money then, finding it, tugged it free with a yank that sent me flying backward. King caught me before I hit the ground.

I looked back at him from my upside down position and said, "Thank you."

He put me back down, stood back and slipped his hands in his pockets. "I'm this close to bein' pissed off."

"Okay, I get that."

I did. His badass biker sense of morals told him that he was the man and I was the woman, therefore he needed to protect me and it was my job to let him. I hadn't told him about

Lysander and his terminal bad luck so he'd been caught unawares by a large, beaten-up man on the front stoop of my house and he'd had no idea how to deal with it.

He nodded curtly, evaded my hand when I offered it to him but followed close behind me as I went back downstairs to my brother.

I gave the money to my brother without a word and watched him painfully swallow his pride before he pocketed it.

"I've got to get going, honey."

"He's goin' with us," King said from behind me.

I spun toward him. "What?"

He ignored me and locked eyes on my brother. "You want a job, I'll get you a job. Want you around to keep my eye on you. My dad's a fuckin' brute so if you think you can pull a fast one of him, think a-fuckin'-gain. You want a chance, you get in your car and follow me and Cress to Hephaestus right now."

God, in that moment, I loved King more than I'd ever loved anything. Even Elvis and Satan. Combined.

Surprisingly, Lysander grew pale and hesitated. "Wouldn't want to put you out, you dating my sister and all. Looks serious."

Before I could respond, King was handing me my school bag, shouldering his backpack and tucking me under his arm. "It is. Wouldn't give you a chance otherwise. My Queen cares about you, I'll make an exception."

"To what?" I asked.

"To my rule. Don't get involved with liars."

My eyes flashed as I fought the instinct to defend my brother but Sander surprised me again by standing up carefully and saying, "Let's go."

We arrived at the characteristically busy garage, which I'd also learned was the biker's base, something called the compound where they also had a clubhouse, the low brick building to the right of the business that had that wicked cool graffiti image of The Fallen logo spray painted on it. Immediately, the guys called out to us as we swung off the bike. From the corner of my eye, I saw Lysander's beat-up Ford truck pull through the open chain-link gate.

"Wanna deal with this myself, babe," King told me as he took my helmet off for me.

I nodded. "I'm okay with that. I'll just go in and drop off the cookies for the guys."

I'd made the men chocolate chip cookies the night before while I'd been waiting for King to get off work at the garage. He'd mentioned before that Maja was currently the Queen of the old ladies because she was Buck's old lady and Buck was VP. If Zeus had a woman, it would be her or, if King had a woman, it could be her. There was no divine right to the Presidency of The Fallen; you had to work hard for that honor—bleed and sweat for your club—but there was something to be said about a biker family, especially one whose ancestors had founded the mother chapter. From what I understood, this fact coupled with King's renowned intellect, made most brothers think that he would one day take the gavel from Zeus. Even though King wasn't sure what he wanted to do when he graduated, I wanted to make sure the bikers liked me (just in case).

I waved at a few of them while they worked on super fly cars as I made my way into the office.

"Mornin', Queenie," Nova greeted me as he leaned over the front desk talking to a gorgeous woman with big, curled black hair and a va-va-voom body that put my elfin form to shame.

"Ah, so you're the famous teacher," she drawled with an

insincere smile. "Heard the Garro men are stickin' their necks out for ya."

Nova snorted. "Don't think it's any skin off the Prez's back to pretend to be datin' a woman as fine as Queenie."

Her eyes studied me from head to toe but she remained unsatisfied. I had the feeling she wanted to stare at me under a microscope until she could identify every single strand of my flawed DNA. Of course, I didn't think someone like her would know how to use a microscope even if she had one, so I didn't worry about it too much.

"Just came to drop off some cookies for you hardworking biker boys." I put the big Tupperware container on the desk and evaded Nova's arm as it lassoed out to catch me around the waist.

In the past week, he'd been caught being too familiar with me by both King and other brothers but even after King had threatened him with castration, Nova didn't seem to be fazed. So, I was careful around him even though I knew he was harmless.

"Name's Paula," the awful woman from behind the front desk told me with a saccharine smile. "I'm a real good friend of King's."

Violence ignited in my belly, great gusts of hatred billowing up my throat tasting like ash in my mouth.

"Name's Cressida," I mimicked her with an equally sweet smile. "I'm King's old lady."

Her lips thinned instantly and she turned to Nova as if he'd betrayed her. "She's what?"

The biker shrugged, rolling an unlit cigarette between his pink, pink lips. "You heard 'er."

"The fuck?" she asked.

"We do," I agreed, nodding somberly. "A lot."

Nova burst out laughing but Paula turned beet-red. I decided to cut out while I was ahead and waved at the biker as I turned to leave.

"Can't wait to see you at the party this weekend, *Queenie*," Paula sneered at my back. "We can really get to know each other then."

I let the glass door shut with a slam behind me and made my way over to Bat, who was working alone on a bike out front. We spoke while I surreptitiously kept an eye on the side wrought iron fire escape that led up to Zeus's loftlike office overlooking the garage bays from inside the massive warehouse.

Bat was a good guy. He was married to a "Grade-A bitch" (according to Harleigh Rose who was my biker life encyclopedia) but he loved his twin boys more than anything and he talked about them all the time. I was going to meet them at the BBQ and I couldn't wait because they sounded like badass bikers in the making. He entertained me with stories about their antics on the weekend, how they'd stolen a poor neighbor's bike, painted it with chrome paint they'd begged their dad to bring home from the shop, and tricked it out with a bell shaped like a skull, and then they'd anonymously put it back in the kid's yard.

My heart melted into a puddle.

So, I was in a good mood when I heard King call my name from across the asphalt.

I wouldn't be when I turned around to see him standing beside a little white Honda Civic with a black hood.

"Like it?" he shouted when my gaze landed on it.

"Um, sure?"

Bat chuckled as he stood up and wiped his hands on the rag he kept in his back pocket. "Queenie, it's your car."

"No," I said slowly. "My car is a dirty white Honda Civic

from 1989."

"Get your sweet ass over here, babe," King called again, his body halfway in the driver's seat with his torso hanging over the opened door.

Reluctantly, I made my way across the lot as most of the men abandoned whatever work they were doing to step into the spring sunshine and watch the unfolding drama.

And I was fairly sure the situation that was unfolding would involve drama because I was not happy.

King didn't seem to pick up on that as he jumped off the car and rounded the hood; already talking about what he'd done to the car, how he'd modified it so it could go from zero to sixty in under thirty seconds, that he'd added a sunroof but also updated the A/C so it would actually work and how he'd put seat warmers in so I wouldn't be cold on the drive to school in the winters.

It was badass biker sweet again, which was too bad because I needed to say what I needed to say and he was most definitely not going to be happy about.

"King," I murmured, aware of our audience. "Stop."

He paused in his excited ramblings, his gorgeous face the picture of Christmas morning joy. I loved that doing something nice for me made him so happy, loved how boyish he was in his enthusiasm for the project.

I told him so then added, "But I told you before I even brought my car in, I cannot afford repairs, let alone all this extra car bling."

His lips twitched, fighting back a smile. "Babe, the 'car bling' was necessary. You're dating a Garro. There is no way a Garro would let his woman drive around in a piece-of-shit car. You're lucky I could work with what you had. Thought about takin' her to the junker."

"You thought about taking Betty Sue to the *junker*?" I repeated, in a significantly higher voice than King had.

Finally, his expression flickered. "Yeah, like I said, it's a piece of shit. But some of the guys helped me in their spare time and now it fuckin' purrs, babe."

"That's great, King. Hopefully you can get a good price from it."

"What the fuck are you talkin' about?" he demanded, affecting the same stance as me but with a lot more intimidation factor. We faced off with our arms crossed and feet braced apart like sailors on rocky waters.

"I told you, I can't afford whatever plastic surgery you've given Betty Sue! You knew that so I don't understand why you felt the need to go *behind my back*, keep me from my only method of transportation for *weeks* and pour thousands of dollars of my nonexistent money into my car." I'd forgotten about our audience even though they'd crowded closer, and my voice had risen to a near shout.

"And I told you, I can't have my woman drivin' a piece-of-shit car," King returned, badass biker voice in full force. "And if you try for one fuckin' second to argue with me about being my woman, Cress, I swear to fuckin' Christ that I'll take you on the hood of this fuckin' car just to prove it."

The idea gave me full body shivers but I ignored them to forge on. "You are suddenly so shallow that you care about what my car looks like?"

A low growl rumbled up from the depths of his throat before he exploded. "It's a fuckin' death trap, Cressida! If you want me to be okay with you drivin' a fuckin' death trap then you are *in*sane."

"And you're insane for completely changing my car without talking to me about it. You were supposed to give it a fucking tune-up, for Christ's sake, King. Now I can barely even recognize her." It was true. Betty Sue looked brand-new with shiny paint and those cool wheel rims that spin the opposite way when you drive.

Actually, looking at her, she looked pretty cool.

"I was doin' somethin' nice for you. You're tellin' me I gotta get you to sign off on it every time I wanna do somethin' nice for you, Cress, then you'll find I don't fuckin' do it anymore."

I shifted my gaze back to the man-boy in front of me and realized that I'd hurt his feelings. His cut-glass cheekbones were flushed with rage, his pose that of a hardened biker at war but those glacial eyes were cracked through with hard lines of pain.

My stomach clenched as the invisible fist of my self-hatred battered against it.

"King," I murmured softly. "I'm sorry, I didn't mean that I was unhappy about the gesture. It's easily the nicest thing anyone has ever done for me. It's only *one* of the many things you've done to try to make me happy in the last few weeks and I didn't mean to throw it in your face like this." I moved forward to try to lay my hand against his crossed arms but he moved back out of reach. The move burned through me, worsened when I heard female laughter behind me.

"I reacted instinctively," I continued quietly. "It's important for me to pay my own way now. Men have been buying things for me nearly all my life. It's more than that too; I don't want to feel like I owe you and I don't want you to feel like you need to get my shit together for me."

"If you haven't realized this yet, you're crazy, but I like to get your shit handled for you," King muttered. "You haven't realized this part either, but you left all that Stepford housewife shit behind and entered my world. And in that world, men take care of their fuckin' women because it's their duty and fuckin' pleasure, whether those women need protecting or not. If there's something you need, Queen, it's your King who provides it for you. You don't like that, you need to learn to eat it."

It wasn't his nicest speech to date or even his most eloquent, but there was something about standing in the middle of bikers on their compound with their one-day King that made his words especially poignant. He'd introduced me to this world, I'd unwittingly already become a part of it and only now was I consciously coming face-to-face with that reality.

As far as misogynistic biker behavior went, King's philosophy wasn't all bad.

I told him so, quietly, just for him.

I was looking for it, so I saw the flash of humor before his eyes clouded over once again.

"Gonna be late for school. The keys are in the ignition. Was going to drive with you but think it's best I catch up with you later," he said.

"King," I tried again.

But he was already brushing past me, his shoulder hitting my arm like gunshot. I reeled back from the pain of blatant dismissal and watched him climb aboard his bike, rev the engine twice and peel loudly out of the lot.

"Blow job," Skell said, suddenly in front of my unseeing eyes as I stared after King.

I hadn't spoken to the Latin biker since the day I'd dropped off my car and he'd called me a piece of ass.

"Excuse me?"

"Offer him a blow job. He'll forgive you soon's your mouth's wrapped around his dick. First off, it's just bad sense to fight with a bitch when her teeth are that close to your junk. And really, no man can stay mad at a woman with his cock in her mouth."

I blinked at him.

"Think about it," he suggested with a friendly pat on the back before he ambled off after the others.

King barely spoke in our third-period history class and looked at me all of three times. Our fight tortured me all day, especially because I'd driven Betty Sue 2.0 to school and she was a *dream*. The seats were redone in pale pink leather that matched the rose gold accents on the dashboard and gearshift. It could have been trashy but it was so utterly classy and exactly what I would have wanted if I'd ever thought about "pimping" my ride.

So, I decided to take Skell's advice.

First, just before the IB English class with King in sixth period that day, I went to the restroom and removed my panties. Then I changed my lesson plan so that half of the students went to the library to work on their final papers about *Paradise Lost* while the rest stayed in the classroom to practice their one-on-one presentations with me in preparation for their IB oral exams.

I made King go first. He barely acknowledged me as he walked to the chair I'd set across from mine between my desk and the white board. I didn't mind. The other kids, quietly working on their laptops while they waited, did not look up while King began his presentation. It was excellent, but of course, he was naturally brilliant with straight As in all of his classes, and one of the perks of being the English teacher's lover was being able to practice your presentation with her in bed.

I waited until he was about a minute into it before I spread my legs to either side of my wide desk chair. King sensed the movement, his eyes flickering up before he could catch himself. I felt the nibble and reeled him in by flicking my loose skirt up with my thumb so he could see the tops of my black lace-topped stockings and my bare pussy.

He didn't move an inch but a sharp intake of air through his teeth gave him away.

When he started talking again, I ran my hands on the insides of my thighs, teasing both of us even though I was already wet.

"Satan is the tragic hero of *Paradise Lost*," King recited as I dipped two fingers inside of me, drew out my juices and painted my clit with them. "He's undoubtedly charismatic, which is how he rallies the fallen angels to continue to rebel against the so-called tyranny of God even after their hellacious defeat in the Angelic War, and he's cunning, the primary example being his manipulation of Eve with her apple. His confidence in these abilities is exactly that which makes him weak. His pride is his hamartia, meaning it leads to his eventual banishment."

His voice had grown hoarse, his breathing erratic as I continued to touch myself for him, poorly hidden by just my desk from the roomful of students. It was nerve wracking in a way that pumped the blood through my body on overdrive. My skin felt too tight, my eyes hot in my head and my breathing loud. The thrill of being caught felt good but it felt delicious to know that I affected him, and even better, when he leaned forward with his forearms on his knees to stare intently at the scene between my thighs.

"The irony is," he continued, "the reader can empathize with Satan in a manner that they can't with God. He is a 'plurality of meanings,' a 'multifaceted' presence that speaks to the complexity of basic human nature. No one person is good or evil, and paradoxically Satan, the character who is traditionally meant to embody all that is bad in the world, is the one to illustrate how natural it is to be at conflict with both, to embody the two."

He paused, reached out to grab my slippery clit between the knuckles of his fore and middle fingers and clamped down hard. My head flew back against the seat as he continued talking, his voice drowning out the minute sounds I tamped down as I rode out my orgasm.

I kept my eyes open and on his as they seared me with a promise, a dirty implied oath to fuck me later with his tongue, teeth and hands but maybe not his cock because I didn't deserve it after this morning. I wanted to moan but instead, I smiled shakily at him.

He adjusted himself slightly in his uniform pants, leaned back in his seat, stuck his two knuckles in his mouth to suck off my cum, and stood up to walk back to his seat, done with his presentation and with me.

Somehow, I managed to sit through the rest of class without getting up because I knew there was a wet spot on the skirt of my dress. King stayed in his seat until the last person left the classroom after the bell and then finally lifted his head to glare at me.

"Shut up, lock the door and come here. Detention is in session."

I swallowed thickly but did as I was told. When I'd pulled the curtain down over the door, I stayed there facing it. There was something about his anger that made me feel completely, provocatively, under his control.

"Turn around."

I did.

"Now come 'ere," King ordered, his eyes sparkling with anger.

I'd never seen him angry before. Lust shot through me like Cupid and his stupid bow were watching from the eaves of my classroom.

King watched me shiver and his eyes melted from ice to liquid. He patted the small desktop attached to his seat.

"Come fuckin' here, Miss Irons," he repeated.

My eyes shot to the door of the classroom. The door was locked and the little paper curtain was doing its job, but still someone could come by. If they found my door locked they'd wonder why. It wasn't unheard of, but it certainly warranted an explanation.

"Don't like repeatin' myself," King growled out.

I was walking toward him before I could make the conscious decision not to. My flared skirt was slippery against the laminate wood desktop so I braced my hands on his shoulders as I hopped up. Before I could get settled, King was putting my calves on his shoulders so he had an unobstructed view of my bare pussy.

"You were a bitch today," King told me harshly. "A bitter shrew I didn't even recognize. Think it's time for you to show me some sweet so I remember why it is I put up with you."

I knew he was angry and that he had a reason to be, but I couldn't stop the blush of mortification and the prickle of defensive anger that ignited somewhere in the base of my belly and tangled with the lust that was kindled there.

"King," I tried.

His gaze cut up from between my thighs and sliced into me. "Do it."

I dropped to my elbows, readjusting myself so I didn't fall off the small table and delicately pulled my skirt up over my groin. His eyes marked each minute movement of my fingers as they crawled down my naked folds.

"You're wet already," he told me.

He didn't have to.

I overflowed like a river in spring, my fingers running laps in the current.

"Show me," he ordered.

I spread my lips open for he could see the depth of my depravity. He could make my pussy glisten for him just by being a badass biker asshole. I didn't know if it said good things about me, but I didn't care.

"Fuckin' gorgeous," he said before he reached out to run two fingers down my slit.

My eyes fell to half-mast and stayed there, weighed by the image of King sitting between my legs like a proprietor evaluating his goods. He was so sexy he didn't seem real. His golden curls were pushed back from his face in a sloppy man bun, a few curls springing out to rest on his ears and in his heartbreaker face. Every time he touched me with his eyes, lips or hands I felt absurdly awed, as if it was a fallen angel that sat between my thighs and not just a man.

He leaned forward to rest his cheek on my inner thigh, his gruff voice abrading the tender skin as he said, "Get yourself ready for my cock."

My fingers dipped into the well of ink and scrolled over my shiny folds, drawing a flourish over my clit. I felt free and powerful spread out for him, showcasing my wares to their best advantage so that he would want to take advantage of them.

His hot breath brushed my sensitive skin but it was the feel of his eyes on me as I dipped one then two fingers inside myself that made my back arch off the table. The movement lifted my pussy closer to him and I heard him drag in a deep drag of my scent.

"Sweeter than apple pie," he praised.

I moaned for him.

"Don't got all day though, babe. You're gonna come for me, fast and hard, then I'm going to clean you up with my tongue."

I panted as his words sent electric shocks through my system. "What about you?"

"Holdin' out for tonight," he muttered, staring fixedly on my fingers as they churned in and out of my sloppy cunt.

I gasped as his rough hand slid up my silky thigh before he sank two thick fingers inside me. His fingers stroked my own as he began to pump in and out of me. It was a tight fight, four fingers stretching me wide, his and mine. Together we fucked my pussy until I was so wet, it leaked down my crack and soaked the desk beneath me.

"Feel good?" he asked.

"So full," I panted.

His head descended and two seconds later, my clit was clasped tightly between his lips. He sucked, flicked his tongue like a whip strike against the tender flesh.

I came apart at the seams. My fingers stopped moving inside my clenching sex but King kept coaxing my orgasm higher and higher, pressing his palm hard against my pubis so the pressure was nearly unbearable.

"King," I groaned over and over, my breathing coming out in a sobbing burst.

My legs flailed over his shoulders. He bit down hard on my thigh and I screamed. It was too much; I was drowning beneath the onslaught, my breath stuttering in my lungs.

But King wasn't done.

He slipped a finger down the slippery line of my ass and rubbed at my asshole.

"Gonna take this," he growled, sliding the digit smoothly inside me. "Soon."

“Please,” I sobbed as sensation pounded into me.

I was caught in the riptide, floundering over and over again. The last of my control broke loose and I gave into the descending darkness with a stammering last gasp.

When I opened my eyes again, some minutes later, King was gently easing our fingers out of my body and gathering me into his lap. I was sprawled over the desk and his chair like a used rag, wrung out.

I felt wonderful.

“Wow,” I breathed as I snuggled into his arms.

He chuckled and rubbed his cheek over my hair.

“What’s tonight?” I asked because I could feel his erection like titanium steel against my ass.

He pulled back to look down at me imperviously. “Tonight, you’re the student and I’m the teacher.”

I tried to swallow my gasp and choked a little.

“Pigtails, knee socks, and those sexy white cotton panties you like to wear under a little skirt.”

“Let me guess, a plaid skirt?”

“Doesn’t matter, babe. It’ll be flipped up when I get you bent over the desk about two seconds after I get my hands on you.”

“Ohmigawd,” I murmured.

Even though I’d had the orgasm to end all orgasms just a few minutes before, I felt my swollen sex tingle at the thought of his fantasy.

“You’re going to kill me,” I groaned.

He shrugged, jostling my entire body. “You’ll die a happy woman.”

“That’s for sure,” I agreed. “I should update my will, just in case.”

His body jostled me again as he laughed.

I was so consumed by the sound that at first, I didn't process the horrible cry and subsequent crash as something fell heavily against the locker outside the classroom.

King was on his feet immediately. I stood dumbly as he took my face in his hands, bruised my mouth with a kiss and said in a no-nonsense badass biker going to work kind of tone, "Stay in here and lock the door behind me."

Then he was opening the door and darting into the hallway.

It took me about thirty seconds to follow him.

When I rounded the corner, it was to see King with his forearm against Carson Gentry's throat. The jock was a big guy, stockier than my blond king from his football and soccer playing, yet King had him dangling off the ground and he was currently snarling into his face.

That occupied me for all of two seconds before I noticed the boy on the ground writhing in the midst of a seizure. Another second more and I realized it was my beloved Benny.

I was on my knees beside him the second after that. All the staff at Entrance Bay Academy were required to take first aid training every year but panic was overloading my system, the adrenaline obliterating everything I'd been taught, so I just kneeled, helplessly stroking his sweaty hair back while he convulsed. Visions of my bachelorette party swam through my head; Marcus Whitman bleeding out in my arms while Lysander tried to get rid of his gun and the police sirens began to call from down the street.

"Queenie," King barked over his shoulder at me. "Cradle his head, pull his belt off and put the strap in his mouth so he doesn't bite off his tongue, then call 911."

King's familiar voice kicked me into gear, triggering the natural obedience that sat deep in the heart of my psyche while also reminding me that I was more than capable of dealing with this calamity.

Calmly, I followed his commands. Benny's paroxysms weren't as violent as they had been even thirty seconds ago but his hair was soaked through with cold sweat and his beautiful lips were purple. He was unresponsive when I tried to speak with him, which nearly made sheer terror overtake me again but then Warren was in the hallway, his cell phone to his ear.

Vaguely, I listened to King as I stroked Benny's sweet, clammy forehead.

"What the fuck did you give him?" he ground out.

He sounded horrible, menacing and full of violent fury like one of Satan's vengeful angels. There was a sound of clanging metal as King proved his wrath by slamming Carson back against the lockers.

"I don't know, man. The guy said it was just some ecstasy or some shit like that," Carson whimpered through his tears.

I didn't want to look away from Benny's face because it was the only way I could monitor his thin, reedy breaths but I had no trouble imagining the petrifaction on Carson's face.

Another rattling clang. "Who'd you get it from?"

"I don't know! Some guy at Evergreen Gas."

"What the fuck were you thinkin' doin' random drugs on fuckin' campus?" King growled.

Carson's pause was long and full of something heavy and dark.

Another crash as King threw him brutally against the metal at his back. "Fuckin' talk. That kid is laid low because of you and I want to know why."

"We hook up, okay?" Carson admitted in a broken whisper that ended on a sob. "We meet up at the gas station and usually drive around or come back to campus to find a quiet place to hook up because I don't want anyone knowing we do that shit together, okay?"

Somehow, even through my already considerable shock and horror at the situation, this surprised me and not in a good way. Tears pricked the backs of my eyes as I leaned down to kiss a now still and unconscious Benny's forehead.

"My sweet Benny, why didn't you tell me?" I whispered.

He must have been so confused and excited about his secret hookup with one of the hottest guys at EBA. It made me furious that Carson would subject sweet, loving Benny to secrecy and gross hookups but it made me want to literally (and I was an English teacher so I really did mean *literally*) kill Carson to know that he'd given Benny drugs.

"And the drugs?" King continued, totally unfazed, totally focused on getting the information he needed.

"I don't know, I heard that it made sex better," Carson mumbled.

"Fucking pathetic," King spat out.

There was a spluttering sound and I imagined that King was pressing his arm harder across Carson's throat.

I wanted him to keep it there until Carson couldn't breathe anymore.

"Cressida, the police said they'll be here in ten minutes tops," Warren said to me as he took a crouch beside us.

I looked up briefly to see his eyes wide and his skin pale as he stared down at the prone Benito.

"He's such a good kid," I whispered and only realized that I was crying when tears slipped into my open mouth.

"He's going to be okay," Warren assured me, but he didn't sound sure.

"Is he?" Carson croaked out.

"Shut the fuck up," King roared into his face. "You think you deserve to breathe, let alone talk when you got that kid fuckin' overdosing in a goddamn hallway? You're lucky I don't put your cowardly ass in the hospital too."

"King," I murmured quietly.

He heard, though, and just like he had done with me, my voice brought him calm.

Flashbacks toyed with the edges of my vision as the sound of sirens came from down the street.

# Twenty.

I spent the night at the hospital.

Benny's family told me I didn't have to stay but I could tell that Arturo and Anna Lucia, the proprietors of the fancy La Gustosa restaurant and Benito's guardians after his parents died in a car accident a few years ago, were happy to have me sit with them. They both cried when they saw me, not because we had any special bond but because, apparently, Benny had told them about me. I started crying too when they wrapped me in their semolina-scented arms and prattled on about how much Benny loved me and how grateful they were that he felt he had someone to talk to.

So, we sat together, my hands in Anna Lucia's, while Benny's stomach was pumped and then he was given some kind of anti-fentanyl drug called Naloxone to mitigate the effects of the chemical already in his system. Apparently, the first few hours were the most dangerous in these kinds of situations so it was a relief when the clock struck midnight and Benny was still breathing.

King had disappeared at some point after giving a brief statement, which I was grateful for both because I didn't really want him mixed up with the police and because he would want to comfort me, I would want to accept that comfort and it was not the time or place for that to go down.

The police interviewed Carson but there were no legal consequences to his actions. This enraged me. How could my brother have been sent to jail for protecting me, and Carson didn't even get a ticket when he'd nearly killed an innocent?

I was so angry that when Carson had the gall to walk up to the Lucias to ask for an update on Benny, I took him aside myself.

We walked down the yellow-lit halls, our shoes clacking on the chipped linoleum floors. I wanted to get control over my anger before I opened my mouth but only mildly succeeded. We stopped at a vending machine and stared at it as if we would get something, as if it held the profound answers to all life's important questions and we only had to press the right combinations of buttons to own them for ourselves.

"I didn't know you were gay," I started and somehow my voice was smooth, pretty casing over the hollow words. "I wish you'd felt comfortable talking to someone about it."

"Dad's a homophobe," he muttered.

"That's hard. Not a reason to treat the boy you like the way you have been, sneaking around with him like you're ashamed of him, and it's certainly not an excuse to give him drugs. Honestly, I can't even imagine what you were thinking."

Carson's jaw ticked, his eyes laminated with tears. "I take it when I have sex with girls, makes it, uh, easier for me. I figured if I did it with Benny who I'm actually into, it would be amazing. Plus, I told him about doing it with girls and he got really jealous, wanted to give me the same thing even though I said I didn't need it."

"Shouldn't have made him feel that way in the first place, Carson," I said softly because he'd started to cry, silent tears of shame. "Shouldn't have given into him either."

"Yeah," he croaked. "I know."

"I think this is a wakeup call, buddy. You need to step up and be there for Benny while he gets better and you need to be open with everyone about who you got those drugs from."

"I already told the police that it wasn't one of The Fallen dealers," he said quickly, his eyes darting to me for the first time. "I know you're dating Zeus Garro."

I put my hand on his shoulder because I didn't want him to be afraid of me because of that. "You're not in trouble with them, Carson. It's Benny you need to focus on. If you still can't do right by him then you need to be man enough to tell him, okay?"

"I'll do right by him," he mumbled, looking to the floor for guidance.

"Your parents coming?" I asked because I knew his parents often worked and stayed down in Vancouver.

"Yeah," he tipped his head with his eyes squeezed shut, tears leaking out from under them. "He's gonna kill me."

I didn't want to think of the kind of father who would make his son feel that way but it made it easier to empathize with Carson and I knew that he needed someone in his corner to prop him up while he got his feet beneath him again so he could move forward on the right path.

"You call me if you need me. I'll come pick you up," I offered. "I'll get you a hotel room or something, okay?"

He looked at me then, turned right into my face and stared right into my eyes. I let him search them with his frantic spotlight stare until he found what he needed to find and then, because I knew it was coming and even though I hated him for what he'd done to Benny, he was just a kid and he needed the comfort, I opened my arms to accept his hug when he drooped forward onto my shoulder and burst into tears.

His mother came into the hospital to pick him up and I spoke quietly to her about the events of the evening. She looked sick to her stomach about Carson's fears because she knew her husband would freak out. I pretended not to notice the bruising she wore around both wrists like shackles and she promised me that she would take care of her son, even if it meant leaving her husband. From the frantic determination hardening her face, I knew she meant it.

After, I went back to sit with the two elderly Italian immigrants again and took up Anna Lucia's hand.

Benny woke up at three in the morning and his guardians let me see him. His throat was too sore to speak but I sat on the edge of his bed, stroking back his dark floppy hair and reading to him from the copy of *Zen and the Art of Motorcycle Maintenance* that I'd stuffed in my bag that morning. He fell asleep again shortly and, soon after, I followed, my head cocked uncomfortably against the orange plastic chair.

I woke up at seven o'clock, said goodbye to the Lucia family and left the hospital to go home for a quick change of clothes before heading to school.

When I walked through the automatic glass doors to the parking lot, King was there, standing against his bike with his arms crossed and his eyes shut. I stopped midstep, staring at his beautiful face, creased like bed sheets from a sleepless night tangled up in them.

Feeling my eyes on him, he looked up and right into them.

My breath left my body in a long whoosh and then I was sprinting across the driveway. He caught me without effort, braced and ready for my full body impact into his arms. I wrapped my arms and legs around him immediately, tighter than vines and just as unyielding. My face planted in his neck, in that fragrant spot just behind his ear where I could soothe myself with the scent of his hair, scented with fresh sea salted air, and the familiar warm laundry aroma of his clothes.

"Got you, Queenie," he murmured, his hand diving under my hair to enclose the back of my neck in his hold. "Got you."

I just clung to him, incapable of speech after the long night without sleep, after the long hours worrying about Benny. It was impossible in that moment to care if anyone we knew could see us embracing in the middle of the hospital parking lot.

All that mattered was being in King's arms. I needed that feeling more than I needed my next breath of air. There were limits to the human body, five days without food, three without water. I'd just learned that mine was twenty-four hours without King.

"Let's get you home, babe," he murmured, gently peeling me off him so he could settle me in the "bitch seat" on his bike.

As soon as he was situated, I slumped against him pressed groin to cheek on his back and wrapped myself around him again, even my legs, which I hitched up and over his thighs. It was a precarious position. I was entirely reliant on King to balance the weight of the bike and keep me from tipping over but I didn't care and apparently, neither did he.

When we reached Shamble Wood Cottage, it was obvious to me that he'd spent the night there even though I'd stayed at the hospital. The dishes we'd left in the sink the morning before were put away and there was a giant bouquet of flowers on the dining room table that King told me were from Maja and Buck. There were fresh sheets on my bed, pale pink instead of cream, and it was made with all the little pillows I only bother with if I had company over.

King steered me into the bathroom, turned the shower to scalding and shucked off my clothes. I was numb to everything but his touch, which seared me each time it landed. I was tired of feeling so I shied away from it and was grateful when he shoved me into the shower but didn't join me.

When I emerged there was a pretty white polka dot red dress with a cream cardigan on the basin. The sound of King murmuring to someone on the phone in the other room filtered under the crack of the door but I ignored it and focused on pulling myself together.

I wore more makeup than usual, but a girl's got to do what a girl's got to do to feel pretty, especially on the bad days.

King stared at me long and hard when I finally left the bathroom, assessing my mindset, probably.

"I'm ready to go," I told him, surprised by how hollow my voice sounded.

He strode forward, grabbed my hair hard in a fist and jerked my head back as he pressed himself hard against me. I gasped, instantly and inappropriately turned on by the gesture when I should be grieving.

"Know you're hurting, my Queen," he said softly despite his intractable expression and dominant stance. "But Benny is alive and gettin' better in the hospital. You've got nothing to grieve for, you hear me? He's *alive*. And that's probably because you and me were foolin' around in detention and overheard him. That asshole Carson didn't have a fuckin' clue what to do. *You* and me, babe, we helped Benny. That's somethin' you need to hold on to right now, not the bad stuff that happened last night, but the fact he's okay and you helped see to that, yeah?"

King's words coated my skin, sat on the surface of me for a long minute while I fought their meaning, tried to stay helplessly lost in overwhelming exhaustion and an overindulgence of empathy. When my eyes started to slide through him, he pulled harder on my hair and, when that didn't work fast enough, he kissed me.

He kissed me the way little girls dream about being kissed at their weddings, the way teenagers like to see in movies. The way most grown women have given up on wishing for.

I lost myself to the kiss, to King's strong hold on me, and when I emerged on the other side, I was once again the Cressida I'd been trying so hard to be.

King watched me with his moonshine eyes. "Good?"

I pressed my lips softly to his then spoke against them, "Thank you."

"Told you, I got you, babe."

"Now, I know it, King," I replied, running one hand down his arm so we could link fingers.

"Ready for school?"

"You'll be there, right?"

He grinned and squeezed my hand. "Until June eighteenth, babe."

I laughed a little and it felt really good. "Then, yeah, babe, I'm ready.

Classes were going well. Everyone was deeply rattled by what had happened to Benny but very few students or faculty knew the full story, mostly because Carson Gentry's family owned half the town and I was sure he had a part in keeping his son out of the narrative.

My IB English and history classes were especially subdued by the news but I put on movies in both classes so they could zone out and relax. Everything was going well until the end of the day when an announcement went out that there would be a town hall meeting at six that night, and that it was mandatory for both students and faculty to attend.

"Is that normal?" I asked Tayline and Rainbow as we had a cup of tea after school in the teacher's lounge.

Before EBA, I never would have thought I'd enjoy hanging out in a teacher's lounge but the academy was superbly funded so the teachers enjoyed a mahogany-paneled, multi-room space on the ground floor of the main building that included a beautifully appointed kitchen, a full bathroom and an enormous lounge decorated with plush leather chairs and couches, plaid pillows in the school colours of navy blue, green and yellow, and a media centre on the other side of the room from where we sat.

Our trio liked the window banquette tucked away at the narrow end of the communal area because it afforded us a grand view of the room (perfect for gossip target practice) but also the privacy we needed to properly talk (gossip).

"It's happened twice before," Rainbow answered after sharing a concerned look with Tay. "Once, after a kid went missing and the town pitched in to find him. That was probably, oh, twenty years ago? And then again when two girls at EBA got pregnant in the same year, this was probably 2010, and the pastor and his son, the mayor, joined forces to warn about the perils of sex before marriage."

"Wow."

Tayline nodded. "I'm telling you right now, it's not going to go well for The Fallen."

"It shouldn't go well for them," Warren cut in, appearing by our table with a suddenness that disturbed me. I wondered where he had been lurking to overhear our conversation. "They've been causing problems in Entrance for years."

"Oh please," Tay said while rolling her huge, chocolate-brown eyes. "The Fallen have protected us from tons of crime. We have one of the lowest rates of drug abuse, drug-related crime and murder in small town Canada. It's their protection that buys us that statistic."

Warren was a handsome man, clean-cut and brunet with blue eyes in a way that most women liked, but when he looked at Tayline as he did then, eyes narrowed and mouth pursed over the sour lemon of thought perched on his tongue, I thought he was hideous.

"They're thugs and they've been given free reign for too long this town. I'm a personal friend of Mayor Lafayette's and I think you'll find he has some very…persuasive things to say about your darling MC tonight."

Rainbow snorted. "Come on, Warren. You grew up here same as me and Tay did. You know they aren't bad guys."

"Sure, that's why Benito Bonanno is in the hospital after a drug overdose," he quipped.

The blood drained from my face both at the reminder of last night's horrors and at the reality of what Warren was saying. They were going to pin the accident on the MC.

I didn't know what that meant for King or Zeus, but it couldn't be good.

As it turned out, it wasn't.

"We need to reaffirm governmental and legal authority in this town," Mayor Lafayette preached later that night from his chestnut podium in Town Hall.

I'd never been to the massive ivy-covered brick building in the centre of town. I wished I were there under more auspicious circumstances because everything about it was old and beautiful. Instead, I sat in one of the packed rows of the main auditorium listening to a tall, middle-aged man with great hair talk about the evils of the MC and the laziness of Entrance citizens in giving them free sovereignty over society.

"We have let these bikers run roughshod over our town for too long. It's time to take it back from them," he finished, which prompted an uneasy round of clapping.

It was uneasy, Tayline informed me from my right side, because The Fallen were actually great for the town. They supported local economy, kept drugs (hardcore ones at least) out of the city proper and brought a lot of foreign business into town because of the popularity of their custom car and motorcycle outfit. The MC had been unpopular until nearly ten years before, when the President who preceded Zeus tried to get into the narcotics game and, thankfully, failed.

"And how do you propose we do that, Mayor?" Stella stood up, her back ramrod straight and her voice hard. She was the owner of the diner in town. People loved her and respected her so they all listened to her, waiting to take their cue from her tone.

"We increase funding to the police department, for one," Mayor Lafayette said with a winning smile. He gestured toward the lineup of policemen standing to his left side on the stage. They were all relatively young and absurdly beautiful. I knew the mayor himself had probably gone down to Entrance Bay Police station to handpick the prettiest cops for his dog and pony show.

"We will also be urging establishments to take down their 'biker friendly' signs," the mayor continued.

"That's horseshit," someone called from the audience.

There was a chorus of agreement.

The mayor opened his mouth to respond when the old oak doors at the back of the hall swung open with an atmospheric creak and the bikers appeared.

Zeus led the small collection of The Fallen down the central red carpet, through the rows of civilians until he stopped directly at my row. The hushed interest of the congregation was thick around us as he put a hand on my shoulder before glaring at the people sitting in the row next to Tayline and me.

Immediately, they scrambled to their feet and moved toward the edges of the hall where the overflow of people remained standing.

"Scoot over, teach," Zeus told me in his super badass biker growl.

I immediately did as I was told.

Harleigh Rose peered around her dad's shoulder to grin at me. "Sup, Queenie?"

"Hey, honey," I whispered as she moved onto the wood bench beside me.

She took my hand immediately between two of her own. I felt the tremor in her hold and squeezed her tighter.

King nodded at me as he took his seat beside Zeus. His eyes were perforated with unease as Nova, Bat, Buck and Priest settled in after him. I wondered if it was because, in sitting with me so publically, they were inexorably linking me to the MC and given the current climate, King was worried about what that would mean for me, or if I would be angry over the display of ownership.

I wasn't. My righteous fury had been ignited by the mayor's witch-hunt against The Fallen. Not only did I want everyone to know where I stood, which was interminably beside the bikers, beside King, but also that I would tear into anyone who claimed they were involved with Benny's incident.

"Yes, good to see you taking part in the community in a legal and civil manner, Mr. Garro," Mayor Lafayette finally said, addressing the elephants that had stomped in the room in their loud motorcycle boots. "Maybe you'd like to say something about your part in the increase of narcotics in this town."

"Mayor, this isn't the time or the place," a handsome blond policeman stepped forward to say quietly.

"Danner, if I wanted your opinion, I'd ask your daddy for it," the mayor ground out.

*Ouch*. That was not only unnecessary but also cruel.

I *really* didn't like Mayor Lafayette.

"I'm happy to talk to folks, Mayor," Zeus spoke clearly, loud enough to reach the far sides of the auditorium and not need a microphone. "They know I'm always up at Hephaestus Auto or at Eugene's havin' a beer. They got somethin' to say, I'm around."

"Do you have anything to say now that one of our children is in the hospital recovering from a drug-related incident?" the mayor said between his teeth.

Zeus affected a hurt expression. "Well, of course I feel for the boy and his family. Queenie"—he dropped his arm around Harleigh Rose so his fingers could sweep over my shoulder—"and my boy, King, were the ones to find him. Cress stayed at the hospital all night 'cause she's real close to the kid."

"And *your* involvement?" the mayor prompted.

Officer Danner shifted uncomfortably behind him.

The auditorium was quiet as a gravesite, watching the standoff between the two leaders of their community.

A slow, predatory smile cut through Zeus's harsh, handsome features. Light glinted off his teeth, set fire to his pale eyes so that he seemed like the Devil sitting in a church, daring God to smite him.

"Don't got any involvement other than that, Mayor Lafayette, and don't much appreciate your insinuation. I'm an active member in this community. I'm a business owner and a father. My daughter goes to Entrance Public and my son goes to EBA. I even pay my fuckin' taxes on time each year. I hope you're not insinuatin' that just 'cause I'm a member of a recreational motorcycle club, I'd be involved in somethin' like drug distribution?"

"I think that's exactly what he was insinuating, Zeus," Stella said, still standing.

"You haven't had problems with the MC in years, Benjamin," an older man stood up to say.

"Yeah, well, we're having them now, John," someone else yelled out from behind us.

"You got questions for me, Sergeant," Zeus said, his low voice undercutting the increasing chatter. "You come ask 'em. This public fuckin' defamation is grounds for me to sue the city."

I pursed my lips because I wasn't sure that was true but it seemed like a good threat.

The staff sergeant stepped forward from the lineup with his thumbs in the belt loops of his uniform. He was the officer in charge of the small RCMP outpost in town and from what I heard, he was a member of the old school policing mentality. He did not like Zeus or The Fallen and it was obvious by the displeasure that creased the plethora of lines across his face that this apathy had reached new heights.

"Trust me, I'll find a way to get you into the station for some questions," he promised darkly, leaning over Mayor Lafayette to speak into the microphone.

"We have a list of businesses who will no longer accept your bikers as clients," the mayor added. "You might want to spread the word to the rest of your gang. Entrance is no longer putting up with drug dealers and ruffians. Until our streets are clean, you're the ones we're looking at."

"Now," Mayor Lafayette announced before Zeus could respond. "Let's open the floor to questions."

As chaos erupted around us, Zeus turned to his crew and said quietly, "You heard the motherfucker, we find whoever is selling kids fuckin' fentanyl and we end this."

A shiver ripped up my spine like something had taken a knife to my vertebrae. I locked eyes with King and saw the violence in his, the promise to enact the kind of retribution I'd only read about in novels or seen on TV. I didn't feel in any way prepared to deal with this side of biker life, but it seemed I had to be ready whether I wanted to or not.

Nervously, I waited for King later that night in the second bedroom I'd made into a little office. The room was cold because the entire back wall of windows extended into the room and the insulation was poor, though King had mentioned bringing in a few of the brothers to help us fix it.

I shook my head at my use of the plural. Since I'd given into his sinful temptations, we hadn't spent a single night apart. It was strange to spend so much domestic time with a man other than William. I'd known everything about my husband and had taken most of it for granted just as he did with me. I wanted to say it was something that happened gradually over time, but that obsessive passion that made even the little moments together glow like faceted jewels had never existed between us, not even when I was young and especially eager to please.

It was not this way with King. I was fascinated, time after time, by his nightly routine. Mostly, he didn't have one. Each evening when he arrived at my house, always after me because he had club business and his job at Hephaestus to attend to after school, we did something different. One night, he stormed into the house, literally threw me over his shoulder and took me for a ride up and down the Sea to Sky Highway, all the way to Whistler and back. The next, he brought home burgers from Stella's because he had remembered I wanted to try them, and we watched *Sons of Anarchy* on Netflix because I'd told him I was doing research and it had made him laugh. One night, we went to Eugene's and shot the shit (a term I learned from Tayline who was my biker babe guru) with some of the guys and their old ladies, including Maja, Lila and Skell's woman, Winona (who was horrible, but I still felt badly for her because Skell was an animal and slept with anything in a skirt).

It was only just before bed that King succumbed to routine like a normal person and it was this that I loved to watch. He peeled out of his clothes in under twenty seconds as if once he had made the decision to undress, he couldn't bear to have the clothes on him any longer. He always left them in the same corner of the closet (because he wasn't a pig, he'd told me when I asked him about it) and then moved into the bathroom to brush and, I couldn't believe it either, floss his teeth.

My badass biker king flossed his teeth.

It explained why he had such pretty canines but still, it always made me laugh to see him dutifully care for his teeth.

I was tugged from my contemplation as the screen door at the side of the house opened with a soft screech, then the main door after that. King never used the front door. When I'd asked him why, he explained that only guests use the front door. It was a weird philosophy but I kind of liked it.

"Cress babe?" he called out.

Even in the two words, I could hear his frustration with the events of the past thirty-six hours. I wanted to take his burden away from him and I thought I had the perfect idea of how to do it, which was why I was perched on the edge of my desk in the freezing study.

"In here," I called, my voice unintentionally husky with anticipation.

My heart palpitated unevenly as the steady thump of his boots grew closer. When he rounded the corner, I had to catch my breath at how stunning he was. The impact of his masculine beauty affected me the same way every time I saw him, whether it was minutes, hours or days since I last laid eyes on him. He was just that beautiful, and I was just that sunk.

"What do we have here?" he asked, leaning against the doorframe in a grease-smeared tee and his favorite old blue jeans. His hair was in disarray, loose around his shoulders but so blond it glowed even in the low light from the single desk lamp I'd turned on.

I licked my lips at the thought of the game I'd set in motion.

"I came to talk to you about that extra credit you said I could earn," I said, looking up at him through my eyelashes as I wiggled my hips coquettishly back and forth. The movement swished my little plaid skirt over the sensitive skin of my thighs and made me shiver.

He hadn't specified plaid in his fantasy but I thought it was appropriate.

I watched his eyes crackle and burn, like fire caught in ice. They swept over my outfit from head to toe, taking in the tight blouse tied under my breasts, the knee-high, navy blue socks and little Mary Janes I wore because I didn't own sexy heels. His gaze lingered over my pigtails, tied with navy blue ribbon into big bows at each end.

"Well, little Miss Irons, I'm not sure you're up for the assignment. It's quite…hard," he said, humor and desire ripe in his voice.

I loved that about him, that he could make sex delicious

as well as fun.

He walked with purpose around me to sit down in the chair behind the desk.

"Well, did you do as I asked?" he asked.

I fidgeted. "What do you mean, Mr. Garro?"

"Are you wearing panties?"

I swallowed. "No, sir, I'm sorry. I didn't have any clean cotton panties so I thought it best I didn't wear any at all."

His face darkened, his beautiful mouth twisting into an ugly sneer that made my thighs quiver. "That's very disappointing, Miss Irons. I'm going to have to punish you for that. You say you want extra credit but then you don't come prepared… How does that show me that you're committed to getting better grades?"

"I'm so sorry," I whispered and I found that I was, desperately sorry and so eager to please that my mouth watered at the thought of how he might use me.

He sighed as if I were an annoying child. "Come here and lay across my lap."

I shivered as I made my way to him and awkwardly placed myself over his groin. The feel of his thick cock under my belly made me wiggle against it.

"Be still," he ordered as he flipped up my skirt to reveal my bare ass. He tsked, but his hand came out to rub over the naked globes. "Was really lookin' forward to those panties."

I bit my lip to keep from groaning when I saw him reach out to grab the wooden ruler I'd purposely left on the desk earlier.

He tested it on his palm, the harsh snap making me jump, and he chuckled.

"I'm going to spank you for each time you disobeyed me in class, Miss Irons. Do you remember how often that was?"

"I think it was twenty times," I answered immediately.

"Hmm, don't think so. Let's try ten."

The first crack of the wooden ruler slapped against my ass with a loud *thwack*. It rocked me forward against King's erection in a delicious way that had me thrusting back for the next strike.

"Good fuckin' girl," he growled, losing his character as he beat back and forth over my ass cheeks with the wicked little ruler.

My ass was on fire by the time the tenth spank landed and I was about to beg King to fuck me, but he was already lifting me off his lap to stand before him.

He stared up at me with his desire bright in his eyes, a flush streaked high across his brutal cheekbones. "Take out my cock and ride me. Wanna see you fuck yourself on my cock."

Immediately, my hands were at his belt and I was straddling his lap, hissing when I slammed myself down on his cock. I couldn't take him all the way, a fact that made me writhe and moan helplessly on top of him.

"So fucking tight," he gritted out, his hands going to my hips to help pull me up and down over him. "Need to loosen that tight little pussy. Want you to take me to the root."

I threw my head back and moaned at his words. Eager to help, I wrapped my fingers in his thick hair as leverage to throw myself down on his thrust.

He reached up to play with my nipples, rolling them between his fingers.

"Harder," I begged, riding him faster now.

His cock stretched me so full that my legs were already shaking with the need to come.

"God, harder," I begged again then hissed when he reared up to bite hard on one nipple while he twisted the other in a tight pinch.

"Come in the next thirty seconds, I'll give you that extra credit," he ground out between biting my diamond-hard peaks.

I made it there in ten.

I shrieked as I came hard all over his big cock, my legs shaking, pussy clenching against him like a vise.

"That's it, come all over me, show me how much you love it," he goaded me as I slammed my hips down over and over.

He slapped his hands over my ass, one at a time on each cheek. The pain made me come harder, longer. I was sobbing, begging him to stop.

"No," he laughed then pinched my clit tight between his fingers so that I shouted and another, smaller orgasm raced through me.

"Cress," he shouted, slamming into me one last time as he found his own climax.

"Fuck," I gasped after a few minutes, collapsing on top of him.

King ran his fingers soothingly over my tingly bottom and pressed kisses to my shoulders.

"Never would have thought, lookin' as pretty as royalty like you do with all that golden hair and those big, innocent eyes, in those sweet little teacher outfits that you'd fuck as hard as you do. Gotta say, babe, I fuckin' love it."

I smiled into his hair, my exhaustion making me honest. "Are you sure it'll be enough to satisfy you? You're a young stud. I'm keeping you from sowing your wild oats and all that."

His laughed vibrated through me. "Don't wanna make you mad when I got you all sweet in my lap but, babe, trust me, I sowed a ton of fuckin' oats before I met you."

I harrumphed, but his laugh eased the edge of my grumpiness. "Might get tired of me, is all I'm saying," I mumbled, both embarrassed and sleepy.

His hands stroked up my back and wound me in a full body hug. "Might get tired but never of you."

"Meant to tell you," I said as my eyes drifted closed, secure enough in his arms to fall asleep like a baby. "William keeps calling me. He's even leaving me messages at the front desk at EBA. Today there was a present on the front steps."

"Did you open it?" he asked, now tense as a board beneath me.

I was too tired to do anything but move my hands lazily through his masses of soft, curly hair and hum. "So sleepy."

"Where did you put it, Cress?" he demanded.

"It's in the kitchen," I said but I was already mostly asleep.

I woke up again when he settled into bed, much later, beside me. The alarm clock read 3:43 in bold, green numbers.

"Where'd you go?" I whispered with my eyes closed as he dragged me across the sheets and settled me over his body like a second blanket.

His skin was cold and he smelled of the cold night outside.

"Just takin' care of somethin' that needed fixin'," he told me in a voice that was hoarse, as if he'd been yelling.

"Did you leave the house?" I asked, frowning and wanting to talk about it but my eyes wouldn't open and sleep was pulling me back into its deep embrace.

"No one sends my woman presents but me," he murmured softly some minutes later, squeezing me tight and pressing a kiss to the top of my head.

But I was too far gone, so I didn't respond.

# Twenty-One.

It was late, sometime in the hours pressed like a book between the pages of night and morning, a pause of time each day where nothing is supposed to happen but quiet contemplation and sleep.

In The Fallen clubhouse, neither of those things were happening.

Old-school rock music throbbed through the clubhouse like a heartbeat, keeping the ebb and flow of movement through the brick, windowless house and its surrounding areas in cadence. It was easy to get caught up in that beat, to lose sight of your inhibitions to the hedonistic currents riding like a subliminal message on the coattails of the Rolling Stones, AC/DC and Guns 'N Roses.

The Saturday night party heralding the start of spring break had long ago dissolved from a spirited family type BBQ into something much darker and more debased.

Bikers lounged across available surfaces making out (or worse) with the biker groupies. More loitered in little groups blazing their grade A marijuana and more still had retired for the night, passed out on couches or were shut away in the rooms they reserved at the back of the building. Most of the bikers with kids had left a long time ago and only the truly hardcore remained.

I was, weirdly, one of them.

King sat on a stool at the bar with me perched on one of his thighs, one arm hooked around my waist to keep me balanced while the other palmed a Blue Buck beer. I'd never seen him drink so much in one night but if he was drunk, I couldn't tell. He spoke with Zeus, Nova, Mute and Bat easily, his smile wide and easy. Every once in a while, his thumb would brush back and forth over the exposed skin of my belly, I would shiver and he'd duck down to press a soft bite to the junction of my neck and shoulder.

We'd had a good night, but not exactly an easy one.

I'd been nervous just putting on my "biker babe" clothes that afternoon. The white cropped Harley Davidson tee revealed a large expanse of my flat, pale gold belly, especially with the low-riding (and I meant low) pair of faded blue jeans I wore. On threat of biker babe wrath, I'd promised the girls that I would finish off the look with dramatic makeup, big hair and wicked-looking spiked-heeled, leather ankle boots.

When I went teetering down the stairs from my bedroom, both King and Mute, who had been murmuring together, stopped talking to stare at me. I fidgeted, hoping I didn't look ridiculous because I didn't *feel* ridiculous. I felt sexy and cool, like a woman you'd think twice about crossing and thrice about fucking. It was a great feeling after a lifetime of feeling like a pretty pawn to be shown off by my mother and William. Today, I felt like a freaking queen.

King seemed to think so too because he practically rushed me at the bottom of the stairs, told Mute to fuck off for a bit, and then kissed me. Mute had fucked off for a bit and King had taken me on the stairs. It had given me rug burn at the base of my back but I didn't care. The resulting sex glow suited my new look.

It also made me a lot less nervous to be formally introduced to The Fallen as King's old lady.

Apparently, my nerves were misplaced anyway. There was nothing formal or intimidating about the BBQ Zeus was hosting at the clubhouse. Men, women and children milled about the asphalt, enjoying the spring sunshine and the jovial company. The smell of charred meat billowed out of the smoker and over the two grills they had going in the back of the clubhouse. There were two picnic tables laden with the salads, sides and desserts the various old ladies and teenage daughters had made, and six coolers filled with various local beers as well as three kegs. One of the prospects, a pimply kid the club had named Pigeon for reasons unknown, was manning the bar inside for anyone (mostly the women) who wanted a cocktail. Two more "hangarounds" were at the bikers' beck and call to run various chores throughout the night, but it seemed that everyone else had decided to take the night off from the drama and the intrigue of the new dealers in town and just enjoy themselves.

Enjoying themselves, I learned, was something bikers did very well.

The kids ran themselves silly through sprinklers set up on the grass and the older children took turns caring for them and hanging with the adults so the parents could take a load off and focus on socializing and boozing.

I was having so much fun that I forgot to be uptight, even when Skell started mauling a much younger woman right in front of me, or when some of the brothers started passing around a joint. King left me, for the most part, with my new group of biker babes, but when I caught eyes with him nearly every time I looked for him, he gave me his boyish grin and it made my heart swell so big it actually *hurt*. The music was great, the booze was bountiful and the food was to die for—greasy and fattening and *yum*.

"Look at that tramp," Lila said, cutting off everyone's conversation about where to shop in Entrance and Vancouver.

Needless to say, I was finding out that the babes and I did *not* shop at the same stores. I was happy with my style but also eager to incorporate more leather and lace into my closet because the women around me looked awesome in it, I thought King would die a special death to see me in it, and I'd always secretly wished I was cool enough to pull it off. The girls were in the middle of reassuring me that I was, when Lila interrupted with her angry comment.

"Huh?" Tayline asked around the mouth of the beer bottle she was in the middle of draining.

She was five-foot-nothing and maybe one hundred and ten pounds soaking wet, but that woman could seriously drink. Meanwhile, even though I was inches taller than her, I was already delightfully intoxicated after five Hey Y'all hard iced teas.

"Riley?" Cleo clarified.

I followed their combined gazes over to a seriously pretty redhead who could have starred in an Herbal Essences commercial. She was striding across the grass in fantastic red cowboy boots, swinging her round hips in a way that had all the men staring at her as she passed.

"Wow, she's seriously pretty," I said.

"She's also seriously talented with her mouth and most of The Fallen men know it," Lila muttered.

I was surprised by her jealousy because I was fairly sure Lila didn't have a man to be possessive of.

"Jesus, Li, when are you going to pony up and tell Nova you want his dick in *your* mouth?" Maya asked. She was crass as ever but somehow maternal, her eyes soft as they stared at the younger woman.

Lila ignored her as she sucked at her teeth. "Shit, heads up, Queenie, Riley's got your man in her sights."

My eyes shot instantly back to the hair commercial girl. She had set those swinging hips at King who was across the yard talking to Mute, Lab Rat and an older biker named Smoke who ran a gun range. He was laughing his beautiful laugh and when Riley stopped in front of him he turned to her, still laughing. I watched her absorb his humor-heightened good looks like a lightning strike, watched her shiver through it. Anger sparked over my skin as they began to talk. Every time Riley touched his corded forearm, the wrath and despair in the pit of my belly burned brighter.

"You need to go up to that bitch and show her what's what," Maja urged me.

"At least go and interrupt their conversation," Cleo said.

I chewed on my bottom lip. King had been so distant with me all day and then, there he was flirting with a gorgeous girl. It made all the insecurities I had flare to life so I didn't feel comfortable approaching him to stake my claim. I didn't even feel comfortable watching them anymore.

"Going to the restroom," I muttered.

"Cress…" Lila called after me, but I ignored her.

I was preoccupied with the sight of King and Riley burned into my eyelids so, I was unprepared for the drama of seeing Paula and her posse when they entered the clubhouse.

She was sitting at the bar talking to three other incredibly scantily clad women. Paula herself had her large dark hair done up even higher than I'd seen the other day and she wore a fishnet top with a skimpy bra and itty-bitty jean shorts. It was spring now but the days were still cool, so she had to be absolutely freezing.

The instant she spotted me, a cruel smile slashed across her face.

"If it isn't the teacher who seduced her student. We were just discussing you. Tell us, did you have to blackmail King to get him to fuck your boring, bony ass? The girls and I were taking bets and I'm feeling lucky." Her words splattered across the floor like filth, coating me in dirty shame.

"I know you're probably used to blackmailing men for money when they get tired of paying for it, but not all of us are that hard up," I returned, surprised by the ease in which the venom spilled from my tongue.

The other women gasped, but Paula's beautiful eyes just narrowed and she swung from her seat to stalk toward me as she said, "Oh, sugar, I'm not hard up. The Fallen Men line up to get their chance with me, but I made an exception for King. *I* went to *him* because Zeus gave me the honor of taking that sweet boy's V-card when he was just a boy."

Rage and disgust hurtled through me. I didn't care that King had slept with her, Paula was gorgeous and I knew that even as young as he was before he'd found me, King had racked up an alarming amount of bed partners. No, what I did absolutely care about was the idea of this viperous woman owning anything of King's, especially something as beautiful as his virginity.

"Well, you can't blame him, then. He didn't know better," I qualified, pleased enough with my comeback and my burgeoning biker babe 'tude that I took an aggressive step forward to meet her as she came at me. She faltered on her high heels, surprised by the move.

Point for me.

Unfortunately, Paula was a seasoned bitch so she recovered

quickly. "So sweet, so fucking naïve. You think that was the only time he dipped his wick in me, Miss Priss? Told you, the men line up to tap this ass. Only reason King didn't have to was because I liked teaching 'im the ways of loving a woman." She leaned right into my face, her boozy breath all over me. "Come to think of it, you and me aren't so different, are we? We both love to school that boy."

"Get out of my face and shut your mouth before I do it for you," I growled through the hot rage that boiled in my gut and threatened to burn over my tongue like dragon's breath.

I was nearly out of control with fury, but some lingering, respectable part of me wanted to give her fair warning before I went crazy on her.

"Maybe we should trade notes," she continued, brazenly reaching out to run her hand down my arm. "Between the two of us, we can see he's getting the best education money can buy. Although, I bet if we asked him, he'd tell you that he prefers my womanly curves to your little girl tits, that he loves how good I take his cock in all my holes."

There was an audible snap as my control collapsed under the weight of her insult and my insides fell into the inferno at the pit of my gut. My stomach flamed, my throat throbbed and I could feel the fire licking at my lips, waiting to turn Paula into ash.

Before, I could understand what I was doing, I'd shoved her against the wall with my forearm across her throat. When she screeched and reached out to scratch me with her fake talons, I maneuvered so that my shoulder pinned one arm and my free hand the other. I leaned into her delicate neck, felt the throb of her pulse against my blazing skin. It made dark notes of laughter coil in my belly, so I indulged in a manic giggle before I leaned into her face like she had done with me.

"I don't know you and I haven't done anything to you, so I'm unsure if you just took an instant dislike to me or if you're an honest-to-goodness crazy bitch by nature. Really, I don't care. What I do care about is you gloating over the fact that you slept with my man right in my face. You want to talk about teaching? Because I'm happy to teach you about some respect."

She snorted and rasped out, "Full of shit."

"Yeah?" I asked, reeling back dramatically before lunging at her face with snapping teeth. My blood was singing with power, my mind giddy with violence. I wanted to push against her throat until she was blue in the face and dare her to go after *my* King. The very thought of her hands on him turned me into the cruelest sadist. "Would you say that stuff you just did to King's face? Because if you did, it would be his arm across your throat and he isn't about violence. I'm his old lady, not you, so if I have to use my fists to remind you of that, I don't see him caring all that much."

"She's fuckin' right."

King's voice behind me widened my lens and suddenly I was aware of the huge crowd we'd drawn. A few men were softly chanting *fight, fight, fight* while the rest were silent but emitted excitement like radio waves.

Instantly, my arm relaxed against Paula's thin neck as I felt King literally at my back. Unfortunately, Paula took advantage by shoving me, and then while I was staggering backward, she jumped on me.

I fell back like a bowling pin, my head crashing against the floor in a way that had me seeing stars. Paula screamed as she landed an open palm slap against my left cheek.

The next second, she was pulled off me, screeching and kicking like a banshee. I lifted myself onto my elbows to watch as Mute and Lab Rat dragged her out of the clubhouse. Then

I dropped my head back to stare up at King, who was glaring down at me, practically vibrating with anger.

"I think I just earned a biker babe badge of honor or something," I told him with a big smile as the adrenaline tangoed with the alcohol coursing through my blood and turned my body into a song. "Do girls get patches too?"

"No, babe, they don't," Hannah said over King's shoulder where she stood with at least a dozen other people. "But I'll see about getting one done for you at the shop, okay?"

"I think that would be good," I nodded somberly. "We could be like the Pink Ladies but a lot cooler. And our jackets should be black!"

There was a low murmur of laughter that ended when King let out a growl and ducked down to scoop me in his arms. Happy to be there, I wound my hands around his neck and called over his shoulder to Zeus, who was lingering by the bar and laughing at me, "Make sure that bitch doesn't get near me again or I'll put her in the ground!"

This time no one tried to hide their laughter.

"You've been watching way too many episodes of *Sons of Anarchy*," Tayline told me as we moved past her and down the hall to the brothers' apartments at the back of the clubhouse.

I tried to shrug but King was holding me too tightly.

It took me a moment after we left the group, after I'd banked my anger and my resulting badass biker babe in training pride, to realize that King hadn't said a word to me.

Nerves danced in my throat. "King?"

"Quiet," he ordered.

I swallowed thickly and wondered for a moment if I'd acted entirely inappropriately. I knew holding a woman, however bitchy, against a wall was not *normally* appropriate behavior but I had reason to believe it would be acceptable in the new biker world I inhabited. So, it occurred to me that while I probably hadn't acted inappropriately, I could have angered King by telling Paula that he was my man and I was his old lady.

When we reached King's room (he had one because he was the Prez's son even though it was biker only), he pried open the door, dropped me on my feet, then slammed a palm against the door to shove it closed.

Then he was on me.

I could taste the hot, metallic anger on his tongue as he used it to sear the inside of my mouth with his possessive, plundering kiss.

He ripped himself away from me after a minute and wiped his mouth with the back of his hand. I stood mute against the wall, watching as he glared at me, his chest heaving.

"King?" I asked in the same little girl's voice I used to apply to William and my father when they were disappointed in me.

I couldn't help it even though I hated it. King's wrath was squeezing the new life out of me, devolving me into the Cressida of old who avoided conflict at all costs.

"Are you fuckin' kidding me with that shit, Cress?" he demanded.

"Um, you mean fighting Paula?" I confirmed then winced. "I know it wasn't my finest moment but—"

King stepped forward to slam his palm against the wall just beside and above my face so he could lean down into me. "Why the fuck is it that I always hear you tellin' other people how you feel 'bout me but you can never tell me that shit to my face, huh?"

I blinked into his face.

He continued, "First you tell the girls at Eugene's that I changed your life just by breathin' and made you leave your husband and I didn't even know you yet. Then you get in some bitch's face 'cause she's disrespecting you but more, 'cause she's disrespecting *me* and you shout in her face that I'm your man and you've never even fuckin' told me that."

"King, honey—" I tried again, reaching out to place my palms flat on his chest to soothe him.

It didn't work and I knew it wouldn't when I felt the hard knock of his staccato pulse against my fingers.

"Been layin' it out for you since the first time I called you babe, Cress. I fuckin' lied to you, skipped classes when you know how much I wanted to be at that school, just so I could have a chance at you. Even when you took that away from me, when you judged me for my brotherhood, when you told me to stay the fuck away from you after I told you I was your student, I kept at you. Wrote you poems that might as well have been penned in my own blood, you cut right at the heart of me. Can see it in your eyes, you're addicted to me, can feel it in that sweet body of yours that you crave me. Wouldn't hurt to hear it from those lips that you want me even half as much as I want you."

Wow. I closed my eyes as his words sunk in, sobering me in an instant. Had I really been so remiss? It seemed so obvious to me that I was more than just in love with him, that I lived and breathed only when he was near. How could I have failed to mention that?

It was an easy question to answer actually.

Because I'd been afraid.

I swallowed thickly because I still was. "How can I trust you with how I feel when I don't even know what you want from me? What am I to you, King? A hot cougar, a plaything, a power trip? You're asking me to risk everything."

"I am," he said immediately, leaning even closer so that I could hear his words in my ear, feel them against my mouth and see them scrawled in his bold, block print across his eyes. "And I'm not asking you to do that because you're a fuckin' hot lay. I'm asking you to risk everything to be my partner, to stand by my side and rule The Fallen men of Entrance, to lie, cheat and steal, to breathe my fuckin' breath, take my kisses and my cock and reign with me. Be the Iron Queen to my Fallen King."

"Why?" I croaked as my heart beat hard against the cage of my ribs like some rabid animal fighting to be freed.

"Because I love you," he growled. "Because I fuckin' love you enough to tear the world apart if it wrongs you, if it causes even a minute of misery for my girl with the whiskey eyes. Never felt this way about anything and I don't want to ever again."

He was so fierce standing over me, intimidating me with his stance, threatening me somehow at the same time that he wooed me. It wasn't a threat of violence but of challenge. He wasn't going to let me take the cowardly way out of this situation or any other. That was one of the reasons I both loved and feared him, because he always forced me to live hard.

Looking up into his warrior eyes, I decided that even if I had to die young as a result it would be worth it to spend the rest of that time with him.

"Loved you since the first day I saw you," I said, clear and loud, looking right into his eyes.

A ragged groan tore from his throat as I slid my hands up from his chest and into his soft-as-silk hair. I fisted it hard and pulled his lips to mine.

Our chemistry exploded between us like lightning, crackling through the room until our hair stood up in the static. I gasped when his hands rooted in my hair and tugged it back roughly so he could warn me, "Want to take you bare, you good with that?"

I nodded manically. He was clean, I knew because he'd gotten checked the week before, and I had an IUD. I'd been begging him for days to take me raw but he was saving it for a special occasion, he'd said. Apparently, this was it.

"I wanna take you hard, Cress babe. Need you to give it to me good, yeah?"

"Yeah, King," I panted, the skimpy thong I wore already soaked with anticipation. "Please."

"You want my cock that badly, babe?" he asked as he skirted his teeth along my jaw and down my neck.

His teeth clamped down there and held me steady as I shuddered.

"Yes, please. Take off your clothes and I'll show you just how much," I begged.

He grinned meanly at me. "No, I don't think so. If you want to see my big cock, you have to earn it. Take off your clothes."

"Oh my God," I breathed, swaying toward him as he let me go to walk over to the single bed in the corner of the small room.

He lay on top of it with his hands behind his head, his biceps bulging out to frame his mess of sexy rumpled hair and the dark look in his pale eyes.

"Show me your body," he ordered again, his voice like smoke as it twined around me. "Show me what no other man will ever fuckin' see again."

I shivered again as I moved to the end edge of his bed so he would have the best vantage point. My eyes locked to his because I wanted to see the way the currents of desire running through them changed the blue to grey to black and back again.

I drew my hands in from my hips bones over the skin bared between my cropped tee and low jeans until they met in the middle at my belly button, then arrowed one up under my shirt while the other went to work at my big belt buckle.

My fingers rolled and pinched my nipples under the flimsy lace of the bra I wore until they were stiff peaks. I tipped my head back slightly so my hair tickled the base of my back, but I could still see King, touching himself through his jeans as he watched me.

With my belt and jeans undone, I delved down into my warm, wet centre and gasped as my fingers dragged over my clit.

"Show me how wet you are," King demanded.

I pulled my index and middle fingers out to show him how they glistened in the light spilling in from the small window.

"Taste how sweet you are."

The groan that escaped my mouth as I opened my lips to obey him might have embarrassed me once, but now I didn't care. I was happy for him to know how much I loved being this dirty for him.

My skin was slick and slightly salty against my tongue as I swirled them over it, my mouth open so he could see.

"Fuck, my Queen is sexy," King rasped, his head pressed back hard into the one hand that cupped it against the wall.

The other squeezed brutally against the enormous length of his erection beneath his jeans. My mouth watered at the sight. I wondered if he would let me handle him that roughly and wetness slipped down my inner thighs to soak the crotch of my pants.

Unable to take it slow any more, I cupped both hands over my breasts under my shirt, pinched my nipples hard, but not as hard as King could and therefore not hard enough, then lifted it over my head.

I unclipped the delicate black lace bra at my back and tipped forward to let it slide down my arms, slowly revealing my small, plump breasts to his hungry eyes. He licked his lips and I licked mine in an echo.

"Show me your cunt."

I shoved my tight jeans down my hips like they were on fire but took my time standing up to reveal my panty-clad pussy. King growled at the sight of the tiny black G-string covering my newly waxed sex. Teasing him, I hooked my thumb under each thin strap at my hips and wiggled them back and forth.

"Off," he barked, jack-knifing off the bed.

I watched, paralyzed, like something soft and sweet—a rabbit cornered by a big, sleek wolf. His teeth were bared, his gait a slow roll of powerful muscles shifting and clenching in delicious unison. Fear lodged in my throat, made me want to cry out and run from the creature that stalked me. So I did. I turned tail and raced for the door.

King caught me just as my hand closed over the knob. He pressed me hard against the door, his hard body pressed flush against mine, his denim-covered erection digging hard into my ass.

"Told you I got you," he snarled softly into my ear. I thrashed hard against the door as he ran his tongue up my neck, nipped my earlobe between his teeth and then, without warning, snatched the placket of my panties in his fist and tore them away from my body. "And I got you. You're mine, little Queen. And I'm going to take everything from you."

I tried to arch back against him but he kept my head pinned to the door by a hand in my hair. The other hooked three fingers into my pussy and kept me still. It was demeaning and sexy and I was already so close to coming that my legs were shaking almost violently.

"You want my cock, Cress?"

"Yes, yes, *yes*," I begged shamelessly as I tried to gyrate on the fingers inside me.

He tightened his grip in my hair so I hissed and went still. Then his thumb hooked under the fingers already inside my pussy and pressed against my ass.

"Gonna take every part of you. Gonna fuck you every day, in each hole so that you're always aching from my cock, so that the only thing that'll ever bring you relief is my dick slidin' back inside of you."

His thumb circled then pressed just inside, repeating the pattern over and over until I writhed and panted against him.

"What do you want, my Queen? Where do you want me to put my big cock?"

"Anywhere," I cried out desperately, getting irritated.

"Even in this tight ass? You sure I'll fit?"

"God, I don't care," I snapped. "Please, for fuck's sake, just take me."

He chuckled darkly, then without warning, he thrust balls-deep in my pussy.

I screamed loudly, convulsing instantly around the hard, brutal length of him. It hurt and soothed at the same time, took me to a place in my head that was dark and wicked and more addictive than any drug.

"That's it, babe, come all over my cock and scream my name. Want everyone to know what a hot fuckin' woman I got in my bed. How much she loves my cock."

"Yes," I shouted, in love with the idea. "Yes, King, please, fuck me. Fuck me harder!"

His hand clamped down harshly over my hip, drilling me down and back against his merciless thrusts. He pressed his sweaty forehead against my neck and took a large bite out of my shoulder as he thrust up, ground deep and ordered, "Fuckin' come for me."

"King," I sobbed as I broke apart around him.

My thoughts scattered to the ground, my body dissolved to dust so only the piston of his hips kept me upright against the door. I went slack and fought to remember more than just King's name.

"Fuck, Cress," I heard him growl through the roaring in my ears, then felt the hot rush of him coming inside me.

"Fucking love you," I told him minutes later when I had the breath to do so.

The hand still holding my hip spasmed as he burrowed his head in my neck and pressed an openmouthed kiss to my pulse. "Fuckin' love you too."

# Twenty-Two.

King hadn't let me out from under his arm for the next three hours. He carted me from group to group as he made his rounds, seamlessly dropping into conversation that I was his girl, and even that we were practically living together. It made me blush the first ten to twelve times because even though he didn't mention it to them, I knew they were aware that I was his teacher. If they cared, which they genuinely seemed not to, they didn't show it. Everyone was nice to me, or at least, polite. When I asked Tayline about it at some point that evening, she'd explained that as King's woman, I was bestowed with a special level of respect.

He was their biker King-in-training and I was his Queen.

It sent a dark thrill through me to be marked with power like that.

I pressed a kiss to King's neck as he spoke with the guys, turning in his arms to do so, before I made my way to the bathroom down the hall. It was occupied, and I could hear the grunts and moans from inside, so I quickly diverted down the hall back to King's rooms farther down the hall. As I went, I passed a room with a light on and the door cracked, the sound of creaking floors and rustling papers inside sitting wrong with me.

I pushed into the room.

It was a study, a rather large and clean one actually, with floor-to-ceiling bookshelves and a big black desk absolutely covered in clearly sorted papers and files.

Behind the desk, stood Lysander.

He was standing, but bent low over the desk with his phone at his ear. I recognized the cracked phone case because I'd bought him the *Jungle Book*-themed accessory for his last birthday (he had a surprisingly adorable weakness for Disney movies).

"What the fuck are you doing?" I asked.

His face was blank with shock for a minute before he broke into a smile. "Needed a quiet place to take a call."

"You were barely around all night," I accused him with a small pout.

I'd been looking forward to spending more time with him now that he worked for Hephaestus but, if anything, he was even more distant. King told me that he kept to himself at the garage but worked hard and had a natural talent with body work (whatever that meant).

"Still adjustin'," he admitted with a grimace.

He'd been out for two years, but I knew it was hard for him to integrate back into society, especially when he'd never been great with people.

"I'm here to help, Sander," I said softly.

He shrugged his shoulders awkwardly.

"Come here, you big lug," I said with a laugh.

He did, bending his big body nearly double to take me into his arms in a tight hug.

"Love ya," he told me, an unusual sentiment from him to speak aloud but one I'd never, not even for a minute, doubted in my life. "Do anything for ya."

"I know," I said, patting his back and breathing in his familiar tobacco and mint scent. "Ditto."

A loud sound rent the night air and minutes later, we heard the thunder of many booted feet tramping outside the clubhouse. Shouting followed.

We broke apart to look at each other.

"Stay here," he growled.

I turned around and ran out of the room. His curse and heavy steps followed me.

There were women speaking in a little huddle in the corner of the main room when I passed through and Tay called my name, but I raced through the door to the front yard where the commotion had come from.

There were men everywhere.

The Fallen brothers were spread out in some kind of loose formation over the asphalt that led down the chain-link fence. It hadn't been locked yet because of the party and through the open gates had come at least six enormous GMC trucks and ten motorcycles. An MC logo jumped out at me, painted on vehicles and patched on to the back of jackets.

Nightstalkers MC.

Most of the men looked dark in the low light, probably Mexican, and all of them wore guns exposed on their hips and sticking out of their boots.

It was not a friendly visit.

"Heard you were looking for us?" one of the strangers stepped forward.

They were all backlit by the high beam lights on their cars and bikes so it was hard to make out his features, but his Spanish accent carried clean and true over the lot.

No one responded to him.

So, he laughed. "Don't be shy now, Fallen brothers! We

wanted you to come looking, there's no shame in pleasing us. In fact, that's why I'm here tonight, to offer you a one-time-only deal. Curious?"

Again, no one spoke.

I spotted Zeus at the head of The Fallen. He was easy to spot, the largest, broadest man on the lot but he also had two silver guns in his hands, steadily pointing at the newcomers. They glinted in the artificial lights.

"I'll tell you anyway because I can see the cat has got your tongues. We have come to take over your operations. You can give them up now or we can take them from you. Trust me, you want to choose the first option."

"Fuck you," Mute, of all people, growled before lobbing a glob of spit at them.

"Fine," the leader said with a dramatic shrug, it was clear that he loved this. "Don't trust me, trust them."

At his cue, three of his brothers stepped forward with an enormous cooler and placed it on the hood of the truck closest to the clubhouse. They blocked the light as they removed whatever it was from the cooler and then stepped back.

The Fallen didn't react to the sight of the four severed heads placed in a row on the hood but I gasped and took a step back to find myself pressed up against my brother.

His hand came down on my shoulder to hold me there. "Don't move and don't draw attention to yourself."

I nodded slightly.

"These are the Presidents and Mafia leaders who chose the second option," the leader said with faux sadness. "It would be a shame to add to my collection. You can't imagine how hard it is to find a cooler big enough to hold them all."

His hyena-like yip and cackle pierced through the night.

"Enough." Zeus's low, thunderous voice stopped

everything, even the cackle, even my breath as it tried to leave my body. "Get the fuck off our land. By now the fuckin' police will be on your heads and I doubt you want to be around with your sick-as-fuck severed heads when they arrive."

"Now, you must be Zeus Garro," the man clapped. "I'm so excited to meet you. Heard so much."

"I'm going to give you five minutes to roll out," Zeus said calmly.

There was a pout in the man's voice when he said, "Oh, you really are no fun. They warned me. Okay, if you want to do it this way, let me tell you how it is going to go. You're going to look for us again, harder this time. You won't find us. Meanwhile, kids are going to keep overdosing from that awful fentanyl that keeps finding its way into drugs these days and who are people going to blame? Well, the villains they know. So, while we slowly pull your business out from under you, your own city will start to run you out of town. It really is a simple plan but you'd be amazed at its efficacy."

I shivered at his pleasant voice reciting his plan like some kind of evil villain in a Bond film. The scary thing was that I believed he could do it.

The sound of sirens merged with the night air and quickly grew closer.

"You got less than two fuckin' minutes," Zeus drawled.

The man laughed manically again. "You think we're scared of the police? Of course, we have some in our pockets. Are you saying you don't? It's a surprise you lasted this long, it really is."

The Fallen brothers hummed with tension and I could tell they wanted to rip the rival gang apart with their bare hands but they had to follow Zeus and he was smart enough to know better.

The sirens drew even closer.

"Well, this was fun. I can't say I have much hope for your continued survival but *buena suerte* and happy fucking hunting!" he crowed.

Gunshots sliced open the dark night, shot upward for the effect and nothing else, the way one might use fireworks or trumpets. As one, the Nightstalkers rounded themselves up and peeled out of the lot in under two minutes.

As soon as they were gone, the brothers moved. Some went to the gate, closing and locking it up tight while others whipped out their phone flashlights to shine it on the tire treads left behind in the gravel and grass. Others disappeared past Sander and me into the clubhouse.

King came to me.

"Should have taken her back inside," he growled at my brother.

"It was too late, he would have noticed her," he responded.

King seemed to find that acceptable because he started ignoring Lysander and paying attention to me. I wrapped my arms tight around him as he kissed the top of my head.

"That was totally fucked up," I murmured into his shirt.

"Yeah."

"I thought The Fallen didn't have rivals."

"They didn't."

"Who was that guy?"

"The crazy motherfucker who thought he was a fuckin' Bond villain? That was Luis Elizondo, the Prez of Nightstalkers MC."

I shivered.

"Let's get you inside," he said, pulling away to lead me into the clubhouse.

I followed. "What's going to happen now?"

"Now, I'm going to put you to bed."

"You're not going to join me? Why aren't we going home?"

He stopped at the mouth of the hallway to the backrooms and tugged me into his arms for a hard kiss.

"Love that you called it our place," he said against my lips when he was done kissing them.

"Well," I grumbled, "you're there all the freaking time."

He laughed and moved forward again with me under his arm.

"I want to stay here tonight. I'm going to sit in on a meeting in church to talk with the brothers about what to do with those fuckers."

"What does that mean?" I asked again.

He pushed open the door to his room and immediately started to undress me. I let him, searching his face as he stripped me and retrieved an old EBA sweatshirt for me to wear.

"King?" I asked again when I was dressed and he'd swung me into his arms to literally tuck me into his bed.

He sighed as he sat on the edge of the mattress and smoothed my hair back from my head. "It means that my plans to fuck you twenty-four-fuckin'-seven for the next two weeks of school break are going to be a little different than I thought. It'll have to be twenty-two-fuckin'-seven so I can spend some time helpin' with this mess."

"Will you be in danger?" I asked.

The adrenaline rush, the alcohol and the amazing orgasms I'd had earlier were combining under the gentle stroke of King's hand in my hair to make me sleepy.

Too sleepy to pay attention to the way his lips thinned as he lied to me.

"No, babe. Everything's gonna be fine."

# Twenty-Three.

It was a little strange to be back at school after the two-week sexcation I'd indulged in with my favorite student. We were a real couple in all the ways that truly mattered so the secrecy and wrongness of our relationship seemed trivial and, at this point, annoying. King was an adult and more than capable of making his own decisions. Anyone could see that just by looking at him. So, would it be so wrong for him to take a teacher eight years his senior for his lover?

Well, when I thought about it like that, the optics weren't exactly good.

Still, I didn't like passing him in the halls without touching him, teaching him with two desks and three metres of space between us instead of over the dinner table or in bed before the sun came up, when our naked skin was cooling but our brains were buzzing with sex-induced adrenaline.

If King's flashing eyes were any indication, he didn't like it any more than I did. He was nearly done though. It was the end of April and technically, because he was an International Baccalaureate student, he would be done in mid-May after his two-week period of rigorous exams. He told me he was taking me away immediately even though I would still have my two junior classes to teach. I'd booked a sub because it was either that or face King abducting me and leaving my classes in the lurch. Besides, I'd caught him doing research on his computer for Graceland and there was no way I was going to miss the opportunity to go there.

We just had to get through the next two months and we could be together for real. I didn't let myself think too much about what that actually meant given that most everyone in Entrance thought I was dating Zeus and that his son was only my student. How they would react when they found out I was actually dating King, I couldn't know, and frankly, I was beginning not to care. The biker mentality was, apparently, contagious.

I was thinking about all of this while my fourth-period junior history class took a pop quiz when a commotion erupted out in the hall. Immediately, I flashed back to two weeks ago when I'd found Benny writhing on the floor. It still haunted me in my idle moments and I imagined that it would for a long time to come.

Louise burst through the door, her huge blue eyes wide with exhilaration. "There's a fight!"

Immediately, the class erupted into chaos as everyone jumped out of their seats, bottlenecking the door as they raced into the hall.

I followed them.

Carson Gentry was on the floor with another football player, Tom Anton, on top of him beating away at his face with two huge fists.

"Fuckin' faggot," he was snarling.

Rage exploded within me but before I could start forward through the crowd, King was there behind Tom, pulling him off Carson as easily as someone might remove lint from their jacket. Then he was on him, lifting Tom against the lockers with a hand at his throat.

"What the fuck?" he garbled, trying to kick out at King.

King leaned his body out of reach and squeezed tighter so Tom's voice was cut off to a wheeze. "What the fuck? That's what I'm askin' you, motherfucker. You got a problem with a man likin' another man, you keep it in your bigoted head and keep your ignorant mouth shut. You can't do that, this day and fuckin' age, you'll find it shut for you."

I couldn't understand what I was seeing. It didn't seem possible that King was defending the same guy who, just months ago, he'd had tossed up against a wall in much the same fashion he had Tom strung up now.

"You don't think he has it rough enough at home? That he hasn't fuckin' suffered for it after what happened to Benny? You're fuckin' filth, man." King growled.

"Okay, break it up," Warren ordered as he made his way into the fray, Harry Reynard of all people, behind him.

"Let the kid down, King, before we have to suspend you for being a hero and completely ruin the moment," Harry ordered in his soft British voice.

It was strangely hilarious, the entire situation.

Someone grabbed my hand and I looked over to see Benny. He had just returned to school that day, but I'd gone to visit him over the break and found out that Carson had started a campaign to try to get him back. It was all over school that Carson, the ultimate pretty boy and ladies man, was gay and in love with Benito Bonanno. Most people thought it was delicious gossip and rather sweet if a little awful that Carson had almost gotten Benny killed.

There were some who thought Carson was suddenly diseased.

Tom Anton, one of his best friends, was obviously one of them.

Benny stared up at me with sad eyes so I squeezed his hand in reassurance.

King let go of Tom to turn to the two male teachers and explain himself. It was a mistake. Tom swung out so quickly that no one had time to shout out a warning. He caught King right under the left side of his jaw and sent him staggering back.

My palm spasmed in Benny's as I fought the urge to storm forward and wring the little prick's neck.

"You would defend the cocksucker. Probably feel guilty about being the one to sell him the drugs in the fucking first place. Everyone knows you and your thug ass dad are pushing bad shit," Tom leered.

Harry was behind King, taking his arms firmly behind his back before he could attack, while Warren took Tom in much the same pose.

"That's enough, Tom," Warren bit out.

"You ruin peoples' lives with that shit," Tom shouted. "You think you're some hero but everyone around here knows you and your fuckin' family are scum."

"That's enough!" I shouted, stepping away from Benny and into the fray.

I stormed up to Tom and sneered, "Only cowards result to name calling and violence without provocation. You want to put the spotlight so badly on everyone else, maybe we should take a closer look at what you're hiding, Tom?"

The boy went white as a sheet.

I nodded curtly. "That's what I thought. Now, be quiet and follow Mr. Warren and Mr. Reynard to the office."

"Bring King," Warren said to Harry over his shoulder as he began to escort Tom to the office.

Harry hesitated. "He didn't really do anything wrong, Warren. He was defending the boy."

"He was incendiary. He needs to be punished as well."

"No." Benny stepped forward, in line with me. His full bottom lip quivered but he jerked his chin up and said, "King was one of the people who found me. He saved me. Now, he saved Carson from a disgusting bully. Just because you don't like that he's a biker or whatever doesn't mean you can punish him when he's just being a decent human."

Inside, I clapped uproariously.

Outwardly, I bit my lip and watched.

The students began murmuring their agreement until someone started chanting, *King, King, King*. Soon, the hall vibrated with the call and when they wouldn't stop, not even when Warren ordered them to, he scoffed and went off with Tom dragging behind him.

The group broke into a little cheer, and I caught King's eyes in time to see him stare in awe at his supporters, as if surprised that anyone would be on his side.

It made my heart ache to see it, but I resolved then and there to always be the one beside him, even and especially when it went against popular opinion.

The truth was, he was young, too wild and reckless, filled to the brim with sex and vigor. His eyes promised to burn me alive, incinerate my inhibitions, turn my morals into ash and my soul into tinder. He held the torch, the threat against everything I had ever stood for, and he had the balls to dare me to come closer. Yet somehow, I found myself obeying, willingly laying myself on the pyre at his feet with open arms. Because if I was going to burn, I was going to make sure we did it together.

"Fuck, you know how to a make a man feel like a fuckin' god," King growled as I took him into the back of my throat.

His hands flexed in my hair as he pulled me back and forth over his cock slowly, firmly, so that each thrust was a journey I'd buy tickets to ride over and over again.

He pulled out of my mouth and I immediately held it open for him, my lips wet and swollen from paying homage to him.

"You suck my dick so good, babe," he praised me, rubbing a thumb over my plump lower lip.

I pulled it into my mouth and sucked hard until he grunted and pulled away to replace it with a firm thrust of his cock.

God, I couldn't get enough of the way he tasted, salty and clean, the feel of his silky skin over steely flesh, ribboned with thick veins that begged for the trace of my tongue. I groaned around him, wrapped my hands around his hips so I could grab his firm ass and shoved myself farther down his length.

"Fuck," he shouted, slamming his hand against the tile wall.

We were in the bathroom at Eugene's. I'd brought him into the handicap-accessible washroom when I'd realized that King was still tense and wired from his confrontation at the school earlier. I remembered Skell's words about blow jobs and decided that it was a good time to test that out.

It appeared to be working.

I dragged my tongue over the underside of his shaft, flicked it over the sensitive crown and hummed at the taste of his precum.

"Wanna fuck you," he growled, bending down to grab me.

"No," I protested, flicking my head back and forth over the throbbing end of him. "Want you to come in my mouth."

"Fuck," he stuttered out, wrapping my hair in his hands

like reins.

I covered my teeth with my lips and started to work my wet, clutching mouth up and down over him. Drool edged out of my mouth, ran down his pulsing shaft and dripped off his balls. I reached up to take them in hand, rolling them back and forth in my palm until his legs seized and his hands clenched in my hair.

"God fuckin' damn, Cress, I'm gonna come," he bit out.

I groaned my delight loud and long around him and was rewarded, a few seconds later, by the salty flood of his cum on my tongue. He shouted hoarsely, his eyes squeezed shut, his gorgeous pink mouth slack as he fed me his cock. When he was finished, I cleaned him up with my tongue and placed a kiss to each side of his groin.

"Delicious." I grinned at him as I stood up, my knees creaking in protest.

I loved the sound, loved the ache under my kneecaps the way an athlete may have appreciated a hard-earned sports injury.

"You're fuckin' delicious," King said, tugging me to him to plant a hot, openmouthed kiss on me.

His tongue swept through my mouth, testing to make sure I'd swallowed every last drop of his cum.

"Gotta take care of my woman," he said against my lips as one hand trailed down my torso to cup my wet pussy through my underwear under my dress.

"No, I'm good until later. That was just for you."

"Babe."

"King."

"*Babe.*"

"*King,*" I mocked him then pressed a firm kiss to his lips. "Seriously, when you were wooing me, you went down on me like ten trillion times and I never repaid the favor. Let me have this."

"I like eating you," he told me something I very much already knew because he ate me at least once a day, but it was still something I loved to hear.

"And I love sucking your cock. Besides, we've been in here long enough, everyone is going to know we hooked up in the bathroom."

"Babe, you think Eugene's needs a bathroom this big? It's a fuckin' biker bar. What do you think we use it for?" he asked then burst into raucous laughter at my disgusted expression.

"And I thought I was being so original," I muttered bitterly, which just made him laugh harder.

"Come on, you dork," he said affectionately as he slung his arms around my shoulders. "Let's get back to the crew."

"I'm going to, um, wash up. I'll meet you out there," I said with a blush.

He swiped my pink cheek with a thumb and shook his head. "Can take my cock better than a working girl and she can't even say she has to wash up afterward without blushin' like a virgin."

I slapped his hand away and glared at him, fighting my smile as he sauntered out of the bathroom. I was still smiling when I washed my hands and then while I made my way back to the bar.

"You should have seen him," I told Tayline later that night as we sat at the bar while King, Cy and a few other members played pool. "He was like an avenging angel. It was amazing."

She snorted as she took a sip of her tequila on the rocks. "Your own personal Satan."

I beamed at her. "Exactly, but better because he laughs a lot and it's super sexy."

The other girls at the bar with us, Cleo and Lila, laughed.

"I know most people think bikers are racist, misogynistic, homophobic pigs," Tay said. "And a lot of them are. But for the most part, The Fallen men are good ones. King just proved he's the best of them."

"Zeus always says he is," Cleo added. "Has since he was a boy. Seriously, Queenie, just when I think I can't get anymore jealous of you, you say something else about King that makes me swoon."

I laughed, looking over my shoulder for the man in question but he'd disappeared. The rest of the guys were still shooting around, drinking beer and talking. I frowned, because King didn't smoke or do anything that would take him outside and he was pretty serious about keeping me in his sight at all times, but I figured he'd just gone to the restroom.

Minutes later the girls and I were laughing about Lila's latest disaster date—this one had flirted with anything that moved including the female *and* male servers at the restaurant they went to—when the atmosphere in the bar changed.

"Eugene!" a male voice shouted.

It sounded vaguely like Nova.

Eugene, who had been polishing glasses behind the bar, half listening to Lila's story, moved into action instantly. He moved surprisingly fast for such a big guy. I watched as he quickly unlocked a sawed-off shotgun from under the bar and then disappeared down the back hall.

The other brothers were already mobilizing, the few civilians in the bar staring wide-eyed around them as bikers checked their weapons and moved out the front and back doors.

Cy and Bat came to stand in front of the us at the bar, their stances wide and their posture ramrod straight.

"Fuck," came a shout and then, because everyone had

quieted and someone had turned down the music, I heard the *pop pop* of gunshots.

"It's King," I whispered brokenly, somehow knowing it in my heart.

Tayline's hand found mine and squeezed.

By the time King stumbled in between Mute and Nova, I was on my feet behind Bat and Cy, facing the door with my hand over my rattling heart.

My blond king was completely battered, blood lacquered across his face like some kind of grotesque Halloween mask. His beautiful halo of golden hair was matted with dirt and more blood. The tee he was wearing was torn by a slash mark that had clearly been made by a knife and he was completely unsteady on his feet.

"Oh my God," I tried to yell but there was no breath in my lungs so it came out more like a wheezing gasp.

"What the fuck happened?" Lila demanded as they leaned King up against the bar and moved out of the way.

I took King's sweet, battered face by the chin and cataloged the angry ripple of open, bleeding skin over his left eyebrow that accounted for the amount of blood seeping down his front.

Something in my chest was withering, going hollow and rotten and dying.

"I asked what *the fuck* happened," Lila shouted at the bikers.

Mute glared at her and took one of his signature menacing steps forward but Nova slapped a palm against his chest. He turned to Lila but his eyes were on me, his voice uncharacteristically grim as he said the two words capable of terrifying us all, "The Nightstalkers."

"They came here?" Cleo gasped.

Eugene trundled into the room carrying a prone body and

dropped the leather-clad form to the floor without care. The man didn't groan as he hit the ground with an almighty thump so he must have been knocked out all ready. I stared at the Nightstalkers MC rocker on his leather jacket, the laughing demon that grinned red-faced from the back of the cut.

"Bat, Cy, help me load this fucker in my truck and we'll take 'im down to the compound," Eugene growled.

He wasn't technically part of the club, but I didn't know the specifics other than that, apparently, Eugene was in someway related to the Garros.

The bikers moved to help him.

I slid my fingers into King's wet hair and pushed it behind his ear.

"King, honey," I whispered to him. "What the fuck happened?"

His hand came out and tiredly wound its way through my hair until it found the back of my neck. "Went to the john and four of them jumped me, dragged me out the back door and started beatin' on me. Got one of them in the throat and managed to shake off another long enough to shout."

"Thank fuck I was takin' a leak," Nova muttered, his distressed eyes on King.

"Amen, brother," King agreed.

"Does this happen often?" I asked, my voice still reedy and thin with shock.

King was watching me, his eyes growing sharper and sharper as he recovered from the head banging.

I didn't look at him, couldn't bear to see the blood streaking his gorgeous face. It reminded me too much of Marcus and Lysander, too much of the many times I'd tended to my bleeding brother after he got into yet another scrap.

"Cress," he called softly.

I ignored him to listen to Mute who grunted, "Used to."

"People know not to fuck with The Fallen," Nova explained. "We got complacent. Used to be a time at least one brother was with an officer at all fuckin' times."

"An officer" I parroted, hating how uninformed I was.

"There're ranks in the MC," Tay leaned forward to explain softly. "The higher-ups are officers. King's obviously not an officer but he's still a target because he's the Prez's son."

"So, this happens," I concluded.

Mute nodded. "Happens."

*Fuck.*

Fear solidified its hold on me, embracing me in its cold fingers, locking me in its sticky arms.

"Cress," King called again.

He knew what was happening, I knew he did, but I couldn't stop the panic from overtaking me and overriding the new Cressida with the old.

"Need to get you to the doc," Mute told his best friend.

King ignored him. "Everyone out."

Only the bikers were left inside, the others having been ushered out by Lab Rat, Blade and Boner, who were still out front keeping watch in case one of them decided to call the police.

"What?" Cy barked.

"Everyone. Out." King shouted, his bloody hair flying as he shot unsteadily to his feet. "Nova, Cy, Bat, go help Eugene take the motherfucker to the compound so we can fuckin' question him. Mute, go tell the other brothers they can come in and work cleanup soon as I'm done talking to my woman."

*Fuck.*

All eyes swung to me, most of them confused but Tayline and Eugene's looks were filled with wary condemnation.

They could see it, the fear hugging my back like a hovering mother. It wanted me back, had missed me for the brief time I'd been free.

"Fuckin' now!" King demanded.

They moved.

It took them two minutes to get out and I took those two minutes to deep breathe. King waited beside me, his breath laboring through his lungs, blood dripping off his nose and splattering on the floor at his feet.

"Cress," he said softly when we were finally alone.

But he didn't touch me and I was so grateful, I could have cried.

If he touched me, I'd be done.

"Look at me, babe," he ordered.

I turned to look at him and the sight brought instant tears to my eyes.

"Can't do it," I whispered through my aching throat.

His eyes flared, so blue against the red blood.

"I want to, please understand. I want to be there with you through the thick and the thin and the laughter and the freaking bloodshed but now that I see it can actually be like this…" I shook my head and took an instinctive step backward.

"I might not even patch in, babe," he said, reaching a hand out to me.

But I was too far away for him to grab me, and he needed the support of the bar at his back because he was still too fucked up from the fight to be steady on his feet.

"Doesn't matter, you're not in the club now and look what's happened to your beautiful face." I cupped my hands over my mouth and tried to fight the panic.

I kept thinking of my hands covered with Marcus's blood, of Lysander's face splattered with gore and brain matter after he shot my rapist in the back of the head.

"My bachelorette party," I blurted out, desperate for him to understand why I was collapsing like the inside of an old house. "Sander took me out because I didn't have any friends and he wanted me to have a night of fun before I got married. I was eighteen." I swallowed painfully. "We got really drunk while bar hopping and at the last place, I met this really cute guy. He bought me drinks and stayed with me for over an hour just chatting. I thought he was so pretty, just like someone out of a Nora Roberts book. He asked me to get some fresh air and I didn't think before I said yes."

God, I could still feel his hands on me, the feel of the rough brick against my cheek as he'd slammed me against the wall and wrenched up my skirt.

"I was drunk and stupid and he took advantage. He was all over me and I was screaming. Sander had wondered where I'd disappeared to so, thank God, he came outside and found me. They fought, but Marcus got a good shot in and sent Sander into a pile of crates. I was frozen. So stupidly frozen against the wall, terrified."

King growled, the sound low in his throat. "Come here, Cress."

I shook my head frantically, back in the place that had taught me not to live on the edge. "He came at me again, had my shirt ripped open and my panties torn off in seconds. I really thought he was going to…anyway. The next thing I know there's this loud *pop pop* just like I heard tonight and something wet rained down over me just before Marcus slumped against me *hard* and I fell to the ground with him pinned on top of me.

"People heard the commotion by then and someone tackled Lysander before he could help get Marcus off me, so I just laid there with him bleeding out all over me for minutes before anyone even realized I was under him."

"If he wasn't already dead, babe, I'd hunt that motherfucker down, kill him slow, over years," King said, his voice nearly as low, dark and menacing as his father's.

"Can't do it," I repeated, barely in the room with him, still back in that time with the bloody body covering me like a shroud. "I can't be your Queen because I'm not strong enough to do this, the violence and the possible death. I couldn't stand to lose you and I don't think—No, I know I can't stand by you knowing that the kind of life you lead, so like Sander's, could make that a real possibility."

King stared at me. I didn't look at him, but I could feel his eyes on me, marking every inch of my body, memorizing me because he knew I was about to walk out the door.

"Don't do it," he warned.

"I'm so, so sorry," I repeated, already turning away, the panic in my throat so hot and bitter, I knew I needed to get out of there so I could throw up. "I know you'll be better off without me, King. You need a real queen by your side. I'm smart enough to know that's not me."

I turned and ran out the front door, knowing Tayline would be there waiting to take me home because she already knew me well enough to know she'd have to.

King didn't follow.

# Twenty-Four.

Air echoed through the empty cavern of my chest each time I drew breath, ricocheting off the hollow cavity where my heart used to be. I felt like everyone could hear the sound of my heartbreak, could see it like a dead thing in my eyes, but no one commented on it, not even Tayline, who only watched me with deep, dark eyes while we drank our morning coffees in the teacher's lounge that morning.

My students felt it even though they didn't know what it was. It made them quiet and slightly loopy as they breathed in the noxious fumes that flowed between King and me. He sat at his desk right before me but did not look at me, not once through the first forty minutes of history class. I found myself dropping things just to make a clatter that might draw his eyes, talking loudly so the volume would magnetize his eyes to me. Nothing worked and as the class drew on, I could feel myself becoming more despondent, my soul crushing into dust under the heel of his disregard.

It grew more impossible to believe I had done the right thing by giving him up with every moment that passed that I wasn't in his arms. It had started as soon as he'd left my house and the now beautiful-to-me sound of his motorcycle disappeared.

Now, I hated myself so much I felt sick with it, nauseated

and feverish, constantly about to faint. Every time I caught sight of his beautiful face, the breadth of his shoulders strong enough to hold up my sky as it threatened to come down around my ears and the halo of hair that crowned him like the king he was, I ached with such ferocity, I lost my breath midway through my lesson.

There was only ten minutes left, I told myself as bile surged over my tongue, and then I was going to go to the bathroom and throw up the little lunch I'd eaten.

"Did Eve do the right thing by giving into temptation?" Margaret asked as we reviewed their *Paradise Lost* papers.

"Of course," Benny answered before I could. "If she hadn't eaten the apple, she would have been Adam's slave forever. When she chose to eat the apple, she made her first autonomous decision from Adam."

I pursed my lips, finally drawn into the conversation in a real way, both because he'd made an interesting point and because Benny had been back in class since the start of term but I couldn't get used to my joy at seeing him there, sitting healthy and, unbelievably, happy.

"No, she switched one man for another and listened to Satan," Carson said. It had taken him a while after the fight to get back into class discussions, but he always sat beside Benny now, and his boyfriend was excellent at drawing him into the conversation just as he was now.

"Sure, Satan influenced her, but Adam was her master and even in choosing to obey Satan and not him, she became independent. She did a bad thing and was, ironically, freed by it," Benny said, his eyes on Carson's, his thumb swiping back and forth of their joined hands.

It was obvious he was speaking allegorically about their relationship.

It was also obvious that I could do the same for myself. I'd been held to William by invisible social shackles I'd worn since birth, with no idea that I wore them but for the vague sense that I didn't fit properly in my own life. Then King had appeared in the parking lot, bright, dangerous and shiny as a forbidden fruit and, unbeknownst to me, I'd take that first, delicious bite. By the time I knew how taboo it was, what repercussions that act would reap, it was too late. I'd tasted the kind of life and freedom I'd always wanted to have and just as it was for Eve, there was no turning back

I turned sharply to look at King who, for the first time all class, was staring at me. Our eyes locked with the vibration of a thunder strike and I rocked back on my heels as it resonated through me. I opened my mouth and I knew exactly what I was going to say (that I loved him more than my next breath) and what that would mean (my immediate dismissal from EBA, the instant dissolution of my impeccable reputation) and I did not care.

I opened my mouth to speak, but was interrupted by a knock at the door. It took me a moment to realize that two uniformed policemen stood in the entrance to my classroom.

"Can I help you, gentlemen?" I asked, my manners overriding my disorientation.

My gaze skittered over to King and found him still watching me. I shivered and watched his hands flex into fists on his desk, wondering if that meant he wanted to touch me or wanted to throttle me.

"Sorry to disrupt, Mrs. Irons—"

"*Miss* Irons," the class, led by King, recited at the same time.

The cop from the town meeting, Officer Danner, the beautiful one with tawny blond hair and Clint Eastwood vibe that had most of the girls in the class tittering self-consciously, stepped forward. "*Miss* Irons, we are here to arrest Kyle Garro for the possession of illegal narcotics. Mr. Garro, stand up and put your hands behind your head."

The air in the room solidified and I watched in shock as the officer moved through it as if through plasticine toward King who was already up and out of his seat. Still, his eyes were on me even as he remained quiet and calm while they patted him down and cuffed him.

"There must be some kind of mistake," I said, finally snapping back to reality and stepping forward. "King is a bright, good student. There is no way this can be true."

There was a way, given that The Fallen were the biggest weed distributors on the west coast, but there was no way that King would be caught with any, let alone hardcore narcotics at *school.*

"We had an anonymous tip that Mr. Garro was keeping narcotics on his person, Miss Irons," Danner's partner told me as he located King's backpack tucked under the chair and unzipped it.

Everyone gasped as they caught side of the huge bag of white powder nestled between the textbooks there.

"Do you have a warrant?" I demanded, scrambling to think of any way to stop them.

The cops ignored me as they bracketed King and began to lead him through the desks.

The students all started to whisper to each other and a few of them began to speak up against what was happening, including Benny and Carson. The latter was even standing up and moving out the door with them.

"No way King would do something like that," he was saying, his voice rising to a shout as they moved away from him and down the hall, which was filling with students. "No fucking way!"

I braced a hand on the doorframe to steady myself as I watched King being escorted out the doors, aware of the students and faculty flooding the halls, of the fact that King was gone, gone to prison, gone away before I could tell him I was stupid but also in love, so goddamn in love with him that I would die an excruciating death every day for the rest of my life if it meant I could be with him.

It started with a sound in my head, a cacophonous shatter and crash as my insides collapsed like a demolished house. Every single thing I'd once been and thought important was in that house: my morality polished like Waterford crystal in the cabinets, my poise and elegance painted on the walls with my preconceived notions hanging like designer garments in the closets. I lost everything to the blast, everything razed to my truest foundation.

And at that foundation, I found the Cressida I'd become with King, one strong enough to give into temptation without guilt, one who fought for the things she wanted and spat in the eye of the people who judged her. It was that Cressida who felt fury light her up like the First of July and it was that Cressida who started off down the hallway toward the headmaster's office.

I ignored the looks of shock and the gossip about King, the staff that reached out to me as I powered past them, Tiffany Calloway's cry as I flew around her desk and burst into Headmaster Adams' office without waiting to be announced.

He sat behind his palatial desk smoking a cigar.

I fought hard against the urge to put it out in his eye.

"Mrs. Irons, what in heavens are you doing?" he asked me.

So, I told him. Or more like shouted at him.

"You allowed the police to illegally search a student and arrest him during my class? Even if they came to you with their suspicions, you should have urged them to speak with him first, or at the very least, wait until after school hours to take him in for questioning. That you would allow this kind of thing to happen to one of our students is reprehensible. And don't say that you would have acted this way for anyone. You clearly hate the Garro family for their way of life and you decided to humiliate King because of it."

"I would lower your voice and think before you run that mouth of yours any more, Mrs. Irons," he encouraged me.

"It's *Miss* Irons," I shouted. "You could look the other way for Carson Gentry because his father owns half this fucking town and look where that left us? His habit went unchecked and it ended with beautiful Benny Bonanno having a *drug overdose* in our hallways. Yet, you're looking for any opportunity to toss King out on his ass even though he's an exemplary student, a wonderful young man who cares for his fellow classmates and the only crime he's ever committed is to be born the son of The Fallen MC."

"I told you to watch yourself, Miss Irons, and I meant it. Do not think that you can just storm in here and tell me what to do. I am the headmaster of this establishment, not you. And just because Zeus goddamn Garro thinks he runs this town and *blackmail*ed me into letting his good-for-nothing-son attend this school, do not think that I will continue to turn a blind eye to the fact that you and he are having an entirely inappropriate relationship."

I blinked at him, my heart pumping too much blood to my head so I couldn't think straight.

"Excuse me?" I whispered.

His smile beneath his thick mustache was slick and cruel. It made him look like Santa Claus stumbled into a horror flick. He crossed his hands slowly and propped his fleshy face on them.

"You heard me. I know all about what you and that disgusting thug get up to in 'detention'. Warren first told me about it weeks ago. You should go home tonight and kiss his father for holding my affair over my head or not only would you be out on your ear without a job, I'd have you investigated."

"But you can't," I said, trying to see through the panic and focus on the good. "You can't do *shit* because Zeus is blackmailing you…"

I'd well and truly snapped, obviously, because I threw my head back the way King would and burst into laughter.

When I was done, and I took my time, I wiped my eyes and smiled at the headmaster. I could feel the expression stretch my lips too wide, my eyes giddy with mania like I was the female incarnate of the Joker. I felt crazy, wild and just as dangerous, so I didn't care.

"You are a weak, pathetic man with no real power," I told the seasoned administrator before me. "You're owned by the rich and blackmailed by the corrupt. This may be one of the best schools in the country but a weak man with a narrow mind runs it and I don't want to be a part of that. You can't even *fire* me when you know I've been fucking a student, who is absolutely delicious, by the way." I shook my head and turned to walk out the door. When I was at the doorframe, I shook my hair out behind me dramatically and turned to him again. "So, it's my fucking pleasure to be able to tell you that I quit."

I left his garbled response behind me, ignored Tiffany

Calloway's gaping mouth and the students who called after me as I stormed through the halls of EBA for the last time and pushed open the doors to the parking lot. My mind was preoccupied with only two things: getting to Street Ink Tattoo Parlor, and then, getting King out of prison and back to me.

# Twenty-five.

It wasn't my first visit to prison and, given that I was in love with an outlaw, I knew it wouldn't be my last. They were technically called "correctional centres" in British Columbia, but jail was jail no matter what they called it. Although, Ford Mountain Correctional was set between beautiful forest and snow-capped mountains just outside of Chilliwack, a strangely tranquil and stunning setting for a medium security prison. It soothed me slightly to know that King was somewhere like that, at the very least.

I was also well acquainted with the visiting protocols so I made sure I called ahead for an appointment and wore conservative clothing. I knew what it was like to go through the body scanner and a pat down, to wait in the cold, drab visitation room for the correction officers to bring prisoners in to visit their family and friends. I knew it because I'd done it all before with Lysander. Driving my new and improved Betty Sue down from Entrance, I told myself that knowing this, I would be unfazed by the sight of King in a prison jumpsuit.

That was not the case.

The sight of King in a prison jumpsuit eviscerated me.

The orange of the rough fabric was garish and combined with the yellow fluorescent lights that hummed overhead made him look gaunt and hollow-cheeked. All his magnificent hair was scraped back into a ponytail at the base of his neck so, for a moment, I thought they'd cut it all off and I nearly burst into tears.

"King," I said, my tongue thick in a mouth full of sand.

"Cressida," he replied cautiously as he took the seat across from me.

His impartiality glanced off my heart like a blow but I absorbed the pain and moved on because I deserved it.

I tried to speak without sobbing, realized that wasn't an option, then swallowed convulsively a few times until I felt I could try again. King watched me, unsmiling, his face hard. I remembered Lysander's face growing hard like that after years in prison, petrifying more and more every time I saw him until he seemed made entirely of marble. I couldn't imagine King like that, my smiling, charismatic, rebel with any cause but me, King rotting away in prison for years of his precious life.

"I can't believe this," I breathed shakily. "I can't believe you're here."

He didn't say anything. I stared at him with everything in my eyes, begging him silently to see my words of apology, the promises of eternal devotion I held for him. He refused. It made me realize how much I'd hurt him when I'd ended things. It seemed like a lifetime ago that I'd been that weak, that cowardly, but I realized with an acute pang that I was being just that pathetic now by not giving him the words, by expecting him to read them the way he normally did, like subtitles beneath my silent lips.

So, I sucked in a deep breath that tasted like prison and tried to write King a verbal apple poem.

"Before you, I lived a boring life without passion or turmoil, just the same quiet existence that so many people spend their entire lives living out. It wasn't enough for me and I didn't know why. My only escape was through my books. They made me think that life could be made of cotton candy castles and white knights in shining armor. They told me that love was always good in the end, and relatively easy to obtain as long as you were a good person, which I was. Then I saw you in the parking lot and I fell in love with you in a way that I've never fallen in love with anyone before. You changed my life, catastrophically and fundamentally, like a warm water hurricane, and you didn't even have to open your mouth to say anything except to laugh.

"I've learned since then that life is messy. It's soaked in sweat and steeped in tears. It stinks of sex and beer. It means loving so much it burns you down and hating until you fly into a rage. It's grotesque but beautiful, a creature you can't even recognize, can't even name until you have it for yourself and then, you aren't ever willing to let it go. You, my eighteen-year-old student, taught me how to live and love until I ached with it all and instead of telling you how terrified that made me, how exhilarated and *alive*, I let fear rule me and I let you down."

I licked my lips, looked up at him from under my eyelashes to see him sprawled in the uncomfortable metal chair the way he would in his desk at EBA. For some reason, the sight made me want to cry.

"You are the king of all the fears that ruled my life, a man of ferocity and passion and balls to the wall determination and endless, boyish enthusiasm. You crack the soul of life open in your palms and drink your fill. A man like that needs a queen by his side," I murmured, repeating my excuse for our breakup back to him in a way that had his eyes clicking to life like flashlights. "And I'm that queen. I will match your ferocity. I will exceed your passion and challenge your balls to the wall determination. I will see your boyish enthusiasm and raise you my newborn love for life. I will stand beside my biker King and be his rough-and-tumble Queen, even if it takes me the next ten years to convince you to take me back."

When I looked up into his eyes again, I saw a passion so fierce I felt his desire echo through my body right down to my toes.

He leaned forward slowly, almost menacingly, until his forearms rested on the table with a clang as his cuffs settled. "Was never gonna let you go, Cress babe. Knew it that day in the parking lot just like you did. There was never a moment after that day that I doubted it."

"Despite everything, *because* of everything, I love you," I whispered as my hands shot out over the table to clutch his.

I ran my fingers over the cold metal shackles, and then spread his hands palms down on the metal surface so I could trace them with a tender touch before doing the same on the other side. I remapped the ridges of calluses on the pads and base of each finger, the life lines that bisected each palm and the tender network of periwinkle blue veins that spread from each wrist into his hands like tangled roots. It was such a strange thing to be sentimental over, his hands and their amazing beauty, but I found myself finally crying as I took them in a firm grip and brought them to my tear-painted lips.

He let me kiss them, cupped one against my cheek while the other found its home around the back of my neck.

I closed my eyes to better absorb his touch.

King's voice was achingly soft, taking my misery into his voice and sucking on it like a candy until it dissolved. "They arrested me before I brought my favorite teacher another apple poem. Was worried I'd have to woo you all over again. Got it with me, you want it?"

"Yes," I breathed, feeling like a dandelion about to face a strong breeze.

He didn't move away to reach for a piece of paper because, I realized just before he opened his mouth, they wouldn't have let him keep any personal effects on him in this horrible place.

So, instead of passing me an apple tied with a poem, he passed me the words written on his tongue.

"Your voice is between the lines, my Queen
Echoed in the white before the black
It is the swell of words that rest
Behind the apex of my throat

Your scent is caught between my teeth
Sinks among the groves there and gives them taste
Of clouds, dew upon my palate,
I hide you under my tongue

Your body walks my lines at night
It warms the skin beneath my arms, settles
Against my chest, a thumb in the hollow of the collarbone
It whispers your breath into mine

Your heart rests in the gaps
Between my ribs it sits and breathes my breath
It webs the links between my toes
And when I swim, my Queen, it is on you I float"

By the time he was finished, I was crying even harder.

He smiled crookedly at me. "Don't think I ever made a woman cry before."

"Oh, shut up," I said, playfully hitting him in the arm.

"With a face like that? Honey, there are girls *still* crying in their beds at night over you."

His grin slipped then fell off his face and his hand tightened around my neck. "Not gonna patch in after school, Cressida. When I get out of here, I'm going to accept at UBC Sauder School of Business."

Elation and worry tore through my chest. "King… honey, I meant what I said about standing by you. Please, don't make this decision based on what you think I want you to do."

I lost my breath at the width of his smile. He was so unbearably handsome, even in an orange jumpsuit and at that moment, I was sure I'd never wanted him more.

"Not about that, Queen, but thanks. It's the right thing to do for me. I got a brain and I want to get better at usin' it, so good that when I graduate and we move back to Entrance I can patch in with somethin' to contribute other than my name."

I loved that he wanted to make something of himself and I loved that he wasn't turning his back on a family who would live and die for him.

I told him so and it was his turn to take my hand and kiss it.

"Also, I quit my job so…yeah. I have no idea what I'm going to do with little to no money and no job, but maybe Eugene would let me work at his bar?" I joked somewhat desperately.

King barked out a short, hard laugh that felt as rewarding as a high five. "Love that you did that for me. Wish I could have seen you rip a fuckin' strip off of Headmaster Adams."

"How do you know I ripped a strip off him?"

"Babe."

"Babe is not an acceptable answer!" I reminded him, but I was laughing because even after two days of being without him, I'd missed this.

"I know you tore into the bastard because my girl is fierce, especially when someone does wrong by her man."

The warmth from his words poured over me like liquid sunshine.

"Okay, I might have yelled at him a little bit," I admitted.

He laughed.

"But he deserved it."

He laughed harder, throat exposed, brown and muscled, more beautiful to me than anything else in the world.

When he finished laughing, his eyes cleared and he said sternly, "Cress babe, there's no way I'm lettin' you work at Eugene's or any fuckin' where else where you gotta wear a skirt. Those legs of yours are exposed to a shit-ton of drinkin' men and I'm not there to clock their fuckin' heads together when they get the hot idea to hit on my woman. Yeah?"

More sunshine, hot rays that tingled over my skin.

"Yeah, King."

He nodded curtly. "You said you've always wanted to go back to school. Get your shit together and apply."

"I don't have the money," I said softly. "And it's too late to apply for scholarships."

"Babe," King used his hand on the back of my head to bring me closer, then brought his other hand to my chin in a firm hold. "I may be eighteen and I may not be one of those trust-fund brats you knew back in Dunbar, but I am a Garro. You think I can't find the money to send you to school?"

"I would be really uncomfortable with that, King, honey," I told him. "It's like I tried to tell you when we fought about the car, I want to be independent. Men have always taken care of me, and through that, manipulated me my whole life."

"You think I want to fuckin' manipulate you?"

"No, I absolutely do not. I'm just trying to tell you why the thought of you or your father paying for my schooling makes me uncomfortable."

"It's not about where the money comes from?" he challenged, pulling back from me so his hands fell with an empty clatter to the table.

"No," I said empathetically because truly, it didn't.

King sighed as he smoothed his hands over his tied back hair and then dropped them with another loud clang. "So, you'll let two bastards who tried to keep you under their thumb your whole fuckin' life take away your opportunity to go back to school, a dream you've had for fuckin' ever? You're gonna let them take away my opportunity to give that to you? That's what you're doin' here, Cress. It isn't about your independence; think you've proven since you left that motherfucker that you're stronger than any woman I ever met. Taking money from the man who loves you, who would fuckin' *love* to give that to you, is not the same exchange you had goin' with William. I'm not askin' you for a trade, for your obedience. I want nothin' back but seein' the smile you'd wear every day you went to school as the student, and not the teacher."

"Damn," I breathed, reaching out to drag his hands back to me. "You really are a biker poet."

The anger dissolved from his features but he still stared at me wearily.

I sighed, pried open his fist and placed his palm against my cheek. "Fine. If it really means that much to you, I'll let you pay thousands of dollars to send me back to university."

His laugh echoed around the room, drawing the attention of the guards, who frowned over at us. When he stopped, he winked at me, "Like winning with you, Cress, but it's never losin' so long as you're the one happy in the end."

Damn, biker boy sweetness could kill a girl.

I realized then that it was almost time to go, so before I lost my nerve, I pulled away from him. "I got something for you. I think you'll like it but I want you to know that I got it for me, not even knowing if you'd take me back."

He nodded, his head cocked in the way that said he was curious and his eyes brighter than star shine with love and interest.

God, a girl could feel like a queen under the mantle of that gaze.

And I did.

So, I carefully rolled up the left edge of my bookish tee (this one with the cover of *1984* because I felt it was fitting for visiting a prison) and exposed the taped white bandage over the side of my ribs.

I heard King's sharp intake of breath as I peeled away the protective covering and unveiled the new tattoo.

It took up about five inches, three of them text written in King's exact handwriting. Above that was a heart and cross-bones, below his poem:

*Fit to me*
*Made for me*
*Bone of my bone*
*Broken*
*Lost or freed*
*You are a state of mine*
*Eternal*
*Bone*
*Of my bone*

When I looked up at him, his face was tight with restraint and his eyes blazed.

"If I never get outta here, I got to marry your sweet ass so we can get us some conjugal visits," he said.

I burst out laughing. It was so him, so inappropriate and boyish and *fun* that I loved him all the more for it.

"You like it," I declared.

"Uh, *yeah*, babe."

"But no need for conjugal visits, okay? We're going to get you out of here. Shamble Wood is empty without its King."

"Won't be for long, babe. Like I said, never gonna let you go. I'm a smart man so I realize I gotta get out of here to keep all the jealous brothers away."

I laughed like he meant me to and for the last ten minutes of our visit, I pretended that I was in love with a boy and we were sitting in a cafeteria like a normal couple. I didn't worry about who had framed him, what the Nightstalkers were planning next, why William kept blowing up my phone or how people were going to react to my affair with a student. I just sat in front of my man and laughed.

# Twenty-Six.

I had thirteen missed calls when I finally checked my cell phone on my way back to Entrance and it started ringing as soon as I picked it up.

"Hello?" I asked through the Bluetooth speakers King had set up in Betty Sue.

She didn't even have a working tape player when I bought her and now, she was wireless. I smiled because it felt like King was with me in the car.

"Miss Irons? It's Officer Danner."

I stiffened, anger and fear seized the air in my lungs like a vacuum. "Yes, Officer, what can I do for you?"

*Keep calm, keep calm. You can't be arrested for sleeping with King. He's legally an adult.*

"I was wondering if you could come into the station today, as soon as possible would be best," he continued.

My hands slipped over the steering wheel, wet with sweat. "May I ask what this is regarding?"

"You may, ma'am, but I'm not at liberty to tell you over the phone."

I chewed so hard on my bottom lip that it began to bleed. Strangely, the taste of my own blood settled me. "I'm just driving back from Vancouver but I'll be there in an hour or so. Do

I need to bring my lawyer?"

"No, Miss Irons. We just want to ask you some questions."

"I'll see you shortly, then." I hung up and immediately asked Betty Sue to dial another number.

"Teach," Zeus answered in his low, thunderous voice.

"Shouldn't call me that anymore, Zeus. I quit," I told him. Nerves flared to life in my belly, reminding me that I had no plans for the future, very little money and a stubborn, mildly unstable husband who refused to let me divorce him.

He laughed, low and slow. "Bat owes me fifty bucks."

"Excuse me?"

"Knew you'd quit. No way you'd stay at a place like that after they fuckin' let that shit happen with the police."

"Did you find out who framed him yet?"

There was an ominous silence. "Not yet. But I had a word with that fuckin' headmaster and if King gets out, he graduates, no problem."

"*If*?"

"He's gettin' out today. Got our fancy lawyer from Vancouver on it who says they had a warrant for his fuckin' locker but they found that shit in his backpack after searchin' 'im. It was clearly fuckin' planted, given no kid of mine is gonna be cartin' drugs to school."

The tension that had been coiled around my heart like the snake from Eden loosened instantly and for the first time in days, I felt able to breathe.

"You call for an update?"

That snake immediately coiled back into place. "Yeah, Officer Danner called me into the police station."

The ensuing silence was a living thing, reaching through the phone to take my neck in its vicious hold. I struggled to speak because I had a feeling that if I didn't, Zeus would get on his motorcycle, go to the station and throttle Officer Danner.

"I'm going there now. I just thought, I don't know, that I should tell someone where I was going and since King is, um, indisposed, I thought I should call you."

The silence slackened just enough for me to breathe again.

"Good. I'm the one you call second every time, yeah?" he affirmed gruffly.

I smiled. "Yeah."

"You go down there and I'll have that fancy lawyer waiting. Name's Gerald White. I'll be down there too but not inside, yeah? We'll talk when you get out."

"Okay, Zeus," I agreed, astonished by the sense of relief.

Then again, it wasn't that surprising. Anyone would feel safe and protected with a man as fierce, cruel and strong as Zeus at their back.

When I entered the station, an older man with what looked like only three strands of hair on his head came forward immediately to introduce himself as Mr. White. A few minutes later, after I was briefed on how to act even though I told him I'd been interviewed by the police before (after Lysander killed Marcus), Officer Danner descended the stairs to the reception area to retrieve me.

It was inappropriate, but I noticed as I did every time I saw him, that he was absurdly handsome. However, unlike the Garro men, Lionel Danner was stern, controlled in a way that spoke of regimented schedules and military education, and he gave off a vibe that told you he would protect you at all costs, he just wouldn't love you while he did it. The contradiction was alluring and I was certain that many women had fallen for the hero in him and ended up in love with a bastard.

It was the hero that approached me, the handsome creases in his tanned face flexed into a smile as he took first Mr. White's and then my hand in his own.

"Miss Irons, it's unfortunate that we keep meeting under less than exemplary circumstances."

"Stop involving me in them, then?" I asked with sarcastic hope.

His lips twitched then flat lined. "I just have a few questions for you, if you'll follow me this way." He looked with mild distaste at Mr. White. "You don't need The Fallen's lawyer, Miss Irons, this is a friendly chat."

"Forgive me for thinking that no chat with a police officer is 'friendly,'" I said as I followed him down a hallway and into a small interrogation room. "I have enough experience to know better."

"You don't like the police," Danner noted grimly.

I smiled contemptibly, channeling my inner biker. "Maybe a long time ago I thought you all were heroes in blue armor, maybe before you arrested my brother for killing the man who tried to rape me, before you arrested King Kyle Garro in the middle of my classroom after illegally searching his belongings, but now, no, I don't like the police."

"Miss Irons, I urge you to let me speak on your behalf," Mr. White murmured to me.

He didn't seem annoyed though, only exhausted, and it occurred to me then that being the MC's lawyer would be a relatively difficult job just given the nature of bikers.

"Sorry," I told him sincerely, "I'm a biker babe in training."

He blinked at me but Danner had to cough to hide his startled laugh.

"Now, Officer Danner, if we could get to the point here? I want to be home when King gets out of jail."

"You're close with Garro's kids?" he asked, and I could tell it was more than professional curiosity that had him asking.

I filed that interesting tidbit away for another time.

"I'm close with King's family," I corrected even though I was terrified to do so.

There was no point in hiding it anymore though. I was no longer a teacher at EBA and people would know soon enough because they would see that we were together in a very biblical sense.

Danner raised his eyebrows. "No kidding."

"Nope, not kidding," I replied firmly.

I tried to affect a good biker babe pose, my arms crossed under my breasts and my eyes narrowed. I couldn't be sure how well it worked when my hair was pulled back into a high curled ponytail tied with a red scrunchy and my *1984* book tee was tucked into a flippy red-and-white checked skirt, but I hoped it would be at least a little intimidating.

"You sure you want to be telling me this as a teacher at EBA?" he asked, leaning in slightly, his stern face suddenly soft with sincerity. "I'd be honor bound to tell the school board about something like that."

Another surprise, Officer Danner liked me. It was the only explanation for why he was giving me an out and it made me wonder, if he hadn't called me in to talk about King, why I was there at all.

"I'm sure. Now, tell me what you want."

He stared at me for another moment before leaning back and rapping his knuckles against the metal desk. "I need to ask you a few questions about your husband, William Trent Irons."

"Excuse me?"

"Your husband. Mr. Irons is being tried for fraud and embezzlement," Danner clarified.

"Um, what?" I asked, my eyes and mouth wide open with shock. "You've got to be kidding me. William is the most upstanding citizen in the province. He works hard, volunteers and goes fishing or golfing at Capilano Golf and Country Club at least twice a week. That is not the kind of man who commits so much as a *minor* infraction, let alone something like fraud."

Danner stared at me then flipped open a folder that had been waiting on the table. He turned to the right page then twisted it to face me.

"Do you recognize these charges?" he asked.

I studied the list but I already knew that I wouldn't. Even while we were living together, I'd known nothing about our finances, not really. I had a credit and debit card for our joint account and I'd known we had a fairly astronomical limit on our credit, but William had handled the money. It was the husband's job, he'd always told me and because I'd grown up hearing the same thing from my father, I'd never questioned it.

Even then, I thought it was strange to see so many small transactions. William never kept cash on hand, because he said it was gauche.

"Did you know he was placed on a ninety-day suspension four years ago for failure to preserve clients' funds in a trust account? It appears that after that, he turned to less savory clients and began to embezzle funds *for* them instead of from them. The reason these statements may look strange to you, is because of the small but frequent cash deposits made over those four years," Danner explained to me.

"I can't believe this," I said, because truly, I couldn't.

The universe was playing some kind of cosmic joke. The man I'd married, who I had thought was too good for me, too boring and straight-laced and moral, had committed felonies while the man I'd fallen in love with, a man I'd thought was too much a boy, too wild and reckless and free to tame, was currently incarcerated for something he hadn't done.

It was too much to take in.

"What does this even mean?" I asked.

"He's being held on bail for two hundred and fifty thousand dollars and he's looking at up to five years in a provincial correction centre. The Vancouver PD asked me to talk to you, see if you could shed any light on the matter but it's obvious you were kept in the dark. Got to tell you, they might want to get more involved in looking at your part in this if they knew you were dating a Garro."

I blinked at him and guessed, "But you won't tell them that."

He blinked at me, too, then shot a look at my attorney. "Listen, Miss Irons, the whole town knows your story. Sad little woman moves to town after leaving her negligent husband, poor and alone in that crumbling wreck of a cottage out on Back Bay Road. People here like you, they think you're a damn fine teacher and a good woman. I'm inclined to agree with the good citizens of Entrance. Despite your obviously poor choice in men, you seem like a good woman. No reason to drag this out for you."

"Thank you," I said, so surprised that my voice was hoarse with it. "You're the kind of man who could make anyone rethink hating men in blue."

His face didn't move but his eyes, which were an extraordinary jade colour, twinkled at me. "Appreciate it. You should also know that most of the evidence against Mr. Irons came from two spectacularly terrified informants, his secretary and one of his small fry criminal clients. The latter was badly beaten but both claimed that a crisis of conscience was their only reason for rolling on Mr. Irons after so many years. Funny that, isn't it?"

*Oh my God.*

My mind flashed back to Nova telling me casually that King and Zeus were "fixin'" my problem with William.

My instinct was to ignore my intuition and chalk it up to the "crisis of conscience" bullshit that they'd told the police. That was what the naïve Cressida B.K. (before King) would have done.

I was not she.

I knew that my new biker family had taken care of the problem for me and instead of fear or horror, I felt giddy with vengeful glee and darkly proud of my men. William had been haunting me since I was a girl, waiting in the wings, grooming me into his perfect doll. He deserved whatever the hell was coming to him, especially if he'd done what the police were saying he had done.

It said more about me, I knew, that I could understand more of the poetic justice of illegally threatening and assaulting someone the way The Fallen had to protect a loved one, than I could why William would use people just to get more money when he already had more than most people ever would.

I smiled politely at Officer Danner and agreed, "Funny indeed. Sometimes the world works in mysterious ways."

"More often, they are not so mysterious." But he dropped it. "Due to the circumstances, you should be able to push through the divorce without his participation. But I would be careful, because your husband is a desperate man involved with dangerous people."

"I think I'll be safe," I said, totally unconcerned.

No one would dare to fuck with The Fallen.

Something ominous turned in my gut as I remembered that someone *had* dared, and that the Nightstalkers MC were still afoot.

I zoned out thinking about this as Danner finished up

talking to Mr. White and only tuned back into real life when we walked out into the parking lot. Zeus was there, leaning against his bike the way King would have been. Of course, the biggest difference between the two was that men and women both would have approached King, drawn by his bike and good looks maybe, but more by his charisma, which emanated from him like a halo. No one approached Zeus. He stood in a deep circle of solitude; his rough-cut face cast in shadows from the waving mass of hair that fell to his shoulders. With his massive, tattooed arms crossed over the impossible expanse of his chest and his big, booted feet crossed at the ankles, but he didn't look like the poster child of a modern-day bad boy the way King might have.

No, if Zeus belonged on a poster, it was as a Wanted one.

I broke into an enormous smile when I saw him and skipped directly to him. He watched me with narrowed eyes as I jumped up to press a kiss on his cheek.

"Thank you," I said quietly, aware that Danner was watching from the doorway and Mr. White was following closely behind to deliver his update.

A spark of surprise, quickly followed by tenderness, lit his silver gaze. "Got your back, Queenie."

It was the first time he'd called me by the nickname the other bikers had bestowed upon me.

I beamed at him. "You totally like me."

His surprised laugh erupted from him like a bark. "Sure, teach."

"Not a teacher anymore," I reminded him.

"It's stuck," he told me with dancing eyes. "King should be back at the clubhouse in an hour. Follow me back in your cage, yeah?"

I rolled my eyes because I thought it was stupid that bikers thought all cars were "cages," but I was too excited to see King again to give him any sass.

"Race you," I called as I ran toward my car.

"King's right, you really are a dork!" he called at my back.

I laughed as I slid into Betty Sue and peeled out of the police station in a move that was not very smart (given my proximity to police) but also was totally badass biker.

I was determined to beat Zeus back to the compound but I noticed that poor Betty Sue was basically out of gas, so I made a quick stop at Evergreen Gas Station on the way there. William's name lit the screen of my cell phone in the passenger seat as I swung out of the car. Pumping my own gas was one of the bizarre things that I loved to do now that I was no longer with William, who had always insisted on the full-service stations. It was kind of ironic that he was calling just as I was doing it.

I was humming along to "Ain't No Rest for The Wicked" by Cage the Elephant ringtone as it blasted through my epic new car speakers but stopped when my voicemail connected to the Bluetooth and William's voice came through.

"Cressida, call me immediately. You don't understand what you've done and I'm willing to forgive you. That *biker* has clearly brainwashed you or something because you keep ignoring me. I'm sorry, my darling, but I need to get you to me soon. My lawyer says it isn't looking good, so I've decided that you and I are going to go away. You were always badgering me about Costa Rica and it has a no extradition treaty. Trust me, you'll love it there. Forgive me, but this was the only way I could think of to get you away from those biker bastards."

I was frowning at my cell phone through the open window when I was suddenly pushed up against the side of my car.

I froze, reminded of Marcus pushing me up against the wall in the back alley.

And just like then, lips descended to my ear, but this time they whispered, “William says he’s sorry.”

Then a crippling pain exploded in my head and I didn’t remember anything anymore.

# Twenty-Seven.

The pain woke me up.

It seared through the centre of my palms like concentrated wildfire. Before I was even fully conscious, I tried to move my hands away from the heat but they were stuck deep in the flames. My eyes flew open and even though my vision was blurry, I could make out the sight of one of my hands affixed to the wooden arms of the chair I sat in. It was nailed there with a thick metal spike that you'd find on a construction site. My mind dissociated from the pain enough to note that it was at least three inches thick and quite long. And it went right through the middle of my hand. Same thing with my other hand.

Someone had knocked me out, dragged me to some kind of warehouse and *nailed* me to a wooden chair.

A sob rose in my throat but I swallowed it down, focusing on the hellacious burn to keep my mind sharp. I took stock of my body, noting the drumbeat of pain at the back of my skull from where the man had clocked me with something hard, the soreness at my wrists and ankles from where they were wrapped tightly in damp rope. There was dirt across my entire left side, which made me think they'd dragged me across the ground before placing me in the chair. Worst of all, my jeans were undone and my underwear was pulled uncomfortably tight over my sex. Someone had checked me out down there while I was passed out.

Another sob crawled up my throat. I thought I might throw up all over myself.

"Comfortable?"

My head snapped back, hitting the exact same place that I'd been struck, and stars exploded in front of my eyes. Through the black spots and colourful flurries, I made out a short, stocky Hispanic man. He stood in front of me, swathed in shadows like a Grim Reaper.

"No," I croaked, noticing that my mouth tasted like ash and blood.

His pockmarked face creased in a bland smile. "What a shame."

Something made a noise behind me. Fear saturated me, yellow and acrid like being doused in urine. I couldn't turn my head enough because my torso was tied to the chair, but I knew someone lingered at my back.

"Aren't you going to ask who I am?" the man in front of me asked, taking a step closer. "Yell 'why me' or start crying? I have to admit, it's my favorite part of this whole thing."

"The whole abducting innocent women thing?" I asked, dredging up the sass that lay deep inside me, under the fear and the pain, lower even than my sense of self-preservation.

I refused to allow this man to scare me. It was the only thing I could focus on through the haze of pain that threatened to take me under again.

My captor laughed his hyena laugh. "Look at her, boys, look how she talks back!" Suddenly, his laughter died and he lunged toward me with bared teeth. "You're nailed to a chair, *puta*, not a throne. Be grateful I've kept you fucking breathing."

"Fuck you," I said with cold calm.

Inside, my body fired like an overheating furnace, sheer terror building the flames too high. I was in overdrive, desperate to flee but literally stuck to the chair. My hands kept trying to jerk away from the pain but it only ripped them open wider.

"Fuck me?" His laugh was like tearing sheet metal. "Fuck *me*? *You* are the one tied to a chair. One of my men already tried to have a go at your sweet white pussy. You want me to let him back in?"

I glared at him. I knew who he was, Luis Elizondo, the President of the Nightstalkers MC, and I knew he wanted information about The Fallen. This knowledge comforted me because it gave me an edge. He didn't expect me to know him just as he wouldn't expect me to stand up to him. He wanted my submission, but I'd become the kind of woman who only gave that gift to one man. If Luis wanted King, wanted the men of The Fallen MC, he'd have to go through me to get to them.

My bravado faltered when Luis lost his patience with me and snarled, an inhumane sound that echoed through the mostly empty warehouse. "Shut the fuck up. Sander, muzzle the bitch."

The fire inside me roared, then died altogether. Ice water flooded my veins as a new kind of terror descended on me.

The body waiting patiently behind my chair stepped closer.

Ice crawled quickly over my skin, inside my ears, nose and gaping mouth to invade my brain, to stop the thoughts that led to only one conclusion.

Huge familiar hands gently appeared at the edges of my vision, a thick length of rope stretched between them. Before I could close my mouth, they jerked the rope between my lips, pressed it tightly to the corners of my mouth so I was semi-swallowing the thick fibers. I gagged at the stress it put on my tongue. The rope was knotted behind my head and the person stepped back.

"Why don't you come show this bitch your face?" the horrible man in front of me ordered.

No.

No, no, no.

As long as I didn't see him, I could stay frozen and numb to the truth.

I squeezed my eyes shut as the heavy thud of booted feet rounded my chair and made their way to the man who spoke.

"Open your eyes, *puta*."

No, no, no.

"Victor," he barked at someone off to the left.

Someone moved out of the shadows. I whimpered when cruel hands gripped my hair and wrenched my head back. The cold, sharp edge of a knife pressed into my throat.

"Open. Your. Eyes." Victor hissed in my ear.

His mordant breath activated my gag reflex. As I shuttled forward with the force of my dry heaves, the knife bit into my neck and a thin trail of blood slipped down to pool wetly in my right collarbone.

"Open your eyes," he ordered again, wiggling the blade against the scratch until it opened wider, spilled more blood down my front.

I opened my eyes.

Even though I'd known who would stand before me, I nearly threw up at the sight of Lysander. He stood beside Luis with his hands behind his back, his posture straight and sure like a soldier before his commander.

"You recognize your brother, of course," Luis began conversationally as he patted Lysander on the back. "He's been a good little informant for me the past few weeks."

I closed my eyes again on a sob but the man holding my hair gave me a little shake, so I peeled them open again.

Lysander stared at me vacantly.

I wanted to scream at him, tear out his hair and slam his head repeatedly against the concrete floor until it busted open and spilled all his secrets across the ground for me to sift through.

My hands tried to fist with rage but pain had me rocking back in the chair.

Fuck, I'd never felt so helpless in my life.

I wished fervently that King and the boys were looking for me. There was no doubt in my mind that if I didn't give Luis what he wanted, he'd kill me. Seeing as I didn't know anything about The Fallen's criminal side, I had nothing to give him. Therefore, I'd be dead sooner rather than later. I just had to give King time to find me.

"Now, maybe, you understand just how serious I am about taking over The Fallen's distribution network. I'm going to get Victor to take that rope out of your mouth and you're going to tell me all about Zeus's operation, aren't you?"

I didn't react but he nodded for Victor to undo the tie. When he did, I spat it into my lap.

"I don't know anything about that, you moron. Old ladies aren't privy to that kind of information and you know it," I rasped through my sore, parched throat.

"I know a man's feeling good after takin' his bitch, he isn't afraid to share things with her," he said.

Fuck, of course he thought that I was with Zeus. Everyone outside of the MC did. What didn't add up was that Lysander knew for a fact that I was with King and not his father. Why would he keep that from his "boss" or whatever Luis was to him?

My eyes darted his way but he was staring through me as if I wasn't even there.

Luis stepped closer and another man materialized out of the shadows to join him. The newcomer cracked his knuckles and smiled at me as Luis said, "We're going to play a game where you tell me what I want to know and Harp here doesn't beat your pretty face in, *sí*?"

I closed my eyes, wishing I had the gag in my mouth again. I tried to find a safe place to rest inside myself, as I couldn't answer question after question and Harp's fists kept coming. There was no such place. But I found that I could let the pain carry me away on dark clouds so that I drifted from ache to ache in mental purgatory. Anything was better than clueing back into reality.

So, it took me a long time to recognize the sound of gunfire even though it ricocheted so close to my head. Through blurry eyes, I watched Harp drop to the ground, half his face blown off by a bullet. Then men were everywhere, wearing the Nightstalkers colours of red, black and green, and some others, others wearing my favorite colours in the whole entire world. Green, black and white.

The Fallen men had arrived.

Through my delirium, I spotted Nova crouched down by one of the doors, covering for King, Zeus and Priest as they ran inside, crouched low and each wielding guns in their hands. Blackness narrowed my vision like a camera filter and I kept dipping in and out of unconsciousness so I saw only flashes. Zeus rugby tackling Luis as he tried to run, his lion roar of fury as he began to pummel the Mexican drug lord's face. Bat appearing from out of nowhere with a huge sniper rifle strapped to his back. He took down two Nightstalkers with his bare hands without any discernable effort.

King. I tried to track his progress across the warehouse but I was too dazed, too dizzy.

"Babe," his voice called, his voice peeling through the heavy curtains of darkness shrouding my mind so that I could see the light.

I opened my eyes to see his face in front of me. He had never looked more like a fallen angel than in that moment, his gorgeous face a mask of vengeful fury.

"King," I breathed but the effort hurt my ribs and I wondered if maybe my tormentor hadn't just aimed his hits at my face.

"Gettin' you out of these ropes," he was saying when I clued in again.

Distinctly, I could feel him loosen them at my chest and ankles. When he got to my hands, he cursed so viciously I jerked and then whimpered as the pain abruptly followed.

"Motherfuckin' *fuckers*," he swore again.

He suddenly had a hammer in his hands, blood speckled over the metal head. I realized they'd probably dropped it to the floor beside me after they'd nailed me in.

I gagged violently again but didn't throw up.

"This is gonna hurt," King said over a particularly loud round of gunfire.

He didn't give me time to brace. With the other side of the hammer wedged painfully under the head of the small spike, he wrenched the metal out of my hand.

I screamed, so hard and loud that I passed out for a few seconds.

Then, I came to just in time for him to pull out the other spike.

I passed out again.

"Shit, she's bleedin' so fuckin' much," King was saying

when I zoned back in but I didn't open my eyes.

"Wrap it tight," someone, Nova I thought, said from my other side as they bound each of my hands with fabric.

The pressure deepened the pain, then my hands felt oddly numb. It was a massive relief. I opened my eyes and mouth to say so and found two Nightstalkers approaching silently from behind King and Nova.

I shouted wordlessly.

They both shifted infinitesimally. Nova evaded his attacker, then threw himself at his torso in a low tackle.

King wasn't so lucky.

He took the edge of a wicked-looking knife to his shoulder, the same blade that had sliced my throat. His face contorted in pain, but then he was trying to wrest the blade out of the man named Victor's hand. I watched them fall hard to the ground, neither one on top as they struggled for supremacy.

My thoughts rushed and whorled like water circling a drain. I could barely feel my body anymore, the pain had washed it clean of sensation, but I recognized that I was free to move.

"Cressida," Zeus bellowed from across the room as he came charging over.

I blinked slowly, not understanding why he was yelling.

A clatter brought my attention to King again and I watched as the knife flew out of Victor's hand and skidded to a stop by my feet. Victor used King's momentum against him and pinned him to the floor with his knees so he could reach into his waistband for a gun.

*No.*

Anything in the world could happen to me, could happen to anyone else. I didn't care if all the kittens, birds and bees had to die, if I had to personally slaughter men, women and children to make it so but nothing could happen to King.

I wouldn't allow it.

The knife was at my feet, I just had to get it. I fell to my knees with a brutal *crack* that vibrated from my kneecaps and up my thighs, but I ignored the pain and tried to clutch the knife in my brutalized hand. It fell through my weak-as-water fingers again and then again.

"Cressida," Zeus shouted, closer now.

I looked up to see him close to Victor, who was about to press the gun against King's thrashing head.

Fury launched through me.

"Give it to me," Zeus ordered, hand out stretched as he lunged toward me.

I wrapped the knife in an excruciating grip and tossed it to him.

He caught it on the fly, sprinted the two steps to where his son lay prone on the ground with a gun at his temple, and without hesitation, he plunged the bloodied blade into the back of Victor's neck, right at the base of his skull.

The sick sound of crushing bones and tearing flesh was louder than the last gunshot that reverberated through the warehouse.

I tried to keep my head up and my eyes open, but moving so much had drained the last of my reserves. With a thin sigh, my head dropped to the concrete and I was out.

I knew before I woke up that I would be in a hospital. The smell was the first thing I noticed, the plastic, medicinal scent of all hospitals everywhere. My body felt strange, not my own, but at least the mind-melting pain was gone. I tried to lift my hand, suddenly terrified that it would still be nailed to the chair. When I succeeded, I opened my eyes to look at the heavily bandaged flesh and burst into tears.

"Babe."

I turned my crying face to King as he moved to lie down beside me and carefully pulled me to him. I wanted to clutch at him, touch him all over to assure myself that he was alive and well but my hands were mittens, so instead, I nuzzled my face hard against his cheek, his neck, his chest.

"I'm here, babe, I got you," he assured me over and over again.

I cried harder, so hard I couldn't breath.

"Shh, babe, I need you to take a deep breath for me, yeah?"

The air rattled around in my open mouth as I tried to suck it into my uncooperative lungs. King took my face gently in his hands and breathed deeply, silently prompting me to mimic him. I tried again and finally found air. We did this, deep breathing together, until my mind cleared and the tears stopped.

"I got you, babe," he said then, each word low and weighty with significance.

"Thought you were going to die," I croaked out because even my throat, teeth and lips hurt.

King's thumb swept tenderly over my swollen mouth before he ducked down to kiss each side where the rope gag had given me a temporary Joker smile.

"Luckily, I had my Queen to keep me alive," he said.

I stared into his eyes, desperate to mark each bubble of air caught beneath the ice of his irises and every colour of pale blue that brightened and darkened them like shapes under glacial caps.

"I want to go home," I told him, suddenly desperate to leave the hospital. "Can I?"

His lips pursed in thought but when I whined low in my throat, he sighed. "We can do whatever the fuck you want, Cress babe. The doc's checked you out. You don't need surgery on your hands but you'll probably have nerve damage and you might need rehab. Otherwise, you have a concussion, a fuckin' laceration on your throat and a fractured jaw. Not to mention your beautiful face is fuckin' black and blue."

"Not great," I murmured.

"No," he bit out.

"Alive," I pointed out. "Both of us."

"Thank fuckin' Christ," he said against my lips before kissing them softly.

"Home?" I asked again.

"Okay, wait here and I'll get everythin' in order." He gave me another kiss before sliding off the bed and made his way to the door. He paused at the door and looked back at me, his hand pulling hard through his curls. "Need a second. Haven't left you since it happened and I'm havin' a hard time doin' it now."

My heart stopped then restarted with a jolt in my chest.

"Love you," I told him.

"Bone of my bone," he replied.

I waited for him while he talked to the doctors (who actively disagreed with my decision to leave but technically they couldn't do anything about it) and brought me papers to sign.

"My parents?" I asked softly, because if they'd been there they would have been given dispensation to sign them for me.

As it was, it was hard to sign papers without the use of your fingers.

"Called 'em. To be fair to the cunts, they wanted to come

but they were freakin' out so much about you gettin' what was comin' to you because you involved yourself with 'riff' fuckin' 'raff' that I ended up hanging up on them before I could tell them where you'd be."

I smiled only slightly because it was sad about my parents, but he was awesome.

"Everyone else is okay?"

His eyes warmed as he helped me sit up on the edge of the bed and then proceeded to dress me. "Priest and Zeus are bruised but fine. Nova got a bullet to the gut. He's in the room down the hall. Puck, Lab Rat and Cy were also there, took care of the guys outside and they're roughed up but cool. I got a nick to the shoulder, not bad. Bat's the only one without a scratch but he was in the navy for ten years before he patched in so go figure."

"Good," I said, placing my hand on his shoulder so I could step into the flip-flops he brought me.

Someone had packed one of King's big sweatshirts that said EBA on it in green and an old pair of jeans I'd left at the clubhouse. They were comfy and they smelled like King, which brought me instant comfort.

"Have lots more questions," I murmured tiredly as I took his hand.

"So do I," a smooth, deep voice said from the doorway.

King growled, but I just sighed and collapsed to the hospital bed again.

"Yeah, Officer, come on in," I said, welcoming Lionel Danner into the room.

He stepped through the doorway, his partner Riley Gibson behind him.

"Sorry to do this when you're still recovering, but I just have to ask you some questions," Danner said. To his credit, he really did sound contrite.

If I were still the old Cressida who liked rules and regulations, I'd probably have fallen for Lionel. He was gorgeous, loyal, dutiful and tough like a Wild West sheriff. So, in short, female catnip.

As it was, because he was Zeus's enemy, he was also mine.

And, needless to say, I was head over heels in love with the teenage biker who stepped slightly in front of me to argue with the cops about interrogating me while I was injured.

"Just a few questions," Danner urged.

"It's fine, King," I said. "Just hurry up. I'm exhausted and I want to go home."

Gibson nodded, stepping forward. "We just wanted to clear up the timeline. Two nights ago—"

"Two?" I asked.

King squeezed my hand. "You were concussed and out of it for a long time, babe. Happy to see those whiskey eyes again."

I leaned heavily into his side as I turned to the cops again. "Go on."

"Two nights ago, you were at Evergreen gas station when you were hit over the head by a man named Hector Alonso and transferred to a warehouse just off Highway 99. They kept you for three hours before Zeus and his… friends—" he hesitated over what to call them but continued "—found you."

"Correct."

"In the ensuing fight, did you witness Zeus Garro kill a man named Victor Hernandez?"

My heart seized as I was thrown back to the night of my bachelorette party. The cops had asked me the same exact thing about Lysander killing Marcus Whitman. No matter what I said about my brother defending me from rape, they had still cuffed him, carted him away and put him in jail for six years of his life.

Then I remembered that Lysander had been in the warehouse, had stood beside a man who wanted to kill me and had done nothing. I couldn't reconcile the one image of him with the other. How could he go from being my defender to my persecutor?

I shoved those thoughts to the back of my mind and focused on the irrefutable fact that I did not trust the police and I adored Zeus.

So, I told them, even though it made my jaw ache, "I'm sorry, Officers. I don't think I can be much help. As you can see," I held up my heavily wrapped hands, "I was preoccupied at the time and in and out of consciousness."

King slipped an arm around my shoulders and I knew he was happy with my answer.

"You're sure?" Gibson pressed, even taking a step forward in an attempt to physically pressure me.

It was a low move after the trauma I'd already endured and both Danner, who held his partner back with an arm and a glare, and King, reacted. My man bared his teeth and declared, "This conversation is over. Cressida is concussed and she has a fuckin' fractured jaw. Asking her to talk to you in this condition is physically painful for her."

The pain in my jaw was nothing compared to the pain in my hands, but I was done with the conversation so I allowed King to pull me to my feet and I followed him when he grabbed his bag and started for the door.

The cops let us go but I could hear Danner murmuring to Gibson to let us be. I was grateful to him because exhaustion hit me like a physical blow as we stepped into the fresh air. Thankfully, King had thought ahead and my car was waiting for us instead of his bike. We were silent on the ride home, mostly because I slept.

He took us to the compound but I didn't question him. Truthfully, I was happy he'd made that decision. I was still shaken and I liked the idea of being on the compound, one of the safest places in BC if not the world.

"No one else is here except for my dad, Bat and Buck. They're in the garage and I need to take you to them before I put you to bed," King said as he let me out of the car.

My intuition prickled. "You have him, don't you?"

King's full lips thinned. "Yeah."

I nodded. "I take it he isn't in the kitchen drinkin' tea with the guys?"

"No, babe, he isn't."

I sighed, not sure how I felt about my brother being held at the hands of The Fallen, however badly he may have betrayed me.

"If he hadn't called us, I don't know if we would have found you," King told me as he closed the passenger door and swung me up on the hood of the car.

He stepped between the legs I spread for him and one of his hands found its place at my neck. His thumb reached around to rub at the taped-together blade wound just under the midline of my throat.

"He called?" I asked to pull King out of his memories and what-ifs.

He nodded. "He called just after you were taken. We knew because Benny Bonanno spotted you getting hit over the head at the gas station and called Tayline who called me. We'd barely begun to mobilize with no fuckin' idea where to look when your fuckin' brother calls me, tells me the Nightstalkers got you and they're takin' you to a warehouse off the highway behind the gas station at the base of the mountains."

"Why would he do that?" I asked because I didn't have one clue how to process the information.

"That's what I need you to find out. We got him here, babe, for two reasons. The man's got to pay for fuckin' with The Fallen but more, for fuckin' with our Queen. And we need to know what the fuck kind of game he was playing. We roughed him up but he won't talk, he says, unless it's to you."

He stared at me hard and long, his pale gaze burrowing to the heart of me. I wondered, probably because I was high on painkillers, if he found a mirror there that reflected his face back at him.

"I'm not patchin' in. I meant what I said to you when I was in the clink. But, babe, this *is* my fuckin' world and one day, I'm gonna rule it. I need you to know what you're getting into if you take me on." He closed his eyes and pressed his forehead to mine. "Can't lose you, won't lose you, but I don't know if I can walk away from my brothers, especially after what they just did to get you home to me."

"I don't want you to," I admitted softly, pressing my own hand to the back of his neck in mimicry of his habit. "When you were lying there about to take a bullet to the head, I swore that I would kill anyone and anything that got in the way of you living, or you being in my arms every single day for the rest of our lives. It was awful but I meant it. I know I've told you a thousand times that I'm not the kind of woman who can deal with the MC life but I think I was wrong. Or, even if I wasn't, I want to be that woman for you, with you. The rough-and-tumble Queen to your biker King."

His smile nearly took my sight, it was so dazzling, but I kept my eyes on it, glaring happily into the sun, uncaring if it blinded me.

"I won't show you anything like this again, you need to

know that too. MC business is kept between brothers, and I don't want you held accountable for anything. Unfortunately, this involves you and I need your help."

"I understand."

He pulled me fully into his arms to hug me.

"Made from me, for me," he murmured into my hair. "The perfect Queen."

I kissed him, my mouth open and soft because it hurt to kiss, but I needed to kiss him more than I cared about the pain. Gently, he pinched my chin so he could control the movement and he kissed me back.

When we parted, I slid silently down his body and took his hand so he could lead me to the garage.

They were in the last bay, the garage door pulled down but the industrial lights on so everything was in stark white and yellow relief. This included my brother, who was bound to a hook in the ceiling that normally hoisted cars. His hands were shackled with chains and his feet dangled just off the floor. There was blood on his face, down his throat and in the weave of his shirt. They had clearly already gone over him once or twice.

My eyes flicked to Bat, Buck and Zeus, who stood closest to Lysander, still wearing brass knuckles that were wet with blood.

I looked up and caught Zeus watching me, his face cruel and guarded. He was waiting for me to freak out, I realized.

So, to prove him wrong, I turned to my brother and walked closer, aware that he watched me between the slits in his swollen face.

"Why did you do it?" I asked simply.

His answer was not so simple.

"I owed them money," he warbled through his split lip.

"Lied to you about the gambling but it's the same story. Took their money to get on my feet after getting outta the slammer and with the interest, I just couldn't get back out from under it. I won pretty good at the races one day a while back but you needed the money for the house, so…" He tried to shrug but grimaced when the movement was cut short by the chains. "They found out you were my sister. My fault, I don't keep much but I got that picture of you from your graduation in my wallet because I'm an idiot. They knew you were datin' Zeus so they had an eye on you, but I was keepin' my eye on them and they didn't care about you in a big way.

"Then fuckin' William. The crazy motherfucker talks to some of his fucked-up clients and asks one of them to kidnap you for him. Wanted to run away with you to fucking Indonesia or some shit. The Nightstalkers heard, took the job and the ridiculous fucking payout, and decided to kill two birds with one stone. They knew you'd probably have information they could use, and if you didn't and they ended up killing you, it would drive Zeus into making a bad mistake."

Wow.

I had trouble digesting everything that he was saying, had trouble believing that my soon-be-ex-husband could "love" me enough to pay for me to be kidnapped, that my brother could have kept such a massive secret double life from me.

"Why did you need the job at Hephaestus, to spy on my friends?" I asked.

"I told them no like six hundred times but they were having too much trouble cracking into the drug trade up here, so they got desperate and threatened me."

"The morning you showed up at my house," I whispered.

He groaned miserably. "Yeah. Decided it wasn't worth it, involving you, but then King got involved and it was so easy. I figured I would take the job but wouldn't give them anything important and I swear to fucking Christ, I didn't, Cress. I would rather die than put you in danger. You know that."

"Do I?" I asked softly. "You killed a man for me once, Sander, but does that mean I need to forgive you for every other bad thing you ever do?"

He was quiet. A smart move because there was nothing he could say to save himself from my condemnation.

"They won't kill you," I said, gesturing to the mean looking bikers with Sander's blood on their hands. "You're my family and I'm theirs so they won't kill you. What they'll do to you otherwise, I don't know and I don't really care. You almost got me and the people I care about killed. I can't—I won't—forgive you for that. I hope you get your act together, Sander, I really do, but I don't want to see you ever again." I ignored the gurgle of hurt that sounded in his throat, the way he flinched so hard against his bounds that his body rocked in the air. "I'm done with people who take from me and don't give anything back. I'll always be thankful that you saved me, but this is goodbye."

Quickly, because I was aware that I was about to burst into tears, I walked forward to press a kiss to his bloody cheek. When I turned away, I moved to Zeus and wrapped him in a full body hug.

"Thank you," I whispered with my heart in my mouth.

He'd stiffened at first, but at my words, his body melted slightly and a hand came around to pat me on the back. He didn't say anything, but he was a badass biker and he didn't have to.

Zeus Garro had my back and now, he knew I had his.

I didn't look back as I collected King's hand and walked out the door, my head held high, blood on my lips and my King at my side.

# Epilogue.

"A dirty chai latte and dark roast coffee, please," I asked the barista at Loafe Café.

"Sure thing," she replied with a bubbly smile.

I returned the expression, which wasn't difficult because these days, all I did was smile. Accepting the dark roast coffee and my change, I went to the coffee station to add cream and an unhealthy amount of sugar, then picked up my dirty chai latte from the counter and found a table outside even though it was a cold day in late October.

It was a gorgeous autumn afternoon in Vancouver, the grey sky the perfect backdrop to the riot of violent orange, red and yellow foliage clinging to treetops and littering the ground. The air was crisp and spiced with the sweet musk of decaying leaves that crunched underfoot. I took out my tattered copy of *Paradise Lost* and read while I waited.

It wasn't long.

"Bone of my bone," King murmured as his cold hands cupped my face to tilt it back for his kiss.

I accepted his mouth with a long hum of pleasure, loving the feel of his lips on mine, loving that no one cared if I kissed him or not. Now that we were free from the chains that bound us in Entrance, I found we erred on the side of too much PDA but I didn't really care. I'd embraced my inner biker a lot over the past six months even though, technically, King and I were not a part of The Fallen. We were just two civilian students at UBC, him in the renowned Sauder Business program and me in my Master's English program doing my dissertation on Satan of *Paradise Lost* as an untraditional hero. I drew daily inspiration from my own untraditional hero, whom I tugged close to me by his long hair so I could deepen our kiss.

When we broke apart, King grinned into my face. He'd grown a short beard in the time we'd been on campus and it made him look even sexier, like a lumberjack that had accidentally wandered onto campus. Women watched him wherever he went and I knew he got asked out a ton, both because he told me and because some women were ballsy enough to ask even when I was standing right next to him. If I wasn't, King turned them down without blinking an eye. If I was, he let me sear them with my possessive wrath because my territorial behavior turned him on.

"Good day, babe?" he asked before gently nipping my chin with his teeth.

"Better now," I said, shamelessly happy and unafraid to be cheesy about it.

Like Milton once wrote about good things coming from evil, the horror of King's arrest and my abduction had grown mild over time and the light we created together had far overcome the dark. My hands still ached when it was damp, which in Vancouver was often, but the scars had been reduced to thin pink slashes that King kissed every morning when we woke up.

He'd obsessed over the scars until one morning that summer, he'd woken me up and dragged me to Street Ink Tattoo Parlor. Now, we had matching tattoos on the inside of our middle fingers, him a King of Hearts and me the Queen. They lined up perfectly when we linked our fingers together, which was often.

He may have kissed the scars every morning when we woke up but his middle finger I now kissed every time after, to remind him that we were alive, free and together.

"You ready to head out?"

I nodded, standing up and swinging my old messenger bag over my shoulder. It was still strange to me that it held *my* essays and not those of my students. King caught my hand as we walked toward the parking lot and I couldn't help myself from looking around at all the students walking by us, feeling like a child holding her first trophy. I would never get used to displaying our relationship, to holding the hand of a man who was as beautiful and magnetic as a fallen angel.

"Did you tell Benny and Carson that we'd be back in time for their party on Sunday?" I asked when we reached his Harley.

King nodded, handed me my helmet (a wicked cool "brain bucket" that had the words *Property of The King* scrawled on the back in gold script) and swung over the bike. "They know, babe."

"I just feel so bad that I won't be there to help them set up," I tried to explain as I settled behind him.

"Babe, it's a fuckin' Halloween party and you already spent the last three days helpin' 'em decorate the house. It's for university students, they don't need you to set out snacks and fuckin' fruit punch."

I blushed but planted my hands on my hips. "This is their first party as a couple, King. It's important they know we support them."

"We see 'em every week, babe. Think they know it."

Strangely, maybe, King and I had become really close with Benny and Carson, who had also moved to UBC in September to start their undergraduate degrees. They fought all the time because Carson still had a hard time being openly gay and Benny was an affectionate guy but it was clear to everyone who knew them that there was a lot of love there. They lived off campus like us, on the main level of a little bungalow with Carson's mum living in the basement. She'd left her husband and didn't want to be far from the son she'd neglected for the first eighteen years of his life. I was fairly close to her too, and we went to hot yoga every Sunday morning.

I settled behind King on the bike, pressed my cheek to him and dragged in a deep breath of his leather, fresh air and laundry scent. We did our laundry together now and I loved the smell of that clean scent on my own clothes, but nothing was the same as taking a hit directly from the source.

"You are such a dork," King chuckled when he heard my deep inhale.

"You love it."

"Yeup, makes me fuckin' crazy. Don't know what's sexier, you in your geeky book tees or you in nothing."

He felt my aroused shiver against his back and laughed.

"Dad needs us or he wouldn't'a called. Need you to be prepared for anything, yeah?" he asked after he'd sobered.

Zeus had called in the middle of the night requesting that King come home for the weekend. It wasn't a usual request since Zeus wasn't a helicopter parent and he'd been really good about giving King his space from The Fallen. Still, when Zeus called, you answered. So, here we were.

"Do you think it's the Nightstalkers?" My scarred hands flexed involuntarily at the reminder.

The rival MC hadn't taken off after Luis died. They'd only regrouped, and after lying low for the summer, I had to wonder if they were making their comeback.

"Don't know, babe."

"It could just be he met a woman and he wants us to meet her?" I asked, jokingly.

Zeus Garro did not date. Not ever.

King snorted.

"Maybe Harleigh Rose is dating someone and he wants us to meet him?" I hoped.

H.R. was more beautiful every day and a sixteen-year-old girl in high school, so it would be expected for her to have a boyfriend.

Zeus Garro did not let his little girl date. Not ever.

"You done talkin' crazy now, babe? Wanna get home and assess the damage myself."

"For now," I muttered, but only so he would laugh again, which he did.

"Don't be afraid to scratch or bite," he said, reminding me of the first time I'd climbed onto his bike, and followed him onto the Sea to Sky Highway with no idea of where he'd take me. "I'm gonna ride hard so hold on tight, Queenie, yeah?

"Always," I said under the roar of the engine as he pulled out of the lot.

**The End.**

See more of King and Cressida in Zeus Garro's book, *Welcome to the Dark Side*, LIVE now.

# Playlist

"Raising Hands Raising Hell Raise 'Em High"—The Wind & The Wave

"Jailhouse Rock"—Elvis Presley

"My Girl"— The Temptations

"Burnin' Love"—Elvis Presley

"Ticking Bomb"— Aloe Blacc

"Lovers in a Dangerous Time"— Barenaked Ladies

"Sail"—Awolnation

"Ain't No Rest for the Wicked"—Cage the Elephant

# Thanks Etc.

*Lessons in Corruption* was a seriously difficult journey for me. Two friends of mine, two of the *absolute* best friends in my life, were involved in a student/teacher relationship that hurt a lot of people, myself included. I never planned to write a love story about that particular romantic trope but then I saw a picture of model Christopher Mason straddling a motorcycle and the story of King Kyle Garro hit me right between the eyes. The process of writing about their romance, the questions that I was forced to ask myself about right and wrong, about how to make their love seem pure and good under questionable circumstances, was incredibly complicated for me. Now, looking back on the process, I realized it was therapeutic. The hurt that my friends caused is easier to emphasize with now, hurts me a little less. I'll never have them in my life again but I feel like I can finally move on and I have King and his rough-and-tumble Queen Cressida to thank for that.

As usual, I have so many people to thank for supporting me so bear with me.

To Amber Hamilton, my amazing PA. You joked once about how you felt like we were having a baby together and look, we've done it! Our baby is out in the world and I can't thank you enough for telling me to breath and holding my hand while I gave birth to this beauty.

Kiki and the ladies at The Next Step PR, you keep me sane and running smoothly on task. I've loved you since the moment I told you my mother had cancer and you listened to me cry. I'll never be able to express how much you personal and professional support means to me.

Najla Qambar is my cover designer and all-around graphics magician. Thank you so much for putting up with my flood of emails and last-minute asks, and for making my imagination come to life.

Amber Hodge, you wonderful lifesaver, thank you for taking my very rough draft and turning it into polished gold. I would have quite literally been lost without you and I can't wait to work with you again.

Every day that I interact with my readers in Giana's Darlings, I feel so blessed. Thank you to my loyal Darlings for assuaging my doubts, reading my works and sharing your passion with me. You literally keep me sane every single day.

To Olive Teagan, who once again endured the mess of my manuscripts to tackle the errors and eradicate them from my finished books. Thank you for being such a wonderful friend and supporter. I love you so much <3

To Serena McDonald who joined #teamGiana after she read this book. Thank you for taking a chance on King and Cress and thank you for loving them enough to support me and ride by my side on this crazy book adventure. Your friendship means more to me than I could ever express adequately with words.

When your family isn't very supportive of what you do, it can be really hard but I'm so thankful to the entire Indie community for supporting me. For the authors who participated in my Release Party—K.J. Lewis, Carian Cole, Saffron A. Kent, Kristi Beckhart, Shanora Williams, Kathryn Nolan, Lucia Franco, L.D. Dunbar, Lizzie Hart Stevens, Ella Fox, L.J. Shen, K Webster and Charleigh Rose—you ladies motivate me every day to be a better writer and I honestly adore you all! I can't list all the book bloggers who make my day with their reviews and teasers but special thanks goes out to Liv Nina, Stacey L. Atwin, Kcee Bomer, Aurora Hale, Nan Ruffo, Maria Rosiesbook Heaven Poli, Krystel Allen, and the ladies at The Fab Readers. Thank you as well to my burgeoning author friends Olive Teagan, A.R. Hadley, and Lee Piper for always supporting me.

My boys, the seven mid-twenty-something-year-old men who I surround myself with on a nearly daily basis, thank you for teaching me about how beautiful men can be. You are my inspiration and my attestation that dream men really do exist.

Finally, to my ultimate boy; the love of my life and my best friend. I know you think every hero is based on you and you'll be happy when you read this to see that, in a way, I agree with you. Because every word of love I've ever written was inspired by you; all of King's apple poems, all of Sinclair's epic speeches. I become my truest self with you just as Cressida does with King and Giselle does with Sinclair. You're the only man I've ever loved and I hope, from the depths of my soul, that one day we will get a happy ending to rival any that I might write.

# About Giana Darling

Giana Darling is a Canadian romance writer who specializes in the taboo and angsty side of love and romance. She currently lives in beautiful British Columbia where she spends time riding on the back of her man's bike, baking pies, and reading snuggled up with her cat, Persephone. She loves to hear from readers so please contact her at gianadarling[at]gmail.com if you have any questions or comments.

**Other Books By Giana:**

*The Affair (The Evolution of Sin #1)*
*The Secret (The Evolution of Sin #2)*
*The Consequence (The Evolution of Sin #3)*
*The Evolution of Sin Trilogy Boxset*
*Lessons in Corruption (The Fallen Men, #1)*
*Welcome to the Dark Side (The Fallen Men Series #2)*
*Good Gone Bad (The Fallen Men Series #3)*

**Coming Soon:**

*Enthralled (The Enslaved Duet, Book 1)*
*Enamoured (The Enslaved Duet, Book 2)*
*After the Fall (The Fallen Men, #4)*

Join my Reader's Group:
www.facebook.com/groups/819875051521137

Follow me on Twitter:
twitter.com/GianaDarling

Like me on Facebook:
www.facebook.com/gianadarling

Subscribe to my blog:
gianadarling.com

Follow me on Pinterest:
www.pinterest.com/gianadarling

Follow me on Goodreads:
www.goodreads.com/author/show/14901102.Giana_Darling

Follow me on Book + Main Bites:
bookandmainbites.com/users/9078

Newsletter:
eepurl.com/b0qnPr

IG:
www.instagram.com/gianadarlingauthor

Printed in the USA
CPSIA information can be obtained
at www.ICGtesting.com
LVHW051743281023
762324LV00014B/408

9 780995 065079